国内外经典教材辅导系列·英语类

吴伟仁《美国文学史及选读》(重排版)

笔记和考研真题详解

主编：圣才考研网
www.100xuexi.com

中国石化出版社

内 容 提 要

本书是英美文学经典教材《美国文学史及选读》(重排版)(吴伟仁主编)的学习辅导书。全书完全遵循该教材的章目编排，共分为五部分，35章，每章由两部分组成：第一部分为复习笔记(中英文对照)，总结本章的重点难点；第二部分是考研真题与典型题详解，精选名校近年考研真题及相关习题，并提供了详细的参考答案。

圣才考研网(www.100xuexi.com)提供吴伟仁《美国文学史及选读》辅导方案【视频课程、电子书、题库】。购书即可享受大礼包增值服务【本书电子书(电脑版、手机版)+全国名校真题详解电子书】。手机扫码(本书封底)领取本书大礼包。

图书在版编目(CIP)数据

吴伟仁《美国文学史及选读》(重排版)笔记和考研真题详解/圣才考研网主编．—北京：中国石化出版社，2016.6(2021.9重印)
国内外经典教材辅导系列·英语类
ISBN 978-7-5114-4155-3

Ⅰ.①吴… Ⅱ.①圣… Ⅲ.①英语-阅读教学-研究生-入学考试-自学参考资料②文学史-美国 Ⅳ.①H319.4：I

中国版本图书馆CIP数据核字(2016)第142302号

中国石化出版社出版发行
地址：北京市东城区安定门外大街58号
邮编：100011　电话：(010)84271850
读者服务部电话：(010)84289974
http://www.sinopec-press.com
E-mail：press@sinopec.com
武汉市盛宏源印务有限公司印刷
全国各地新华书店经销
*
787×1092毫米16开本14.25印张352千字
2016年7月第1版　2021年9月第2次印刷
定价：48.00元

序　言

我国各大院校一般都把国内外通用的权威教科书作为本科生和研究生学习专业课程的参考教材，这些教材甚至被很多考试(特别是硕士和博士入学考试)和培训项目作为指定参考书。为了帮助读者更好地学习专业课，我们有针对性地编著了一套与国内外教材配套的复习资料，并提供配套的名师讲堂和题库。

《美国文学史及选读》(重排版)(吴伟仁主编)一直被用作高等院校英语专业英美文学教材，被许多院校指定为英语专业考研必读书和学术研究参考书。作为该教材的学习辅导书，本书具有以下几个方面的特点：

1. 梳理章节脉络，浓缩内容精华。每章的复习笔记以该教材为主并结合其他教材对本章的重难点知识进行了整理，并参考了国内名校名师讲授该教材的课堂笔记，因此，本书的内容几乎浓缩了经典教材的知识精华。

2. 中英双语对照，凸显难点要点。本书章节笔记采用了中英文对照的形式，强化对重要难点知识的理解和运用。

3. 精选考研真题，补充难点习题。本书精选名校近年考研真题及相关习题，并提供答案和详解。所选真题和习题基本体现了各个章节的考点和难点，但又不完全局限于教材内容，是对教材内容极好的补充。

购书即可享受大礼包增值服务【本书电子书(电脑版、手机版)＋全国名校真题汇编电子书】。手机扫码(本书封底)领取本书大礼包。

圣才考研网(www.100xuexi.com)是圣才学习网旗下的考研考博专业网站，提供考研公共课和全国500所院校考研考博专业课辅导【一对一辅导、网授精讲班等】、电子书、题库、全套资料(历年真题及答案、笔记讲义等)、国内外经典教材名师讲堂、考研教辅图书等。

考研辅导：kaoyan.100xuexi.com(圣才考研网)
官方总站：www.100xuexi.com(圣才学习网)

圣才考研网编辑部

目　录

第一部分　殖民地时期的美国文学

第二部分　理性时代和革命时期文学

第三部分　浪漫主义文学

第四部分　现实主义文学

第五部分 20 世纪美国文学

第一部分　殖民地时期的美国文学

第1章　约翰·史密斯

1.1　复习笔记

Ⅰ. Historical Introduction	**Ⅰ. 历史背景**
(1) It was not until the beginning of the 17th century that the vast continent where the United States was located was stepped into by explorers from Britain and a few European countries. In the early 17th century, the British eventually settled in Virginia and Massachusetts, laying the foundation for the well-known mainstream American culture.	(1)直到17世纪初，美国所在的广袤大陆才被英国及少数几个欧洲国家的探险家涉足。17世纪早期，英国人最终在弗吉尼亚和马萨诸塞定居，奠定了人们熟知的美国主流文化的基础。
(2) The colonies that became the first federation were mostly maintained by British traditions, governed by British law, relied on British commerce, and were named after British monarchs and territories.	(2)成为第一个联邦的殖民地大部分是由英国的传统维系，受英国法律管辖，依靠英国商贸，以英国君主和领地命名。
(3) Early American literary works were mostly narratives and diaries written by the colonists. The content was mainly about their voyage to this new continent, how to adapt to the new life on the island, and how to deal with the local Indians. There were also letters, contracts, government charters, religious and political declarations.	(3)美国早期文学就是这些殖民者写的叙述文和日记，主要是关于他们来到这块新大陆的航海历程，如何适应岛上的新生活，如何和当地印第安人打交道；还有信件、契约、政府宪章、宗教和政治声明。
(4) In 1607, British colonists established the first permanent colony in Jamestown, Virginia, North America. The British mercenary Captain John Smith was one of these colonists. In the early 17th century, his report on exploring the New World was considered the first American literary work written in English.	(4)1607年，英国殖民者在弗吉尼亚詹姆斯敦建立了第一个在北美的永久性殖民地。英国雇佣兵约翰·史密斯上尉就是这批殖民者中的一员。17世纪初，他发表的关于探寻新大陆的报告被认为是第一部用英语写作的美国文学作品。
Ⅱ. Early New England Literature	**Ⅱ. 早期新英格兰文学**
New England literature embodies a variety of ideas from the very beginning. Its content involves topics such as theology, morality, history, and politics. The Puritans came to New England for religious freedom. They endured hardship and the harsh church rules for a long time. Through years of hard work, they developed a lifestyle which was compatible with	新英格兰文学打一开始就充满了各种各样的思想，内容涉及神学、道德、历史和政治等话题。清教徒来到新英格兰是为了获得宗教自由，他们长期地忍受着困苦和教堂严酷的教规。通过多年的努力，他们养成了一种与他们忧郁的宗教

their melancholy religion, that is, hardworking, thrifty, piety, and temperance. These main values were fully reflected in their works, including sermons, books and letters of some famous pastors such as John Cotton and Cotton Mather.

相适应的生活方式，即勤劳、节俭、虔诚和节制。这些主要价值观充分体现在他们的作品中，包括一些著名的牧师如约翰·科顿和科顿·马瑟等的布道词、书籍和信件等。

Ⅲ. Puritan Thoughts

(1) Literally speaking, the Puritans wanted to purify their beliefs and behaviors. The Puritan was a "would-be purifier." The term was coined by their opponents to mock them. It is used to mock those who think they were holier and better. These fearless Puritans accepted this title and regarded it as a symbol of honor.

(2) The Puritans wanted to restore the simplicity and holiness of the church and the theological authority of the Bible. They saw the corruption of the Anglican Church, so they wanted to break away from it.

(3) Puritans included people from the humblest to the loftiest ranks of English society, educated and uneducated, poor and rich. Their common shortcoming was that they viewed things too extreme. The Puritans believed that they were chosen by God, and those who lived differently from them were against God's will and were not accepted. They were keen to defend their beliefs, and they often could not tolerate other beliefs.

(4) The Puritans lived a hard life of self-discipline. They tended to regard happiness and laughter as a manifestation of sin.

(5) The religious education of the Puritans tended to overemphasize the harsh side of God while ignoring the benevolent side of God.

Ⅲ. 清教徒的思想

(1)从字面上讲，清教徒想要净化他们的信仰和行为，他们是“灵魂将要得到净化的人”。这一词是由他们的对手造出来讽刺他们的，用来嘲讽那些自认为更圣洁、更美好的人。这些无畏的清教徒接受了这一称呼，并视其为荣誉的象征。

(2)清教徒希望恢复教堂的朴素和圣洁，以及《圣经》的神学权威。他们看到英国国教的腐败，因此想脱离国教。

(3)清教徒涵盖英国社会中最卑微到最高贵的人，受过教育的和没受过教育的人，贫穷的和富裕的人。他们共同的不足是对事物看法过分极端。清教徒认为自己是上帝选定的人，而那些与他们生活方式不同的人就是违背上帝的意愿，不被接受。他们热衷于为自己的信仰辩护，而通常难以容忍其他信仰。

(4)清教徒们过着一种自律艰苦的生活，他们倾向于将快乐和欢笑看成是一种罪恶的表现。

(5)清教徒的宗教教育倾向于过分强调上帝严厉的一面，而忽略了上帝仁慈的一面。

Ⅳ. John Smith (1580—1631)

(1) Captain John Smith became the first American writer. His first work is *A True Relation of Such Occurrences and Accidents of Note as Hath Happened in Virginia Since the First Planting of That Colony* (1608). The letter responded to the opinions on opening up the colony and praised the superiority of the New World. His next book was *A Map of Virginia: with a Description of the Country* (1612). The book was a guide to

Ⅳ. 约翰·史密斯(1580—1631)

(1)约翰·史密斯成为第一位美国作家。他的第一个作品是寄给在伦敦的弗吉尼亚公司的一封信：《自殖民地第一次在弗吉尼亚垦荒以来发生的各种事件的真实介绍》，信中回应了关于开辟殖民地的意见，赞扬了新大陆的优越之处。他随后又写了《弗吉尼亚地图：一个

the country and an invitation for adventurers to come to the New World to further expand the cultivation industry here.	乡村的描述》。这本书是一本指南，也成为了冒险家来新大陆进一步扩大这里的种植业的邀请函。
(2) Smith published eight in all, some of which explored the history of New England. Smith's work reflected the idea that America needs "workers" instead of "gentlemen" in the face of the difficult task of establishing colonies and pushing the frontiers westward. This kind of thinking slowly evolved into the basic idea of American history.	(2)史密斯共出版了8部作品，部分是关于新英格兰的历史。史密斯作品中反映的思想——面对建立殖民地和"西进"的艰巨任务，美国需要"工人"而不是"绅士"——慢慢演变成了美国历史的基本思想。

1.2 考研真题与典型题详解

Ⅰ. Fill in the blanks.

1. The most enduring shaping influence in American thought and American literature was __________.
2. The first permanent English settlement in North America was established at __________, Virginia.
3. Among the members of the small band of Jamestown settlers was __________, an English soldier of fortune, whose reports of exploration, published in the early 1600s, have been described as the first distinct American literature written in English.
4. Hard work, thrift, piety and sobriety, these were the __________ values that dominated much of the early American writing.
5. The term "Puritan" was applied to those settlers who originally were devout members of the Church of __________.
6. *The General History of Virginia* contains Smith's most famous tale of how the Indian princess named __________ saved him from the wrath of her father.
7. __________ was a famous explorer and colonist. He established Jamestown.
8. The Puritan philosophy known as __________ was important in New England during colonial time, and had a profound influence on the early American mind for several generations.

Ⅱ. Multiple Choices

1. Early in __________, the English settlements in Virginia and Massachusetts started the main stream of the American national history. (北二外 2007 研)
   A. 14th century　B. 15th century　C. 17th century　D. 16th century
2. The first settlers who became the founding fathers of the American nation were quite a few of the __________. (北二外 2008 研)
   A. Quakers　B. Anglicans　C. Catholics　D. Puritans
3. The first permanent English settlement in North America was established at __________. (北二外 2009 研)
   A. Jamestown　B. New York　C. Boston　D. Concord
4. American Colonial literature is longer than any other literary period, which started when the first

settlers kept diaries and sermons and developed till __________.（北二外 2010 研）

A. the mid of 18th C　　B. early 17th C

C. the end of 17th C　　D. the end of 18th C

5. The ship "__________" carried about one hundred Pilgrims and took 66 days to beat its way across the Atlantic. In December of 1620, it put the Pilgrims ashore at Plymouth, Massachusetts.

A. Sunflower　　B. Armada　　C. Mayflower　　D. Titanic

Ⅲ. Explain the following term.

American Puritanism（南开大学 2008 研；厦门大学 2011 研）

Ⅳ. Essay question

What is the significance of American Puritanism in American literature?

参考答案及解析

Ⅰ. Fill in the blanks.

1. American Puritanism

（美国文化源于清教文化，由清教徒移民时传入北美。美国主流价值观都可以追溯到殖民地时期一统天下的清教主义，并且清教思想对美国文学有着根深蒂固的影响。）

2. Jamestown

（1607 年在北美弗吉尼亚詹姆斯敦定居的殖民者是第一批美国永久居民。）

3. Captain John Smith

（约翰·史密斯上校（1580. 1—1631. 6. 21）因在北美弗吉尼亚州建立了英国第一个永久殖民地詹姆斯敦而扬名天下。他的《自殖民地第一次在弗吉尼亚垦荒以来发生的各种事件的真实介绍》则是美国文学的"第一书"，其实也是整个美国历史的"第一书"。）

4. Puritan

（勤劳、节俭、虔诚、持重是引领早期美国文学的清教价值观。）

5. England

（清教徒（Puritan），是指要求清除英国国教（Church of England）中天主教残余的改革派。该词于 16 世纪 60 年代开始使用，源于拉丁文的 Purus，意为"清洁"。）

6. Pocahontas

（约翰·史密斯在《弗吉尼亚通史》中讲述了他与印第安公主波卡虹塔斯（Pocahontas）之间的故事。公元 1608 年史密斯与当地印第安部落的一位叫波瓦坦的酋长谈判，这位酋长年轻的女儿波卡虹塔斯挽救了史密斯船长的性命。）

7. Captain John Smith

（约翰·史密斯上校，新英格兰的舰队司令，是英国军人，探险家和作家。他因在北美弗吉尼亚州建立了英国第一个永久殖民地詹姆斯敦而扬名天下。）

8. Puritanism

（清教主义，起源于英国，在北美殖民地得以实践与发展。清教徒构成了当时北美移民的主体，在新英格兰北部更是清一色的清教徒。清教主义奠定了美国社会的基础，塑造了美国人的性格，从各个方面影响着美国社会。）

Ⅱ. Multiple Choices

1. C　17 世纪初，英国人在弗吉尼亚和马萨诸塞定居，这也是美国历史的开端。

2. D　早期来到北美的殖民者有不少是清教徒，因而殖民时期的文学深受清教思想影响。

3. A　詹姆斯敦是英国人在北美的第一个永久定居地。

4. A　美国殖民地时期文学起止时间为 1607 年—1765 年。

5. C　1620 年 100 多名清教徒前辈乘坐“五月花”号船到达美国马萨诸塞州的普利茅斯。

Ⅲ. Explain the following term.

The word Puritanism is originally used to refer to the theology advocated by a party within the Church of England. The term Puritanism is also used in a broader sense to refer to the attitudes and values considered characteristic of the Puritans. It has been employed to denote a rigid moralism, or the condemnation of innocent pleasure, or religious narrowness adhered by the early New England Puritans. The American Puritanism as a cultural heritage exerted great influence over American moral values. And this Puritan influence over American Romanticism was conspicuously noticeable. In addition, a preoccupation with the Calvinistic view of original sin and the mystery of evil marked the works by such famous writers as Hawthorne and Melville.

Ⅳ. Essay question

The British began to immigrate to North America in the first half of the 17th century. Many early American immigrants were Puritans, and they came to the United States for a variety of reasons. The Puritanism they believed in later took root in the New World and had a profound impact on American thought and American literature.

The American Puritans were idealists, believing that the Church should be restored to the “Purity” and religion was a matter of primary importance. They accepted the doctrine of predestination, original sin, total depravity, and limited atonement. Overall, American literature, at least white American literature, is based on the myth of the Garden of Eden in the Bible. To a large extent, it is a literary form of pious idealism as the legacy of American Puritanism. The Puritans longed to live in a perfect order. With great courage, they hope to establish a new Garden of Eden in the United States so that they can finally live an ideal life. Encouraged by this sense of mission, they were very optimistic in the face of difficulties and obstacles. These have become important nourishment for the production and development of American literature. Optimism is embodied in the works of many American writers.

Furthermore, Puritan theology and Puritan literary practice are the main reasons for the development of native symbolism in the United States. To the pious Puritans, the reality of the world is just the symbol of God. All phenomena in life are part and concrete manifestation of God's intention. It is easy to spot this symbolic process which often occurred in Puritan thinking. Over time, this process became part of the cultural traditions on which the American people and writers grew up. Symbolism is commonly used by Jonathan Edwards, Emerson, Hawthorne, and Melville. This unique way of observing the world by the Puritans is a basic component of their education.

In terms of the writing skills, the conciseness of Puritan works also profoundly affected American literature. The works of Puritan writers show a fresh and concise style. They use simple and sincere rhetoric, with the noble temperament under the direct influence of the Bible. Their works have left a lasting influence on American literature.

第2章 威廉·布拉德福德和约翰·温思罗普

2.1 复习笔记

Ⅰ. William Bradford (1590—1657)	**Ⅰ. 威廉·布拉德福德(1590—1657)**
(1) William Bradford was the first governor of Plymouth, and his representative work is *Of Plymouth Plantation.*	(1)威廉·布拉德福德是普利茅斯的第一任总督，代表作品是《普利茅斯种植园》。
(2) Bradford wrote many personal experiences in his works. His language was concise, sincere, and straightforward, making his work easy to read and touching. In addition, he also wrote a lot of poems, prose and narrative poems.	(2)布拉德福德在其中写下了很多自己亲身经历的事件。本书语言简洁，情感真挚，平铺直叙，易读又感人。此外，他还写了大量的诗歌、散文和叙事诗等。
(3) When he died, the entire New England colonies mourned him. Cotton Mather later wrote an inscription for him, calling him "a common blessing and father to them all".	(3)他去世时，整个新英格兰殖民地都为他哀悼。科顿·马瑟后来为他题词，称他是"众人之福，众人之父"。
Ⅱ. John Winthrop (1588—1649)	**Ⅱ. 约翰·温思罗普(1588—1649)**
(1) John Winthrop was the first governor of Boston, and his notable work is *The History of New England from 1630 to 1649*. His works are frank, simple and true.	(1)温斯罗普是波士顿的第一任总督，代表作是《新英格兰史》。他的作品坦率、质朴、真实。
(2) These two books are very precious historical materials, recording important historical events of the author's era. The author wrote them out of a need to permanently record important events rather than out of creative interest.	(2)《普利茅斯种植园史》和《新英格兰史》是非常珍贵的历史资料，记录了作者所处时代的重大历史事件。作者的写作不是出于创作的兴趣，而是出于一种将重大事件永久记录下来的需要。

2.2 考研真题与典型题详解

Ⅰ. Fill in the blanks.

1. In 1620, __________ was elected Governor of Plymouth, Massachusetts.
2. *The History of New England* is a priceless gift __________ left us.
3. In 1620, led by William Bradford, a group of Pilgrims arrived in present-day Massachusetts on a ship called __________. (暨南大学2013研)
4. William Bradford himself used a word " __________ " to describe the community of believers who sailed from Southampton, England, on the Mayflower and settled in Plymouth, Massachusetts in 1620.

Ⅱ. Multiple Choices

1. Who was called "a common blessing and father to them all"?

   A. John Winthrop. B. William Bradford. C. Philip Freneau. D. Thomas Paine.

2. Which is not the feature of John Winthrop's writing style?

   A. Candidness. B. Simplicity. C. Honesty. D. Humor.

Ⅲ. Explain the following term.

Literary Journals

参考答案及解析

Ⅰ. Fill in the blanks.

1. William Bradford

   (1620年威廉·布拉德福德被选为普利茅斯殖民地的第一任总督。)

2. John Winthrop

   (约翰·温思罗普(John Winthrop)(1588—1649),美国殖民地领导人,马萨诸塞湾清教徒总督。他著名的作品是《新英格兰史》(*The History of New England*)。)

3. Mayflower

   (1620年9月16日,在牧师布莱斯特率领下乘"五月花号"前往北美。此次航行的主要领袖是威廉·布拉德福德(William Bradford) 和 威廉·布鲁斯特(William Brewster)。)

4. Pilgrims

   (威廉·布拉德福德是普利茅斯的首任总督。1620年他率领100多名英国移民乘坐"五月花号"大帆船到达北美的普利茅斯。他把其率领的信徒称为朝圣者(pilgrims)。)

Ⅱ. Multiple Choices

1. B 威廉·布拉德福德被称为"众人之福,众人之父"。

2. D 温斯罗普的作品特点是坦率、质朴、真实。因此答案为D项。

Ⅲ. Explain the following term.

Literary Journals: ①A journal records the personal daily life. It provides valuable details that only participants or witnesses know. A journal can reveal a lot of information about the author. ②Although a journal provides the writer's insights into life, it is not necessarily a reliable record of facts. The author's impression may cause the narration of the event to be inconsistent with the facts, especially when he or she is a participant. Journals written for publication rather than personal use tend to be more subjective. The European encounters with and conquest of the Americas are recorded in the journals of the explorers.

第3章　约翰·科顿和罗杰·威廉姆斯

3.1　复习笔记

Ⅰ. John Cotton (1585—1652)

(1) John Cotton was the first major intellectual spokesman of the Massachusetts Bay Colony and sometimes he was called "the Patriarch of New England".

(2) John Cotton wrote several books that strongly illustrated Puritan theory, but his main influence was in his preaching. After arriving in Boston in 1633, he had always been the spiritual leader of the community. The theocracy he preached, that is, the rule of the country by religion, directly affected the behavior of people at that time.

(3) Through John Cotton we can see an important characteristic of the Puritans. They were more concerned with authority than democracy.

(4) Cotton was partly responsible for Roger Williams's exile from Massachusetts. However, no matter what shortcomings and limitations Cotton had, his firmness and contribution to faith were worthy of admiration.

Ⅱ. Roger Williams (1603—1683)

(1) Williams studied law at Cambridge University, but he did not engage in law-related work. Instead, he entered the church and was immersed in the Puritan school. When he came to the Massachusetts colony in 1631, he held a more democratic religious view. He had a disagreement with the leaders of the colony, resulting in his exile to what is now Rhode Island. He founded a community which he called Providence, because of "God's merciful providence to him in his distress".

(2) Williams heralded the history of religious toleration in America, and the history of the separation of church and state. He held that no political order or church system could identify itself directly with god. As a Puritan, Williams' tolerance came from a simple thought that one should behave with integrity, be faithful, and have no right to impose beliefs on anyone.

Ⅰ. 约翰·科顿（1585—1652）

(1)约翰·科顿是马萨诸塞湾殖民地第一个知识分子的主要发言人，有时被称为“新英格兰的族长”。

(2)约翰·科顿写了几本有力地说明清教徒理论的书，但是他的主要影响在于他的讲道。1633年到波士顿之后，他一直是社区的精神领袖，他所宣讲的由宗教来统治国家的神权思想直接影响了当时人们的行为。

(3)通过约翰·科顿我们可以看到清教徒的主要特点。他们关注更多的是权威而不是民主。

(4)科顿对威廉姆斯被驱逐出马萨诸塞州一事负有部分责任。然而，不管科顿有着怎样的缺点和局限，他对于信仰的坚定和贡献都是值得敬佩的。

Ⅱ. 罗杰·威廉姆斯(1603—1683)

(1)威廉姆斯曾在剑桥大学学习法律，但是没有从事法律相关的工作，而是进入教堂，沉浸在清教流派中。当他于1631年来到马萨诸塞殖民地后，他更民主的宗教观点与殖民地的领导人产生分歧，致使他被流放到现在的罗德岛州。他建立了一个叫“天意”的社区，因为“逆境中上帝赐予他仁慈的天意”。

(2)罗杰·威廉姆斯开创了美国宗教容忍异己的历史，也开创了美国政教分离的历史。作为一个清教徒，威廉姆斯的容忍是来自于一种朴素的思想，即行为正直，信仰虔诚，没有任何权力将信仰强加于任何人。

3.2 考研真题与典型题详解

Ⅰ. Fill in the blanks.

1. __________ was the first major intellectual spokesman of the Massachusetts Bay Colony.
2. Roger Williams founded a community which he called __________, because of "God's merciful providence to him in his distress".

Ⅱ. Multiple Choices

1. Who among the following translated the Bible into the Indian tongue?
   A. Roger Williams. B. John Eliot.
   C. Cotton Mather. D. John Smith.
2. Choose the work which is written by Roger Williams.
   A. *A Key into the Language of America* B. *A True Sight of Sin*
   C. *Common Sense* D. *The General Magazine*
3. The following figures were often considered the founding fathers of the American Republic EXCEPT __________. (汕头大学2017研)
   A. George Washington B. Thomas Jefferson
   C. Roger Williams D. John Adams

参考答案及解析

Ⅰ. Fill in the blanks.

1. John Cotton
   (约翰·科顿是马萨诸塞湾殖民地第一个知识分子的主要发言人。)
2. Providence
   (罗杰·威廉姆斯建立了一个叫"天意"的社区，因为"逆境中上帝赐予他仁慈的天意"。)

Ⅱ. Multiple Choices

1. B 17世纪四十年代，约翰·艾略特(John Eliot)牧师开始向印第安人传教，还把《圣经》翻译成万帕诺亚格语(Wampanoag)，并建立了"祈祷之城"，印第安人与白人相邻而居，学习基督教教义和农业技艺。

2. A 罗杰·威廉姆斯对语言很感兴趣，他的其中一本书就是*A Key into the Language of America*。

3. C 罗杰·威廉姆斯是十七世纪北美殖民时代的著名人物。他的一生，都在为建立一个能摆脱宗教战争与宗教迫害的政治体制而奋斗。十八世纪末，美国开国先贤们彻底实践了威廉姆斯的政教分离思想，为美国的宪政奠定了坚实的制度基础。

第4章　安妮·布雷兹特里特和爱德华·泰勒

4.1　复习笔记

Ⅰ. Anne Bradstreet(1612—1672)	**Ⅰ. 安妮·布雷兹特里特(1612—1672)**
(1) Anne Bradstreet is one of the most interesting of the early poets. Both her father and her husband were governors of Massachusetts, and they were the first colonists to arrive by Arbella.	(1)安妮·布雷兹特里特是美国早期最有趣的诗人之一。她的父亲和丈夫都曾当过马萨诸塞州的总督，他们都是第一批乘“阿贝拉”到来的殖民者。
(2) Her first work *The Tenth Muse Lately Sprung Up in America* was published in London.	(2)她的第一部作品在伦敦出版，名为《美国新崛起的第十位缪斯女神》。
(3) Some poems of Anne Bradstreet are too grand. But she was good at describing the simple things in daily life with her piety.	(3)安妮·布雷兹特里特的一些诗歌主题过于宏大，但是她对一些日常生活中的小事描写得很到位，饱含虔诚。
Ⅱ. Edward Taylor(1642—1729)	**Ⅱ. 爱德华·泰勒(1642—1729)**
(1) The best of the Puritan poets was Edward Taylor who came from England. He then became a full-time pastor after studying at Harvard University.	(1)爱德华·泰勒是清教徒诗人中最优秀的一位，青年时期来自英国，读完哈佛大学后成为一位专职牧师。
(2) He is the most accomplished poetic craftsman of the early years. He adopted the writing form and style of the British poets in the mid-17th century.	(2)他是早期诗歌成就最突出的一位诗人。他采用的是17世纪中期英国主流诗人的写作形式和风格。
(3) Most of Taylor's work treated religious themes, with many poems based directly on the Psalms.	(3)泰勒的大部分作品是以宗教为主题的，并且许多作品直接是基于《圣经》中的诗篇而作的。
(4) Taylor did not publish any of his work. It was not until 1937, more than two hundred years after his death, that his manuscript was discovered. This discovery immediately made Taylor an important representative of American colonial literature and enriched the American poetry tradition.	(4)泰勒没有出版任何作品。直到他去世两百余年后的1937年，他的手稿才被发现。这一发现立刻使得泰勒成为美国殖民时期文学的重要代表人物，丰富了美国的诗歌传统。

4.2　考研真题与典型题详解

Ⅰ. Fill in the blanks.

1. Many Puritans wrote verse, but the works of two writers, Anne Bradstreet and ________, rose

to the level of real poetry.

2. *The Tenth Muse Lately Sprung Up in America* is a collection of poems composed by __________.

3. A complete edition of Edward Taylor's poems appeared in __________.

Ⅱ. Multiple choices.

1. Anne Bradstreet was a Puritan poet. Her poems made such a stir in England that she became known as the "__________" who appeared in America.

   A. Ninth Muse　B. Tenth Muse　C. Best Muse　D. First Muse

2. __________ is generally considered as the best of the Puritan poets in the literature of colonial America. (西南大学 2009 研)

   A. Edward Taylor　B. Anne Bradstreet　C. John Cotton　D. Roger Williams

Ⅲ. Read the following quotations and answer the questions.

Passage 1

I heard the merry grasshopper then sing.
The black-clad cricket bear a second part;
They kept one tune and played on the same string,
Seeming to glory in their little art.
Shall creatures abject thus their voices raise
And in their kind resound their Maker's praise
Whilst I, as mute, can warble forth no higher lays?

Questions:

1. This is the ninth of the "Contemplations" written by an early American woman writer. What is her name?

2. Make a brief comment on this short poem.

Passage 2

Huswifery

Make me, O Lord, thy spinning wheel complete.
Thy holy word my distaff make for me.
Make mine affections thy swift flyers neat,
And make my soul thy holy spool to be.
My conversation make to be thy reel, and reel,
the yarn thereon spun of thy wheel.

Questions:

1. Identify the poet of this poem.

2. Make a brief comment on this poem.

Ⅳ. Short answer question

Who was Anne Bradstreet? What were her literary achievements?

Ⅴ. Essay question

Do you agree that in colonial America there was no poetry at all? Give your reason.

参考答案及解析

Ⅰ. Fill in the blanks.

1. Edward Taylor

（美国殖民时期最著名的诗人是安妮·布雷兹特里特和爱德华·泰勒。）

2. Anne Bradstreet

（安妮·布雷兹特里特是美国殖民时期著名的诗人。其代表作是诗集《美国新崛起的第十位缪斯女神》。）

3. 1960

（泰勒没有出版任何作品。直到他去世两百余年后的1937年，他的手稿才被发现。这一发现立刻使得泰勒成为美国殖民时期文学的重要代表人物，丰富了美国的诗歌传统。1960年，泰勒的一部完整的诗歌集出版问世。）

Ⅱ. Multiple Choices

1. B 安妮·布雷兹特里特被誉为"美国出现的第十个缪斯"。

2. A 爱德华·泰勒通常被认为是美国殖民时期文学中最优秀的清教徒诗人。

Ⅲ. Read the following quotations and answer the questions.

Passage 1

1. Anne Bradstreet.
2. This stanza, written by Anne Bradstreet, is taken from her best known and most attractive poem, "Contemplations". This short poem offers the reader an insight into the mentality of the early Puritan pioneering into a new world. When the poet heard the grasshopper and the cricket sing, she thought of this as their praising their creator and searched her own soul accordingly. It is evident that she saw something metaphysical inhering in the physical, a mode of perception which was singularly Puritan.

Passage 2

1. Edward Taylor.
2. The poem indicates that the poet saw religious significance in a simple daily incident like a housewife spinning. The spinning wheel, the distaff, the flyers, the spool, the reel and the yarn have all acquired a metaphorical significance in the symbolic, Puritan eyes of Edward Taylor.

Ⅳ. Short answer question

Anne Bradstreet is one of the most interesting of the early poets. Her first work *The Tenth Muse Lately Sprung Up in America* was published in London. She was good at describing the simple things in daily life with her piety. Mrs. Bradstreet's works also serve as a document of the struggles of a Puritan wife against the hardships of New England colonial life.

Ⅴ. Essay question

①The strenuous life of the pioneer left little time for cultivating any of the arts, and the spirit of New England was too serious and too stern to permit indulgence in what was merely pleasant or beautiful. Even after the first critical years of danger and struggle were past, the intellectual life of the people was bounded by the narrow limits of religious discussion and theological debate. That the Puritan was not without imagination, however, is abundantly proved by the forceful figures and impassioned rhetoric of the prose writers who did only occasionally slip into rhyme. Anne Bradstreet and Edward Taylor are such examples.

②Anne Bradstreet was a Puritan who wrote ponderous verses of interminable, inter-locking poems. Her poems made such a stir in England that she became known as the "Tenth Muse" who appeared in America. Her famous "Contemplations" offers the reader an insight into the mentality of the early Puritan pioneering in a new world.

③Edward Taylor was a meditation poet. In his splendid, exotic images, Taylor came nearest to the English baroque poets. He was, first and last, a Puritan poet, concerned about how his images speak for God. He has faith in God who can save the erring, or possibly sinful, humankind from the evil designs of Hell.

第二部分　理性时代和革命时期文学

第5章　本杰明·富兰克林

5.1　复习笔记

Ⅰ. Historical Introduction	**Ⅰ. 背景介绍**
(1) Theology dominated American literature during the Puritan period. After that, politics became the main subject of literary works.	(1)神学在清教徒时期的美国文学中占主导地位。而后，政治成为作家们的主要题材。
(2) In the middle of the 18th century, the United States became a prosperous colony with a rapidly growing population and continuous integration. In people's minds, the word "state", which symbolizes an independent government, began to replace "colony".	(2)18世纪中期，美国成为人口迅速增长、不断融合的相互毗邻、繁荣的殖民地。在人们的思想中，象征独立政府的词语"国家"，开始取代"殖民地"。
(3) The War of Independence lasted for eight years (1776—1783) and finally established a Federative bourgeois democratic republic—the United States of America.	(3)独立战争持续了八年(1776—1783)，最终建立了联合的资产阶级共和国——美利坚合众国。
(4) American bourgeois Enlightenment opposed to old colonial order and religious obscurantism. It dealt a fatal blow to the Puritan tradition and brought secular education and literature to life. American readers were very fond of the works of English scientists, philosophers and writers.	(4)美国资产阶级启蒙运动反对旧殖民地秩序和宗教蒙蔽主义，给予清教传统致命打击，使世俗的教育和文学焕发生机。美国读者对英国科学家、哲学家及作家的作品很感兴趣。
(5) Although the American literature of this century largely imitated the British literature of the 18th century, the brave and enterprising Americans created excellent political pamphlets and domestic newspapers with great ambition.	(5)尽管本世纪的美国文学很大程度上模仿了18世纪英国文学，但此时英勇进取的美国人怀着雄心壮志，创作了极好的政治小册子和国内报纸。
Ⅱ. Benjamin Franklin (1706—1790)	**Ⅱ. 本杰明·富兰克林(1706—1790)**
1. Life	**1. 生平**
Benjamin Franklin was born in Boston in 1706. He was versatile and energetic throughout his life. He was well known as a writer, a statesman, an inventor as well as a preeminent scientist of his day. He was also a humanist and humanitarian who believed in the possibilities of human progress and the	1706年，富兰克林出生在波士顿。他一生多才多艺，能量充沛。他不仅是一名作家、政治家、发明家，他也是当时著名的科学家。同时他也是一个人文主义者和人道主义者，相信人类进步和物质财富的

comforts of material success. He signed *the Declaration of Independence*. He was one of the founders of the United States. Franklin died in 1790 at the age of 84. As a highly respected figure, he was mourned by the people of many countries.

2. Literary Status

Franklin not only made great social achievements, he was also one of the first major American writers. He was talented in writing with a touch of humor and irony. His articles were flat and straightforward, reflecting the clarity, restraint, simplicity and balance advocated by neoclassicism.

3. Major Works

Poor Richard's Almanac
The Autobiography
The Way to Wealth
Collected Works

4. Selected Work

◆*The Autobiography*

The Autobiography is an excellent work in autobiographical literature. It is a concise and extremely fascinating narrative of Franklin's leaping from poor and humble to rich and famous. It faithfully records the glorious career of the first self-reliant person in the United States. He represents that in the United States, human beings are inherently kind and free, possessing the inalienable freedom granted by God and the right to pursue happiness. The book celebrates the realization of the American dream by telling the story of success through self-reliance.

The Autobiography fully illustrates that Franklin was the spokesperson of the American Enlightenment in the 18th century. This is also a Puritan document that records the self-reflection and self-improvement of the Puritans. It is also the best illustration of the moral principles of the Puritans, that is, in order to succeed, one must be diligent, simple, and cautious.

The style of *The Autobiography* reflects the simple, straightforward and concise style of the Puritans.

舒适。他签署过《独立宣言》，是美国的缔造者之一。1790 年富兰克林去世，享年 84 岁，作为一位备受崇敬的人物，被多国人民哀悼。

2. 文学地位

除了他的社会功绩，富兰克林也跻身于美国第一批主要作家之列。他具有写作天赋，表达有力，带有一丝幽默和讽刺。他的文章平铺直叙，反映了新古典主义崇尚的明晰、节制、朴素和平衡。

3. 主要作品

《穷理查历书》
《自传》
《致富之道》
《全集》

4. 选读作品

◆《自传》

《自传》是自传体文学中的上乘佳作。它简明而极其引人入胜地叙述了富兰克林由穷苦卑微跃至富有、闻名的故事。它忠实地记录了美国第一位自力更生者光辉灿烂的职业生涯。他代表着，在美国，人本质是善良自由的，拥有上帝赋予的不可剥夺的自由及追求幸福的权力。该书通过讲述自力更生而获取成功的故事，歌颂了美国梦的实现。

《自传》充分说明了富兰克林是 18 世纪美国启蒙运动的代言人。这也是一本清教文献，记录了清教徒的自我反省和自我完善。它也是清教徒道德原则的最好说明，即为了取得成功，人必须勤劳、简朴、谨慎。

《自传》的文体体现出清教徒朴素、直率、简洁的风格。

5.2 考研真题与典型题详解

Ⅰ. Fill in the blanks.

1. In his autobiography, ________ creates the image of a self-made man and demonstrates his belief that the new world of America was a land of ________ which might be met through hard work and wise management.（天津外国语学院 2011 研）
2. If we say Jonathan Edwards represents the upper levels of the American mind, ________ represents the lower levels.
3. Franklin's claim to a place in literature rests chiefly on his ________ and ________.
4. In American literature, the eighteenth century was an Age of ________ and Revolution.
5. Franklin was the epitome of the ________, the versatile, practical embodiment of national man in the 18th century.
6. Benjamin Franklin's best writing is found in his masterpiece ________.
7. Benjamin Franklin also edited the first colonial magazine, which he called ________.

Ⅱ. Multiple Choices

1. Benjamin Franklin is not merely an outstanding politician, a talented inventor but also a famed literary giant. His autobiography set the example of practicing ________ moral disciplines which gave profound influences as the national spirit.（北二外 2007 研）

   A. Quaker's　　B. Puritan
   C. Anglican Christian　　D. Easter's

2. The first symbol of self-made American man is ________.（北二外 2009 研）

   A. George Washington　B. Washington Irving　C. Thomas Jefferson　D. Benjamin Franklin

3. The English colonies in North America rose in arms against their parent country and the Continental Congress adopted ________ in 1776.

   A. the *Declaration of Independence*　　B. the Sugar Act
   C. the Stamp Act　　D. the Mayflower Compact

4. During the Reason and Revolution Period, Americans were influenced by the European movement called the ________.

   A. Chartist Movement　　B. Romanticist Movement
   C. Enlightenment Movement　　D. Modernist Movement

5. "God help those who help themselves" is found in ________'s work.（北二外 2016 研）

   A. Paine　B. Franklin　C. Freneau　D. Jefferson

6. The secular ideals of the American Enlightenment were exemplified in the life and career of ________.

   A. Thomas Hood　　B. Benjamin Franklin
   C. Thomas Jefferson　　D. George Washington

7. From 1732 to 1758, Benjamin Franklin wrote and published his famous ________, an annual collection of proverbs.

   A. *The Autobiography*　　B. *Poor Richard's Almanac*
   C. *Common Sense*　　D. *The General Magazine*

8. Which statement about Benjamin Franklin is not true?

A. He instructed his countrymen as a printer.

B. He was a scientist.

C. He was a master of diplomacy.

D. He was a Puritan.

9. Benjamin Franklin shaped his writing after the ________ of the English essayists Joseph Addison and Richard Steele.

A. *Spectator* B. *Walden*

C. *Nature* D. *The Sacred Wood*

Ⅲ. Explain the following term.

The literary form of autobiography(北二外 2008 研)

Ⅳ. Read the following quotation and answer the questions.

It was about this time I conceived the bold and arduous project of arriving at moral perfection. I wished to live without committing any fault at any time; I would conquer all that either natural inclination, custom, or company might lead me into. As I knew, or thought I knew, what was right and wrong, I did not see why I might not always do the one and avoid the other. But I soon found I had undertaken a task of more difficulty than I had imagined. While my care was employed in guarding against one fault, I was often surprised by another; habit took the advantage of inattention; inclination was sometimes too strong for reason. I concluded, at length, that the mere speculative conviction that it was our interest to be completely virtuous was not sufficient to prevent our slipping; and that the contrary habits must be broken, and good ones acquired and established, before we can have any dependence on a steady, uniform rectitude of conduct. For this purpose I therefore contrived the following method.

In the various enumerations of the moral virtues I had met with in my reading, I found the catalog more or less numerous, as different writers included more or fewer ideas under the same name. Temperance, for example, was by some confined to eating and drinking, while by others it was extended to mean the moderating every other pleasure, appetite, inclination, or passion, bodily or mental, even to our avarice and ambition. I proposed to myself, for the sake of clearness, to use rather more names, with fewer ideas annexed to each, than a few names with more ideas; and I included under thirteen names of virtues all that at that time occurred to me as necessary or desirable, and annexed to each a short precept, which fully expressed the extent I gave to its meaning.

Questions:

1. Which work is this passage taken from?
2. Who is the author of this book?
3. What is your understanding of the book?

Ⅴ. Short answer questions

1. What is a proverb? Which writer in this period liked to use proverbs?
2. Analysis of *Poor Richard's Almanac*.

Ⅵ. Essay question

What are the characteristics of Benjamin Franklin's literary work?

参考答案及解析

Ⅰ. Fill in the blanks.

1. Benjamin Franklin, opportunities

（富兰克林是美国启蒙时期与独立战争时期的代表人物。他的《自传》是美国第一部成功的传记体作品，文中树立的主人公形象激励了一代又一代的美国人去追求美国梦。）

2. Benjamin Franklin

（美国文学评论家范·威克·布鲁克斯（Van Wyck Brooks）在《美国的成年》（*America's Coming of Age*）中指出乔纳森·爱德华兹和本杰明·富兰克林是美国18世纪的两位重要的哲学家，他们是不同层次思想的代表。）

3. *Poor Richard's Almanac*, *The Autobiography*

（富兰克林在文学上的地位主要取决于《穷查理历书》和《自传》。）

4. Reason

（18世纪的美国处于理性与革命时期。这一时期的美国深受法国启蒙思想的影响，且处于独立革命时期。）

5. Enlightenment

（富兰克林是启蒙思想的缩影，是18世纪理性的代表。）

6. *The Autobiography of Benjamin Franklin*

（本杰明·富兰克林文学上最大的成就体现在他的作品《本杰明·富兰克林自传》上。该书以平易的文风叙述了富兰克林艰苦创业、自学成才、坚持不懈的奋斗历程。）

7. *the General Magazine*

（本杰明·富兰克林（1706—1790）——十八世纪美国最伟大的科学家和发明家，著名的政治家、外交家、哲学家、文学家和航海家以及美国独立战争的伟大领袖。他编辑了美国殖民时期第一份杂志 *the General Magazine*。）

Ⅱ. Multiple Choices

1. B　富兰克林是一位虔诚的清教徒，他的《自传》是奉行清教道德标准的典范，对塑造美国精神产生了重大影响。
2. D　富兰克林是第一个自力更生、白手起家的美国人的标志。
3. A　1776年13个英属北美殖民地奋起反击英国的殖民统治，并且1776年7月4日，大陆会议通过了一份由托马斯·杰斐逊起草的《独立宣言》（*Declaration of Independence*）。
4. C　18世纪的美国处于理性与革命时期，这时的美国深受同时期欧洲启蒙运动的影响。
5. B　“自助者天助之”出自富兰克林的作品。
6. B　作为美国财富和智慧的象征，美国人民把富兰克林的头像印在100美元纸钞的正面。200多年来，这位智者的思想一直被那些希望拥有美德并过上富足生活的人们所遵循和实践着。他的个人生活和职业生涯代表了美国启蒙运动中世俗化的理想。
7. B　《穷理查历书》（*Poor Richard's Almanac*）它是由美国资本主义精神最完美的代表——本杰明·富兰克林所写。该出版物从1732年至1758年不断出现。它幽默、睿智、形式奇特，通篇贯彻着人类的智慧精华，书中的名言警句与人生箴言即使在现在看来也具有很积极的作用。
8. A　本杰明·富兰克林有一连串的头衔——作家，发明家，出版商，科学家，外交家。他没有显赫的家世，没有富裕的生活，仅仅靠自己对宗教的虔诚，对教育的重视，生活的简朴，以及不屈的奋斗获得了在各个领域的成功，他是美国“清教主义”的杰出代表。所以选项 A 对本杰明·富兰克林的陈述显然是不对的。

9. A 本杰明·富兰克林的作品深受英国散文家约瑟夫·艾迪生(Joseph Addison)和理查德·斯蒂尔(Richard Steele)的《旁观者》的影响。

Ⅲ. Explain the following term.

The literary form of autobiography: An autobiography is a person's account of his or her life. It is generally written in the first person, with the author speaking as "I". Autobiography presents life events as the writer views them, and offers insights into the beliefs and perceptions of the author. Representative writer is Benjamin Franklin with his work *The Autobiography*.

Ⅳ. Read the following quotation and answer the questions.

1. *The Autobiography*
2. Benjamin Franklin
3. ①The book is probably the first of its kind in literature. It is the simple yet immensely fascinating record of a man rising to wealth and fame from a state of poverty and obscurity in which he was born, the faithful account of the colorful career of America's first self-made man. The book contains four parts, written at different times.

   ②This is also a Puritan document that records the self-reflection and self-improvement of the Puritans. It is also the best illustration of the moral principles of the Puritans, that is, in order to succeed, one must be diligent, simple, and cautious.

   ③*The Autobiography* fully illustrates that Franklin was the spokesperson of the American Enlightenment in the 18th century. It is a concise and extremely fascinating narrative of Franklin's leaping from poor and humble to rich and famous. It faithfully records the glorious career of the first self-reliant person in the United States. He represents that in the United States, human beings are inherently kind and free, possessing the inalienable freedom granted by God and the right to pursue happiness. The book celebrates the realization of the American dream by telling the story of success through self-reliance.

   ④The style of *The Autobiography* reflects the simple, straightforward and concise style of the Puritans. The lucidity of the narrative, the absence of ornaments in wording and complex, involved structures in syntax, and the Puritan abhorrence of paradox are all well graphically demonstrated here and in the whole of the book. Taken as a whole, it is safe to say that the book is an exemplary illustration of the American style of writing.

Ⅴ. Short answer questions

1. ①A proverb is a short popular saying expressing some general truth or superstition. As expressions of basic principles of folk wisdom drawn from the daily experiences of a group of people, proverbs exist in all societies. They reflect a particular culture's view of the world and convey feelings about fate, the seasons, the natural world, work and effort, love, death, and other universal experiences. These memorable bits of wisdom have survived for centuries; perhaps they reflect unchanging truths about human nature.

   ②Most of Benjamin Franklin's aphorisms are adapted from anonymous traditional or folk sayings, known as proverbs. Franklin, who believed that clarity and brevity were two of the most important characteristics of good prose, rewrote many proverbs, crafting short, direct, witty sayings that taught a lesson.

2. Benjamin Franklin created a character, Poor Richard, in whose name the work appeared, and whose real existence was debated humorously and seriously. For almost a quarter of a century, he kept publishing *Poor Richard's Almanac*, expanding its literary part to the intense delight of its readers.

   Apart from poems and essays, he managed to put in many adages, and commonsense witticisms which became household words and many mottos of the most typical kind. He did not always write the maxims himself. He borrowed from others and made good use of his own wit and wisdom to simplify and enrich their axiom. There are many similar statements filled almanac, and taught as much as amused. The practical wisdom of Franklin shone forth rays of grandeur from its pages.

Ⅵ. Essay question

The predominant quality in all of Benjamin Franklin's writing is its genuine humanness; this is what brought the Almanac into instant popularity, and what makes the Autobiography an enduring American classic. It is a quality that had been extremely rare in the earlier colonial literature. He was talented in writing with a touch of humor and irony.

Franklin's literary work was thoroughly typical of himself. To him the matter of "getting on" in the world was a duty; and to enable others to see the advantages of integrity, application, and thrift was his self-appointed task. The absence of ideality is obvious in all his compositions. His articles were flat and straightforward, reflecting the clarity, restraint, simplicity and balance advocated by neoclassicism. The works which have been mentioned possess a universal charm.

第 6 章　托马斯·潘恩

6.1　复习笔记

<table>
<tr>
<td>

Thomas Paine (1737—1809)

1. Life

Thomas Paine was the most influential ideologist and writer during the Age of Reason and Revolution. His life was a life of unremitting struggle for human rights. Thomas Paine was born in the American Revolutionary War, with a natural writing ability and a rebellious spirit. As a tax collector, he had a deep understanding of society and witnessed the suffering of people under the burden of heavy taxes and the helplessness of humble workers of the same class as him. Paine then published *Common Sense*, which became the strongest voice of the American Revolution. On May 21, 1792, Paine was accused of treason for writing *Rights of Man* and fled to France for asylum. In 1802, he returned to the United States, but found that his patriotic behavior had been forgotten by people. In his last few years, no one remembered him except his detractors, and most of the time he lived in obscurity on the farm in New Rochelle. Paine died in 1809 and was buried in New Rochelle.

2. Major Works

The Case of the Officers of the Excise (1772)
Common Sense (1776)
The American Crisis (1776—1783)
Rights of Man (1791)
The Age of Reason (1794—1795)

3. Selected Work

◆ ***The American Crisis***

The American Crisis shows Paine's strong belief in deism and informs the world that the British are trying to exercise rights that only God can exercise.

Paine believes that British political and military behavior in the United States is "impious".

Paine states that God would support the cause of independence in the United States. He maintains an optimistic attitude and hopes that the US crisis can be resolved as soon as possible.

</td>
<td>

托马斯·潘恩(1737—1809)

1. 生平

托马斯·潘恩是理性与革命时期最富有影响的思想家和作家，他的一生是为人的权利不懈奋斗的一生。托马斯·潘恩出生于美国独立战争年代，具有天生的写作才能和叛逆精神。当税务员时，他深入了解社会，目睹了重税负担下人们的疾苦和与自己同一阶层的卑微工人的无助。之后潘恩出版了《常识》，成为美国独立战争的最强音。1792 年 5 月 21 日，潘恩因写《人权》被指控叛国罪，逃到法国避难。1802 年，他回到美国，但是发现他曾经的爱国行为都被人们遗忘了。在他最后的几年里，除了他的诋毁者外，没有人再记起他，大多时候他默默无闻地生活在新罗谢尔的农场上。潘恩于 1809 年去世，并被安葬在新罗谢尔。

2. 主要作品

《税务官的状况》(1772)
《常识》(1776)
《美国危机》(1776—1783)
《人权论》(1791)
《理性时代》(1794—1795)

3. 选读作品

◆**《美国危机》**

《美国危机》表现出潘恩强烈的自然神论信仰，告知世人英国试图行使只有上帝才可行使的权力。

潘恩认为英国在美国的政治和军事行为是"不虔诚的"表现。

潘恩声明他相信上帝会支持美国的独立事业。他保持着乐观的态度，希望美国危机能够尽快解决。

</td>
</tr>
</table>

6.2 考研真题与典型题详解

Ⅰ. Fill in the blanks.

1. Except *Common Sense*, Paine's the other two famous works were ________ and ________.
2. On January 10, 1776, Thomas Paine's famous pamphlet ________ appeared.
3. Thomas Paine, with his natural gift for pamphleteering and rebellion, was appropriately born into an age of ________.
4. Thomas Paine's second most important work ________ was an impassioned plea against hereditary monarchy.
5. A series of sixteen pamphlets by Thomas Paine was entitled ________.

Ⅱ. Multiple Choices

1. It was not until January 1776 that a widely heard public voice demanded complete separation from England. The voice was that of ________, whose pamphlet *Common Sense*, with its heated language, increased the growing demand for separation.

   A. Thomas Paine　　B. Thomas Jefferson

   C. George Washington　　D. Patrick Henry

2. Which is not connected with Thomas Paine?

   A. *Common Sense.*　　B. *The American Crisis.*

   C. *Rights of Man.*　　D. *The Autobiography.*

3. "These are the times that try men's souls", these words were once read to Washington's troops and did much to spur excitement to further action with hope and confidence. Who is the author of these words?

   A. Benjamin Franklin.　　B. Thomas Paine.

   C. Thomas Jefferson.　　D. George Washington.

4. Thomas Paine's *Common Sense* ________. (对外经贸 2014 研)

   A. blamed the Parliament for the colonies' problems, but maintained the colonies should be loyal to the king

   B. blamed the king for the colonies' problems and urged Americans to declare their independence

   C. insisted that the British allow the colonies to elect their own representatives to Parliament

   D. urged the overthrow of the British king and the establishment of democracy in England

Ⅲ. Read the following quotation and answer the questions.

These are the times that try men's souls: The summer soldier and the sunshine patriot will in this crisis, shrink from the service of their country; but he that stands it now deserves the love and thanks of man and woman. Tyranny, like hell, is not easily conquered; yet we have this consolation with us, that the harder the conflict, the more glorious the triumph. What we obtain too cheap, we esteem too lightly—This dearness only that gives everything its value. Heaven knows how to put a proper price upon its goods.

Questions:

(1) Which book is this passage taken from?

(2) Who is the author of this book?

(3) Whom is the author praising? Whom is the author criticizing?

(4) What do you think of the language used in the book?

Ⅳ. Essay question

Analyze *The American Crisis*.

参考答案及解析

Ⅰ. Fill in the blanks.

1. *Rights of Man*, *The Age of Reason*

(潘恩著名的作品包括,《常识》《人权论》《理性时代》。)

2. *Common Sense*

(1776 年美国独立的风潮开始,托马斯·潘恩支持美国独立,反对英国的殖民专政,撰写了他的成名小册子《常识》,为美国从英国殖民中独立出来辩论,批评英国国王残暴无能,认为独立后的美国应该建立共和国。)

3. revolution

(潘恩是美国独立革命时期著名的作家之一。)

4. *Rights of Man*

(1791 年 3 月,托马斯·潘恩在伦敦出版《人权论》,激烈抨击埃德蒙·伯克(Edmund Burke, 1729—1797)的《法国革命感言录》(*Reflections on the Revolution in France*)(1790)。《人权论》的可贵之处还在于,它冲破了当时笼罩于整个西方思想界对英国君主立宪政体的迷信,深入骨髓地批判了这一政体,给当时还处于摸索状态的法国革命指明了共和主义的崭新方向。)

5. *The American Crisis*

(在 1776—1783 的戎马生涯中,托马斯·潘恩忙中偷闲,以笔代剑,先后发表 16 篇文章,最后集结为一册并定名为《美国危机》(*The American Crisis*)。)

Ⅱ. Multiple Choices

1. A　潘恩的《常识》号召美国摆脱英国的统治。

2. D　《自传》是本杰明·富兰克林的代表作,其余三项都是潘恩的主要作品。

3. B　"这是考验人的灵魂的时刻"选自潘恩的《美国危机》。

4. B　托马斯·潘恩的《常识》主要谴责了英国的殖民统治,呼吁美国人反抗,争取独立,建立自己的共和政府。

Ⅲ. Read the following quotation and answer the questions.

(1) *The American Crisis*

(2) Thomas Paine

(3) Paine is praising those who stand "it", it referring to "the service of their country". In the meantime, Paine is criticizing those who shrink from the service of their country in this crisis.

(4) The language is plain, impressive and forceful. Paine himself once said that his purpose as a writer was to use plain language to make those who can scarcely read understand.

Ⅳ. Essay question

①*The American Crisis* is a series of pamphlets which published at one of the darkest moments of the revolution when Washington's troops had just suffered one of the worst defeats in the war and were in the process of retreating. This work boosted the morale of the soldiers and brought them confidence and courage.

②"These are the times that try men's souls," "The harder the conflict, the more glorious the triumph." Paine maintains that consolation for those Americans who support the overthrow of tyranny is the belief that they will win "more glorious" victory and people must appreciate what they believe in and fight for. Paine states that God would support the cause of independence in the United States. He maintains an optimistic attitude and hopes that the US crisis can be resolved as soon as possible. The American Crisis shows Paine's strong belief in deism and informs the world that the British are trying to exercise rights that only God can exercise.

③Paine quotes the Tory who states, "Give me peace in my day". He is concerned only with immediate results so that he can reap the benefits, perhaps without care for the permanence of peace. Paine thinks that speakers need to struggle and suffer throughout their lives to ensure that future generations enjoy permanent peace.

④*The American* Crisis is also a Enlightenment document. Man relies on reason and indomitable optimism, not salvation, for liberty. However much the soldier, the scholar, the common man struggling for victory wants the support of God, he must rely on his devotion to his cause and to his fellow man first and foremost.

第7章　托马斯·杰斐逊

7.1　复习笔记

Thomas Jefferson (1743—1826)	托马斯·杰斐逊(1743—1826)
1. Life	**1. 生平**
Thomas Jefferson was an active leader and organizer of the American Revolution of Independence. He was also a bourgeois democratic thinker, advocating equality of human rights, as well as the speech, religion, and personal freedom. He was born in Albemarle County, Virginia, April 13, 1743. This Virginian planter-aristocrat had vigorous humanitarian sympathies and he was just as much a product of the Enlightenment. He has a wide range of knowledge and has made considerable achievements in law, philosophy, government, architecture, education, science, agriculture, mechanics, etc. In 1776, along with John Adams, Benjamin Franklin, Roger Sherman, and Robert R. Livingston, he drafted *The Declaration of Independence*. In 1800, he was elected president of the United States and served two consecutive terms. Jefferson died in 1826, which coincided with the fiftieth anniversary of the signing of *The Declaration of Independence*.	托马斯·杰斐逊是美国独立革命的积极领导者和组织者，是资产阶级民主主义思想家，主张人权平等，言论、宗教和人身自由。托马斯·杰斐逊于1743年4月13日出生在弗吉尼亚夏洛茨维尔县。这位贵族式的种植园主有着强烈的人道主义同情心，他几乎是启蒙运动的产物。他所学知识广泛，在法律、哲学、政府、建筑、教育、科学、农业，力学等方面都颇有建树。1776年，他与约翰·亚当斯、富兰克林、罗杰·谢尔曼以及罗伯特R. 利文斯顿共同起草了《独立宣言》。1800年，他当选美国总统，并连任两届。杰斐逊于1826年去世，恰逢《独立宣言》签署五十周年。
2. Influence	**2. 影响**
Thomas Jefferson's thoughts and personality deeply affected the era of his life, and he may be the person who brought the most extensive influence to the United States. To this day, people can still see the profound influence he has brought to American society.	托马斯·杰斐逊的思想和人格深深地影响了他生活的时代，他可能是给美国带来最为广泛影响的人物。一直到今天，人们仍然可以看到他给美国社会带来的深刻影响。
3. Major Works	**3. 主要作品**
The Declaration of Independence (1776) *Notes on the State of Virginia* (1785)	《独立宣言》(1776) 《弗吉尼亚日记》(1785)
4. Selected Work	**4. 选读作品**
◆***The Declaration of Independence***	◆《独立宣言》
The Declaration of Independence is generally considered to include five parts: Introduction, the Preamble, the Indictment of George III, the Denunciation of the British people, and the Conclusion. It has been regarded as an important human rights	《独立宣言》通常被认为包括五个部分："引言""序文""对乔治三世的控告""对英国人的谴责"以及"总结"。它已被认为是一则重要的人权宣言。尤其是第二句话：

declaration. Especially the second sentence: We hold these truths to be self-evident, that all men are created equal, that they are endowed by their Creator with certain unalienable Rights, that among these are Life, Liberty and the pursuit of Happiness.	我们认为这些真理是不言而喻的，即人人生而平等，造物主赋予他们若干不可剥夺的权利，其中包括生命权、自由权和追求幸福的权利。

7.2 考研真题与典型题详解

Ⅰ. Multiple Choices

1. Thomas Jefferson's attitude, that is, a firm belief in progress, and the pursuit of happiness, is typical of the period we now call ________.

A. Age of Evolution　　B. Age of Reason

C. Age of Romanticism　　D. Age of Regionalism

2. ________ carries the voice not of an individual but of a whole people. It is more than writing of the Revolutionary period, it defined the meaning of the American Revolution.

A. *Common Sense*　　B. *The American Crisis*

C. *Declaration of Independence*　　D. *Defence of the English People*

Ⅱ. Explain the following term.

Jefferson, Thomas(天津外国语 2007 研)

Ⅲ. Essay question

Write an analysis of *Declaration of Independence*.

参考答案及解析

Ⅰ. Multiple Choices

1. B　托马斯·杰斐逊生活在美国理性时代，他深信人生而平等、人具有不可剥夺的生命、自由和追求幸福的权利。

2. C　《独立宣言》是一个伟大的政治文件。《独立宣言》虽然是北美殖民地上层讨论的结果，但却代表了广大殖民地人民的心声。它在人类历史上第一次以政治纲领的形式提出了如下原则：人人生而平等、人具有不可剥夺的生命、自由和追求幸福的权利，以及政府必须经人民的同意而组成，应为人民幸福和保障人民权利而存在，人民有权起来革命以推翻不履行职责的政府。这些原则成为以后美国的意识形态，为美国此后 200 多年的发展奠定了思想基础。

Ⅱ. Explain the following term.

Jefferson, Thomas: Thomas Jefferson was an active leader and organizer of the American Revolution of Independence. He was also a bourgeois democratic thinker, advocating equality of human rights, as well as the speech, religion, and personal freedom. In 1776, he drafted *the Declaration of Independence*. In 1800, he was elected president of the United States and served two consecutive terms.

III. Essay question

Declaration of Independence not only announced the birth of a new country, it also proposed the philosophy of human freedom, which plays an important role in the Western world. It inspires ordinary people to fight for personal freedom, autonomy, and dignity in society.

In addition, the declaration drafted by Jefferson became a model for other parts of the world and became a moral force for mankind. The principles of decentralization of authority, agrarian economy, public education and flexible laws were all by products of the central doctrine of Lockian perfectibility.

Alexander Hamilton and the other founders of the Federal Party opposed this doctrine and formal statement, claiming that freedom is achieved through obedience to authority. In this case, a clear and strong civil law system is derived from nature based on experience. But once it was formulated, it was almost rigid. Man is not consistent in design or action, and the Constitution of the United States, with its added "Bill of Rights" by reflecting two such opposite views as those of Jefferson and Hamilton. It is probably a description of basic human nature. These views have appeared in American national literature time and time again in different forms.

第 8 章　菲利普·弗瑞诺

8.1　复习笔记

Philip Freneau (1752—1832)

1. Life

Philip Freneau was the most prominent poet and political journalist of the post-Revolutionary period in the United States. He was an important figure in the transition from neo-classicism to romanticism. He was born on January 2, 1752, in New York, of French Huguenot and Scottish stock. While studying at Princeton University, he established a deep friendship with future President James Madison and future novelist Hugh Henry Breckenridge. Later he turned from poetry to political journalism. Reduced in fortune and political ambition, in 1794, Freneau settled in the Mount Pleasant near Freehold, New Jersey, and worked as an editor for a New Jersey newspaper. In order to survive, he returned to the farm. In 1818, his home was destroyed by a fire. He had to pack up some of the leftovers and moved to a small farmhouse near the town. In 1832, the impoverished Freneau froze to death in obscurity at the age of 80.

菲利普·弗瑞诺(1752—1832)

1. 生平

菲利普·弗瑞诺是美国革命后时期最杰出的诗人和政治新闻记者，是新古典主义向浪漫主义过渡的重要人物。1752 年 1 月 2 日弗瑞诺出生于纽约，有着法国胡格诺派教徒和苏格兰人的血统。他在普林斯顿大学学习时与未来的总统詹姆斯·麦迪逊以及未来的小说家休·亨利·布雷肯里奇建立了深厚的友谊。之后他从诗歌转向政治报刊。随着财富和政治抱负的减少，1794 年，弗瑞诺到新泽西福利霍尔德附近的快乐山种植园定居，并曾为一家新泽西报社做编辑。为了生存，他又回到了农场，1818 年，他家被一场大火烧毁，他只好收拾一些所剩的家什，搬到了城镇附近的一所小农舍里。1832 年，贫困潦倒的弗瑞诺默默无闻地冻死了，享年 80 岁。

2. Literary Achievements and Status

(1) He was called "Poet of the American Revolution". He was also called the "Father of American Poetry", and was considered to have an important position in the American literary world.

(2) As a poet, Freneau heralded American literary independence; his careful observation of nature makes his treatment of themes about native wild life different from other native writers.

(3) He dedicated his poetry creation ability to the country's struggle for independence. His poems praised the people's righteous cause and exposed the atrocities of the British colonists. In addition, he is also one of the prominent representatives of initiating American literary nationalism.

2. 文学成就和地位

(1)他被称为"美国革命诗人"。他被称为"美国诗歌之父"，最终被认为在美国文坛上占有重要地位。

(2)作为一位诗人，弗瑞诺预示了美国文学的独立；他对自然的细致观察使其对有关本土野生生命主题的处理与其他本土作家有所不同。

(3)他把自己的诗歌创作才能奉献给了国家的独立斗争事业，其诗歌歌颂了人民的正义事业，揭露了英国殖民者的暴行。除此之外，他还是开启美国文学民族主义的突出代表之一。

3. Major Works "The Power of Fancy" (1770) "The Rising Glory of America" (1772) "The House of Night" (1776) "The Beauties of Santa Cruz" (1776) "The British Prison Ship" (1781) *The Poems of Philip Freneau Written Chiefly During the Later War* (1786) "The Wild Honey Suckle" (1786) "The Indian Burying Ground" (1788)	**3. 主要作品** 《想象的力量》(1770) 《美洲光辉的升起》(1772) 《夜之屋》(1776) 《圣诞老人之美》(1776) 《英国囚船》(1781) 《战争后期菲利浦·弗瑞诺主要诗歌集》(1786) 《野忍冬花》(1786) 《印第安人的墓地》(1788)
4. Selected Works	**4. 选读作品**
◆"The Wild Honey Suckle" "The Wild Honey Suckle" is probably Freneau's most famous poem, which is widely read. In the poem, the poet expresses a deep understanding of the lovely and fleeting nature of life. He loves nature and feels sorry for the shortness of the life. However, the poet is optimistic because he knows that life and death are natural.	**◆《野忍冬花》** 《野忍冬花》或许是弗瑞诺最有名的一首诗，被人们广泛阅读。诗中，诗人表达了一种对自然生命的可爱和短暂易逝的深刻认识。他热爱大自然，又为大自然生命的短暂感到惋惜。然而，诗人是乐观的，因为他知道生死乃自然之道。
The poem shows the poet's dedication to describing the subject matter of the United States.	该诗显示了诗人致力于描写美国本土的题材。
◆"The Indian Burying Ground" This poem is about Indian funeral, which is very different from the white's. The dead Indian is dressed in special cloth and buried in a sitting posture as if celebrating a happy event. Death has a special meaning in the Indian tradition. It is no longer a sad and terrifying thing. Those who die become warriors who guard the earth.	**◆《印第安人的墓地》** 这首诗写的是与白人大有不同的印第安人殡葬。死去的印第安人穿上特别的衣服，以坐姿埋葬，像是在庆祝欢庆的事。死亡在印第安人传统中具有特殊的意义，它不再是令人悲伤、恐惧的事情。去世的人成为守护大地的勇士。
The rhyming scheme of the poem is abab.	这首诗的韵律是 abab。
◆"To a Caty-Did" "Caty-did" is an onomatopoeia, the call of a famous insect. It will grow up to about two inches long and is dressed in a green leaf-like coat.	**◆《致纺织娘》** "凯提-迪德"是拟声词，是一种有名的昆虫的叫声，这种昆虫长大后身长约两寸，披着绿叶般的外衣。
This poem reveals the poet's love of nature and careful observation of the creatures, and at the same time shows the mystery of nature.	这首诗揭示了诗人对大自然的热爱和对自然界生物的细致观察，同时显示出了大自然的神秘之处。

8.2 考研真题与典型题详解

Ⅰ. Fill in the blanks.

1. __________ was noteworthy first because of the nature of his poems. They were truly American and very patriotic. In this respect, he reflected the spirit of his age. Therefore, he has been called the "Father of American Poetry".
2. Philip Freneau's famous poem __________ was written about his imprisoned experience.
3. The most outstanding poet in America of the 18th century was __________.
4. In 1791, probably with Jefferson's support, __________ established in Philadelphia the *National Gazette*.

Ⅱ. Multiple Choices

1. Who was considered as the "Poet of American Revolution"?

   A. Michael Wigglesworth.　　B. Edward Taylor.

   C. Anne Bradstreet.　　D. Philip Freneau.

2. Which poem is not written by Philip Freneau?

   A. "The British Prison Ship"　　B. "The Wild Honey Suckle"

   C. "The Indian Burying Ground"　　D. "The Day of Doom"

3. As a poet in the early Republic of the United States, Philip Freneau's poems are familiar to readers. __________ is the poet's meditations on the imaged afterlife. (武汉理工大学2010研)

   A. "The Wild Honey Suckle"　　B. "The Indian Burying Ground"

   C. "To an Author"　　D. "The Hurricane"

Ⅲ. Read the following quotations and answer the questions.

Passage 1

From morning suns and evening dews
At first thy little being came:
If nothing once, you nothing lose,
For when you die you are the same;
The space between, is but an hour,
The frail duration of a flower.

Questions:

1. Who is the writer of these verses?
2. What is the title of this poem?
3. Give a brief comment on this poem.

Passage 2

In a branch of willow hid
Sings the evening Caty-did:
From the lofty locust bough
Feeding on a drop of dew,
In her suit of green array'd
Hear her singing in the shade
Caty-did, Caty-did, Caty-did!

Questions:

1. Who is the writer of these verses?
2. What is the title of this lyrical poem?
3. What is a "Caty-did"?

参考答案及解析

Ⅰ. Fill in the blanks.

1. Philip Freneau

   (菲利普·弗瑞诺是开启美国民族主义的突出代表之一，他被称为"美国诗歌之父。")

2. "The British Prison Ship"

   (作为著名的"革命诗人"，菲利普·弗瑞诺的诗歌充满了战斗的激情和尖锐的攻击性，强烈且分明的爱憎是弗瑞诺革命诗歌的一大特色。1780 年，一艘美国船遭英国船队的袭击，他作为一名乘客被捕入狱。1781 年他便据此写下了名诗《英国囚船》。这是一首充满抨击色彩的诗作，揭露了英国对俘虏的血腥与残忍。)

3. Philip Freneau

   (菲利普·弗瑞诺是 18 世纪美国最杰出的诗人。)

4. Philip Freneau

   (1791 年在托马斯·杰斐逊的支持下，弗瑞诺在费城创办了《国民公报》(*National Gazette*)。)

Ⅱ. Multiple Choices

1. D　菲利普·弗瑞诺(Philip Freneau)(1752—1832) 美国殖民时期著名诗人，美国革命战争后期最杰出的作家。他被誉为"美国独立革命的诗人"。

2. D　《判决日》是新英格兰牧师、诗人迈克尔·威格尔斯沃斯(Michael Wigglesworth)的作品，其余三项都是菲利普·弗瑞诺的诗歌。

3. A　弗瑞诺对野忍冬花充满了喜爱之情，他通过自己的想象从环境的变迁出发探寻野忍冬花的一生的历程，从开放到凋零，我们能看到的不仅是永恒不变的自然之美与客观无情的自然法则，更是弗瑞诺那超然的人生感悟与态度。

Ⅲ. Read the following quotations and answer the questions.

Passage 1

1. Philip Freneau.
2. "The Wild Honey Suckle".
3. It is probably Freneau's most famous poem, which is widely read. In the poem, the poet expresses a deep understanding of the lovely and fleeting nature of life. He loves nature and feels sorry for the shortness of the life. However, the poet is optimistic because he knows that life and death are natural. The poem shows the poet's dedication to describing the subject matter of the United States.

Passage 2

1. Philip Freneau.
2. "To a Caty-Did".
3. "Caty-did" is an onomatopoeia, the call of a famous insect. It will grow up to about two inches long and is dressed in a green leaf-like coat. It can sing such a song as Caty-did in the evening, towards autumn.

第三部分 浪漫主义文学

第9章 华盛顿·欧文

9.1 复习笔记

Ⅰ. Historical Introduction (1) During this period, the United States experienced population growth, westward movement and the abolition of voting restrictions. The egalitarian belief that all white men were created equal prevailed.	**Ⅰ. 历史背景** (1)在这一时期内，美国经历了人口增长、西进运动以及选举投票限制的废止。白人生而平等的理念盛行。
(2) Before 1860, due to technological progress, the United States had already started the process of industrialization and urbanization. New York replaced Boston and Philadelphia, became the economic and cultural center of the United States, and also developed into the largest city in the United States.	(2)1860年之前，由于技术进步，美国就已开始了工业化和城镇化进程。纽约取代波士顿和费城，成为了美国的经济文化中心，也发展成美国最大的城市。
(3) However, the gap between the rich and the poor in America has widened. Transcendentalists, Baptists, Presbyterians, and Methodists all provide believers with a new way to believe in God. Various social movements seeking reform, freedom and fairness emerged, including the abolitionist movement and feminist movement.	(3)然而美国人民贫富差距扩大。超验主义者、浸礼会教徒、长老会教徒、循道宗信徒都向教徒们提供了信仰上帝的新道路。各种寻求改革、自由和公平的社会运动兴起，包括废奴运动和女性主义运动。
(4) By the 1950s, the level of education and literacy had greatly improved. Subsequently, American native writers gradually gained a good reputation both at home and abroad.	(4) 到19世纪50年代，教育和识字水平大幅度提高。随后，美国本土作家逐渐享誉国内外。
Ⅱ. Literary Characteristics (1) Romanticism: It opposes traditional art forms and rationalism, and conforms to the revolutionary pioneering spirit and egalitarianism of American tradition. During this period, most writers' thoughts were influenced by the environment of the New World itself and the early romanticism in Europe. The general characteristic of romanticism is that it pays attention to morality, emphasizes individualistic values and intuitive feelings, and thinks that nature is the source of beauty, while human society is the source of corruption.	**Ⅱ. 文学特征** (1)浪漫主义：反对传统的艺术形式和理性主义，符合美国传统的革命开拓精神和平等主义。这一时期大部分作家的思想都受到了新大陆本身所处环境以及欧洲早期浪漫主义思潮的双重影响。浪漫主义的一般特征是注重道德，强调个人主义价值观及直觉感受，认为自然是美的源头，而人类社会则是腐败之源。

(2) Transcendentalism (1830s—the Civil War): exalted feeling over reason, individual expression over the constraints of norms and conventions. It is a belief in the transcendence of "Oversoul", a ubiquitous force for goodness, which is both the source of all things and contains all things.

(2)超验主义：感觉胜于理性，个人表达胜于规范和惯例的约束。它宣扬"超灵"，一种无处不在的向善的力量，既是万物之源，又包含万物。

(3) Literature is no longer mainly used for preaching, and no longer serves politics and religion. Novels, short stories and poems replaced sermons and declarations as the main literary forms.

(3)文学不再主要用于说教，不再为政治和宗教服务。小说、短篇故事和诗歌取代布道和宣言成为主要的文学形式。

(4) The major themes of the novel are:

①the desire to escape from society and return to nature;

②Gothic novels: excavating the psychological state of characters, as an important literary form, have been passed down to this day.

(4) 小说的主要主题有：

①逃离社会，回归自然的欲望；

②哥特小说：挖掘人物心理，作为一种重要的文学形式流传至今。

(5) Nationalism stimulated American writers' interest in native languages and ordinary people. Noah Webster's *An American Dictionary of the English Language*. Literature began to celebrate American farmers, the poor, illiterate people, children, and primitive people untainted by society.

(5)民族主义进一步激发了美国作家对本土语言和普通民众的兴趣。韦伯斯特词典出版。文学开始颂扬美国农民、穷人、目不识丁的人、儿童以及没有被社会污染的原始人群。

Ⅲ. Washington Irving (1783—1859)

Ⅲ. 华盛顿·欧文(1783—1859)

1. Life

Born into a wealthy family in New York, Irving loved reading since childhood, and began to write poetry, prose and drama in his youth. He began to study law at the age of 16, but he preferred unique literature. At the age of 19, he published a satirical work about New York people in the newspaper founded by his brother, "Jonathan Oldstyle". Irving was a writer, a merchant and a diplomat. His life, like his works, is unique and has made extraordinary achievements.

1. 生平

欧文生于纽约一个富商的家庭，自幼酷爱读书，少年时代便开始写诗歌、散文和戏剧。16 岁时开始学习法律，但是他更喜欢别具一格的文学。19 岁时就在他兄长创办的报纸上发表了名为《乔纳森·欧尔德斯泰尔》的对纽约人加以讽刺的作品。欧文不仅是一位作家，还是商人和外交官。他的人生如同其作品一样，别具特色，而且成就非凡。

2. Literary Achievements and Status

(1) He was the first great prose stylist of American romanticism, whose prose style doomed him to be more enduring than other contemporary writers, such as Scott and Cooper, and to provide a foundation for the prevailing prose narrative of the future.

(2) He was the first great belletrist, writing always for pleasure, and to create fun.

2. 文学成就及地位

(1)他是第一位伟大的美国浪漫主义散文家，其随笔风格注定了他比同时期的其他作家，如斯科特和库柏，更经久不衰，同时也为后来盛极一时的叙事散文奠定了基础。

(2)他是第一位伟大的纯文学作家，他一直为乐趣和创造乐趣而写作。

(3) He was one of the first modern writers to combine history and biography for entertainment. By the 1830 s, Irving was considered the greatest American writer.

(4) He was the father of American literature. As a type of American literature, short stories are originated from Irving's *The Sketch Book*. This book also marked the beginning of American Romanticism.

3. Major Works

The Sketch Book(1819—1820)

"The Legend of Sleepy Hollow"

"Rip Van Winkle"

A History of New York(1809)

Tales of a Traveller(1842)

Life of Oliver Goldsmith(1840)

Life of George Washington(published in 1855—1859)

4. Selected Works

◆"The Author's Account of Himself"

It seems to be a self-introduction to Irving himself, including his life experience, habits, hobbies, thinking, etc. By reading this article, readers can better understand the author.

◆"The Legend of Sleepy Hollow"

"The Legend of Sleepy Hollow" is selected from *The Sketch Book*, which also contains his famous short story "Rip Van Winkle". "The Legend of Sleepy Hollow" is one of the earliest novels in America and is still widely read.

The creation of archetypes is one of Irving's consummate craftsmanship. Ichabod is the representative of the accommodating New Englanders. He is a city slicker in the village and a destructive force who wants to cheat. He was finally driven out of the village that did not belong to him, and the village was restored to peace and tranquility. Brom, on the other hand, is a peasant of Huck Finn's style, rude, energetic and self-reliant in the frontier. It can be seen from this that the love dispute between Ichabod and Brom can be regarded as the competition between two moral groups under specific historical conditions.

The style of the piece represents Irving at his best.

(3)他是首批将历史和传记结合起来进行娱乐文学创作的现代作家之一。到19世纪30年代，欧文被认为是美国最伟大的作家。

(4)他被称为"美国文学之父"。短篇小说作为美国文学的一种类型源于欧文的《见闻札记》。该书也象征着美国浪漫主义文学的开始。

3. 主要作品

《见闻札记》(1819—1820)

《睡谷的传说》

《瑞普·凡·温克尔》

《纽约外史》(1809)

《旅客谈》(1824)

《哥尔德斯密斯传》(1840)

《华盛顿传》(1855-1859出版)

4. 选读作品

◆《作者自叙》

这似乎是欧文的一篇自我介绍，包括他的人生经历，生活习惯，爱好，想法等等，通过阅读本篇文章，读者可以更好地了解作者。

◆《睡谷的传说》

《睡谷的传说》选自《见闻札记》，与《瑞普·凡·温克尔》同是其中的名篇。《睡谷的传说》是美国最早出现并至今仍被广泛阅读的小说之一。

原型的创造是欧文高超的造诣之一。伊卡包德是通权达变的新英格兰人的代表，他是村子里的城市滑头，一种欲行欺诈的破坏性力量。他最后被赶出本不属于他的村庄，于是小村子又恢复平静祥和。布鲁姆则是哈克·费恩式村野之夫，粗鲁、精力充沛，在边疆自食其力。由此可看出，伊卡包德和布鲁姆的情场之争又可以看作是特定历史条件下两个道德群体之间的竞争。

该故事的写作风格也代表了欧文的最高水准。

9.2 考研真题与典型题详解

Ⅰ. Fill in the blanks.

1. "The Legend of Sleepy Hollow" was written by ________. (大连外国语 2008 研)
2. Ichabod Crane, the schoolmaster, is a character in the short story ________ collected in *The Sketch Book*. (首师大 2008 研)
3. The Romantic period in the American literary history covers the time between the end of the ________ century to the outbreak of the ________. It started with the publication of Irving's ________ and ended with Whitman's ________. This period is also called ________.
4. In the early nineteenth century, Washington Irving wrote ________ which became the first work by an American writer to win financial success on both sides of the Atlantic.
5. ________ was regarded as Father of the American short stories.
6. Washington Irving also wrote two biographies, one is *Life of Oliver Goldsmith*, and the other is ________.
7. ________ was regarded as the first great prose stylist of American romanticism.
8. In Washington Irving's work ________ appeared the first modern short stories and the first great American juvenile literature.
9. Washington Irving's first book appeared in 1809. It was entitled ________.
10. In Paris, Washington Irving met John Howard Payne, the American dramatist and actor, with whom Irving wrote his brilliant social comedy ________, or *The Merry Monarch*.
11. ________ was the first American to achieve an international literary reputation after the Revolutionary War.

Ⅱ. Multiple Choices

1. It is on his ________ that Washington Irving's fame mainly rested.

   A. tales about America　　B. early poetry
   C. childhood recollections　　D. sketches about his European tours

2. Washington Irving's social conservation and literary for the past is revealed, to some extent, in his famous story, ________.

   A. "The Legend of Sleepy Hollow"　　B. "Rip Van Winkle"
   C. "The Custom-House"　　D. "The Birthmark"

3. The following selection is taken from ________. (大连外国语 2007 研)

   A. "The Cask of Amontillado"　　B. "The Legend of Sleepy Hollow"
   C. " A Rose for Emily"　　D. " Babylon Revisited"

   In the bosom of one of those spacious coves which indent the eastern shore of the Hudson, at that broad expansion of the river denominated by the ancient Dutch navigators the Tappan Zee, and where they always prudently shortened sail and implored the protection of St. Nicholas when they crossed, there lies a small market town or rural port, which by some is called Greensburgh, but which is more generally and properly known by the name of Tarry Town.

4. Which of the following words does not describe the features of Irving's writings? (天津外国语学院 2009 研)

A. decorum. B. humor. C. musicality. D. imagination.

5. Washington Irving's first book appeared in 1809, titled ________.

A. *The American Scholar* B. *The Marble Faun*

C. *The Pioneers* D. *A History of New York*

6. Choose Washington Irving's works from the following items.

A. *Self-Reliance* B. *Sister Carrie*

C. *Walden* D. *A History of New York*

Ⅲ. Explain the following term.

Romanticism(北外 2011 研)

Ⅳ. Read the following quotations and answer the questions.

Passage 1

"There was, as usual, a crowd of folk about the door, but none that Rip recollected. The very character of the people seemed changed. There was a busy, bustling, disputatious tone about it, instead of the accustomed phlegm and drowsy tranquility. He looked in vain for the sage Nicholas Vedder..."

Questions:

1. From which work is this passage taken?
2. How do you understand this selection?

Passage 2

"From the listless repose of the place, and the peculiar character of its inhabitants, who are descendants from the original Dutch settlers, this sequestered glen has long been known by the name of SLEEPY HOLLOW, and its rustic lads are called the Sleepy Hollow Boys throughout all the neighboring country. A drowsy, dreamy influence seems to hang over the land, and to pervade the very atmosphere. Some say that the place was bewitched by a high German doctor, during the early days of the settlement; others, that an old Indian chief, the prophet or wizard of his tribe, held his powwows there before the country was discovered by Master Hendrick Hudson. "

Questions:

1. Who is the writer of this short story from which the passage is taken?
2. What is the title of this short story?
3. Give a definition of "short story".

Passage 3

Rip Van Winkle

On awaking, he found himself on the green knoll from whence he had first seen the old man of the glen. He rubbed his eyes—it was a bright sunny morning. The birds were hopping and twittering among the bushes, and the eagle was wheeling aloft and breasting the pure mountain breeze. "Surely," thought Rip, "I have not slept here all night." He recalled the occurrences before he fell asleep. The strange man with a keg of liquor—the mountain ravine—the wild retreat among the rocks—the woe-begone party at ninepins—the flagon—"Oh! That flagon! That wicked flagon!" thought Rip— "what excuse shall I make to Dame Van Winkle?"

He looked round for his gun, but in place of the clean well-oiled fowlingpiece, he found an old firelock lying by him, the barrel incrusted with rust, the lock falling off, and the stock worm-eaten. He now suspected that the grave roysters of the mountain had put a trick upon him, and having dosed him with liquor, had robbed him of his gun. Wolf, too, had disappeared, but he might have strayed away after a squirrel or partridge. He whistled after him and shouted his name, but all in vain; the echoes repeated his whistle and shout, but no dog was to be seen.

He determined to revisit the scene of the last evening's gambol, and if he met with any of the party, to demand his dog and gun. As he rose to walk, he found himself stiff in the joints, and wanting in his usual activity. "These mountain beds do not agree with me," thought Rip, "and if this frolic should lay me up with a fit of the rheumatism, I shall have a blessed time with Dame Van Winkle." With some difficulty he got down into the glen; he found the gully up which he and his companion had ascended the preceding evening; but to his astonishment a mountain stream was now foaming down it, leaping from rock to rock, and filling the glen with babbling murmurs. He, however, made shift to scramble up its sides, working his toilsome way through thickets of birch, sassafras, and witch-hazel, and sometimes tripped up or entangled by the wild grape vines that twisted their coils or tendrils from tree to tree, and spread a kind of network in his path.

At length he reached to where the ravine had opened through the cliffs to the amphitheatre; but no traces of such opening remained. The rocks presented a high impenetrable wall, over which the torrent came tumbling in a sheet of feathery foam, and fell into a broad, deep basin, black from the shadows of the surrounding forest. Here, then, poor Rip was brought to a stand. He again called and whistled after his dog; he was only answered by the cawing of a flock of idle crows, sporting high in air about a dry tree that overhung a sunny precipice; and who, secure in their elevation, seemed to look down and scoff at the poor man's perplexities. What was to be done? The morning was passing away, and Rip felt famished for want of his breakfast. He grieved to give up his dog and gun; he dreaded to meet his wife; but it would not do to starve among the mountains. He shook his head, shouldered the rusty firelock, and, with a heart full of trouble and anxiety, turned his steps homeward.

As he approached the village, he met a number of people, but none whom he knew, which somewhat surprised him, for he had thought himself acquainted with every one in the country round. Their dress, too, was of a different fashion from that to which he was accustomed. They all stared at him with equal marks of surprise, and whenever they cast their eyes upon him, invariably stroked their chins. The constant recurrence of this gesture induced Rip, involuntarily, to do the same, when, to his astonishment, he found his beard had grown a foot long!

He had now entered the skirts of the village. A troop of strange children ran at his heels, hooting after him, and pointing at his gray beard. The dogs, too, none of which he recognized for his old acquaintances, barked at him as he passed. The very village was altered; it was larger and more populous. There were rows of houses which he had never seen before, and those which had been his familiar haunts had disappeared. Strange names were over the doors—strange faces at the windows—everything was strange. His mind now misgave him; he doubt whether both he and the world around him were not bewitched. Surely this was his native village, which he had left but the day before. There stood the Catskill Mountains—there ran the silver Hudson at a distance—there was every hill and dale precisely as it had always been. Rip was sorely perplexed—"That flagon last night," thought he, "has addled my poor head sadly!"

It was with some difficulty that he found the way to his own house, which he approached with silent awe, expecting every moment to hear the shrill voice of Dame Van Winkle. He found the house gone to decay—the roof fallen in, the windows shattered, and the doors off the hinges. A half-starved dog, that looked like Wolf, was skulking about it. Rip called him by name, but the cur snarled, showed his teeth, and passed on. This was an unkind cur indeed—"My very dog," sighed poor Rip, "has forgotten me!"

He entered the house, which, to tell the truth, Dame Van Winkle had always kept in neat order. It was empty, forlorn, and apparently abandoned. This desolateness overcame all his connubial fears—he called loudly for his wife and children—the lonely chambers rung for a moment with his voice, and then all again was silence.

Questions:

1. When Rip Van Wrinkle woke up from his twenty-year sleep, he started to doubt whether he was himself or another man. Does it mean that identity of a man is closely related to time? If so, do we have a definite answer to the question "who am I"?
2. *Rip Van Winkle* has been seen as a symbol of several aspects of America. For example, the village itself symbolizes America-forever and rapidly changing. Then what do you think Rip and his wife symbolize respectively?
3. In this short story Rip drinks and falls asleep. The noise of his daily life becomes only "distant thunder". Life goes on even in his deathlike sleep. Discuss the purpose of the author to arrange for Rip to sleep for twenty years.

V. Short answer questions

1. In American literature history, the Romantic Period, during which many famous writers and their masterpieces came into being, played an important role. Washington Irving, Nathaniel Hawthorne and Walt Whitman, etc, all of whom are not ignored by us. According to their writings, discuss the features of American literature in this period.
2. What is the theme of "Rip Van Wrinkle"? List the major works of Washington Irving and discuss the artistic characteristics of his works.
3. How to define the Romantic period in American history?
4. What is the historical and socio-cultural background of the Romantic Period in America?

VI. Essay questions

1. What's Washington Irving's main contribution to American Literature?（大连外国语学院 2007 研）
2. Analyze "The Legend of Sleepy Hollow".（大连外国语学院 2007 研）

参考答案及解析

I. Fill in the blanks.

1. Washington Irving

（华盛顿·欧文，美国著名作家，被称为“美国文学之父”。《睡谷的传说》是欧文的著名短篇小说，收在他的著名散文集《见闻札记》中。）

2. “The Legend of Sleepy Hollow”

（Ichabod Crane 是一个小学校长，欧文《睡谷的传说》中的人物。）

3. 18th；Civil War；*The Sketch Book*；*Leaves of Grass*；the American Renaissance

（美国浪漫主义时期开始于十八世纪末，到内战爆发为止，是美国文学史上最重要的时期。华盛顿·欧文出版的《见闻札记》标志着美国浪漫主义文学的开端，惠特曼的《草叶集》是浪漫主义时期文学的压卷之作。浪漫主义时期的文学是美国文学的繁荣时期，所以也称为“美国的文艺复兴”。）

4. *The Sketch Book*

（美国作家华盛顿·欧文被英国作家萨克雷称为“新世界文坛送往旧世界的第一使节”。《见闻札记》被当时的英国评论界誉为“美国富有想象力的第一部真正杰作”，它“组成了它所属的那个民族文学的新时代”。）

5. Washington Irving

（华盛顿·欧文被誉为“美国短篇小说之父”。）

6. *Life of George Washington*

（华盛顿·欧文撰写了两部传记：《哥尔德史斯密斯传》和《华盛顿传》。）

7. Washington Irving

（华盛顿·欧文是美国著名作家，他被誉为美国第一位浪漫主义散文文体作家。）

8. *The Sketch Book*

（华盛顿·欧文的作品《见闻札记》是现代文学史上第一部短篇小说集和美国第一部伟大的青少年文学读物。）

9. *A History of New York*

（1809 年，华盛顿·欧文的第一部作品《纽约外史》以“迪德里希·尼克博克（Diedrich Knickerbocker）”的笔名出版。《纽约外史》出版后，欧文便成为纽约文坛风靡一时的人物。）

10. *Charles the Second*

（华盛顿·欧文在巴黎遇到美国剧作家兼演员约翰·霍华德·佩恩，欧文同佩恩合写的社会喜剧《查理二世》曾风靡一时。）

11. Washington Irving

（华盛顿·欧文是美国著名作家，他是美国独立战争后美国文学史上最早赢得国际声誉的作家。）

Ⅱ. Multiple Choices

1. A　欧文的声望主要体现在关于美国的小说上。
2. B　《瑞普·凡·温克尔》在一定程度上反映了欧文的保守思想。
3. B　题中片段选自美国著名小说家 Washington Irving《睡谷的传说》。此段文章交代了故事的背景。文章大意为：哈德逊河东岸有很多宽阔的小河湾，在一个河湾的深处，很久之前荷兰航海家们曾占领水域，并在那里小心地靠岸，寻求圣尼古拉斯的保护。现在，那里有个小镇，或者农村的港口，有些人叫它格林斯堡，而更多人叫它泰瑞镇。
4. C　华盛顿·欧文的作品具有幽默风趣的笔调，活跃而优雅的写作风格，富于幻想的浪漫色彩。

5. D　欧文的第一部作品是《纽约外史》，发表于1809年。

6. D　*Self-Reliance*(《论自助》)是爱默生的作品，*Sister Carrie*(《嘉莉妹妹》)是西奥多·德莱塞的作品，*Walden*(《瓦尔登湖》)是Thoreau(梭罗)的作品，只有*A History of New York*(《纽约外史》)是欧文的作品。

Ⅲ. Explain the following term.

Romanticism: (1) It refers to the literary and artistic movements of the late 18th and early 19th century in Europe. (2) It was characterized by a rejection against the precepts of order, calm, harmony, balance, idealization, and rationality that were held by the neoclassicists. Instead romanticism emphasized the individual, the subjective, the irrational, the imaginative, the personal, the spontaneous, the emotional, the visionary, and the transcendental. Romanticists also showed interest in the medieval, exotic, primitive, and nationalistic. (3) Romanticism prevailed in England from the publication of *Lyrical Ballad* in 1798 to the death of Walter Scott in 1832. The English Romantic Period is an age of poetry. Major romantic poets include William Blake, Wordsworth, Coleridge, Byron, Shelley and Keats.

Ⅳ. Read the following quotations and answer the questions.

Passage 1

1. This passage is taken from Washington Irving's "Rip Van Winkle".
2. It shows the change that Rip sees as he enters the village after the 20-year sleep and the destructive effect of the change. It also reveals, to some extent, the conservative attitude of its author.

Passage 2

1. Washington Irving
2. "The Legend of Sleepy Hollow"
3. A short story is a brief prose fiction, usually one that can be read in a single sitting. It generally contains the six major elements of fiction—characterization, setting, theme, plot, point of view, and style.

Passage 3

1. Man must have an identification to communicate with others in society. But man cannot be treated in a labeled way. In the naturalistic view, man is dynamic and constantly changing. If the change is too radical, man may lose his identity, because he fails to adapt himself to the radical change.
2. Rip is good-natured, simple, anti-intellectual, imaginative, and jolly as the overgrown child, which symbolizes the immature America. His wife symbolizes the puritanical discipline and the work ethic of Franklin.
3. Washington Irving has Rip sleep through his own country's history, through what we might call the birth of America. Rip lives in peace and harmony before but return to the busy, bustling, self-consciously adult United States of America. His purpose is to show us clearly the conflicts of the nations—the conflict of innocence and experience, work and leisure, the old and the new, the head and the heart. The story reveals the conservative attitude of its author. It also tells us that a man who has looked toward the beginning of civilization in America can make a choice in his analysis of his own life.

Ⅴ. Short answer questions

1. The whole nation had a strong sense of optimism and the mood of "feeling good", giving birth to the spectacular outburst of romantic feelings. The English counterpart, especially the cultural heritage, exerted a stimulating impact on the writings of the young nation. Taking foreign influence into consideration, the great works of American writers still carried typically American romanticist color. The young nation had brought forth its own Philosophy, Transcendentalism, stressing man's capacity of knowing truth intuitively, and of attaining knowledge beyond the scope of the senses.
2. ①Washington Irving (1783—1859) is the first American author to achieve international renown. "Rip Van Wrinkle" is a short story embraced in Irving's *The Sketch Book of Geoffrey Crayon, Gent*, which dealt with the nostalgia for the unrecoverable past. The story reveals, to some extent, the conservative attitude of its author. It might be taken as an illustration of Irving's argument that changeand revolutionupset the natural order of things and of the fact that Irving never seems to accept a modern democratic American.

   ②His major works include *A History of New York* , *The Sketch Book of Geoffrey Crayon, Gent*, of which the most famous and frequently anthologized are "Rip Van Winkle" and "The Legend of Sleepy Hollow," *Life of Oliver Goldsmith* and *Life of George Washington.*

   ③Irving was the great prose stylist of American romanticism. His familiar prose narrative juxtaposes the Old World and the new one, adding his own antiquarian interest with artistic perspective. Irving put his focus on American subject, American landscape, and he treated his subject with imagination.
3. ①The Romantic Period in the history of American literature stretches from the end of the 18th century to the outbreak of the Civil War. It started with the publication of Washington Irving's *The Sketch Book* and ended with Whitman's *Leaves of Grass.*

   ②Being a period of the great flowering of American literature, it is also called "the American Renaissance".
4. ①The development of the American society nurtured "the literature of a great nation." The young Republic, devoid of a heavy burden of the inherited past and history, was flourishing into a politically, emotionally and culturally independent country.

   ②Historically, it was the time of westward expansion. Emotionally, the whole nation was experiencing an industrial transformation, which affected the rural as well as the urban life. Politically, democracy and equality became the ideal of the new nation.

   ③With the founding of the American Independent Government, the nation felt an urge to have its own literary expression and to make its new experience known in a way that no other country had. In addition, the literary environment of this country was ready for the Romantic movements that occurred in the first half of the 19th century.

Ⅵ. Essay questions

1. Washington Irving's contribution to American literature is unique in more than one ways. He did a number of things which have been regarded as the first of their kind in America.

   He was the first American writer of imaginative literature to gain international fame. When he returned home in 1832, he was hailed as the only American writer known to Europeans, and Americans saw this as a sign of the emergence of American literature as a separate entity. It is not too much to say that he is the father of American literature.

The short story as a genre in American literature probably began with Irving's *The Sketch Book*, a collection of essays, sketches, and tales, of which the most famous and frequently anthologized are "Rip Van Winkle" and "The Legend of Sleepy Hollow". The book touched the American imagination and foreshadowed the coming of Hawthorne, Melville, and Poe, in whose hands the short story attained a degree of perfection as a literary tradition. It also marked the beginning of American Romanticism. The Gothic, the supernatural, and the longing for the good old days are evident in some of its works, romantic enough thematically if not entirely stylistically, for Irving wrote in the neoclassical tradition of Joseph Addison and Oliver Goldsmith. Looking at a picture of Irving surrounded by his nieces, one does sometimes think of the old man, benign and pleasant and refined, as the uncle of American authors.

2. Washington Irving's short story "The Legend of Sleepy Hollow" is about the memorable event in which an apparently headless knight throws his head at his love interest, and the unforgettable character of Ichabod Crane, who is at once shrewd, gullible, confident and coward.

The creation of archetypes is a particularly subtle feat of Irving's superb craftsmanship. As described in the story, Ichabod Crane is a school teacher who travels to Sleepy Hollow to teach the children of the area. He is an outsider of the village while Brom Bones is the native villager. In Ichabod Crane, we see a precocious, soft-spoken New Englander, shrewd, commercial, a city man, an intruder, a somewhat destructive force who comes to deceive the villagers.

His bookish knowledge excites him, and he is driven out of the place where he does not belong, so that this quiet village remains forever beautiful and happy. On the other hand, Brom Burns is a Huck Finn type of hick, rude, energetic and boisterous, but very kind at heart, a pioneer who changes for himself. Thus, seen in this way, the love rivalry between Ichabod and Brom suddenly presents two moral groups caught in a kind of historical competition.

As to the style of the piece, it represents Irving at his best. The association between a certain local and the inner activities of a character, the emotional loading of almost every line of the story, their effect on the five senses of the reader whose attention is so fully engaged and who feels so much involved in what is happening—all these have placed this and other Irving stories among the best of American short stories.

第 10 章　詹姆斯·费尼莫尔·库柏

10.1　复习笔记

James Fenimore Cooper (1789—1851)	**詹姆斯·费尼莫尔·库珀(1789—1851)**
1. Life James Fenimore Cooper was born in New Jersey in 1789. He is the first famous novelist in America to enter the literary world with courage. Once, while reading a boring English novel, Cooper suddenly told his wife that he could write better novels than this. His wife defiantly said that he was talking big. In this way, the 30-year-old Cooper started his literary career, which brought him wealth and world reputation.	**1. 生平** 1789 年库柏出生在新泽西州。他是美国第一位凭着胆识走上文坛的著名小说家。一次，库柏在读一本枯燥的英国小说时，突然对妻子说他能够写出比这更好的小说。他的妻子却挑衅地说他是在说大话。就这样，30 岁的库柏便开始了之后为他带来财富和世界声誉的文学事业。
2. Literary Achievements (1) Cooper created two popular novel genres: the sea adventure tale and the frontier saga. The best of his sea romances was *The Pilot* (1824).	**2. 文学成就** (1)库柏开创了两种极受欢迎的小说体裁：海上冒险故事和边疆传奇。在众多海上传奇小说中，1824 年出版的《领航者》最为成功。
(2) Cooper's enduring popularity in the literary world is largely due to his frontier stories, especially the five novels that comprise *The Leatherstocking Tales* (1832—1841).	(2)库柏在文坛经久不衰很大程度上得益于他的边疆小说，尤其是由五部小说组成的《皮袜子故事集》(1823—1841)。
(3) Some leading roles and a large number of supporting roles created by Cooper are both good and evil, which not only make Americans know their past, but also make Europeans know America.	(3)库柏塑造的一些主角和大量配角，既有善良的也有邪恶的，不但使美国人认识了他们的过去，也使欧洲人认识了美国。
3. Major Works *The Spy* (1821) *The Pilot* (1824) *The Leatherstocking Tales* (1832—1841): *The Deerslayer* *The Last of the Mohicans* *The Pathfinder* *The Pioneers* *The Prairie*	**3. 主要作品** 《间谍》(1821) 《领航者》(1824) 《皮袜子故事集》(1832—1841)： 《杀鹿者》 《最后的莫希干人》 《探路人》 《拓荒者》 《大草原》

4. Selected Work ◆***The Last of the Mohicans*** *The Last of the Mohicans* is the best among *The Leatherstocking Tales*, from the conception of the work to the characterization to the specific plot. *The Last Mohican* is a famous book about race, friendship, love of nature and virtue. In the story, Cooper highly praised the noble quality of "the last of the Mohicans".	**4. 选读作品** ◆**《最后的莫希干人》** 《皮袜子故事集》中最出色的一部应推《最后的莫希干人》，无论是从作品的构思到人物性格塑造再到具体情节。《最后的莫希干人》是一部关于种族、友谊、热爱大自然、美德等的名著。故事中，库柏高度赞扬了"最后的莫希干人"的高贵品质。

10.2　考研真题与典型题详解

Ⅰ. Fill in the blanks.

1. *The Spy* was written by __________. （大连外国语 2007 研）
2. James Fenimore Cooper's novel __________ was a rousing tale about espionage against the British during the Revolutionary War.
3. The central figure in *The Leatherstocking Tales* is __________, who goes by the various names of Leatherstocking, Deerslayer, Pathfinder and Hawkeye.
4. In 1823 Cooper James Fenimore wrote *The Pioneers*, the first of the five novels that make up __________. The remaining four books: *The Last of the Mohicans* (1826), *The Prairie* (1827), *The Pathfinder* (1840), and *The Deerslayer* (1841), continue the story of Natty Bumppo, one of the most famous characters in American fiction.
5. The best of James Fenimore Cooper's sea romances was __________. The hero of the novel represents John Paul Jones, the great naval fighter of the Revolutionary War.
6. The first important American novelist was __________.
7. __________ by __________ records the history of modern civilization advancing on the receding wilderness, and its basic conflict is between the protagonist who insists on man's old forest freedom and the judge who believes that man remains savage without law and order. （天津外国语 2012 研）

Ⅱ. Multiple Choices

1. Natty Bumppo is the protagonist appearing in a series of five novels written by __________. （四川大学 2011 研）
   A. Mark Twain　　B. Theodore Dreise
   C. Nathaniel Hawthorne　　D. James Fenimore Cooper
2. Which ONE of the following is the author of *The Leatherstocking Tales*? （四川大学 2008 研）
   A. Henry David Thoreau.　　B. Washington Irving.
   C. Edgar Allan Poe.　　D. James Fennimore Cooper.
3. James Fennimore Cooper's novel __________ is the first to reveal the west and Native Americans' life in a passionate way. （北二外 2007 研）
   A. *Go Down, Moses*　　B. *The Last of the Mohicans*

C. *Winesburg, Ohio* D. *O, Pioneers!*

Ⅲ. Read the following quotation and answer the questions.

"Arms and the clarion for the battle, but the song of thanksgiving to the victory!" answered the liberated David. "Friend," he added, thrusting forth his lean, delicate hand forwards Hawkeye, in kindness, while his eyes twinkled and grew moist, "I thank thee the hairs of my head still grow where they were first rooted by Providence; for, though those of other men may be more glossy and curling, I have ever found mine own well suited to the brain they shelter. That I did not join myself to the battle was less owing to disinclination, than to the bonds of the heathen. Valiant and skillful hast thou proved thyself in the conflict, and I hereby thank thee, before proceeding to discharge other and more important duties, because thou hast proved thyself well worthy of a Christian's praise."

…

Questions:

1. This novel was written by the first American novelist. What is his name?
2. What is the name of the novel?
3. The central figure in this novel appeared in this passage. It is __________.

Ⅳ. Short answer questions

1. Make an introductory comment on James Fenimore Cooper's frontier saga *The Leatherstocking Tales*.(四川大学2009研)
2. What are the artistic achievements of James Fenimore Cooper? And what are his major works?

Ⅴ. Essay questions

1. The desire to escape from society and return to nature has become a permanent convention of American literature since the 19th century. Please discuss this literary motif in social and cultural contexts, and illustrate it with two or three examples from the 19th and 20th American literature. (厦门大学2011研)
2. The American frontier and wilderness plays a significant symbolic role in American literary imagination. Please discuss the issue in an essay within about 400 words and relate your discussion to TWO to THREE individual works in the history of American Literature.(武汉大学2012研)

参考答案及解析

Ⅰ. Fill in the blanks.

1. James Fenimore Cooper

(《间谍》是美国早期作家James Fenimore Cooper的一篇小说。)

2. *The Spy*

(詹姆斯·费尼莫尔·库柏(James Fenimore Cooper)认为他的小说《间谍》"应当是一部纯粹美国式的以爱国为主题的书"。)

3. Natty Bumppo

(《皮袜子故事集》是美国作家詹姆斯·费尼莫尔·库柏的系列小说。该故事集中的主要人物是Natty Bumppo。在不同的故事中他有皮裹腿、杀鹿者、探路人及鹰眼等别名。)

4. *The Leatherstocking Tales*

(《皮袜子故事集》包括《拓荒者》《最后的莫希干人》《大草原》《探路人》和《杀鹿者》五部

小说。)

5. *The Pilot*

(小说《领航者》是詹姆斯·费尼莫尔·库柏(James Fenimore Cooper)最好的海上传奇故事。小说主人公影射了美国独立战争期间的伟大的海军斗士——约翰·保罗·琼斯。)

6. James Fenimore Cooper

(詹姆斯·费尼莫尔·库柏是美国首位重要的小说家。他最有成就的作品，如《皮袜子故事集》五部曲，对美国的西部小说产生很大影响。)

7. *The Leatherstocking Tales*; James Fenimore Cooper

(《皮袜子故事集》反映了野蛮与文明、自然法律与社会法律、好与恶等对立关系之间的冲突与斗争。)

Ⅱ. Multiple Choices

1. D James Fenimore Cooper 是美国浪漫主义时期早期的代表作家之一，Natty Bumppo 是他的五部曲 *The Leatherstocking Tales* 的主人公。同时代的代表作家还有 Washington Irving。Nathaniel Hawthorne 是这一时期后期出现的代表作家，其代表作是 *The Scarlet Letter*(《红字》)。

2. D James Fenimore Cooper，美国早期作家，《皮袜子故事集》是他的经典之作。

3. B 《最后的莫希干人》描写的是美国西部边疆和美洲土著印第安人的生活。选项 A《去吧，摩西》的作者是 William Faulkner(威廉·福克纳)；选项 C《小城畸人》的作者是 Sherwood Anderson(舍伍德·安德森)；选项 D 的作者是女作家 Willa Cather(薇拉·凯瑟)。

Ⅲ. Read the following quotation and answer the questions.

1. James Fenimore Cooper
2. *The Last of the Mohicans*
3. Hawkeye

Ⅳ. Short answer questions

1. *The Leatherstocking Tales* is a series of novels by American writer James Fenimore Cooper. Natty Bumppo is the protagonist of the series. Although he is the child of white parents, he grows up with Native Americans, becoming a near-fearless warrior skilled in many weapons, one of which is the long rifle. He respects his forest home and all its inhabitants, hunting only what he needs to survive. When it comes time to fire his trusty flintlock, he lives by the rule, "One shot, one kill." He and his Mohican "brother" Chingachgook champion goodness by trying to stop the incessant conflict between the Mohicans and the Hurons. He is known as "Deerslayer" in *The Deerslayer*, "Hawkeye" and "La Longue Carabine" in *The Last of the Mohicans*, "Pathfinder" in *The Pathfinder*, "Leatherstocking" in *The Pioneers*, and "the trapper" in *The Prairie*. The novels recount significant events in Natty Bumppo's life from 1740 to 1806.

2. ①James Fenimore Cooper is regarded as the first great American writer of fiction. He initiated three genres of fiction: historical novel, sea novel, and frontier novel. His novels are filled with action-packed plots and vivid portrayal of American life in frontier and wilderness. He turned whatever American history can offer—the west and the frontier as a usable past—to good account and helped to introduce the "Western" tradition into American literature.

②Cooper's claim to greatness in American literature lies in the fact that he created a myth about the formative period of the American nation. In 1823 Cooper wrote *The Pioneers*, the first of the five novels that make up *The Leatherstocking Tales*. The remaining four books: *The Last of the Mohicans* (1826), *The Prairie* (1827), *The Pathfinder* (1840), *and The Deerslayer* (1841), continue the story of Natty Bumppo, one of the most famous characters in American fiction. *The Leatherstocking Tales* are noted for their portrayal of American subject matter in American settings. The hero of the tales, Natty Bumppo, embodies the conflict between preserving nature unspoiled and developing the land in the name of progress.

V. Essay questions

1. Since the American Romanticism in 19th century, the desire to escape from society and return to nature has become a permanent convention of American literature. This convention is closely related to American social and cultural contexts.

   Socially, at the time of Romanticism, America was experiencing a great time of westward expansion. The confrontation with the Indians, the Wild West and the frontier's life, all these give an impression of nature and serve as the materials for writing. In addition the great success of industrial transformation and nation independence urges the coming out of America's own literature.

   Culturally, the influence of England Romantic movement in England and Europe and the cultural heritage of American Puritanism and the "newness" of a nation endow the American literature its own features.

   This desire is particularly evident in Cooper's *The Leatherstocking Tales*, in Thoreau's *Walden* and, later, in Mark Twain's *Adventures of Huckleberry Finn*. In these works, the authors give nature some romantic and mysterious motif.

2. The importance of the frontier and the wilderness in American literature was first well articulated in Cooper's *The Leatherstocking Tales* and was to remain a major concern for many later authors. Cooper's claim to greatness in American literature lay in his creation of a myth about the formative period of the American nation. He wrote with increasing awareness of the importance to fiction of the Western frontier, where American society may be conceived as passing from one set of principle to another in two directions. Cooper's power lay in his assurance that one direction was morally right and the other practically inevitable. Here lies Cooper's conflict of allegiance. He was devoted to the principles of social order and responsible to the idea of nature and freedom in the wildness. His masterpiece The Leatherstocking Tales contains a five volume biography of the protagonist Natty Bumppo, who lives in a mysterious wild country and has a legendary career. The fact that he had never been to the frontier and among the Indians and yet could write five huge epic books about them is an eloquent proof of his rich imagination. His Indians were the first to appear in American fiction and probably the first group of noble savages. He was the quintessential simple, na? ve, generous, intelligent, brave frontiersman with a love of people and of life.

   Later on, Emerson advocated that American literature should pay attention to the Wilderness. To some extent, it reflects the spirit of American frontier and wilderness in literature. He held that the universe is composed of Nature and Soul. He regarded nature as the purest, and the most sanctifying moral influence on man, and advocated a direct intuition of a spiritual and immanent God in nature.

In the modern period, Mark Twain's masterpiece, *Adventures of Huckleberry Finn*, is a work that reflects the conflicts between society and wilderness, civilization and savage. The Mississippi River is the symbol of wilderness, in opposition to the society symbolized by the family and social environment in the novel. Tired of his state of life, Huck escapes from his father to the river and floats along it with Jim, a black man who has also escaped from his master. For them, the Mississippi River is a pleasant wilderness which satisfies their longing for freedom and liberation.

Thus, we can see that American literature of frontier and wilderness shows Americans' pioneering and freedom-pursuing spirit.

第 11 章 威廉·卡伦·布莱恩特

11.1 复习笔记

William Cullen Bryant (1794—1878)	**威廉·卡伦·布莱恩特(1794—1878)**
1. Life	**1. 生平**
William Cullen Bryant was born in Cummington, Massachusetts. Bryant was considered a gifted child, publishing his first poem at the age of 10 and his first book at the age of 13. His literary career was largely influenced by his father as a doctor. After giving up his hard work as a lawyer, he became deputy editor of *New York Evening Post*. After his wife died in 1866, he continued to translate the *Iliad* and subsequently the *Odyssey* into English blank verse. After his death, the people of New York mourned for this most respected citizen, and there was no one else since Irving.	威廉·卡伦·布莱恩特生于马萨诸塞卡明顿。布莱恩特被认为是天才儿童,十岁时出版第一首诗,十三岁时出版第一本书。他的文学生涯很大程度上受作为医生的父亲的影响。放弃辛苦繁重的律师工作后,他成为了《纽约邮报》的副编辑。1866 年妻子逝世后,他继续将《伊利亚特》和《奥德赛》翻译成英语无韵诗。他死后,全纽约民众为这位最受尊重的公民哀悼,所致悼词之多自欧文以来别无他人。
2. Literary Achievements and Status	**2. 文学成就和地位**
Bryant was one of the best poets in America at that time. In addition to being a poet, Bryant is also well-known as one of the most outstanding editors in American journalism. He supported freedom of speech, free trade and the abolition of slavery.	布莱恩特是美国当时最优秀的一位诗人。布莱恩特除了是一位诗人外,还当之无愧地被誉为美国新闻界最出色的编辑之一。他支持言论自由、贸易自由和废除奴隶制。
There are more and more great poets than Bryant, but no one can be more imaginative.	比布莱恩特更伟大的诗人越来越多,但没有人能比布莱恩特更富有想象力了。
Just as Owen ushered in a new era of American prose, Bryant also proved to European readers that American poetry is attracting people's attention. He was the first American to win the stature of a major poet.	正如欧文开创了美国散文新时代一样,布莱恩特也向欧洲读者们证明了美国诗歌正在受到人们的关注。他是第一位赢得杰出诗人地位的美国人。
3. Major Works	**3. 主要作品**
"Thanatopsis" (1817) "To a Waterfowl" (1818)	《死亡随想》(1817) 《致水鸟》(1818)
4. Selected Works	**4. 选读作品**
◆"Thanatopsis"	**◆《死亡随想》**
"Thanatopsis", was Bryant's best-known poem. When he wrote it, he was only 16 years old.	《死亡随想》是布莱恩特最著名的诗歌,做诗时他只有 16 岁。

The title of the poem means "view of death", which should be read in the context of literary tradition and the poet's own religious belief. From some English poets, he learned the writing method of blank verse and the theme of the "graveyard school" of writers.	诗歌标题的意思是"死亡观"，应该在文学传统和诗人本身的宗教信仰背景下来读这首诗。他从一些英国诗人那里学到无韵诗的写法和"墓园诗派"诗人的主题。
◆"To a Waterfowl"	**◆《致水鸟》**
"To a Waterfowl" not only describes the poet's pleasant sight of seeing lonely birds flying in the twilight when people have self doubt and despair, but also expresses his feeling of a sacred power to guide and protect all creatures in nature. The clear images and concise and powerful moral analogy in the poem have been admired by readers, and even recognized by those who hate "preaching".	《致水鸟》不仅描绘了诗人在令人产生自我怀疑和绝望的日暮时分看到孤鸟飞翔的悦目景象，也表达了自己所感受到的一种引导、保护自然界一切生物的神圣力量。诗中清晰的意象和简明有力的道德类比一直为读者所钦佩，甚至得到了那些讨厌"说教"的人的认可。

11.2 考研真题与典型题详解

Ⅰ. Fill in the blanks.

1. "To a Waterfowl" is perhaps the peak of ________'s work; it has been called by an eminent English critic "the most perfect brief poem in the language."
2. ________ was the first American to gain the stature of a major poet in the world literature.
3. Among William Cullen Bryant's most important later works are his translations of the *Iliad* and the ________ into English blank verse.

Ⅱ. Multiple Choices

1. In 1817, the stately poem called *Thanatopsis* introduced the best poet ________ to appear in America up to that time.
   A. Edward Taylor　　B. Philip Freneau
   C. William Cullen Bryant　　D. Edgar Allan Poe
2. Choose William Cullen Bryant's poem from the following ones.
   A. "Thanatopsis".　　B. "Song of Myself".
   C. "Ligeia".　　D. "Voices of the Night".

Ⅲ. Explain the following term.

Fireside poets

Ⅳ. Read the following quotation and answer the questions.

To him who in the love of Nature holds
Communion with her visible forms, she speaks
A various language; for his gayer hours
She has a voice of gladness, and a smile
And eloquence of beauty, and she glides
Into his darker musings, with a mild

And healing sympathy, that steals away
Their sharpness, ere he is aware. When thoughts
...

Questions:

1. What is the title of the poem from which the selection is taken?
2. What does the title mean?
3. What is the meter of the poem?
4. According to this selection, to whom does nature speak? To what two different human moods does nature respond?

参考答案及解析

Ⅰ. Fill in the blanks.

1. William Cullen Bryant
(威廉·卡伦·布莱恩特(William Cullen Bryant)是美国首位著名的抒情诗人。抒情诗《致水鸟》是其最好的诗歌，被英国某知名评论家誉为“用美国英语写作的最完美的短诗”。)
2. William Cullen Bryant
(威廉·卡伦·布莱恩特(William Cullen Bryant)创作了大量优美的诗歌，自然风物在他的诗中显得和谐而柔美，静谧而有节制，反映了他在那个时代所追求的理想。正是这些特点，使他成为美国的第一位浪漫主义诗人，而且也是获得世界性声誉的第一位美国诗人。)
3. *Odyssey*
(威廉·卡伦·布莱恩特(William Cullen Bryant)晚年将荷马的两部长篇史诗《伊利亚特》和《奥德赛》译成了英语无韵诗(blank verse)。)

Ⅱ. Multiple Choices

1. C 威廉·卡伦·布莱恩特 William Cullen Bryant(1794—1878)，美国诗人和报纸编辑。1817 创作了《死亡随想》。
2. A 《死亡随想》是威廉·卡伦·布莱恩特的作品。B 项《自我之歌》是惠特曼的著名诗作，C 项《丽姬娅》是爱伦·坡的短篇小说，D 项《夜之声》是朗费罗的组诗。

Ⅲ. Explain the following term.

Fireside poets: ①William Cullen Bryant, Henry Wadsworth Longfellow, James Russell Lowell, Oliver Wendell Holmes, and John Greenleaf Whittier constituted a group sometimes called the Fireside Poets. ②They earned this nickname because they frequently used the hearth as an image of comfort and unity, a place where families gathered to learn and tell stories. These tremendously popular poets also were widely read around the hearthsides of 19th-century American families. ③The consensus of American critics was that the Fireside Poets first put American poetry on an equal footing with British poetry.

Ⅳ. Read the following quotation and answer the questions.

1. “Thanatopsis”
2. View of death.
3. Iambic pentameter
4. Nature speaks to him who in the love of nature holds communion with nature's visible forms. Nature responds to two human moods. One is gladness; the other is gloominess, or sadness.

第 12 章　埃德加·爱伦·坡

12.1　复习笔记

Edgar Allan Poe (1809—1849)	埃德加·爱伦·坡(1809—1849)
1. Life	**1. 生平**
Poe was born in Boston in 1809 to poor street actors. Two years after he was born, his parents died and he was adopted by Richmond, Virginia businessman John Allen. Poe was later added by himself.	1809 年坡出生于波士顿，父母是贫穷的流浪演员。他出生两年后父母就去世了，被弗吉尼亚州里士满富商约翰·爱伦收养，坡则是他后来自己加上的。
In his early years, Allan Poe worked as an editor in the *Southern Literary Messenger*. During his work in the newspaper, he showed outstanding abilities in editing, poetry, literary criticism and novel creation. However, because of his low salary, he resigned and planned to take a chance in New York and Philadelphia. Allan Poe had been wandering for many years and lived a very hard life. In 1849, he died in miserable circumstances.	爱伦·坡早年在《南方文学新报》里做编辑，在报社工作期间，他显示出了在编辑、诗歌、文学批评和小说创作方面的突出才能。然而，因为薪资太低，他辞职打算去纽约和费城碰碰运气。爱伦·坡漂泊了许多年，生活得很清苦。1849 年他在凄惨的境遇中去世。
2. Literary Achievements and Status	**2. 文学成就和地位**
Ironically, when he struggled for life in the United States, his works caused a huge shock in Europe, and were praised as the pioneer of poetry and novel writing skills. Detective stories are generally regarded as the founder of his horror stories. His influence on French writers is particularly strong.	讽刺的是当他在美国为生活苦苦挣扎时，他的作品却在欧洲引起了巨大的震撼，被人们誉为诗歌和小说创作技巧的先锋。坡因其神秘恐怖的故事闻名，他被普遍认为是侦探小说的开创者。他对法国作家的影响尤为强烈。
3. Major Works	**3. 主要作品**
Tales of the Grotesque and Arabesque (1840)	《怪异故事集》(1840)
The Raven (1845)	《乌鸦》(1845)
"The Fall of the House of Usher"	《厄舍府的倒塌》
"The Black Cat"	《黑猫》
"The Masque of the Red Death"	《红死病的假面具》
"Annabel Lee"	《安娜贝尔·李》
"To Helen"	《致海伦》
"The Raven"	《乌鸦》
4. Selected Works	**4. 选读作品**
◆"To Helen"	**◆《致海伦》**
"To Helen" is one of the most famous of Poe's lyrics.	《致海伦》是坡最著名的抒情

The poem was inspired by the beauty of a classmate mother who was at school in Richmond, Virginia. The poem is famous for its rhythm, changeable sentence length, the metaphor of maritime travel and the frequently cited poem line "To the Glory that was Greece / And the grandeur that was Rome."	诗之一。这首诗的灵感来源于坡在弗吉尼亚州里士满上学时的一位同学母亲的美貌。该诗以其韵律、多变的句子长度、海上旅行这一比喻以及经常被引用的诗行"光荣属于希腊，伟大属于罗马"等而著称。
◆"The Raven"	**◆《乌鸦》**
"The Raven" is an illustration of Poe's poetic theory. This poem has about one hundred lines (108 lines in particular), and readers can read it completely in one go. The whole poem is filled with the melancholy atmosphere caused by the death of the beloved young beauty. The poem describes a young man mourning the passing of Lenore. The bird in the beginning of the poem repeats a word repeatedly. Under this influence, his sadness turns into madness.	《乌鸦》体现了坡的诗歌创作理论。这首诗大概有一百行(具体是108行)，读者可以一气呵成，读完全诗。整首诗弥漫着因心爱的年轻美人逝去而忧郁的气氛。诗歌描写了一位年轻人哀悼逝去的丽诺，诗歌开篇出现的鸟儿反复重复一个词，在此影响下，他的悲伤继而转化为疯狂。
The young man's spirit is on the verge of collapse, half asleep and half awake, in the face of birds to pour out their sadness. The phantom of birds is a poetic imagination, which enhances the tragedy of losing one's lover. Poe's poems are heavily tinted in a dreamy, hallucinatory color. And the narrator is in a state of semi-stupor.	这位年轻人的精神濒临崩溃的边缘，在半梦半醒之间，面对鸟儿倾吐自己的悲伤。鸟儿的幻影是一种诗意的想象，增强了失去爱人的悲剧性。坡的诗歌中梦幻的色调较重，叙述者处于一种半昏迷的状态。
◆"Annabel Lee"	**◆《安娜贝尔·李》**
This poem obviously reveals the theme of Poe's writing the sadness for the death of beauty.	这首诗明显揭示了爱伦·坡为美人的消逝而悲伤的写作主题。
◆"The Fall of the House of Usher"	**◆《厄舍府的倒塌》**
"The Fall of the House of Usher" is considered as Poe's most famous work of Gothic style and best embodiment of Poe's "totality". All the elements and details in it are connected with each other.	《厄舍府的倒塌》被认为是坡最具哥特式特征的小说，是他的"整体性"写作原则的最佳体现，其中的所有元素和细节都相互联系在一起。
This novel shows Poe's ability to create an emotional tone in his works, especially a sense of fear, destruction and guilt.	这篇小说说明坡有能力在作品中创造一种感情基调，尤其是恐惧感、毁灭感和罪恶感。

12.2 考研真题与典型题详解

Ⅰ. Fill in the blanks.

1. Author ________ Title ________(南京大学2009研；南京大学2008研)

It was now midnight, and my task was drawing to a close. I had completed the eighth, the ninth and the tenth tier. I had finished a portion of the last and the eleventh; there remained but a single stone to be fitted and plastered in.

2. Edgar Allan Poe's stories fall into two categories: __________ and "tales of ratiocination". (天津外国语 2010 研)
3. In consideration of the beauty of poems, __________ concludes that "the death of a beautiful woman is unquestionably the most poetical topic in the world." (天津外国语学院 2007 研)
4. __________ is regarded as the father of psychoanalytic criticism and the detective story. (首师大 2008 研)
5. __________'s poems have the musical quality and romantic beauty. "The Raven" is his best-known poem.
6. Edgar Allan Poe's poem __________ is perhaps the best example of onomatopoeia in the English language.
7. Write down the name of the author of the following work. (厦门大学 2009 研)
   The Raven and Other Poems
8. __________ is generally thought of as the true beginner of the short stories because he was the first writer who formulated poetics of the short stories.
9. Edgar Allan Poe's poem __________ was published in 1845 as the title poem of a collection.

Ⅱ. Multiple Choices

1. Which ONE of the following is also an influential writer of detective stories? (四川大学 2007 研)
   A. Harriet Beecher Stowe.　　B. William Dean Howells.
   C. Edgar Allan Poe.　　D. Herman Melville.
2. Mark the novelist whose major works are characterized by the elements of the "grotesque"? (四川大学 2008 研)
   A. Philip Freneau.　　B. Edgar Allan Poe.
   C. Washington Irving.　　D. Emily Dickson.
3. Edgar Allan Poe's first collection of short stories is __________.
   A. *Tales of a Traveller*　　B. *The Leatherstocking Tales*
   C. *The Canterbury Tales*　　D. *Tales of the Grotesque and Arabesque*
4. In 1831, Edgar Allan Poe published his third book *Poems by Edgar A. Poe in New York*, which consisted of some of his best poems, like __________ and The City in the Sea.
   A. "To a waterfowl"　　B. "To a Caty-Did"
   C. "To Helen"　　D. "The Wild Honey Suckle"

Ⅲ. Explain the following terms.

1. Edgar Allan Poe(北航 2007 研)
2. Gothic novel(南开大学 2004 研)
3. internal rhyme (上海交大 2002 研)

Ⅳ. Read the following quotations and answer the questions.

Passage 1(人大 2007 研)

"Prophet!" said I, "thing of evil! —prophet still, if bird or devil! —
Whether tempter sent, or whether tempest tossed thee here ashore,

Desolate yet all undaunted, on this desert land enchanted—

On this home by horror haunted—tell me truly, I implore—

Is there—is there balm in Gilead? —tell me—tell me, I implore!"

Questions:

1. Give the title of the work and the full name of the author.
2. Explain the implications of the underlined parts.

Passage 2(北航 2010 研)

During the whole of a dull, dark, and soundless day in the autumn of the year, when the clouds hung oppressively low in the heavens, I had been passing alone, on horseback, through a singularly dreary tract of country; and at length found myself, as the shades of the evening drew on, within view of the melancholy House of Usher. I know not how it was—but, with the first glimpse of the building, a sense of insufferable gloom pervaded my spirit. I say insufferable; for the feeling was unrelieved by any of that half-pleasurable, because poetic, sentiment, with which the mind usually receives even the sternest natural images of the desolate or terrible. I looked upon the scene before me—upon the mere house, and the simple landscape features of the domain—upon the bleak walls—upon the vacant eye-like windows—upon a few rank sedges—and upon a few white trunks of decayed trees—with an utter depression of soul which I can compare to no earthly sensation more properly than to the after-dream of the reveler upon opium—the bitter lapse into everyday life—the hideous dropping off of the veil. There was an iciness, a sinking, a sickening of the heart—an unredeemed dreariness of thought which no goading of the imagination could torture into aught of the sublime. What was it—I paused to think—what was it that so unnerved me in the contemplation of the House of Usher? It was a mystery all insoluble; nor could I grapple with the shadowy fancies that crowded upon me as I pondered. I was forced to fall back upon the unsatisfactory conclusion, that while, beyond doubt, there are combinations of very simple natural objects which have the power of thus affecting us, still the analysis of this power lies among considerations beyond our depth. It was possible, I reflected, that a mere different arrangement of the particulars of the scene, of the details of the picture, would be sufficient to modify, or perhaps to annihilate its capacity for sorrowful impression; and, acting upon this idea, I reined my horse to the precipitous brink of a black and lurid tarn that lay in unruffled lustre by the dwelling, and gazed down—but with a shudder even more thrilling than before—upon the remodelled and inverted images of the grey sedge, and the ghastly tree-stems, and the vacant and eye-like windows.

Nevertheless, in this mansion of gloom I now proposed to myself a sojourn of some weeks. Its proprietor, Roderick Usher, has been one of my boon companions in boyhood, but many years had elapsed since our last meeting.

Questions:

1. Why does the author deliberately describe the architecture or mansion?
2. What is the author's artistic view on literature?

Passage 3

Lo! in you brilliant window-niche

How statue-like I see thee stand,

The agate lamp within thy hand!
Ah, Psyche, from the regions which
Are Holy Land!

Questions:

1. This is the last stanza of a poem "To Helen". Its writer is __________.
2. Whom is Helen associated with?
3. Who is Psyche?

Passage 4

Although, as boys, we had been even intimate associates, yet I really knew little of my friend. His reserve had been always excessive and habitual. I was aware, however, that this very ancient family had been noted, time out of mind, for a peculiar sensibility of temperament, displaying itself, through long ages, in many works of exalted art, and manifested, of late, in repeated deeds of munificent yet unobtrusive charity, as well as in a passionate devotion to the intricacies, perhaps even more than to the orthodox and easily recognizable beauties, of musical science. I had learned, too, the very remarkable fact, that the stem of the Usher race, all time-honored as it was, had put forth, at no period, any enduring branch; in other words, that the entire family lay in the direct line of descent, and had always, with very trifling and very temporary variation, so lain. It was this deficiency, I considered, while running over in thought the perfect keeping of the character of the premises with the accredited character of the people, and while speculating upon the possible influence which the one, in the long lapse of centuries, might have exercised upon the other—it was this deficiency, perhaps, of collateral issue, and the consequent undeviating transmission, from sire to son, of the patrimony with the name, which had, at length, so identified the two as to merge the original title of the estate in the quaint and equivocal appellation of the "House of Usher"—an appellation which seemed to include, in the minds of the peasantry who used it, both the family and the family mansion.

Questions:

1. Which fiction is this excerpt from?
2. Who is the author? What are the artistic features of the author?
3. What literary technique is the fiction famous for, as embodied in this excerpt?

Ⅴ. Short answer questions

1. How does Edgar Allan Poe anticipate the 20th-century literature? (国际关系学院 2007 研)
2. As a theorist of short story, Edgar Allan Poe proposes that the first sentence should help bring out the single effect of the story. Explain what is the single effect of "The Fall of the House of Usher" and how it is achieved through the beginning sentence. (天津外国语 2012 研)
3. Describe and make a comment on the following character. (厦门大学 2007, 2009 研)
   Montresor (from: "The Cask of Amontillado")

Ⅵ. Essay questions

1. Discuss Edgar Allen Poe's contribution to the genre of short fiction. (大连外国语 2008 研)
2. Analyze Edgar Allan Poe's poem "To Helen".

参考答案及解析

Ⅰ. Fill in the blanks.

1. Author：Edgar Allan Poe　　Title：“The Cask of Amontillado”
（题目节选自爱伦坡的《阿芒提拉多的酒桶》。《阿芒提拉多的酒桶》是美国作家爱伦·坡的一部短篇小说佳作。）
2. “tales of mystery and the macabre”
（埃德加·爱伦·坡(Edgar Allan Poe)，十九世纪美国诗人、小说家和文学评论家，他的小说分为“神秘恐怖故事”和“推理故事”两类。）
3. Edgar Allan Poe
（爱伦·坡认为，美的效应在于使灵魂激动而变得高尚；无论哪种美，其最高形式必然使敏感的灵魂悲泣。因此，诗的基调应该是“忧郁”。人最感到忧郁的事莫过于死，而最富于诗意的死莫过于心爱的年轻美女离世。）
4. Edgar Allan Poe
（爱伦·坡被认为是精神分析批评之父和侦探小说的鼻祖。）
5. Edgar Allan Poe
（爱伦·坡的诗歌富有音乐感和浪漫主义色彩，《乌鸦》是最知名的一首。）
6. “The Bells”
（埃德加·爱伦·坡(Edgar Allan Poe)(1809—1849)的诗《钟》是英语语言中成功运用拟声法的范例。）
7. Edgar Allan Poe
（爱伦·坡是美国著名诗人、短篇小说家和文学评论家。《乌鸦及其它诗》是他的诗集。）
8. Edgar Allan Poe
（爱伦·坡被视作短篇小说的真正始祖因为他是第一个在小说中赋予了诗意的作家。）
9. “The Raven”
（《乌鸦》是美国作家埃德加·爱伦·坡所著的一首叙事诗，于 1845 年 1 月首次出版。它的音调优美，措辞独具风格，诗句中有着超自然的氛围。）

Ⅱ. Multiple Choices

1. C　题目考查下列作家中谁还是一位有影响的侦探小说家，毫无疑问是爱伦·坡，他是西方侦探小说的鼻祖。
2. B　Edgar Allan Poe(爱伦·坡)，美国著名诗人、短篇小说家、文学评论家。他的短篇小说着意描写人的内心世界，对表现人的思想病态尤其感兴趣。其后期的短篇小说，经常充满一种恐怖气氛，情节阴森古怪，令人毛骨悚然。
3. D　埃德加·爱伦·坡(Edgar Allan Poe)十九世纪美国诗人、小说家和文学评论家，在世时长期担任报刊编辑工作。《怪异故事集》(*Tales of the Grotesque and Arabesque*)是爱伦·坡的第一部短篇小说集。
4. C　1831 年，爱伦·坡出版了第三本诗集《爱伦·坡纽约诗集》，其中最有名的诗是“The City in the Sea”(《海中城市》)和“To Helen”(《致海伦》)。

Ⅲ. Explain the following terms.

1. Edgar Allan Poe：Edgar Allan Poe (1809—1849) was an American writer, poet, editor and lit-

erary critic, considered part of the American Romantic Movement. Best known for his tales of mystery and the macabre, Poe was one of the earliest American practitioners of the short story and is considered the inventor of the detective-fiction genre. He is further credited with contributing to the emerging genre of science fiction. He was the first well-known American writer to try to earn a living through writing alone, resulting in a financially difficult life and career.

2. Gothic novel: Gothic novel is a type of romance popular in the late eighteenth and early nineteenth centuries. The form was inaugurated by Horace Walpole's *The Castle of Otranto* (1764), whose popularity attracted many imitations, among the best known of which were Ann Radcliffe's *The Mysteries of Udolfo* and Matthew Lewis's *The Monk*. These stories, usually set in medieval castles complete with secret passageways, mysterious dungeons, peripatetic ghosts, and much gloom and supernatural paraphernalia, were thrillers designed to evoke genteel shudders, although Mary Shelley's *Frankenstein* (1817), one of the most original of the Gothic novels, had a more serious purpose. The influence of this genre extended to such works as Coleridge's "Christabel," the novels of the Brontës, the mysteries of Edgar Allan Poe, and the writings of innumerable imitators. Recent critics have interpreted the Gothic elements not only as melodramatic devices calculated to evoke terror in the reader but also as symbolic manifestations of the characters' own unconscious fears or spiritual confusion.

3. internal rhyme: The internal rhyme is the rhyme that occurs within a single line of verse. An example is in the opening line of Edgar Allan Poe's "The Raven": "Once upon a midnight dreary, while I pondered weak and weary." Here, "dreary" and "weary" make an internal rhyme.

Ⅳ. Read the following quotations and answer the questions.

Passage 1

1. "The Raven" by Edgar Allan Poe
2. Prophet: The speaker here calls the raven as a prophet, who can give him some clues to his puzzle of his beloved one.

   Implore: This word means that the speaker appeals the raven to tell him whether there are ways to cure his pain.

   Balm in Gilead: This sentence is quoted from the Bible, which means that whether there are some medicines to reduce the speaker's pain.

Passage 2

1. This passage is selected from Edgar Allan Poe's short story "The Fall of the House of Usher". The House of Usher, itself doubly referring both to the actual structure and the family, plays a significant role in the story. It is the first "character" that the narrator introduces to the reader, presented with a humanized description: its windows are described as "eye-like" twice in the first paragraph. The fissure that develops in its side is symbolic of the decay of the Usher family and the house "dies" along with the two Usher siblings. The house foreshadows doom and gives feelings of fear, and guilt.
2. Poe believes that the short story must be of such length as to be read at one sitting (brevity), so as to ensure the totality of impression. The very first sentence ought to help to bring out the "single effect" of the story. No word should be used which does not contribute to the "pre-estab-

lished" design of the work (compression). A tale should reveal some logical truth with "the fullest satisfaction," and should end with the last sentence, leaving a sense of finality with the reader.

Passage 3

1. Edgar Allan Poe
2. Psyche
3. Psyche is the goddess of the soul in Greek mythology.

Passage 4

1. This excerpt is from "The Fall of the House of Usher".
2. The author is Edgar Allan Poe. As a remarkable poet and critic, Poe stresses rhythm, defines true poetry as "the rhythmical creation of beauty," and declares that "music is the perfection of the soul, or idea, of poetry." As a short-story writer, Poe is a fascinating man of imagination. In his psychological fiction, he places the subconscious condition of the mind under investigation and probes beneath the surface of normal existence. He was the first author in American literature to turn the neurotic into heroic figure, the protagonist, in his stories. He is the father of many things, one of which is psychoanalytic criticism, the other being the detective story.
3. "The Fall of the House of Usher" possesses the essential features of the Gothic fiction. It is a genre of literature that combines elements of both horror and romance. Prominent features of Gothic fiction include terror (both psychological and physical), mystery, the supernatural, ghosts, haunted houses and Gothic architectures, castles, darkness, death, decay, doubles, madness, secrets, and hereditary curses.

V. Short answer questions

1. Edgar Allan Poe led 20th century literature, and his influence in modern literature is worldwide. He was one of the earliest American practitioners of the short story and is considered the father of psychoanalytic criticism and the detective fiction. Poe is also credited with contributing to the emerging science fiction genre. His aesthetics and conscious craftsmanship, his attack on "the heresy of the didactic," and his call for "the rhythmical creation of beauty" have influenced French symbolists and the devotees of "art for art's sake."
2. "The Fall of the House of Usher" is a very famous and representative work of Poe, in which he successfully creates the effects of horror, madness, morbidity, mystery and so on. The first sentence of this work introduces the background and setting of the story and strives to reveal the single effect of it. The story begins at dusk on an autumn day, "clouds hung oppressively low in the heavens", which gives us an impression of gloom, dullness, desolation, and melancholy. And throughout the whole story, we can find the same atmosphere, which makes people feel tense. So, the first sentence successfully illustrates the single effect of the story.
3. Montresor is the protagonist in "The Cask of Amontillado", a short story by Allan Poe. Montresor tells the story of the night that he took his revenge on Fortunato, a fellow nobleman. Angry over some unspecified insult, Montresor murders his friend during Carnival when the man is drunk, and hangs his body by chains.

VI. Essay questions

1. Poe's theories for the short story are remarkable in their clarity. His principles for the short story

are best illustrated in his review of Hawthorne's *Twice-Told Tales*. The short story, he says, must be of such length as to be read at one sitting, so as to ensure the totality of impression. The very first sentence ought to help to bring out the "single effect" of the story. No word should be used which does not contribute to the "pre-established" design of the work. A tale should reveal some logical truth with "the fullest satisfaction," and should end with the last sentence, leaving a sense of finally with the reader.

As a short-story writer, Poe was a fascinating man of imagination. He places the subconscious condition of the mind under investigation and probes beneath the surface of normal existence. What interests him most is the deep abyss of the unconscious and subconscious mental activity of the people, the subterranean recesses of the mind at work. This area of human experience Poe reveals sometimes is with alarming accuracy. His assumption seems to be that every mind is half mad or capable of slipping into insanity. As a result of all these, his fictional characters are mostly neurotics. He was the first author in American literature to make the neurotic the heroic figure, the protagonist, in his stories. Poe's most enduring tales are those of horror, the horror coming from the working of an irrational or criminal mind, driven to evil or insanity by a perverse, irrational force which, to Poe, is an elementary impulse in man. A number of Poe's tales treat a number of different people who, going mad, are all along aware that they are going mad, thus exhibiting the believable stages of mental disintegration. Poe's best known fiction works are Gothic, a genre he followed to appease the public taste. His early detective fiction tales starring the fictitious C. Auguste Dupin, laid the groundwork for future detectives in literature. Poe's work also influenced science fiction.

（本题考查爱伦·坡对短篇小说这种文学体裁的贡献，可从理论和创作两方面进行阐述。）

2. ①"To Helen" is one of Edgar Allan Poe's most famous lyrics. It is inspired by the beauty of the mother of a schoolmate of Poe's in Richmond, Virginia. The poem is famous for a number of things, for example, its rhyme scheme, its varied line lengths, its metaphor of a travel on the sea, and its oft-quoted lines.

②In the first stanza, Helen's beauty is soothing. It provides security and safety. Perhaps the reader is expected to associate Marlowe's famous line: "Was this the face that launched a thousand ships?" to Helen's beauty, for her beauty is as hypnotic for the speaker as were the ships that transported another wanderer—Ulysses home from Troy.

③Throughout the poem, Poe uses allusions of classical names and places, as well as certain kinds of images to create the impression of a far-off idealized, unreal woman, like a Greek statue. Words that support the image of an ideal woman are "hyacinth" and "classic" (line 7), "Naiad airs" (line 8), and "statue-like" (line 12). Helen stands, not like a real woman, but like a saint in a "window-niche" (line 11). She becomes a symbol both of beauty and of frustration, a romantically idealized, yet inaccessible image of the heart's desire.

第13章 拉尔夫·沃尔多·爱默生

13.1 复习笔记

Ralph Waldo Emerson (1803—1882)	拉尔夫·沃尔多·爱默生(1803—1882)
1. Life In 1803, Emerson was born in a prominent New England pastor's home in Boston. He studied at Harvard University. After a period of time as a teacher, he accepted the doctrine of Unitarianism and became a Unitarian minister to the Second Church of Boston. Soon after, he resigned because he disagreed with some old-fashioned rituals and began to write literature. When traveling to Europe, he was influenced by European Romanticism. After returning home, he formed an informal Transcendentalists' club with some friends and edited for a time the Transcendentalist journal, *The Dial*, to explain their ideas. He was the most outstanding spokesman of Transcendentalism in New England.	**1. 生平** 1803年，爱默生出生于波士顿的一个显赫的新英格兰牧师之家。他曾在哈佛大学就读。做过一段时间的老师，后接受上帝一位论，并成为波士顿第二礼拜堂一神教牧师。不久，因对该教一些古板仪式持异议而辞职，开始文学创作。赴欧洲旅行时受到欧洲浪漫主义的影响。回国后跟朋友结成非正式的“超验主义俱乐部”，编辑超验主义专刊《日晷》，传播超验主义思想。他是新英格兰超验主义最杰出的代言人。
2. Literary Influence Emerson believed in individualism, independence of mind and self-reliance. Now the harsh rhythm and unusual images in his poems are also praised. He was regarded as one of the best American writers, the most influential philosopher and writer of his time. As a prophet of that era, he had different degrees of influences on later writers such as Thoreau, Whitman and Hawthorne.	**2. 文学地位** 爱默生相信个人主义，思想独立和自立。如今他诗中刺耳的韵律和不同寻常的意象也被称赞。他生前被认为是美国最优秀的作家之一，是同时代最具影响力的哲学家和文豪。他是那个时代的先知，对梭罗、惠特曼、霍桑等后来作家产生了不同程度的影响。
3. Major Works *Nature* (1836) "The American Scholar" (1837) *Essays* (1841) "Self-Reliance" "The Divinity School Address" (1838) *Representative Men* (1850) *English Traits* (1856)	**3. 主要作品** 《论自然》(1836) 《美国学者》(1837) 《论文集》(1841) 《论自助》(1841) 《神学院演说》(1838) 《代表》(1850) 《英国人的特性》(1856)

4. Selected Works	4. 选读作品
◆*Nature*	◆《论自然》
(1) Published in 1836, *Nature* is generally regarded as the Bible of New England Transcendentalism.	(1)《论自然》发表于1836年，它通常被认为是新英格兰超验主义的圣经。
(2) In this book, Emerson emphasizes the transcendence of the "Oversoul". He thinks that the universe is composed of nature and human soul. Nature is the purest and can sanctify the mind. It advocates that people directly experience the ubiquitous God in nature.	(2)在这本书中，爱默生强调超灵的无处不在。他认为宇宙由自然和人类灵魂组成。自然是最纯洁无瑕的，能够圣化人的心灵。倡导人们直接体验自然界无处不在的上帝。
(3) The spiritual God exists in the soul of man, and that man is divine. The divinity of man became a favorite subject in Emerson's speech and writing. Everyone should think that the world belongs to him and the world exists only for him. Emerson wants to convey the idea of "self-reliance". At a deeper level, "self-reliance" is a reflection of the rising spirit of the times.	(3)神圣的上帝存在于人的灵魂之中，因而人也是神圣的。人的神性成为爱默生演讲和写作挚爱的话题。每个人都应认为世界是属于他的，世界只为他而存在。爱默生要传达的思想是"自助"。在深层次上讲，"自助"是时代上升精神的反映。
(4) Nature is the symbol of God. It coordinates the relationship between man and God. Emerson's view of nature shows that the world around human beings is symbolic.	(4)自然是上帝的象征，他协调人和上帝的关系。爱默生关于自然的观点表明，人类周遭的世界具有象征意义。
◆**"Self-Reliance"**	◆《论自助》
(1) The core point of Emerson's "Self-Reliance" is also the theme of American Transcendentalism movement. This article also makes us know a lot of new ideas, and makes readers realize that they want to be independent, only in this way can we successfully become an independent person.	(1)爱默生在《论自助》中所阐述的核心观点也是美国超验主义运动的主题。这篇文章也使我们知道了很多新的想法，并使读者意识到自己要自立，只有这样才能成功的成为一个独立的人。
(2) The distinction of "Self-Reliance" lies in its elegant prose style and the ability to express ideas vividly: Emerson's articles capture people's imagination. At the same time, he also used a lot of rhetorical devices.	(2)《论自助》的出彩之处在于其优雅的散文风格及生动表达思想的能力。爱默生的文章能抓住人们的想象。同样他也在文中运用了很多修辞手法。

13.2 考研真题与典型题详解

Ⅰ. Fill in the blanks.

1. Ralph Waldo Emerson wrote __________, which has been called "the Manifesto of American Transcendentalism," and __________, which has been regarded as America's "Declaration of Intellectual Independence." (南开大学2007研)

2. Author __________ Title __________（南京大学 2008 研）

Virtues are, in the popular estimate, rather the exception than the rule. There is the man and his virtues. Men do what is called a good action, as some piece of courage or charity, much as they would pay a fine in expiration of daily non-appearance on paradise.

3. Ralph W. Emerson believes in the concept of the __________. It is the __________ within which every man's particular being is contained and made one with all other.（国际关系学院 2009 研）

4. In 1836, a little book came out which made a tremendous impact on the intellectual life of America. It was entitled *Nature* by __________.

5. "To speak truly, few adult persons can see nature. Most persons do not see the sun. At least they have a very superficial seeing. The sun illuminates only the eye of the man, but shines into the eye and the heart of the __________." These lines are taken from *Nature* by __________.（天津外国语 2012 研）

6. The great work __________ not only demonstrates Emersonian ideas of self-reliance but also develops and tests Thoreau's own transcendental philosophy.

Ⅱ. Multiple Choices

1. Which ONE of the following is generally believed to be the main idea of American Transcendentalism?（四川大学 2010 研）

A. Glorification of the environmental forces.

B. Advocating the notion of the futility of human efforts.

C. Stressing hard-work, piety and sobriety.

D. Emphasis on spirit or the Oversoul—an all-pervading power for goodness.

2. The following selection is from Emerson's work entitled __________.（大连外国语 2008 研）

A. "Self-Reliance" B. "The American Scholar"

C. *Nature* D. *English Traits*

A foolish consistency is the hobgoblin of little minds, adored by little statesmen and philosophers and divines. With consistency a great soul has simply nothing to do...Speak what you think today in words as hard as cannon balls, and tomorrow speak what tomorrow thinks in hard words again, though it contradict everything you said today.

3. __________ was the most leading spirit of the Transcendental Club.

A. Henry David Thoreau B. Ralph Waldo Emerson

C. Nathaniel Hawthorne D. Walt Whitman

4. "The universe is composed of Nature and the soul...Spirit is present everywhere". This is the voice of the book *Nature* written by Emerson, which pushed American Romanticism into a new phase, the phase of New England __________.

A. Romanticism B. Transcendentalism

C. Naturalism D. Symbolism

5. Transcendentalist doctrines found their greatest literary advocates in __________ and Henry David Thoreau.

A. Thomas Jefferson B. Ralph Waldo Emerson

C. Philip Freneau D. Oversoul

6. Which essay is not written by Ralph Waldo Emerson?

A. "Of Studies" B. "Self-Reliance"

C. "The American Scholar" D. "The Divinity School Address"

Ⅲ. Explain the following terms.

1. Oversoul(武汉大学 2008 年)
2. Ralph Waldo Emerson(北航 2007 研)
3. "Self-Reliance"(北二外 2009 研)

Ⅳ. Read the following quotations and answer the questions.

Passage 1

Make comments on the following passage.(浙大 2007 研)

Speak what you think now in hard words and tomorrow speak what tomorrow thinks in hard words again, though it contradicts everything you said today. —"Ah, so you shall be sure to be misunderstood?"—Is it so bad then to be misunderstood? Pythagoras was misunderstood, and Socrates, and Jesus, and Luther, and Copernicus, and Galileo, and Newton, and every pure and wise spirit that ever took flesh. To be great is to be misunderstood.

Passage 2(北航 2008 研)

To speak truly, few adult persons can see nature. Most persons do not see the sun. At least they have a very superficial seeing. **The sun illuminates only the eye of the man, but shines into the eye and the heart of the child.** The lover of nature is he whose inward and outward senses are still truly adjusted to each other; who has retained the spirit of infancy even into the era of manhood. His intercourse with heaven and earth becomes part of his daily food. In the presence of nature, a wild delight runs through the man, in spite of real sorrows. Nature says, —he is my creature, and maugre all his impertinent griefs, he shall be glad with me. Not the sun or the summer alone, but every hour and season yields its tribute of delight; for every hour and change corresponds to and authorizes a different state of the mind, from breathless noon to grimmest midnight. Nature is a setting that fits equally well a comic or a mourning piece. In good health, the air is a cordial of incredible virtue. Crossing a bare common, in snow puddles, at twilight, under a clouded sky, without having in my thoughts any occurrence of special good fortune, I have enjoyed a perfect exhilaration. Almost I fear to think how glad I am. In the woods too, a man casts off his years, as the snake his slough, and at what period soever of life, is always a child. In the woods is perpetual youth. Within these plantations of God, a decorum and sanctity reign, a perennial festival is dressed, and the guest sees not how he should tire of them in a thousand years. In the woods, we return to reason and faith. There I feel that nothing can befall me in life, —no disgrace, no calamity, (leaving me my eyes,) which nature cannot repair. Standing on the bare ground, —my head bathed by the blithe air, and uplifted into infinite space, —all mean egotism vanishes. I become a transparent eye-ball; I am nothing; I see all. The currents of the Universal Being circulate through me; I am part or particle of God. The name of the nearest friend sounds then foreign and accidental. To be brothers, to be acquaintances, —master or servant, is then a trifle and disturbance. I am the lover of uncontained and immortal beauty. In the wilderness, I find something more dear and connate than in streets or villages. In the tranquil landscape, and especially in the distant line of the horizon, man beholds somewhat as beautiful as his own nature.

1. Identify the author and the work from which the passage is selected.
2. Explain the sentence "The sun illuminates only the eye of the man, but shines into the eye and the heart of the child."
3. What kind of philosophical school does the author belong to? And define the term.
4. In the line "I become a transparent eye-ball; I am nothing; I see all", why the eye-ball is transparent?
5. Compare and contrast Emerson and British Romanticism.

Ⅴ. Short answer questions

1. How to understand Ralph W. Emerson's statement "What I must do is all that concerns me, not what the people think. This rule, equally arduous in actual and in intellectual life, may serve for the whole distinction between greatness and meanness," in terms of American characteristics? (南京大学 2007 研)
2. Emerson states: "Let a man then know his worth, and keep things under his feet." This indicates the author's belief in real virtue. Please make comments on this line. (南京大学 2009 研)

参考答案及解析

Ⅰ. Fill in the blanks.

1. *Nature*; "The American Scholar"
   (爱默生的《论自然》被称为"美国超验主义的宣言"，其《美国学者》则被誉为美国知识分子的独立宣言。)
2. Author: Ralph Waldo Emerson   Title: "Self-Reliance"
   (题目节选自爱默生的《论自助》。爱默生是思想家、散文作家、诗人，是超验主义运动的主要代表。)
3. Transcendentalism; Oversoul
   (爱默生信奉超验主义，在他看来，超灵为人所共有，每个人的思想存在于超灵之中，人能以直觉官能与之交融。)
4. Ralph Waldo Emerson
   (拉尔夫·沃尔多·爱默生(Ralph Waldo Emerson, 1803—1882)美国散文作家、思想家、诗人。1836 年出版处女作《论自然》。《论自然》的发表为美国思想界吹来一股清风，一扫机械主义自然观的乌烟瘴气。)
5. child; Ralph Waldo Emerson
   (此句为爱默生代表作《论自然》中的名句。)
6. *Walden*
   (梭罗的代表作《瓦尔登湖》表明梭罗不仅接受了爱默生的超然主义哲学，而且进一步亲身实践阐明自然界的泛神特性。)

Ⅱ. Multiple Choices

1. D　超验主义的核心思想是超灵(Oversoul)，认为真理超越人的有限感觉之外，不能通过理性认识，而要以直觉来领悟普遍真理。

2. A　题目中的段落节选自爱默生的《论自助》，节选部分的大意是：愚蠢地坚持随众随俗是心胸狭小的幽灵的表现，是低级的政客、哲学家和神学家崇拜的东西。伟大的灵魂根本不会随波逐流……今天你想说什么就说什么，像放连珠炮一样；明天你想说什么，照样斩钉截铁地说什么，哪怕跟你今天说的一切都是互相矛盾的。

3. B　爱默生是超验主义的倡导者，爱默生经常和他的朋友梭罗、霍桑、阿尔柯、玛格利特等人举行小型聚会，探讨神学、哲学和社会学问题。这种聚会当时被称为“超验主义俱乐部”，爱默生也自然而然地成为超验主义的领袖。

4. B　《论自然》是爱默生的第1部重要哲学著作，最初发表于1836年。它集超验主义思想之大成，有新英格兰超验主义宣言的美称。《论自然》中强调精神，或超灵，认为这是宇宙至为重要的存在因素。超灵是一种无所不容、无所不在、扬善抑恶的力量，是万物之本、万物之所属，它存在于人和自然界内。

5. B　美国超验主义(American Transcendentalism)是美国的一个重要思潮，它兴起于十九世纪三十年代的新英格兰地区。它是与拉尔夫·沃尔多·爱默生以及梭罗相关的一种文学和哲学运动，宣称存在一种理想的精神实体，超越于经验和科学之处，通过直觉得以把握。

6. A　《论读书》是英国杰出的哲学家、科学家及散文家弗朗西斯·培根(Francis Bacon)撰写的一篇探讨读书问题的散文札记。其余三个选项均是爱默生的作品。

Ⅲ. Explain the following terms.

1. Oversoul: “The Over-Soul” is an essay by Ralph Waldo Emerson, first published in 1841. For Emerson, the term denotes a supreme underlying unity which transcends duality or plurality, much in keeping with the philosophy of Advaita Vedanta. Oversoul has more recently come to be used by Eastern philosophers such as Meher Baba and others as the closest English language equivalent of the Vedic concept of Paramatman. The term is used frequently in discussion of Eastern metaphysics and has also entered western vernacular. In this context, the term “Over-soul” is understood as the collective indivisible Soul, of which all individual souls or identities are included.

2. Ralph Waldo Emerson: Ralph Waldo Emerson (1803—1882) was an American essayist, philosopher, and poet, best remembered for leading the Transcendentalist movement of the mid 19th century. He gradually moved away from the religious and social beliefs of his contemporaries, formulating and expressing the philosophy of Transcendentalism in his 1836 essay, *Nature*. As a result of this ground breaking work, he gave a speech entitled “The American Scholar” in 1837, which Oliver Wendell Holmes, Sr. considered to be America's “Intellectual Declaration of Independence”.

3. “Self-Reliance”: “Self-Reliance” is an essay written by American Transcendentalist philosopher and essayist, Ralph Waldo Emerson. It contains the most solid statement of one of Emerson's repeating themes, the need for each individual to avoid conformity and false consistency, and follow his or her own instincts and ideas. Emerson's ideas are considered a reaction to a commercial identity; he calls for a return to individual identity.

Ⅳ. Read the following quotations and answer the questions.

Passage 1

This paragraph is taken from Ralph Waldo Emerson's "Self-Reliance". In this paragraph, Emerson advocates that people should live truly and bravely, being not afraid of being misunderstood. Emerson points out in "Self-Reliance" that a person ought to go upright and speak truth in all ways. First, the author speaks loudly that human should speak the truth in hard words even though it may contradict everything that you said before. Then he quotes others' doubts. Here Emerson gives some examples to demonstrate his opinion, some great figures that have ever been misunderstood but are actually right. He also points out that greatness will inevitably be misunderstood.

Passage 2

1. The passage is selected from Emerson's *Nature*.
2. The man can only see the sun, but the child can feel the sun. That is to say, adults usually arenot aware of the nature, only little children can enjoy nature from the bottom of their hearts.
3. Emerson belongs to the Transcendentalist school. Transcendentalism is a New England movement, which flourished from about 1835 to 1860. It had its roots in romanticism and in post-Kantian idealism by which Coleridge was influenced. It had a considerable influence on American art and literature. Basically religious, it emphasized the role and importance of the individual conscience, and the value of intuition in matters of moral guidance and inspiration. The group of people was also social reformers. Some of the members, besides Emerson, were famous, including Bronson Alcott, Henry David Thoreau and Nathaniel Hawthorne.
4. Because this is a moment of "conversion", when one feels completely merged with the outside world, when one has completely sunk into nature and become one with it, and the soul has gone beyond the physical limits of the body to share the omniscience of the Oversoul. In a word, the soul has completely transcended the limits of individuality and become part of the Oversoul.
5. (1) Similarities: ①They both respect nature. British Romanticists claim that they can get a lot of aspiration from nature, and they appreciated natural beauty. Emerson believes that nature is ennobling. ②They both stress the importance of the individual. British Romanticists see the individual as the very center of all life and all experience; Emerson thinks that the individual is divine and, therefore, self-reliant.

   (2) Difference: Emerson emphasized the concept of the "Oversoul". The Oversoul was an all-pervading power for goodness, omnipresent and omnipotent, from which all things came and of which all were a part.

V. Short answer questions

1. The quotation is from Emerson's essay "Self-Reliance", one of the clearest and most memorable examples of Emerson's philosophy of individualism, an idea deeply rooted in American culture. His variety of individualism stems from the self's intuitive connection with the Over-soul, and is not simply a matter of self-centered assertion or immature narcissism. Emerson expresses the romantic idea of individualism, with an emphasis on being self-sufficient. Emerson believed that each person has a unique gift that can only be revealed when the individual has the courage to believe in his or her own thoughts, attitudes, and inclinations against all public opposition.
2. This line is a representation of Emerson's transcendental ideas that the individual is the most important of all and an individual should know about his own worth and give full to it. If man de-

pends upon himself, cultivates himself and brings about the divine in himself, he can hope to become better and even perfect. He tries to convince people that doing things according to their knowledge of their worth is a perfect way to develop and improve themselves. Each man should determine his own existence. Men should and can be self-reliant. Self-reliance is also an expression of the hope that man can become the best person he hopes to be. "infinitude of the privates man". He tried to convince people that the possibilities for man to develop and improve himself are infinite. Men should and could be self-reliant.

To Emerson, the physical world was vitalistic and evolutionary. Nature was emblematic of God. It mediates between man and God, and its voice leads to higher truth. "Nature is the vehicle of thought," and "particular natural facts are symbols of particular spiritual facts." In a word, "Nature is the symbol of spirit."

第14章 亨利·戴维·梭罗

14.1 复习笔记

Henry David Thoreau (1817—1862)

1. Life

Thoreau was a famous New England Transcendentalist. He was born in Concord, Massachusetts. After graduating from Harvard University, he became friends with Emerson and began to accept Emerson's ideas. As Emerson's most faithful believer, he moved to Walden Pond in 1845 and lived in seclusion for more than two years. During this period, he sometimes visited visitors, and once he was detained overnight for refusing to pay taxes. This inspired him to write a famous political essay "Civil Disobedience". After returning to Concord, Thoreau wrote the famous *Walden* based on his life experience in Walden Pond for more than two years, and spent the rest of his life till the age of forty-five.

2. Literary Achievements and Status

There are three great 19th-century writers who were left out in the history of American literature and won fame in the 20th century, namely Thoreau, Herman Melville and Emily Dickinson. Thoreau is now regarded as an important writer in the 19th century, and his literary achievements are even higher than Emerson's. His influence goes beyond the United States. In 1969, the statue of Thoreau was put into the Hall of Fame in New York.

3. Major Works

"Civil Disobedience"(1849)

Walden (1854)

"A Plea for Captain John Brown"(1859)

4. Selected Work

◆ ***Walden***

Thoreau's masterpiece *Walden* is a great Transcendentalist work. It faithfully recorded Thoreau's reflection when he communicated with nature alone. It shows that Thoreau not only accepted Emerson-s transcendentalism philosophy, but also

亨利·戴维·梭罗(1817—1862)

1. 生平

梭罗是著名的新英格兰超验主义者，他出生于马萨诸塞州的康科德镇。从哈佛大学毕业后和爱默生成为好友并开始接受了爱默生的思想。作为爱默生最忠实的信徒，1845年他搬到瓦尔登湖畔居住，过了两年多简朴的隐居生活。这期间他有时接访来客，一次他因拒绝交税而被拘留了一夜。这激发他写成了著名的政论文《论公民的不服从》。回到康科德后，梭罗根据两年多在瓦尔登湖的生活经历写成了著名的《瓦尔登湖》，并在那里度过余生，直至45岁时逝世。

2. 文学成就和地位

在美国文学史上生前备受冷落、在20世纪才赢得盛名的19世纪伟大作家有三位，即梭罗、赫尔曼·麦尔维尔和艾米莉·迪金森。现在梭罗被认为是19世纪重要的作家，甚至文学成就高于爱默生。他的影响超出了美国范围。1969年，梭罗的塑像被放进了纽约的“名人堂”。

3. 主要作品

《论公民的不服从》(1849)

《瓦尔登湖》(1854)

《为约翰·布朗上校请愿》(1859)

4. 选读作品

◆**《瓦尔登湖》**

梭罗的代表作《瓦尔登湖》是一部超验主义巨作。他忠实地记录了梭罗独自与自然界交流时的反思。它表明梭罗不仅接受了爱默生

expounded the pantheistic characteristics of nature by personal practice. *Walden* is all-encompassing and can be interpreted from various angles.	的超验主义哲学，而且进一步亲身实践阐明自然界的泛神特性。《瓦尔登湖》包罗万象，可以从多种角度去解读。
(1) It is a book about man: what he is, what he should be and must be. Thoreau thinks that the most important thing in life is self-sufficiency and striving for spiritual perfection. Thoreau is known as the forerunner of individualism in the history of American literature.	(1)它是一本关于人的书，阐述人应该而且必须成为什么样的人。梭罗认为生活中最重要的事情是自给自足，努力实现精神上的完美。梭罗被誉为美国文学史上个人主义的先导。
(2) In this book, Thoreau lashed out at modern civilization. He believes that modern civilization has made people lose their humanity and put people in spiritual predicament.	(2)在该书中梭罗猛烈抨击了现代文明。他认为现代文明使人失去了人性，将人置于精神困境中。
(3) In addition, the book shows that Thoreau wants his compatriots to get rid of their smug complacency. He records his efforts to minimize his own needs at Walden Pond. He holds that spiritual richness is real wealth. Human spirit may not help people to make great achievements, but it helps people to make real progress in the process of self-improvement.	(3)此外，该书表明梭罗希望国人摆脱自鸣得意、沾沾自喜的情绪。他记录了自己在瓦尔登湖上尽量将个人需求降到最低的情况。他认为精神上的富有才是真正的富有。人的精神或许不能帮助人飞黄腾达，却有助于人在自我完善的过程中取得真正的进步。
(4) Thoreau's purpose in living in the forest is to test a new way of life for himself and his compatriots. When he came out of the forest, he was reborn and reinvigorated. Thus, regeneration became one of the important themes in *Walden* and it determined the structural framework of the book.	(4)梭罗去森林居住目的是为自己和同胞们试验一种新的生活方式。他从林中出来时获得了重生，整个人面貌焕然一新。重生成为《瓦尔登湖》中重要的主题之一，并且决定了该书的结构框架。

14.2 考研真题与典型题详解

Ⅰ. Fill in the blanks.

1. Ralph Waldo Emerson's truest disciple, the man who put into practice many of Emerson's theories, was __________.
2. A superb book entitled __________ came out of Henry David Thoreau's two year experiment at Walden Pond.
3. Write down the name of the author of the following work. (厦门大学 2008 研)
   A Week on the Concord and Merrimack Rivers
4. In 1845, Henry David Thoreau began a two-year residence at __________ Pond.
5. Another renowned New England Transcendentalist was __________, a friend of Ralph Waldo Emerson's and his junior by some fourteen years.

Ⅱ. Multiple Choices

1. Point out the work that was written by Henry David Thoreau. ________(四川大学 2009 研)

   A. "The Fall of the House of Usher"　　B. *The Rise of Silas Lapham*

   C. *Walden*　　D. "The Legend of Sleepy Hollow"

2. Transcendentalist doctrines found their greatest literary advocates in ________ and Henry David Thoreau.

   A. Thomas Jefferson　　B. Ralph Waldo Emerson

   C. Philip Freneau　　D. Oversoul

3. From Henry David Thoreau's jail experience, came his famous essay, ________, which states Thoreau's belief that no man should violate his conscience at the command of a government.

   A. *Walden*　　B. *Nature*

   C. "Civil Disobedience"　　D. *Common Sense*

Ⅲ. Short answer questions

1. What is the major thematic concern of *Walden*? (国际关系学院 2007 研)
2. What is the main idea of Henry David Thoreau's *Walden*?

参考答案及解析

Ⅰ. Fill in the blanks.

1. Henry David Thoreau

   (亨利·戴维·梭罗(Henry David Thoreau)是美国作家、哲学家，他最著名的作品为著名散文集《瓦尔登湖》和论文《论公民的不服从》。梭罗是爱默生最忠实的追随者并且将爱默生的许多理论付诸实践。)

2. *Walden*

   (《瓦尔登湖》出版于 1854 年，梭罗在书中详尽地描述了他在瓦尔登湖湖畔一片再生林中度过两年零两月的生活以及期间他的许多思考。)

3. Henry David Thoreau

   (《康科德和梅里麦克河上的一周》是梭罗的重要作品。该书 1849 年出版，记载了 1839 年夏末梭罗与兄长约翰自制小舟，驾船漂游家乡附近两条河流的见闻和感想。)

4. Walden

   (1945 到 1947 年亨利·戴维·梭罗居住在瓦尔登湖岸的小木屋里，并根据这段经历写作了《瓦尔登湖》。)

5. Henry David Thoreau

   (亨利·戴维·梭罗，美国作家、哲学家，新英格兰著名的超验主义者。他比爱默生小 14 岁，是爱默生思想忠实的追随者。)

Ⅱ. Multiple Choices

1. C　梭罗是美国超验主义作家之一，其代表作是《瓦尔登湖》。选项 A《厄舍府的倒塌》是 Edgar Allan Poe(爱伦·坡)的作品；选项 B《塞拉斯·拉帕姆的发迹》是 William Dean Howells(豪威尔斯)的小说；选项 D《睡谷的传说》的作者是 Washington Irving(华盛顿·欧文)。

2. B　美国超验主义(American Transcendentalism)是美国的一个重要思潮，它兴起于十九世纪三十年代的新英格兰地区。它是与拉尔夫·沃尔多·爱默生以及梭罗相关的一种文学和哲学运动，宣称存在一种理想的精神实体，超越于经验和科学之处，通过直觉得以把握。

3. C　在瓦尔登湖生活期间，梭罗因为反对黑奴制拒交“人头税”而被捕入狱。友人替他代交了税款保其出狱，但这一亲身体验却激发他写成了著名的政论《抵制公民政府》(“Resistance to Civil Government”)，后改名为《论公民的不服从》(“Civil Disobedience”)。

Ⅲ. Short answer questions

1. *Walden* is informed by American Transcendentalism, a philosophy developed by Thoreau's friend and spiritual mentor Ralph Waldo Emerson. It emphasizes the importance of solitude, contemplation, and closeness to nature in transcending the "desperate" existence that he believed was the fate of most people. Thoreau was putting into practice the Transcendentalist belief that one can best transcend normality and experience the Ideal, or the Divine, through nature.
2. Henry David Thoreau is an American transcendentalist writer, he was by no means an "escapist" or a recluse, but was intensely involved in the life of his day. *Walden* is a great transcendentalist work.

   In this work, Thoreau saw nature as a genuine restorative, wholesome influence on man's spiritual well-being and regarded it as a symbol of the spirit. Indeed, *Walden* is a faithful record of his reflections as he communed with nature alone, eloquently demonstrating that he not only embraced Emerson's transcendentalist philosophy, but further articulated the pantheistic quality of nature.

   Walden can be many things and can be read on more than one level. It is, first and foremost, a book on self-culture and human perfectibility. It is about man, what he is and what he should be and must be. Second, Thoreau was very critical of modern civilization. It was, in Thoreau's opinion, an insult and an enslavement of man. He felt that man should seek truth directly by leaving the life of hurry and bustle to get ahead in worldly affairs and sinking himself in the wholesome atmosphere of nature. Furthermore, the book is full of ideas expressed in jostle his neighbors out of their smug complacency. And he goes on to prescribe a panacea for the fatal modern craze for monetary success that comes in the wake of mechanization and commercialization of life.

第 15 章　纳撒尼尔·霍桑

15.1　复习笔记

Nathaniel Hawthorne (1804—1864)	纳撒尼尔·霍桑(1804—1864)
1. Life	**1. 生平**
Hawthorne was born in Salem, Massachusetts. One of his ancestors was a colonial magistrate, who was notorious for his involvement in persecuting the Quakers. Another ancestor was a judge who tried witch cases in Salem in 1692. The family gradually declined. Hawthorne was keenly aware of the viciousness of his ancestors, which also made him understand that evil exists in the core of human life. During his stay at Bowden College, he made friends with Henry Wadsworth Longfellow and Franklin Pierce. He collected writing materials by wandering around Salem town, observing people's livelihood and listening to public opinion. In the 1930s, he once edited magazines in Boston, and later worked in customs. On the way to White Mountain, Hawthorne died in Plymouth in his dream and was buried in the "Authors' Ridge" in Sleepy Hollow Cemetery, Concord, Massachusetts.	霍桑出生于马萨诸塞州的萨勒姆镇。他的一位祖先是殖民地行政官，因参与迫害贵格党人而臭名昭著。另一位祖先则是 1692 年萨勒姆审巫案的法官。家族渐渐走向没落。霍桑强烈地意识到他祖先的恶性，这也让他明白了邪恶存在于人生命的核心部分。在鲍登学院期间，他结交了朗费罗和皮尔斯。他通过在萨勒姆镇闲逛，观察民生，听取民意来收集写作材料。30 年代时他曾一度在波士顿编辑杂志，后来在海关工作。去怀特山途中，霍桑在梦中于普利茅斯去世，葬于沉睡谷墓地的“作者之脊”。
2. Ideas	**2. 思想**
(1) Throughout his life, he was haunted by his sense of sin and evil in life, therefore we see "black vision" in his works—the power of evil. He believed that sin is the mark that everyone is born with. Almost every one of his works involves sin and evil.	(1)终其一生，霍桑心中都萦绕着罪恶感，因此我们可以在他的作品中感受到“黑色视觉”——邪恶的力量。他认为罪恶是人生来所带的标记。几乎他的每一部作品都涉及到了罪与恶。
(2) He opposed the Transcendentalists' purely optimistic attitude towards human nature.	(2)他反对超验主义者对人性持有纯粹乐观的态度。
(3) Sin will eventually be punished. Sin or evil can be passed from generation to generation. In his opinion, sin plays a role of enlightenment.	(3)罪行必遭惩罚，罪或者恶都会代代相传。他相信罪恶起教化的作用。
(4) He believed that romance was the predestined form of American narrative. He had a strong interest in history and cultural relics, and thought that these can nourish the growth of his mind.	(4)他认为传奇是美国小说叙事的注定形式。他对历史和文物古迹有浓郁的兴趣，认为这些可以滋养思想的成长。
(5) Hawthorne had a negative attitude toward science.	(5)霍桑对科学持消极的态度。

3. Writing Style	**3. 写作风格**
(1) Hawthorne is a romantic writer with the most contradictory thoughts and skillful writing skills in the history of American literature. Contradiction is a prominent feature of Hawthorne's writing.	(1)霍桑是美国文学历史上思想最为矛盾、写作手法娴熟的浪漫主义作家。矛盾性是霍桑写作艺术的一个显著特征。
(2) He is good at exploring people's complex psychology, and he is an anatomist of "the interior of the heart". His works are rich in descriptions of psychological activities. For him, telling stories is another way to explore the meaning of life.	(2)他善于探究人的复杂心理，是人物内心的剖析师。他的作品有丰富的心理活动描写。对他来说，讲故事是探讨生命意义的另一种方法。
(3) Allegory is a heavy blow to reality, while symbolism is a weapon to expose and attack. Hawthorne is a master of symbolism. He inherited the Puritan tradition and reinvigorated American literature. His vivid and symbolic images directly hit the root of human morality.	(3)寓言是对现实沉重的打击，象征主义则是揭露和抨击的武器。霍桑是象征主义大师，他继承了清教的传统并光复了美国文学。他生动且具有象征意义的意象直击人性道德的根源。
4. Influence	**4. 影响**
Hawthorne's influence is far-reaching. James Russell Lowell gave him due recognition in *A Fable for Critics*. Hawthorne's ability to make a story exist in its own right but meanwhile appears as a moral symbol, which had a great influence on Merville. He exerted great influence on William Dean Howells, William Faulkner and some Gothic novelists.	霍桑的影响可谓深远。詹姆斯·拉塞尔·洛威尔在《写给批评家的寓言》中给予了他应有的认可。霍桑有能力把一个故事写得好又似一个道德象征，对梅维尔影响甚广。他对威廉·迪安·豪威尔斯，威廉·福克纳和一些哥特式小说家影响深重。
5. Major Works	**5. 主要作品**
"Young Goodman Brown" (1835) "The Minister's Black Veil" (1836) *Twice-told Tales* (1837) *Rappacini's Daughter* (1844) *Mosses from an Old Manse* (1846) *The Scarlet Letter* (1850) *The House of the Seven Gables* (1851) *The Blithedale Romance* (1852) *The Marble Faun* (1860)	《小伙子布朗》(1835) 《教长的黑纱》(1836) 《重讲一遍的故事》(1837) 《拉普奇尼博士的女儿》(1844) 《古屋青苔》(1846) 《红字》(1850) 《有七个尖角阁的房子》(1851) 《福谷传奇》(1852) 《玉石雕像》(1860)
6. Selected Work	**6. 选读作品**
◆ ***The Scarlet Letter***	◆《红字》
(1) Theme—This novel shows the universality of evil and explores the complexity and ambivalence when people are faced	(1)主题——这部小说展现了罪恶的普遍性并探究了人们面临选

with choices. Hawthorne does not intend to tell a story about love or sin, but pays attention to the moral, emotional and psychological influences that guilt brings to ordinary people or some main characters, thus showing the tension between society and individuals. For Hawthorne, everyone is a potential sinner, and moral courage is essential to the improvement of human nature.	择时的复杂与矛盾心理。霍桑无意去讲述一个关于爱情或罪恶的故事，而是关注于罪恶感带给普通人或一些主要角色在道德、情感、心理方面的影响，从而展示了社会与个人之间的紧张状况。对于霍桑来讲，每个人都是潜在的罪人，道义上的勇气对人性的改善是必不可少的。
(2) Symbolism—*The Scarlet Letter* is a hymn on Hester's moral growth. The scarlet letter "A" originally is a symbol of shame, "adultery". Then, because of her sincere sympathy and help to fellow villagers, the meaning of the scarlet letter became "capable"; Finally, the scarlet letter A appears in the sky, which means "angel". When she established a meaningful relationship with her native people, her life finally gained real meaning.	(2)象征主义——《红字》就是一曲歌颂海斯特道德成长的赞歌。红字最初是羞耻的象征，是"通奸"；然后因为她对同乡人真诚的同情和帮助使得红字的意义变为"能干"；最后，红字 A 出现在天空中，意味着"天使"。当她与乡人建立了意义深长的关系时，她的生命最终获得了真正的意义。

15.2 考研真题与典型题详解

Ⅰ. Fill in the blanks.

1. Pearl is a character in __________ written by __________. (大连外国语学院 2007 研)
2. As a reflection of Hester Prynne's moral development, the __________ symbolically undergoes a gradual and imperceptible change from "__________" to "able" and last to "angel". (天津外国语学院 2008 研)
3. In 1850, Nathaniel Hawthorne brought out his masterpiece __________, the story of a triangular love affair in colonial America.
4. The way in which __________ wrote *The Scarlet Letter* suggests that American Romanticism adapted itself to American puritan moralism.
5. Hester Prynne is the heroine in Nathaniel Hawthorne's novel __________.
6. Herman Melville's world classic novel *Moby Dick* was dedicated to __________, a novelist.

Ⅱ. Multiple Choices

1. The most influential novelist in Romantic period is __________. (北二外 2009 研)

   A. Nathaniel Hawthorne　　B. Edgar Allan Poe

   C. Emily Dickinson　　D. Fennimore Cooper

2. The finest example of Nathaniel Hawthorne's symbolism is the recreation of Puritan Boston in __________.

   A. *The Scarlet Letter*　　B. "Young Goodman Brown"

   C. *The Marble Faun*　　D. "The Ambitious Guest"

3. "There is evil in every human heart, which may remain latent, perhaps, through the whole

life; but circumstances may rouse it to activity. " The thought is reflected in __________.

A. Nathaniel Hawthorne's "Young Goodman Brown"

B. Mark Twain's *The Adventures of Huckleberry Finn*

C. Walt Whitman's *Leaves of Grass*

D. Herman Melville's *Moby Dick*

4. __________ is an appalling fictional version of Nathaniel Hawthorne's belief that "the wrong doing of one generation lives into the successive ones" and that evil will come out of evil though it may take many generations to happen.

A. *The Marble Faun* B. *The House of the Seven Gables*

C. *The Blithedale Romance* D. "Young Goodman Brown"

5. Which is not Nathaniel Hawthorne's long novel?

A. *The Marble Faun* B. *The Blithedale Romance*

C. *The House of Seven Gables* D. *Dr. Heidegger's Experiment*

6. Herman Melville called his friend Nathaniel Hawthorne __________ in American literature.

A. the largest brain with the largest heart

B. father of American poetry

C. the transcendentalist

D. the American scholar

Ⅲ. Read the following quotation and answer the questions.

"Who is that man, Hester?" gasped Mr. Dimmesdale, overcome with terror. "I shiver at him! Dost thou know the man? I hate him, Hester!"

She remembered her oath, and was silent.

"I tell thee, my soul shivers at him," muttered the minister again. "Who is he? Who is he? Canst thou do nothing for me? I have a nameless horror of the man."

"Minister," said little Pearl. "I can tell thee who he is!"

"Quickly, then, child!" said the minister, bending his ear close to her lips. "Quickly! —and as low as thou canst whisper."

Pearl mumbled something into his ear, that sounded, indeed, like human language, but was only such gibberish as children may be heard amusing themselves with, by the hour together. At all events, if it involved any secret information in regard to old Roger Chillingworth, it was in a tongue unknown to the erudite clergyman, and did but increase the bewilderment of his mind. The elvish child then laughed aloud.

"Dost thou mock me now?" said the minister.

"Thou wast not bold! —thou wast not true!" answered the child.

"Thou wouldst not promise to take my hand, and mother's hand, tomorrow noontide!" (北航 2007 研)

Questions:

1. Which fiction is this excerpt from?

2. Who is the author? What are the major artistic features of the author?

3. Try to comment on the irony in this excerpt.

Ⅳ. Short answer questions

1. Give some different explanations of the symbolic meaning of "A" in *The Scarlet Letter* by Hawthorne.（人大2006研；南京大学2008研）
2. What are the artistic characteristics of *The Scarlet Letter*?

Ⅴ. Essay questions

1. Due to his family background and his understanding of human nature, Nathaniel Hawthorne seems to be haunted by a sense of sin and evil in life. Explain his "black" vision in *The Scarlet Letter*.（天津外国语学院2007研）
2. Nathaniel Hawthorne is often blamed for depicting the Puritans as self-righteous and authoritarian, bent on making everyone conform to a rigid set of rules and ostracizing everyone who disagreed with them. Is the blame justified? Support your argument with detailed analysis of one of his novels or stories.（天津外国语2011研）

参考答案及解析

Ⅰ. Fill in the blanks.

1. *The Scarlet Letter*, Nathaniel Hawthorne
（Pearl是美国作家Nathaniel Hawthorne小说《红字》中的人物。）
2. scarlet letter "A", adultery
（霍桑的小说《红字》中海斯特·普琳经历了道德的洗礼，红字"A"的含义也逐渐由"通奸"转变为"能干"以至后来的"天使"。）
3. *The Scarlet Letter*
（1850年，纳撒尼尔·霍桑发表了他的代表作《红字》。该书讲述的是美国殖民时期的一个三角爱情故事。）
4. Nathaniel Hawthorne
（纳撒尼尔·霍桑的小说《红字》暗示了美国浪漫主义遵循美国清教伦理道德。）
5. *The Scarlet Letter*
（《红字》是19世纪美国浪漫主义作家纳撒尼尔·霍桑的长篇小说，发表于1850年。小说女主人公是海斯特·普琳（Hester Prynne）。）
6. Nathaniel Hawthorne
（麦尔维尔在创作《白鲸》的过程中受到霍桑的诸多指导和建议，因而小说成书后，梅尔维尔在书中提及该书是献给霍桑的。）

Ⅱ. Multiple choices.

1. A　美国十九世纪最有影响的浪漫主义小说家是霍桑。
2. A　《红字》（*The Scarlet Letter*）是美国19世纪影响最大的浪漫主义小说家和心理小说家纳撒尼尔·霍桑（Nathaniel Hawthorne）的代表作。该小说是成功运用象征手法的典范。
3. A　霍桑认为罪恶是人生来所带的标记。几乎他的每一部作品都涉及到了罪与恶。
4. B　《红字》（*The Scarlet Letter*）发表后获得巨大成功，霍桑继而创作了不少作品。其中《有七个尖角阁的房子》（*The House of the Seven Gables*）描写品钦家族的祖先（Colonel Pyncheon）谋财害命而使后代遭到报应的故事，说明财富是祸患，"一代人的罪孽要殃及子孙"；这部小说也反映了资本主义发展初期的血腥掠夺。

5. D 《黑德格医生的实验》(*Dr. Heidegger's Experiment*)是霍桑的中短篇小说。其余三项《玉石雕像》(*The Marble Faun*),《福谷传奇》(*The Blithedale Romance*),《有七个尖角阁的房子》(*The House of the Seven Gables*)都是霍桑的长篇小说。

6. A 赫尔曼·麦尔维尔(Herman Melville)称纳撒尼尔·霍桑(Nathaniel Hawthorne)为美国文学史上"心胸最宽广,最伟大的智者(the largest brain with the largest heart)。"

Ⅲ. Read the following quotation and answer the questions.

1. This excerpt is from *The Scarlet Letter*.
2. The author is Nathaniel Hawthorne. Much of Hawthorne's writing focuses on New England, and many of his works feature moral fables with Puritan overtones. His fiction works are part of the Romantic movement and, more specifically, dark romanticism. His themes often revolve around the inherent evil and sin of humanity, and his works often have moral messages and deep psychological complexity.
3. 3. When Pearl asked Mr. Dimmesdale to stand with her and her mother on the platform the next day, the minister refused. He only promised to stand together with them before the judgment-seat at the great judgment day, and thus "the daylight of this world shall not see our meeting". In fact, he did not want to make known publicly his relationship with Hester and Pearl. So, Pearl's words "Thou wast not bold! —thou wast not true!" are ironic.

Ⅳ. Short answer questions

1. At the beginning, the letter "A", a symbol of adultery, was worn on Hester's chest. This is the puritan way of treating her as a criminal because she had committed adultery. Then it becomes a symbol of loneliness and alienation. Because of her shameful history, Hester's social life was virtually eliminated. And little Pearl is the only companion of her lonely life. Finally it becomes a symbol of able, angel and admirable. The townspeople who condemn her now believe the scarlet letter stands for her ability to her beautiful needlework and for her selfless help to the poor and sick. Hester is a strong admirable woman who goes through more emotional torture than most people experience in a lifetime. "A" may also represent Adamic, or prehistoric, an archetypal vice suggestive of "original sin".
2. *The Scarlet Letter* is a simple but moving story, in which all elements of his thinking and aesthetics seem to be fully expressed. It reveals Hawthorne's masterful craft and powerful psychological insight as he explores the guilt and anxiety in the human soul.

   Hawthorne's extraordinary understanding of Puritan history, his understanding of the colonial history in England, his apparent concern with the moral issue of sin and guilt, and his keen psychological analysis of people are on full display in this novel. With modern psychological insight, Hawthorne explored the secret motivations of human behavior and the guilt and anxiety that he believed result from all the sins against humanity, especially the sin of pride.

   Hawthorne is a master of symbolism. The structure and the form of the novel are carefully designed to cater to the needs of the theme. By using Pearl as a thematic symbol, Hawthorne emphasizes the consequence of the sin of adultery on the community and people living in that community. As a key to the whole novel, the letter "A" takes on different layers of symbolic meanings as the plot develops. This ambiguity is one of the salient features of the work.

V. Essay questions

1. All his life, Hawthorne was haunted by his sense of sin and evil. Reading his tales and romances, one cannot but be overwhelmed by the "black" vision which these works reveal. As a natural corollary, the black vision has become his trademark. It illustrates in part the influence that the Calvinist doctrine of "original sin" and total depravity on his mind. One of the roots of Hawthorne's evil is his conceited intellect. Hawthorne's intellectuals are usually villains, terrible because of the lack of a sense of fellowship.

    In *The Scarlet Letter*, the experience of Hester and Dimmesdale recalls the story of Adam and Eve because, in both cases, sin leads to expulsion and suffering. But it also produces knowledge—specifically, knowledge of what it means to be human. The real villain in *The Scarlet Letter* is Roger Chillingworth, the scholar, the embodiment of pure intellect, who commits "the Unpardonable Sin"—the violation of the human heart. He torments Dimmesdale's conscience until the poor man is tortured to death. The end of Chillingworth is also tragic enough. Dimmesdale declares God's judgment on his deathbed: "Thou, too, hast deeply sinned!" And Chillingworth simply shrivels. The last time we see him, he is kneeling down beside Dimmesdale "with a blank, dull countenance, out of which the life seemed to have departed." Chillingworth's misshapen body reflects (or symbolizes) the evil in his soul, which builds as the novel progresses, similar to the way Dimmesdale's illness reveals his inner turmoil.

2. Nathaniel Hawthorne was born into a rigid Puritan family and was heavily influenced by Puritanism. In his novels, Puritans as a group are often portrayed as self-righteous and authoritarian, bent on making everyone conform to a strict set of rules that exclude everyone who disagrees with them. It is true, in fact, in his writing. For example, in The Scarlet Letter, the heroine Hester Prynne is ostracized by society because of her commitment of adultery. She is forced to wear a scarlet "A" as her punishment because in puritan society, Puritanism is the authority and everyone is supposed to abide by.

    However, this does not mean that Hawthorne held a completely negative attitude toward Puritanism. On the contrary, it is because of the deep influence of Puritanism that he sees its flaws as well as cherishes it unconsciously in his writing. Sin and evil is the most important theme in The Scarlet Letter. Though having great sympathy to Hester, both Hester Prynne and her lover Dimmesdale are on their way to some kind of salvation.

第16章　赫尔曼·麦尔维尔

16.1　复习笔记

Herman Melville (1819—1891)

1. Life

Herman Melville was a famous American novelist and poet. Melville was born in New York City to a poor family. He received a limited education and then began working as a cabin boy. There were three events that influenced his life: going to sea, his marriage and his friendship with Hawthorne. His experiences and adventures at sea provided him with rich material for his novels. In his married life, Melville had to produce inferior works to satisfy his wife's luxurious lifestyle. Melville realized that Hawthorne had gained insight into the evils that existed in American social life. When the two met, the intent of Melville's masterpiece, *Moby Dick*, changed significantly. The rewritten work became a literary classic in the world today. He spent his last two decades in obscurity and was little known when he died in 1891.

2. Major Works

Typee (1846)
Omoo (1847)
Mardi (1849)
Redburn (1849)
White-Jacket (1850)
Moby Dick (1851)
Pierre (1852)
The Confidence-Man (1857)
Battle Pieces (1866)
Billy Budd (1924)

3. Selected Work

◆*Moby Dick*

(1) *Moby Dick*, a tremendous chronicle of the hunt for an imaginary and mysterious white whale. The book reached a creative peak of symbolism and appealed strongly to the readers of the present society.

赫尔曼·麦尔维尔(1819—1891)

1. 生平

赫尔曼·麦尔维尔是美国著名的小说家和诗人。麦尔维尔出生于纽约，家境贫寒。他接受的教育有限，之后便开始做船舱服务员。影响他一生的事件有三个：出海、他的婚姻及其与霍桑的友谊。他在海上的经历和冒险为他的小说创作提供了丰富的素材。在婚姻生活上，麦尔维尔不得不创作劣质作品以满足妻子的奢华生活。麦尔维尔意识到霍桑已洞悉美国社会生活中存在的恶。当两个人相会后，麦尔维尔的代表作《白鲸》的创作意图发生了重大改变。改写后的作品成为当今世界的文学经典。他的最后二十年默默无闻，1891年去世时也鲜为人知。

2. 主要作品

《泰比》(1846)
《欧穆》(1847)
《玛地》(1849)
《雷得伯恩》(1849)
《白外套》(1850)
《白鲸》(1851)
《皮埃尔》(1852)
《骗子》(1857)
《战事集》(1866)
《比利·巴德》(1924)

3. 选读作品

◆《白鲸》

(1)《白鲸》主要讲述一个为追捕一只想象中的神秘白鲸的漫长海上故事。这本书达到了象征主义手法的创作高峰，强烈地吸引了现在社会的读者。

(2) *Moby Dick* represents Melville's pessimistic attitude toward his time. The world described in the book has no God and is meaningless. Melville's work represents the lack of faith, futility, and meaninglessness of modern Western life so well that people in the 20th century finally found it great and fascinating.	(2)《白鲸》代表了麦尔维尔对他所处时代的悲观态度。书中所描述的世界里没有上帝，毫无意义。麦尔维尔的作品淋漓尽致地表现了西方现代生活中信仰缺失、徒劳感及无意义感，因此20世纪人们终于发现了它的伟大和引人入胜之处。
(3) The theme of the novel is alienation. Alienation existed at different levels of Melville's life, between people, between people and society, and between people and nature. Melville also criticizes New England Transcendentalism for its overemphasis on individualism and Oversoul. Another theme of this novel is "rejection and quest".	(3)该小说的主题是疏离。疏离存在于麦尔维尔生活时代的不同层面，如人与人之间，人与社会之间，以及人与自然之间。麦尔维尔同时对新英格兰超验主义过度强调个人主义和"超灵"进行了批判。该小说的另外一个主题是"拒绝与追寻"。
(4) The novel is highly symbolic. The voyage itself is a metaphor for "search and discovery, the search for the ultimate truth of experience." Moby Dick is the most obvious symbol in the book, and it can be interpreted in many ways. Some believe it represents evil, some believe it represents goodness, and some believe it is both. Its white color is self-contradictory, representing both death and decay and purity, innocence and youth. It represents the ultimate mystery of the universe.	(4)该小说富有象征意义。航行本身是探索和发现，寻求最终真相的隐喻。白鲸是全书中最明显的象征，它可以有多种解释。有人认为它代表邪恶，有人认为它代表了善良，也有人认为它二者兼有。它的白色是自相矛盾的颜色，既代表了死亡和腐朽，又代表了纯洁、天真和青春。它代表了宇宙的最终奥秘。
(5) Melville achieves ambiguity by using the narrative technique of multiple perspectives.	(5)麦尔维尔通过运用多重视角的叙事技巧以达到模棱两可的效果。

16.2 考研真题与典型题详解

I. Fill in the blanks.

1. Herman Melville's novel __________ is a tremendous chronicle of a whaling voyage in pursuit of a seemingly supernatural white whale.
2. Author __________ Title __________(南京大学2008研)
The report of his undeniable delirium at sea was likewise popularly ascribed to a kindred cause. And so too, all the added moodiness which always afterwards, to the very day of sailing in the Pequod on the present voyage, sat brooding on his brow.
3. Tashtego, Daggoo and Queequeg are the three main harpooners in the novel __________.(首师大2008研)
4. __________ is famous for writing stories about the sea and the islands of the Southern Pacific. In

his masterpiece ___________, he tells a story of a whaling voyage within which is set a symbolic account of the conflict between man and his fate.

5. ___________ is the narrator in *Moby Dick*.

6. It is said that in his late years, Herman Melville stopped writing novels and stories and turned to poetry, ___________ is his most famous poetic work.

7. Herman Melville is best known as the author of one book named ___________, which is, critics have agreed, one of the world's greatest masterpieces.

8. "Young Goodman Brown" is written by ___________, who held an unceasing interest in the "interior of the heart" of man's being; while *The Confidence-Man* is by ___________, whose monumental work ___________ is regarded as the first American prose epic.（北师大 2005 研）

Ⅱ. Multiple Choices

1. The author of the following selection is ___________.（大连外国语 2007 研）

   A. Herman Melville　　B. Thomas Hardy

   C. Theodore Dreiser　　D. Jack London

   There is a wisdom that is woe; but there is a woe that is madness. And there is a Catskill eagle in some souls that can alike dive down into the blackest gorges, and soar out of them again and become invisible in the sunny spaces. And even if he forever flies within the gorge, that gorge is in the mountains; so that even in his lowest swoop the mountain eagle is still higher than other birds upon the plain, even though they soar.

2. Which of the following is closest to Shakespearean tragedy?（大连外国语 2008 研）

   A. *The Scarlet Letter.*　　B. *Uncle Tom's Cabin.*

   C. *Moby Dick.*　　D. *Wuthering Heights.*

3. In ___________, Captain Ahab is obsessed with the revenge on a whale which sheared off his leg on a previous voyage, and his crazy chasing of it eventually brings death to all on board the whaler except Ishmael, who survives to tell the tale.（天津外国语学院 2007 研）

   A. *Typee*　　B. *White Jacket*

   C. *Moby Dick*　　D. *Billy Budd*

4. In *Moby Dick*, the voyage symbolizes ___________.

   A. the microcosm of human society　　B. a search for truth

   C. the unknown world　　D. nature

5. Herman Melville's ___________ is an encyclopedia of everything: history, philosophy, religion, etc. in addition to a detailed account of the operations of the whaling industry.

   A. *The Old Man and the Sea*　　B. *Moby Dick*

   C. *White Jacket*　　D. *Billy Budd*

6. ___________ was a romanticized account of Herman Melville's stay among the Polynesians. The success of the book soon made Melville well known as the "man who lived among cannibals".

   A. *Moby Dick*　　B. *Typee*　　C. *Omoo*　　D. *Billy Budd*

Ⅲ. Read the following quotations and answer the questions.

Passage 1（北航 2010 研）

The Whiteness of the Whale

Chapter XLII

What the White Whale was to Ahab, has been hinted; what, at times, he was to me, as yet remains unsaid.

Aside from those more obvious considerations touching Moby Dick, which could not but occasionally awaken in any man's soul some alarm, there was another thought, or rather vague, nameless horror concerning him, which at times by its intensity completely overpowered all the rest; and yet so mystical and well nigh ineffable was it that I almost despair of putting it in a comprehensible form. It was the whiteness of the whale that above all things appalled me. But how can I hope to explain myself here, and yet, in some dim, random way, explain myself I must, else all these chapters might be naught.

Questions:

1. Comment on the personality of Ahab, the captain.
2. What are the symbolic meanings of the white Moby Dick?
3. How do you understand the voyage of Pequod the ship in the sea?

Passage 2

Identify the following passage by giving the title of the work and the full name of the author, and explain the implications of the underlined parts of the passage. (人大 2006 研)

It was the private property of three confederate white seamen of that ship, one of whom, it seems, communicated it to Tashtego with Romish injunctions of secrecy, but the following night Tashtego rambled in his sleep, and revealed so much of it in that way, that when he was wakened he could not well withhold the rest. Nevertheless, so potent an influence did this thing have on those seamen in the Pequod who came to the full knowledge of it, and by such a strange delicacy, to call it so, were they governed in this matter, that they kept the secret among themselves so that it never transpired abaft the Pequod's mainmast.

Ⅳ. Short answer questions

1. *Moby Dick* features several seemingly insane characters. How does insanity relate to this story? How do these characters contrast with one another? (北航 2009 研)
2. What does the white whale in *Moby Dick* symbolize? Why do you think so? (国际关系学院 2007 研)
3. Comment briefly on the following character: Captain Ahab(中山大学 2004 研, 厦门大学 2007 研)
4. What are Herman Melville's major works?

Ⅴ. Essay questions

1. Make a comment on Herman Melville's novel *Moby Dick*. (四川大学 2008 研)
2. The ship (or the boat, or the like) has been a key symbol in western literature. W. H. Auden holds that there are mainly two views of a ship: as a vessel isolated in the ocean, thus a microcosm of society; and as a vehicle of escape from the shore, thus an image of freedom. Elaborate on the symbolic meaning of the ship/boat, or a boarded floating object in one American or British novel. (天津外国语 2013 研)

参考答案及解析

Ⅰ. Fill in the blanks.

1. *Moby Dick*

(《白鲸》是一部以捕鲸生涯为题材的小说，一位名叫亚哈(Ahab)的"皮廓德号"(Pequod)

捕鲸船船长带领全体船员，追捕一条叫做“莫比·迪克”的大白鲸的历险过程。)

2. Author: Herman Melville　Title: *Moby Dick*

（题目节选自 Herman Melville 的 *Moby Dick*(《白鲸》)。《白鲸》刻画了捕鲸人与巨鲸搏斗的真实画面，人与宗教之间的关系，以及人性的挣扎与考验。)

3. *Moby Dick*

（这三个人是《白鲸》里的捕鲸手。)

4. Herman Melville; *Moby Dick*

（赫尔曼·麦尔维尔因写南太平洋的大海和岛屿的故事而著名。他的代表作《白鲸》讲述了以人与他自己命运的冲突作为象征的捕鲸航程。)

5. Ishmael

（以实玛利是小说《白鲸》的叙述者。)

6. *Clarel*

（麦尔维尔发表的小说在当时反响平平，晚年他放弃小说改写诗歌。《克拉瑞尔》(*Clarel*)是其最著名的诗作。)

7. *Moby Dick*

（赫尔曼·麦尔维尔以其海上经历为事实依据写成的寓言杰作《白鲸记》被认为是美国乃至世界上最伟大的小说之一。)

8. Nathaniel Hawthorne, Herman Melville, *Moby Dick*

（“Young Goodman Brown”(《小伙子布朗》)是霍桑的作品。*The Confidence-Man*(《骗子》)是麦尔维尔的作品，麦尔维尔最著名的作品是 *Moby Dick*(《白鲸》)。)

Ⅱ. Multiple Choices

1. A　题中片段选自美国著名小说家 Herman Melville 的著名小说《白鲸》。
2. C　《白鲸》是美国著名小说家 Herman Melville(赫尔曼·麦尔维尔)的名作，是一个捕杀白鲸的复仇故事，也是一个人与自然相抗衡的噩梦，既有莎士比亚悲剧的格调，又有史诗般的气势。
3. C　Captain Ahab(亚哈船长)是麦尔维尔的小说 *Moby Dick*(《白鲸》)里的主人公。
4. B　小说《白鲸》中航程象征了对真理的探寻。
5. B　赫尔曼·麦尔维尔的《白鲸》是一部内容丰富的小说，这部捕鲸小说成为当今公认的捕鲸的百科全书。
6. B　赫尔曼·麦尔维尔(Herman Melville)年轻时曾做过捕鲸水手，航行于南太平洋一带，1842 年 7 月在南太平洋马克萨斯群岛(the Pacific islands of the Marquesas group)被波利尼西亚的泰皮族所俘虏。后来麦尔维尔根据这一经历写成了小说《泰比》(*Typee*)。

Ⅲ. Read the following quotations and answer the questions.

Passage 1

1. Ahab, the Pequod's obsessed captain, represents both an ancient and quintessentially modern type of hero. Like the heroes of Greek or Shakespearean tragedy, Ahab has a fatal flaw that he shares with such legendary figures as Oedipus and Faust. His tremendous overconfidence, or hubris, leads him to defy common sense and believe that, like a god, that he can achieve his will and is not subject to the forces of nature. He believes that Moby Dick is the embodiment of evil in the world, and he paranoidly pursues Moby Dick because he believes that the destruction of

this evil is his inevitable destiny. Unlike the heroes of older tragic works, however, Ahab suffers from a fatal flaw that is not necessarily inborn but results from the psychological and physical damage caused by living in a cruel world. He is as much a victim as he is an aggressor, and the symbolic opposition that he constructs between himself and Moby Dick propels him toward what he considers a destined end.

2. Moby Dick is sometimes considered to be a symbol of a number of things, among them God, nature, fate, the ocean, and the very universe itself.
3. Named after a Native American tribe in Massachusetts that did not long survive the arrival of white men and thus memorializing extinction, the Pequod is a symbol of doom. It is painted a gloomy black and covered in whale teeth and bones, literally bristling with the mementos of violent death. It is, in fact, marked for death. Moreover, the themes of rejection and quest are at work throughout this novel, and voyage of Pequod for Ishmael has become a journey in quest of knowledge and values.

Passage 2

Moby-Dick, Herman Melville

"Romish injunctions": This phrase means the most secret part of the secret.

"came to the full knowledge of it": This phrase means that seamen knew the most secret part of the story.

"never transpired abaft the Pequod's mainmast": The main crew didn't know that story. It implies that they kept the secret so well that even now there were still not many people knowing it.

Ⅳ. Short answer questions

1. In *Moby Dick*, Ishmael describes Ahab as mad in his narration, and it does indeed seem mad to try to fight the forces of nature or God. However, some of the other characters in the novel whom Ishmael labels insane—notably Pip and Gabriel—might be viewed as wise rather than crazy, thus calling into question the possibility of making a clear distinction between sanity and insanity. Gabriel, the prophet figure aboard the Jeroboam, behaves irrationally and makes a number of ridiculous-sounding predictions. If viewed in a certain light, however, his prophecies sound not like silly attempts to foresee the future but like cleverly phrased efforts to effect change aboard his ship. Gabriel's prophecies are aimed at obtaining justice for the crew from the ship's officers and to avoid the dangers that would come from trying to hunt down Moby Dick. Like Ahab, he manipulates the superstitions and religious beliefs of the crew to gain support. But while Ahab's obsession was paranoid and selfish, Gabriel's "madness" was a response to the irrational and unjust behavior of those who controlled his ship.
2. For Captain Ahab, the white whale represents evil. After the loss of his leg in his encounter with the white whale, Ahab begins to hate Moby Dick and tries his best to kill the whale. He seems to embody all the evil that he once entrusted to Moby Dick. For the other members of the whaling ship, Moby Dick symbolizes the unknown, mysterious forces of cosmic nature. For the readers, the white whale is capable of many interpretations, for it is "paradoxically benign and malevolent, nourishing and destructive," "massive, brutal, monolithic, but at the same time protean, erotically beautiful, infinitely variable."

3. Ahab is the egomaniacal captain of the Pequod in Melville's *Moby Dick*. He is described as a grand, ungodly, god-like man. Ahab is grand because of his enormous intelligence and ability. He is ungodly because of his refusal to worship anything except his own will just as his name suggested. In Bible, Ahab was a wicked king of Israel punished for his disobedience. In this novel, from the time that his leg is bitten off by Moby Dick, Captain Ahab paranoidly pursues his elusive nemesis. And Ahab is godlike because his doomed fight against the universe is in some way a nobly defiant one that lifts him above mortal men and places him closer to the great forces of nature: lightning, fire, the whale, even the universe itself.
4. American novelist, Herman Melville, is a major literary figure whose exploration of psychological and metaphysical themes foreshadowed 20th-century literary concerns. His works remained in obscurity until the 1920s, when his genius was finally recognized. Melville's early works include *Mardi* , *Redburn*, *White-Jacket* and *Moby Dick*; and his later works include *Pierre*, *the Confidence-Man*, *Billy Budd*.

V. Essay questions

1. *Moby Dick* is often referred to as "the Great American Novel" and is considered one of the treasures of world literature. In *Moby Dick*, Melville employs stylized language, symbolism, and metaphor to explore numerous complex themes. Through the main character's journey, the concepts of class and social status, good and evil, and the existence of gods are all examined as Ishmael speculates upon his personal beliefs and his place in the universe.

   Moby Dick is a symbolic work, but also includes chapters on natural history. Major themes include obsession, religion, and idealism versus pragmatism, revenge, racism, sanity, hierarchical relationships, and politics. All of the members of the crew have biblical-sounding, improbable, or descriptive names, and the narrator deliberately avoids specifying the exact time of the events and some other similar details. These together suggest that the narrator is deliberately casting his tale in an epic and allegorical mode. The white whale has also been seen as a symbol for many things, including nature and those elements of life that are out of human control.
2. The ship in *Moby Dick* is just a microcosm of society. There are all walks of life on this boat. *Moby Dick* is, critics have agreed, one of the world's greatest masterpieces. To get to know the nineteenth-century American mind and America itself, one has to read this book. It is an encyclopedia of everything, history, philosophy, religion, etc. in addition to a detailed account of the operations of the whaling industry. But it is first a Shakespearean tragedy of man fighting against overwhelming odds in an indifferent and even hostile universe. As he had indicated in *Mardi*, we should get to know the extent of evil in life and the human soul to help make life and man better. As he puts it, "The way to heaven is through hell."

   Moby Dick represents the sum total of Melville's bleak view of the world in which he lived. It is at once godless and purposeless. Man in this universe lives a meaningless and futile life, meaningless because futile. As some critics note, man can observe and even manipulate in a prudent way, but he cannot influence and overcome nature at its source. He must, ultimately, place himself at the mercy of nature. Once he attempts to seek power over it he is doomed.

第17章　亨利·沃兹沃思·朗费罗

17.1　复习笔记

Henry Wadsworth Longfellow (1807—1882)	亨利·沃兹沃思·朗费罗(1807—1882)
1. Life Longfellow was born in Portland, Maine, on February 27, 1807, and died in Cambridge, Massachusetts, on March 24, 1882. In 1822, at the age of 15, Longfellow entered Bowdoin College. After graduating, he traveled to Europe and studied the languages and literature of France, Germany, Italy, Finland and Spain, and in 1836 he was appointed professor at Harvard University, where he taught the richness and splendor of European literature. He localized the rhythms of European poetry to tell the story of America. He not only brought European culture to America, but also spread American folk themes. Afterwards, he gathered thousands of honors and even his home was worshipped as a shrine by Americans and visited by many foreign celebrities. After his death, a bust of Longfellow was placed in the "Poet's Corner" of Westminster Abbey, the only American poet to be so honored.	**1. 生平** 1807年2月27日，朗费罗出生于缅因州的波特兰大，1882年3月24日在马萨诸塞的坎布里奇去世。他是当时最受欢迎的美国诗人，也是新英格兰诗人中最著名的一位。1822年，15岁的朗费罗进入鲍登学院。毕业之后，他去欧洲旅行并且研究法国、德国、意大利、芬兰和西班牙等国的语言和文学。1836年，他被聘为哈佛大学教授，讲授丰富绚烂的欧洲文学。他将欧洲诗歌的韵律本土化，来讲述美国。他不仅将欧洲文化带到美国，更将美国民间主题传播开来。之后，他集万千荣誉于一身，连家也被美国人奉为神龛，众多外国名人也争相拜访。去世以后，朗费罗的半身像被放在威斯敏斯特教堂的"诗人角"，他是美国惟一获此殊荣的诗人。
2. Major Works *Voices of the Night* (1838) *Ballads and Other Poems* (1841) *Evangeline* (1847) *The Song of Hiawatha* (1855) *The Courtship of Miles Standish and Other Poems* (1858) "A Psalm of Life" (1838) "My Lost Youth" (1855)	**2. 主要作品** 《夜吟》(1838) 《歌谣及其他》(1841) 《伊凡吉林》(1847) 《海华沙之歌》(1855) 《迈尔斯·斯坦狄什的求婚》(1858) 《人生礼赞》(1838) 《我逝去的青春》(1855)
3. Selected Works **◆"A Psalm of Life"** Longfellow believes that people should approach life in the present world with a positive and optimistic attitude. The	**3. 选读作品** **◆《人生礼赞》** 朗费罗认为人们应以积极和乐观的态度来对待现世的人生。世界正飞速地变化着，人们不应当毫无

world is changing rapidly and people should not do nothing. The word "strife" shows that life is not always easy, but that there are always difficulties and moments of life and death. Longfellow encourages everyone to have faith and to always move forward towards their future goals.	作为。"strife"一词显示出了人生并不会一帆风顺，而是总有一些困难，总会有经历生死关头的时刻。朗费罗鼓励每个人都要有信念并且朝着未来的目标永远向前。
◆"The Slave's Dream"	**◆《奴隶的梦想》**
This poem shows the poet's supportive attitude toward the abolitionist movement. Longfellow expresses his deep sympathy for the slaves by comparing their different living conditions in Africa and America, while revealing the brutality of the slave owners.	这首诗表明了诗人对废奴运动的支持态度。朗费罗通过比较奴隶在非洲和美国的不同生活状况表达了对奴隶的深切同情，同时揭示了奴隶主的残暴。
◆"My Lost Youth"	**◆《我逝去的青春》**
Longfellow spent most of his childhood in his hometown of Portland, Maine. He always loved it deeply, and he wrote about the beautiful scenery, the tranquility and simplicity of his hometown in this poem. The poet's youthful dreams are full of freedom and imagination, and he finds his lost youth in the dreams and will of youth.	朗费罗的童年大多是在家乡缅因州的波特兰大度过的。他一直深爱着那里，他把家乡美丽的风景，宁静、淳朴的生活写在了这首诗里。诗人青春的梦想充满了自由和想象，他在青春的梦想和意愿中找到了自己逝去的青春。
◆*The Song of Hiawatha*	**◆《海华沙之歌》**
The Song of Hiawatha consists of 23 chapters that tell the story of the successes and sorrows of Hiawatha of the Ojibway, a tribe of Indians living along the Lake Superior shoreline in what is now Michigan. Longfellow combined tribal lore with a rich imagination to create this epic poem.	《海华沙之歌》包括23个诗章，讲述的是欧及布威族印第安人海华沙的成功事迹与悲伤故事，欧及布威族生活在现在密歇根的苏必利尔湖沿岸。朗费罗结合部落传说和丰富的想象创造了这部史诗。
Hiawatha represents the ideal blend of wisdom and courageous strength. But Hiawatha, while brave, is no warrior. He is a peacekeeper and reconciler. When the white man brings a foreign religion and heralds the end of the local way of life, Hiawatha accepts the change with optimism, believing it will eventually lead them to a better life.	海华沙代表了智慧和勇气的理想结合体。但是，勇敢的海华沙不是一名战士，他是和平守卫者和协调人。当白人带来异国宗教并预示当地生活方式结束的时候，海华沙乐观地接受了这种变化，相信它最终会使他们过上更好的生活。

17.2 考研真题与典型题详解

Ⅰ. Fill in the blanks.

1. After his death, __________ became the only American to be honored with a bust in the Poet's Corner of Westminster Abbey.
2. Author __________ Title __________（南京大学2007研）

   I breathed a song into the air,
   It fell to earth I knew not where;

For who has the sight so keen and strong
That can follow the flight of a song.

3. Henry Wadsworth Longfellow's first collection of poems entitled __________ appeared in 1838.
4. The most scholarly of Henry Wadsworth Longfellow's writings is his translation of Dante's __________.
5. Write down the name of the author of the following work.（厦门大学2007研）
"A Psalm of Life"
6. Life is real!
Life is earnest!
And the grave is not its goal
Dust thou art, to dust returnest was not spoken of the soul.
These lines are taken from a poem entitled __________.（天津外国语2013研）

Ⅱ. Multiple Choices

1. Which ONE of the following poems is authored by Henry Wadsworth Longfellow?（四川大学2009研）
A. "The Raven".
B. "Wild Nights—Wild Nights!"
C. "The Indian Burying Ground".
D. "The Slave's Dream".
2. The following selection is from __________.（大连外国语2008研）
A. "My Lost Youth"
B. "A Psalm of Life"
C. *Nature*
D. *The Song of Hiawatha*

Footsteps, that, perhaps another,
Sailing o'er life's solemn main,
A forlorn and shipwreck'd brother,
Seeing, shall take heart again.
Let us then be up and doing,
With a heart for any fate;
Still achieving, still pursuing,
Learn to labor and to wait.

3. With the appearance of __________ in 1855, which is about American Indians, Henry Wadsworth Longfellow' s poetical reputation was established.
A. *Evangeline*
B. *The Courtship of Miles Standish*
C. *Song of Hiawatha*
D. *Michael Angelo*
4. The following lines were written by __________.
A. Henry Wadsworth Longfellow
B. Walt Whitman
C. Emily Dickinson
D. James Cooper

Often I think of the beautiful town
That is seated by the sea;
Often in thought go up and down
The pleasant streets of that dear old town,
And my youth comes back to me.

And a verse of a Lapland song
Is haunting my memory still:
"A boy's will is the wind's will,
And the thoughts of youth are long, long thoughts."

Ⅲ. Explain the following term.

Trochee(国际关系学院 2007 研)

Ⅳ. Read the following quotation and answer the questions.

Tell me not, in mournful numbers,
Life is but an empty dream!
For the soul is dead that slumbers,
And things are not what they seem.
Life is real-life is earnest!
And the grave is not its goal;
Dust thou art, to dust returnest,
Was not spoken of the soul.

Questions:

1. Who is the writer of the lines?
2. What is the title of the whole poem from which the two stanzas are taken?
3. Summarize the poet's advice for living.

Ⅴ. Short answer question

What are the artistic achievements of Henry Wadsworth Longfellow's poetry?

参考答案及解析

Ⅰ. Fill in the blanks.

1. Henry Wadsworth Longfellow
(亨利·沃兹沃斯·朗费罗(1807—1882)晚年获得各种荣誉，接受过剑桥及牛津大学颁予的荣誉学位。死后其半身像置于伦敦威斯敏斯特大教堂的诗人角，他是第一个获此殊荣的美国人。)
2. Author: Henry Wadsworth Longfellow　　Title: "I Shot an Arrow"
(题目节选自朗费罗的《我射出一支箭》，作者在这首诗中含蓄而巧妙地歌颂了友谊的地久天长。)
3. *Voices of the Night*
(亨利·沃兹沃斯·朗费罗(Henry Wadsworth Longfellow, 1807—1882), 19 世纪美国最伟大的浪漫主义诗人之一。他是新英格兰文化中心剑桥文学界和社交界的重要人物。1838 年出版第一部诗集《夜吟》(*Voices of the Night*)。)
4. *Divine Comedy*
(1861 年亨利·沃兹沃斯·朗费罗的夫人不幸被火烧伤致死，这一直使他无比悲痛，为了摆脱精神上的重负，他投身于但丁的《神曲》(*Divine Comedy*)的翻译。)
5. Henry Wadsworth Longfellow
(朗费罗的《人生礼赞》写成于 1838 年，副标题为"青年人的心对歌者说的话"。诗中说，人生不是一场幻梦，人要有英雄气概，要不断追求和进取。）

6. “A Psalm of Life”

（该选段选自朗费罗的《人生礼赞》。）

Ⅱ. Multiple Choices

1. D 《奴隶的梦》是朗费罗的一首名诗。选项 A《乌鸦》是爱伦·坡的名诗；选项 B 的作者是艾米莉·狄金森；选项 C 是 Philip Freneau（菲利普·弗瑞诺）的一首诗。
2. B 题目中的诗歌节选自美国诗人 Henry Wadsworth Longfellow（朗费罗）的名作“A Psalm of Life”（《人生礼赞》）。节选部分译文：也许我们有一个兄弟/ 航行在庄严的人生大海，/遇险沉了船，绝望的时刻，/ 会看到这脚印而振作起来。/ 那么，让我们起来行动吧，/对任何命运都敢于担待；/ 不断进取，不断追求，/学会劳作，学会等待。
3. C 美国 19 世纪杰出诗人朗费罗以其充满神话传奇色彩的长篇叙事诗《海华沙之歌》，再现了早期印第安人的历史与文化。该诗奠定了朗费罗在诗歌界的地位。
4. A 题中诗句选自美国诗人 Henry Wadsworth Longfellow 的名诗《我逝去的青春》（“My Lost Youth”）。题中诗句的译文为：我常常思念这美丽的小城，/它就坐落在海边；/常常令我游思不定/这愉快亲切的古城街道，/我的青春回到我身边。/一句拉普兰民歌的诗句/一直徘徊在我记忆里：/“孩子的愿望是风的愿望，/青春的怀念是悠长的，悠长的怀念。”

Ⅲ. Explain the following term.

Trochee：A trochee is a metrical foot used in formal poetry consisting of a stressed syllable followed by an unstressed one. Lines of verse made up predominantly of trochees are referred to as trochaic verse or trochaics. Regular trochaic lines are quite rare in English, Longfellow's *Song of Hiawatha* (1855) being a celebrated example.

Ⅳ. Read the following quotation and answer the questions.

1. Henry Wadsworth Longfellow.
2. “A Psalm of Life”
3. His optimism which has characterized much of his poetry also endeared many critics to him. He seemed to have persevered despite tragedy. In his poem, “A Psalm of Life”, he writes：“Life is real—Life is earnest—And the grave is not its goal”. This is the cry of the heart, “rallying from depression”, ready to affirm life, to regroup from losses, to push on despite momentary defeat.

Ⅴ. Short answer question

①Henry Wadsworth Longfellow was the best known of the Fireside Poets, and it was with him that American poetry began to emerge from the shadow of its British parentage.

②His poetic narrative helped create a national historical myth, transforming colorful aspects of the American past into memorable romances. They include *Evangeline* (1847), which concerns lovers who are separated during the French and Indian War (1754—1763) and *The Song of Hiawatha* (1855), which derives its theme from native American folklore.

③No American poet before or since was as widely celebrated during his or her lifetime as Longfellow. After his death, a bust of Longfellow was placed in the “Poet's Corner” of Westminster Abbey, the only American poet to be so honored.

第四部分 现实主义文学

第18章 沃尔特·惠特曼

18.1 复习笔记

Ⅰ. Historical Introduction	**Ⅰ. 背景介绍**
1. Political Background	**1. 政治背景**
(1) The American Civil War saw the triumph of Northern industrialism and the decline of Southern agrarianism as a result of which a new industrial era dominated by steel and steam, mass consumption and rapid mechanization came into being. In the course of industrialization, urban factories gained momentum with the influx of massive rural immigrant labor force into cities.	(1)美国内战见证了北方工业主义的胜利和南方农业主义的落没。随之而来的是崭新的工业时代，一个由钢铁和蒸汽、大众消费和快速机械化主导的时代。在工业化进程中，随着大量农村劳动力涌向城市，城市工厂得到发展。
(2) Along with the bonus of sharp population increase and accelerated urbanization, there arose serious problems of an ever-expanding gulf between the rich and the poor in striking contrast to the overall national prosperity. It was the beginning of what Mark Twain called "The Gilded Age", an age of excess and extremes, of decline and progress, of poverty and dazzling wealth, of gloom and buoyant hope.	(2)尽管美国人口激增和城市化加速带来红利，越来越严重的贫富分化问题凸显，与这个国家总体的繁荣景象构成鲜明反差。这是马克·吐温所说的"镀金时代"的开端：一个过剩与极端的时代，一个衰落与进步的时代，一个贫穷与炫富的时代，一个阴郁沮丧与满怀希望的时代。
(3) People at the bottom of social ladder demanded greater voting rights, leading to not only a radical shift from traditional political alliances to emerging bossism of big cities, but also unprecedented political patronage and graft at the national level.	(3)下层阶级要求更多的投票权，导致传统的政治联盟转向大城市统治，全国范围内政治庇护和贪污空前。
(4) Newly-built railroads and trans-Atlantic communication infrastructure across the nation liberated Americans from isolation, giving birth to flourishing commercial expansion, facilitated Westward Expansion Movement, and interregional flow of population.	(4)由于跨大西洋交通线和美国国内铁路的建设，美国人不再与世隔绝，刺激了商贸繁荣、西进运动，促进了人口流动。
2. Literary Characteristics of the Age	**2. 文学特征**
(1) Since the 1850s, women became the nation's dominant culture force. An increasing number of women's journalism of various sorts went into public.	(1)19世纪后半叶，女性成为美国文化的主力。各种女性周刊杂志纷纷涌现。

(2) The great age of American romanticism had ended. As the swaying influence of New England's culture faded, New York replaced Boston as the nation's literary centre.	(2)美国伟大的浪漫主义时代已经结束了。新英格兰已经丧失文化统治力，纽约作为美国第一大城市，取代波士顿成为新的文学中心。
(3) A host of new US writers with middle-class and journalistic background emerged to establish a literature of realism.	(3)一大批美国中产阶级、有新闻业背景的新作家涌现，建立了现实主义文学。
①Realism, with its origin in France, stressed the approach to faithful depiction of life, of the "reality and truth" embedded in the ordinary. Realist fiction, having its debut in local literature, reached its zenith in the 1880s and came to decline ever since.	①现实主义来源于法国，主张描写日常生活中的“现实和真实”。它首先出现在乡土文学中，于19世纪80年代达到顶峰，但在世纪之交就开始衰落了。
②American realists intended to describe real American life in which the ordinary and local were as fit for artistic description as the magnificent and the distant. Consequently, they favored rounded characters with display of subtle humanity over idealized characters and events.	②这些现实主义作家试图描写真实的美国生活，坚持认为寻常和当地的事物与壮丽遥远的事物一样适于艺术性描写。他们反对描述理想化的人物和事件，而是力图展现圆形人物性格中的微妙。
③Representatives: Bret Harte, William Dean Howells, Hamlin Garland, Mark Twain and Henry James.	③代表作家：布莱特·哈特、威廉·迪恩·豪威尔斯、哈姆林·加兰、马克·吐温和亨利·詹姆斯。
(4) The end of the 19th century features a generation of American writers who were disturbed by ideas of the conflicted workings of the universe and perception of society's disorder and who shifted to naturalism, a new and harsher realism.	(4)19世纪末，产生了一代美国作家，他们思考混乱的世界，转向自然主义——一种更加严厉的现实主义。
①Regarding the world as amoral, American naturalists attempted to achieve extreme objectivity and frankness by presenting characters of low economic station as vulnerable victims to environment and heredity. Naturalist works had a strong sense of pessimism and determinism.	①美国自然主义作者认为世界是无道德的。他们试图通过描述社会经济地位低下阶层的人物受制于环境和遗传，来实现绝对的客观性和真实性。他们的作品中隐含着悲观态度和决定论。
②Representatives: Stephen Crane, Frank Norris, Jack London, Henry Adams, and Theodore Dreiser.	②代表作家：斯蒂芬·克莱恩、弗兰克·诺里斯、杰克·伦敦、亨利·亚当斯和西奥多·德莱塞。
Ⅱ. Walt Whitman (1819—1892)	**Ⅱ. 沃尔特·惠特曼**
1. Life	**1. 生平**
Whitman grew up and worked in New York as a schoolteacher, an apprentice to a printer, and the editor of various	惠特曼在纽约布鲁克林长大，在那里做过教师、排字学徒工和各

newspapers. Despite limited school education, Whitman was an avid reader himself, reading a large number of literary works. The works of Shakespeare and Milton had an important influence on him.

种报纸的编辑。他接受的学校教育很少，但通过自学博览群书。他对莎士比亚和弥尔顿的作品特别着迷。

When the Civil War began, he worked as a "wound dresser" in a military hospital. In 1873, he suffered a paralytic stroke and moved to New Jersey where he was taken good care of by his friends and where he spent the remaining years revising his *Leaves of Grass*.

内战开始后，惠特曼在战地医院做看护员。1873 年，他患半身不遂迁至新泽西，在那儿得到朋友的照顾，他继续修订《草叶集》直至去世。

2. Poetic Style

2. 写作风格

(1) Discarding the traditional iambic pentameter, Whitman wrote "free verse", poetry without a fixed beat or regular rhyme scheme.

(1) 惠特曼打破了五步抑扬格的传统，并创作"自由体"诗歌，也就是没有固定韵律的诗歌。

(2) Whitman's poetry is rather rhythmical. The musicality of his poems is a result of his use of parallelism and phonetic recurrence at the beginning of lines.

(2) 惠特曼的诗歌有很强的节奏感，诗行前几句排比和语音重复使他的诗歌颇具音乐美感。

(3) Whitman's language is relatively simple, some even rather crude, and colloquial. Moreover, powerful, colorful, and rarely-used words frequently appear in his poetry.

(3) 惠特曼语言相对简单朴实，甚至十分粗犷，另一个特点是口语化。惠特曼词汇惊人，他的用词有力、生动、冷僻。

(4) Combining the ideal of the democratic common man and that of the rugged individual, Whitman envisioned the poet as a hero, a savior and a prophet, one who led the community by his expressions of the truth.

(4)惠特曼在他的诗中将民主人和粗犷的人结合。他把诗人设想成一个英雄、救世主和预言家，表达真理来领导整个群体。

3. Influence

3. 影响

Whitman boasts lasting influence on American modern poetry with his innovations in diction and versification, his frankness about sex, his inclusion of the commonplace and the ugly and his censure of the weakness of the American democratic practice. His *Leaves of Grass* represents America's first genuine epic poem.

凭借他在措辞和诗律方面的创新、对性这一话题的坦率、诗作中反映的平凡和丑陋的题材、以及他对美国民主弊端的指责，惠特曼对美国现代诗歌影响深远。他的《草叶集》的系列诗歌是美国文学史上第一部真正的史诗。

4. Major Works

4. 主要作品

Leaves of Grass
"Song of Myself"
"The Poet"
"When Lilacs Last in the Dooryard Bloom'd"
"O Captain! My Captain!"
"I Hear America Singing"

《草叶集》
《自我之歌》
《诗人》
《当紫丁香最近在庭院开放》
《哦，船长！我的船长!》
《我听到美国在唱歌》

"There was a Child Went Forth" "Out of Cradle Endlessly Rocking" "Two Riverlets" "Drum Traps"	《有 个孩子向前走去》 《从永久摇荡的摇篮里》 《两条小河》 《桴鼓集》
5. Selected Works	**5. 选读作品**
◆"Song of Myself"	**◆《自我之歌》**
Recurring celebration of ideals of equality and democracy, individual dignity, and humanity help shape Whitman's poems. "Song of Myself" reveals a rankles, hierarchy-free world of equality.	惠特曼的诗歌中弥漫着对平等和民主理想、个人价值和人性光辉的赞颂。《自我之歌》呈现了一个没有阶层和等级的平等的世界。
◆"I Sit and Look Out"	**◆《坐观世间》**
This poem conveys the poet's feelings about earthly sorrows and miseries. The last line "See, hear, and am silent" can be interpreted as a message of how the poet responds to worldly suffering: On the one hand, the poet is impotent in removing these sorrows, so he can do nothing but see, hear, and keep silent; on the other hand, despite harsh bitterness and difficulties observed, the poet is still optimistic about human capacity to overcome hardships.	诗歌揭示了深深震撼诗人心灵的世间苦难和悲惨。最后一行"我眼看，耳听，沉默不语"表明了诗人对世间疾苦的态度：一方面，诗人对世间苦难束手无策，只能看、听、保持沉默；另一方面，虽然这些苦难异常深重，诗人仍怀有希望，相信人类能够战胜。
◆"Beat! Beat! Drums!"	**◆《敲吧！敲吧！战鼓！》**
It is an anti-war poem. The poet bitterly criticizes wars in a very ironical tone.	这是一首反战诗。诗人用反讽的语气无情地批判了战争。

18.2 考研真题与典型题详解

Ⅰ. Fill in the blanks.

1. In his cluster of poems called *Leaves of Grass*, __________ gave America its first genuine epic poem.
2. The poetic style Walt Whitman devised is now called __________, which is poetry without a fixed beat or regular rhyme scheme.（天津外国语 2014 研）
3. *Leaves of Grass*, either in content or form, is an epoch-making work in American literature; its democratic content marked the shift from __________ to __________, and its __________ form broke from old poetic conventions to open a new road for American poetry.
4. As a literary movement, __________ came in the latter half of the 19th century as a reaction against the "lie" of romanticism and sentimentalism.（天津外国语学院 2007 研）

Ⅱ. Multiple Choices

1. Which ONE of the following poems is composed in memory of Abraham Lincoln?（四川大学 2011 研）

   A. "The Wild Honey Suckle".　　B. "The Tide Rises, The Tide Falls".

C. "Because I Could Not Stop for Death". D. "O Captain! My Captain!"

2. Which ONE of the following is the author of the poem "Song of Myself"?（四川大学 2008 研）

A. Walt Whitman. B. Stephen Crane.

C. Edgar Allan Poe. D. Henry Wadsworth Longfellow.

3. "By day her meals untouch'd, then at night fitfully sleeping, often waking" is taken from "I Hear America Singing". The female described here is the __________ of the dead person.（首师大 2009 研）

A. mother B. wife C. sister D. daughter

4. "I celebrate myself, and sing myself, /And what I assume you shall assume, /For every atom belonging to me as good belongs to you."

In the above quoted verse lines taken from Walt Whitman's poem "Song of Myself", what does the central image "myself" refer to?（四川大学 2009 研）

A. Merely the poet himself. B. The common people of America.

C. Masculine sublime ego. D. American puritans.

5. __________ divides the 19th century into the age of romanticism and realism in American literature.（北二外 2009 研）

A. The Spanish-American war B. The Civil War

C. WWI D. WWII

Ⅲ. Explain the following terms.

1. free verse（首师大 2009 研）

2. Walt Whitman and *Leaves of Grass*（南开大学 2010 研）

Ⅳ. Read the following quotations and answer the questions.

Passage 1

The following poem is written for the mourning of the Assassination of President Abraham Lincoln. Read it and answer the questions.（北二外 2009 研）

O Captain! My Captain

O Captain! My Captain! Our fearful trip is done,
The ship has weather'd every rack, the prize we sought is won,
The port is near, the bells I hear, the people all exulting,
While follow eyes the steady keel, the vessel grim and daring;
But O heart! heart! heart!
O the bleeding drops of red!
Where on the deck my Captain lies,
Fallen cold and dead.

O Captain! My Captain! Rise up and hear the bells;
Rise up—for you the flag is flung—for you the bugle trills,
For you bouquets and ribbon'd wreaths—for you the shores crowding,
For you they call, the swaying mass, their eager faces turning;
Here, Captain! Dear father!

This arm beneath your head;
It is some dream that on the deck,
You've fallen cold and dead.

My Captain does not answer, his lips are pale and still,
My father does not feel my arm, he has no pulse nor will;
The ship is anchor'd safe and sound, its voyage closed and done;
From fearful trip the victor ship comes in with object won;
Exult, O shores! And ring, O bells!
But I, with mournful tread,
Walk the deck my captain lies,
Fallen cold and dead.

1. The writer of this famous poem is one of the most influential poets at the age of romanticism. Can you give out his name and present his contribution in literature briefly?
2. Can you enlist at least two major figures of speech used in this poem and illustrate their functions respectively?

Passage 2

"I celebrate myself, and sing myself.
And what I assume you shall assume,
For every atom belonging to me as good belongs to you."

Questions:

1. Who wrote these lines? What is the poet celebrating?
2. Whom does "you" refer to?
3. What are the two principle beliefs that the poet set forth on this poem?

Ⅴ. Short answer question

Why is *Leaves of Grass* considered a milestone in American literature?

Ⅵ. Essay question

Why is the publishing history of *Leaves of Grass* particularly interesting? What is the significance of *Leaves of Grass* in American literature? What is the poet's view of himself? How is he viewed by other literati, the critic, and the general public? (人大 2005 研)

参考答案及解析

Ⅰ. Fill in the blanks.

1. Walt Whitman

(《草叶集》(*Leaves of Grass*)是十九世纪美国作家沃尔特·惠特曼(Walt Whitman)所著的诗集。《草叶集》是惠特曼一生创作的总汇，也是美国诗歌史上一座灿烂的里程碑。作品包含了丰富而深刻的思想内容，充分反映了十九世纪中期美国的时代精神。)

2. free verse

(沃尔特·惠特曼(Walt Whitman, 1810—1892)是美国著名诗人、人文主义者，他创造性地运用了诗歌的自由体(free verse)，其代表作品是诗集《草叶集》(*Leaves of Grass*)。自由诗是诗体的一种，其结构自由，段数、行数、字数没有一定规格；语言有自然节奏而不用韵。)

3. Romanticism; Realism; free verse

(《草叶集》无论是从内容上还是形式上都是美国文学划时代的作品，它有关民主的内容标志着浪漫主义到现实主义的转变，它采用自由体，从而打破了旧时诗歌的传统，为美国诗歌独辟蹊径。)

4. Realism

(作为一场文学运动，现实主义作为对浪漫主义和感伤主义的"谎言"的对抗出现在19世纪后半期。)

Ⅱ. Multiple Choices

1. D "O Captain! My Captain!"是Walt Whitman(惠特曼)写的用来纪念林肯之死的诗歌。诗歌中把林肯亲切地称为Captain。

2. A Walt Whitman(沃尔特·惠特曼)，美国著名诗人，"Song of Myself"(《自我之歌》)代表其创作的最高峰，后来收录在他的*Leaves of Grass*(《草叶集》)中。

3. A 这首诗是惠特曼"Come Up From The Fields, Father"里的几句，描写的是母亲接到儿子的死讯以后痛苦的心情。节译：白天她茶饭不思，晚上她无法安睡。

4. B 惠特曼在《自我之歌》里歌颂的是伟大的美国劳动人民。

5. B 内战是美国浪漫主义文学和现实主义文学的分水岭。

Ⅲ. Explain the following terms.

1. free verse: Poems without regular or established rhythm but with recognizable poetic quality. Walt Whitman is a representative innovator of free verse.

2. Walt Whitman and *Leaves of Grass*: Walt Whitman (1819—1892) was a great American poet in the 19th century. He was a major contributor to literary independence and innovation and devoted all his life to the creation of the "single" poem, *Leaves of Grass*. His poems are to a large extent known as acclaims for openness, freedom, and above all, individuality. Whitman's poetic principle is to relieve poems from the traditional iambic pentameter by employing what he called "free verse". His lines interfuse enthusiastic celebration of life and excellence of humanity.

Ⅳ. Read the following quotations and answer the questions.

Passage 1

1. The poem is composed by Walt Whitman. Whitman has his presence in both national and international modern poetry. His best works have been cherished as a common property of the Western culture. Poets across Europe and Latin America have been benefiting from his poetics. Modern American poets such as T. S. Eliot and Ezra Pound were the receiver of Whitman's poetic and literary wisdom as well. Contemporary American poetry also inherits his artistic style and techniques. Whitman has been credited for his innovations in diction and versification, his bold treatment of the sexual, his inclusiveness of the ordinary and the dissatisfying, and his critique of American democracy all contribute to his lasting charm.

2. "O Captain! My Captain!" is a poem by Walt Whitman. It was written in homage to U. S. President Abraham Lincoln after his assassination in 1865. The major figures of speech used in the poem are:

(1) Metaphor. A metaphor is used to compare one thing to another without using words such as "as" or "like." In this poem, "Captain" refers to Abraham Lincoln, and the "ship" symbolizes the United States of America. "The fearful trip" is the Civil War ended up with Lincoln's assassination. The ship is returning home to meet the cheering crowds who have just won "the prize" of victory. In the second stanza, the speaker calls his Captain "father," through which Whitman praises Lincoln as more of a father figure than merely a military leader, one true hero of the great nation whose wisdom and teachings had formative impact on his followers and who directed his children from innocent childhood to mature adulthood. In conclusion, the poem serves as memorization of Lincoln who led the Union to victory during the Civil War and creates in him significant importance as the father of this new, united, post-slavery country.

(2) Apostrophe. As a form of personification, apostrophe is used to address directly to an imaginary or absent listener that can be a person, an object or an abstract concept to convey extreme emotions. In the poem, the speaker repeatedly cries: "O Captain! My Captain!", which indicates his deep love and respect for the Captain. In the second stanza, the speaker speaks to "you", which shows an overwhelming sorrow in the speaker's coming to terms with the Captain's death. In the third stanza, the speaker has finally accepted the cruel fact of his Captain's death, so he can by no means addresses his Captain directly but speaks of him entirely in the third-person.

(本题要求至少列举两项"O Captain! My Captain!"中所用的修辞手法，并分别阐述它们在诗中所起到的作用。惠特曼在诗中主要运用了暗喻、象征、呼语和重复等手法，可任选两项进行阐释。)

Passage 2

1. These lines are taken from Walt Whitman's "Songs of Myself". In the poem, "I" represents neither the poet nor any particular person. By interfusing the first person with the second person perspective, the poet can better free himself in uttering expressions, in communicating the ideal of individualism, and in achieving a better effect of patriotic nationalism.
2. Here "you" refers to the democratic "en-mass" of America.
3. The two beliefs are the theory of universality and the belief in the singularity and equality.

V. Short answer question

Whitman's *Leaves of Grass* has been commended for its singing praises of American democracy.

In this work, the abundance of themes voices freshness. With intense humanistic care for industrious people and the hustle and bustle of cities, Whitman in his poems awakened public awareness of individualism and human dignity with careful design. In "Song of Myself" Whitman let loose of his imagination, perception and description of the physical and, above all, the sexual.

In terms of style, diction in Whitman's poetry is strikingly colloquial and simplistic with the quality of prose rhythm in journalism. With the device of direct speech, Whitman addresses his audience and listeners with "I", a voice that is designed to celebrate himself and human experience in the earthly world. Plus, Whitman invented free verse which gives his poems a taste of flowing and lingering musicality and a unique sense of rhythm.

Ⅵ. Essay question

In *Leaves of Grass*, Walt Whitman boldly depicted human body and extolled the senses, outstanding himself among his literary peers.

Whitman's contribution and innovation in American poetry has a profound influence till today. In *Leaves of Grass*, he broke free from the limitations and restrains of traditional rhyme and introduced what he called free verse. Such poetic technique was not highly thought of during his time but has its shadow in many later poems. The Whitmanian poet is treated as a hero who is preeminent in his community with the force of truthful expressions.

Whitman was not widely well-received when he was alive and was attacked by the majority of critics owing to his unconventional and bold style. Ironically, the reception of Whitman was disappointing during his life despite his initial intention of voicing for the general public.

第 19 章　艾米莉·狄金森

19.1　复习笔记

Emily Dickinson(1830—1886)

1. Life

Miss Dickinson was born in Amherst, Massachusetts, and her father was a prominent lawyer and politician. Emily's family was very closely knitted, and she and her sister remained at home and single. Emily seldom left Amherst; she attended college in a nearby town for one year, and later made one trip as far as Washington and two or three trips to Boston. After 1862 she became a total recluse.

Dickinson's poetic creation began with relatively little formal education. Though doubting the conventional religion of her family, she studied the Bible, and many of her poems resemble hymns in form. The early 1860s saw the summit of her poetic creation. However, she refused to revise her poems to cater to others and took no interest in having them published. Many of her nearly 1,800 poems were finally published posthumously in 1890s.

2. Themes

(1) Dickinson's poems are inspired by her own life experiences and centered on her doubt and thinking about religion, pain and frustration of love, success and failure.

(2) The theme of mortality and immortality occupies much space in Dickinson's poems. For Dickinson, death leads to immortality.

(3) Dickinson sees nature as both gaily benevolent and cruel.

(4) On the ethical level, Dickinson holds that beauty, truth and goodness are ultimately one.

(5) She emphasizes free-will and human responsibility.

艾米莉·狄金森(1830—1886)

1. 生平

狄金森出生在马萨诸塞州艾摩斯特市，父亲是一位知名的律师和政治家。狄金森家庭成员关系紧密，她和姐姐都终身未嫁。艾米莉很少离开艾摩斯特，她在附近镇上读了一年大学，之后最远到过华盛顿一次，到过波士顿两三次。1862年后，她彻底隐居起来。

当她开始写诗的时候，只接受了一点正式教育。虽然她不相信家人所信仰的传统宗教，但是她研究《圣经》，她的许多诗歌是模仿赞美诗的形式写成的。她的创作巅峰期在19世纪60年代早期。然而她不愿迎合批评家而修改诗作，也对出版没有兴趣。因此她创作的1800首诗歌中许多是在20世纪90年代她去世后出版的。

2. 主题

(1)基于她个人的经历和人生悲喜，她的诗歌是关于宗教主题的疑惑和信仰，爱情中的痛苦和挫折，成功与失败。

(2)狄金森的大部分诗歌是关于死亡与永生的。对狄金森来说，死亡导向永生。

(3)在狄金森眼中，自然是仁慈而又冷酷残忍的。

(4)在伦理的层面上，狄金森认为真善美最终是一体的。

(5)她强调自由意志和人类责任。

3. Writing Styles	**3. 写作风格**
(1) Her poetry abounds in telling images. In the best of her poems, every word presents a picture. So, she is regarded as the precursor of Imagist poetry.	(1)她的诗歌充满各种意象。在她最出色的诗歌中，每一个词都是一幅画。所以她被视作意象派诗歌的先驱。
(2) Dickinson's poetic diction has the quality of conciseness, directness and simplicity.	(2)她的诗风简明，直接，善用最平易的词。
(3) Dickinson's poems are usually short. Because the original poems do not have titles, the first line of her poems usually serves as the title. The capital letters in her poems are used for emphatic effect.	(3)狄金森的诗歌通常篇幅较短。因为原诗稿无标题，所以迪金森诗歌中第一句往往被用作诗歌的题目。诗中用大写的词表示强调。
(4) She wrote whimsical, darting verse with sublime indifference to any notion of being a democratic or popular poet. Dickinson's poems are her manifesto of how one could seat in a single household, live an inactive life, and make enchanting poetry out of it.	(4)狄金森的作品古怪而又简洁，她对于大众或流行之类的概念视而不见，往往是通过一件具体的家庭小事和一种闲适的生活来阐明事理，并把这些描写为令人痴迷的诗歌。
4. Major Works	**4. 主要作品**
"The Soul Selects Her Own Society"	《灵魂选择自己的友伴》
"My Life Closed Twice before Its Close"	《我的生命在结束之前已结束了两次》
"Because I Could Not Stop for Death—"	《因为我不能停下来等待死神》
"I Heard a Fly Buzz—When I Died—"	《我死时听到了苍蝇的嗡嗡声》
"Mine—by the Right of the White Election"	《我的——根据白色选举的权利》
"Wild Nights—Wild Nights"	《狂风夜——狂风夜!》
"Death is a Dialogue Between"	《死是一场对话》
"I Died for Beauty—But Was Scarce"	《我为美而死》
5. Selected Works	**5. 选读作品**
◆"I Taste a Liquor Never Brewed"	**◆《我品尝未酿之酒》**
The "liquor" in this poem refers to nature, by which the poet is very fascinated and enchanted. Dickinson uses the metaphor to express how the beauty of nature intoxicates her and cheers her up.	诗中的"美酒"是指令诗人如痴如醉的大自然。迪金森使用隐喻手法通过描写醉酒状态表达了振奋人心的大自然之美。
◆"I Felt a Funeral, in My Brain"	**◆《在脑海，我感受到了葬礼》**
This poem shows the poet's mind state in an obvious and concrete way.	诗歌清晰而具体地显示了诗人的思想状态。
◆"A Bird Came down the Walk—"	**◆《一只鸟儿停在道上——》**
It is a keen observation of the poet when she sees the bird on the road and she tries to feed it some crumb, but it has fear and flies away.	当诗人看到一只鸟儿在路边时，仔细观察了它，并试图喂食面包屑，但是鸟儿却感到了惊吓飞走了。

◆**"I Died for Beauty—But Was Scarce"** This poem shows the poet's firm pursuit for beauty and truth. ◆**"I Heard a Fly Buzz—When I Died—"** It depicts the subtle and sensitive feelings and thought of the speaker on the verge of dying. ◆**"Because I Could Not Stop for Death—"** In this poem, Dickinson reveals the theme by describing death and immortality with the dominant metaphor of a carriage on a journey.	◆**《我为美而死》** 这首诗表明了诗人对美与真理的不懈追求。 ◆**《我死时听到了苍蝇的嗡嗡声》** 诗歌描写了主人公弥留之际细致、敏感的情感和思想。 ◆**《因为我不能停下来等待死神》** 诗中狄金森将死亡和永恒隐喻为旅程中的马车，揭示了诗歌的主题。

19.2　考研真题与典型题详解

Ⅰ. Fill in the blanks.

1. In Emily Dickinson's poem "Because I could not stop for Death", she uses personification to compare death to ________. （天津外国语 2010 研）
2. Author ________ Title ________（南京大学 2008 研）

   Not one of all the purple host
   Who took the flag today
   Can tell the definition,
   So clearly, of victory.
3. For the whole 19th century ________ was the only woman poet who enjoys high academic esteem today. She has been acclaimed as a poet of philosophical and tragic dimensions, a poet who was responsive to the challenging questions of man, nature and human consciousness.

Ⅱ. Multiple Choices

1. Which ONE of the following is an influential poet whose poems often express a thematic concern about the issue of death and eternity?（四川大学 2009 研）

   A. Walt Whitman.　　B. Ralph Waldo Emerson.
   C. Henry Wadsworth Longfellow.　　D. Emily Dickinson.
2. The following selection is from a poem written by ________. （大连外国语 2007 研）

   A. Robert Burns　B. Emily Dickinson　C. Carl Sandburg　D. John Keats

   I willed my Keepsakes—Signed away
   What portion of me be
   Assignable—and then it was
   There interposed a Fly—

   With Blue—uncertain stumbling Buzz—
   Between the light—and me—
   And then the Windows failed—and then

I could not see to see—

3. The first line of the following poem is __________. （大连外国语 2008 研）

A. Because I could not stop for Death
B. I felt a Funeral, in my Brain
C. I taste a liquor never brewed
D. Success is counted sweetest

Not one of all the purple host
Who took the flag today
Can tell the definition,
So clear, of victory!

As he, defeated—dying—
On whose forbidden ear
The distant strains of triumph
Burst agonized and clear!

4. Emily Dickinson's poetic idiom is noted for the following except __________.

A. brevity
B. directness
C. plainest words
D. obscure

5. The main theme of Emily Dickinson is the following except __________.

A. religion
B. love and marriage
C. life and death
D. war and peace

Ⅲ. Read the following quotations and answer the questions.

Passage 1（北航 2008 研）

I heard a Fly buzz—when I died—
The Stillness in the Room
Was like the Stillness in the Air—
Between the Heaves of Storm—

The Eyes around—had wrung them dry—
And Breaths were gathering firm
For that last Onset—when the King
Be witnessed—in the Room—

I willed my Keepsakes—Signed away
What portion of me be
Assignable—and then it was
There interposed a Fly—

With Blue—uncertain stumbling Buzz—
Between the light—and me—
And then the Windows failed—and then
I could not see to see—

Questions:

1. Identify the author of the passage.
2. What are the effect and the meaning of "I heard a Fly buzz—when I died—"?
3. What is the meaning of the last two lines?

Passage 2（南开大学 2011 研）

Because I could not stop for Death

Because I could not stop for Death—
He kindly stopped for me—
The Carriage held but just Ourselves—
And Immortality.

We slowly drove—He knew no haste,
And I had put away
My labor, and my leisure too,
For his Civility—

We passed the School, where Children strove
At Recess—in the Ring—
We passed the Fields of Gazing Grain—
We passed the Setting Sun—

Or rather. He passed Us—
The Dews drew quivering and chill—
For only Gossamer, my Gown—
My tippet—only tulle—

We paused before a House that seemed
A Swelling of the Ground—
The Roof was scarcely visible—
The Cornice—in a Ground

Since then—'tis centuries—and yet
Feels shorter than the Day
I first surmised the horses' heads
Were toward Eternity.

1. Why did Death stop for me?
2. Why couldn't I stop for Death?
3. What did the Death's carriage hold?
4. What three things did the speaker and Death pass?
5. What is the "House" in the ground in stanza 5? Why do the centuries seem shorter than the Day?

6. What is the theme of the poem?

Passage 3

Read the following poem and write a short essay based on the following questions in about 100 words. (厦门大学 2012 研)

I'm Nobody

By Emily Dickinson (1830—1886)

I'm nobody, who are you?
Are you nobody too?
Then there's a pair of us.
Don't tell—they'd banish us, you know.

How dreary to be somebody,
How public—like a frog—
To tell your name the livelong June
To all admiring bog.

Questions:

1. What, in your opinion, is the theme of this poem?
2. What is the meaning of each stanza?
3. What is your attitude towards fame?

Ⅳ. Short answer question

Identify the following two poems and make a brief summary of their main points to compare their attitudes toward death. (武汉大学 2007 研)

Poem 1

Death be not proud, though some have called thee
Mighty and dreadful, for, thou art not so;
For those whom thou think'st thou dost overthrow
Die not, poor Death, nor yet canst thou kill me.
From rest and sleep, which but thy picture be,
Much pleasure; then from thee much more must flow,
And soonest our best men with thee do go,
Rest of their bones, and soul's delivery.
Thou art slave to fate, chance, kings, and desperate men,
And dost with poison, war, and sickness dwell,
And poppy, or charms can make us sleep as well,
And better than thy stroke; why swell'st thou then?
One short sleep past, we wake eternally,
And death shall be no more; Death, thou shalt die.

Poem 2

Death is a Dialogue between
The Spirit and the Dust.

"Dissolve" says Death—The Spirit "Sir
I have another Trust"—

Death doubts it—Argue from the Ground—
The Spirit turns away
Just laying off for evidence
An Overcoat of Clay.

V. Essay questions

1. What are the thematic concerns and the artistic characteristics of Emily Dickenson's poetry?
2. Emily Dickinson's poetry abounds in images. In the best of her poems every word is a picture seen. Comment on the images in either "Because I Could Not Stop for Death" or "I Like to See It Lap the Miles".（天津外国语 2008 研）

参考答案及解析

I. Fill in the blanks.

1. a gentleman who took me with his carriage
（《因为我不能停下来等待死神》是美国诗人艾米莉·狄金森的代表诗歌之一。其中，诗人运用拟人的手法将死亡比作"赶着马车带'我'离开的人"。）
2. Emily Dickinson; "Success is Counted Sweetest"
（题目节选自狄金森的《成功最甜美》。艾米莉·狄金森，美国最富传奇性的抒情诗人。生前只发表了7首诗，诗作几乎全部在她死后才发表。她被视为20世纪现代主义诗歌的先驱之一，和美国文学之父欧文、诗人惠特曼比肩。）
3. Emily Dickinson
（贯穿整个19世纪，艾米莉·狄金森是唯一一位至今仍备受推崇的女诗人。）

II. Multiple Choices

1. D　艾米丽·狄金森的诗歌表达了一种对于死亡和永恒的关注，如"因为我不能停下来等待死神"。
2. B　题中诗句选自美国著名诗人 Emily Dickinson 的诗《我死时听到了苍蝇的嗡嗡声》，译文为：我立了遗嘱——分掉关于我的/所有可以分掉的/部分——然后我就看见了/一只苍蝇闯了进来/蓝色的——带着忧郁、不确定踌躇蹒跚的嗡嗡声/在我——与光——之间/然后窗户关闭——然后/我眼前漆黑一片。
3. D　题目中的诗歌选自 Emily Dickinson（艾米丽·狄金森）的"Success is Counted Sweetest"，该诗的第一行即 Success is counted sweetest。节选部分的译文：身穿紫服的王者之师/今日虽高扬凯旗/ 却无一人能把胜利的/ 含义，说清道明。/战败者奄奄一息，/凯乐在远处奏响，/冲破阻隔，飞到他的/ 耳际，悲痛而嘹亮。
4. D　艾米丽·狄金森的用词简洁、直率、平易，而非晦涩。
5. D　艾米丽·狄金森诗歌的主题不涉及战争与和平。

III. Read the following quotations and answer the questions.

Passage 1

1. The author is Emily Dickinson.

2. The speaker is lying on her deathbed and waiting for the last moment. The room still and the tears of her relatives running dry, an atmosphere of solemnity and woe permeates the air. The speaker patiently waits to behold the "King", namely the holy spirit, but all of a sudden she hears a fly buzzing around. Often seen as disgusting and annoying, the fly sometimes gathers around corpses. As the image of flies disconcerts people, the speaker intends to show doubt about the idea of "immortality" in the poem.
3. The fly's wings cutting the speaker off from the light, she closes her eyes and dies. In seeing the light which the speaker deems as coming from heaven, she imagines her ascent to the paradise with the holy. At the very moment, a fly shows up and interferes with the speaker's vision because of which her previous faith in immortality and transcendence shakes. Now, the speaker is not sure whether she can really go to heaven with the "King".

Passage 2

1. In the first line of the poem, Dickinson explains why she "could not stop for death": because death appears benign and seems to offer her ease and assurance. The speaker depicts Death as kind and considerate.
2. In the whole poem, Dickinson regards life as a journey only through which can we stop for death. Therefore, to the speaker's mind, death is not the terminal of life but an interchange station after which we travel all the way to immortality.
3. Death's carriage holds immortality, "I" and "death".
4. They pass three places: the School which symbolizes childhood, the Fields of Gazing Grain which symbolize maturity and the Setting Sun which symbolizes the old age.
5. "House" means the grave, of which what is visible on the ground is the tomb like a roof. So, the "house" means death. However, instead of being the terminal station on our life's journey, death is nothing more than a pause of the journey. In the light of Christine tenets, death ushers in eternity. Thus, compared with the journey before death, a century is even shorter than a day.
6. By compared life to a journey, Dickinson tells the reader that death is not as painful and terrible as commonly imagined. It is just like a friend and comes to accompany you to eternity. Nevertheless, it seems that death has cheated her and finally deserted her in eternity. It is Emily Dickinson's impression of death and the essence of life that stirs meditation in us.

   (此文需要抓住死亡和旅程这两个概念来回答，同时注意作者对死亡的态度。

   参考译文：因为我不能停下来等待死神/他和善地停下来等我——/那辆车只能容我们两个——/还有不朽。//我们慢慢驱车——他不慌不忙/我也把我的劳与闲/统统丢到一边，/为了他的礼让——//我们走过校园，孩子们你推我搡，/在休息时间，在圆形广场——/我们走过在田间凝眸的麦秆——/我们走过落日旁——//或毋宁说，他走过我们身旁/寒露降，身子冻得打颤——/因为我的长衫落纱般——/我的披肩如丝网——//我们停步在一所房子前，/那似乎是隆起的土地一片/屋顶几乎看不见——/屋檐在地里面——//离那时已是几个世纪/过了还不到一天，/我首次猜测到，马头/在朝向永恒奔窜。)

Passage 3

1. This poem shows the poet's attitude towards fame. Instead of having strong desires for vain fame as many do, Dickinson prefers "obscurity" and satirizes the so-called "somebody" who restlessly

chases after fame and blows his own trumpet.

2. The first stanza is saying that the poet meets a "nobody", possibly her friend. Together, the two nobodies can enjoy each other's company, this valuable bosom friendship and their shared anonymity. In the second stanza, the speaker becomes confident after becoming aware of the defects and vanity of making painful efforts to become "somebody". She realizes that true friendship is all the way more important than admiration from crowds of irrelevant strangers who do not really care to understand you.

3. In my opinion, this poem serves as enlightenment, reminding us of what is the most precious in life and of virtues worth striving for such as love, faith, friendship, joy of life and so on. Fame is only a small portion of the beautiful scenery in one's life, but it is transitory and should not be one's ultimate goal of work and life.

Ⅳ. Short answer question

1. "Death Be Not Proud" has earned wide popularity due to its message of hope couched in eloquent language. The speaker informs the reader that death has no firm grounds of pride in that death leads not to a definite ending of human spirit but to eternity. Though regarded as potent and irritable by many people, death is really a pathetic slave that can do nothing but prey on human misfortune, diseases, and so on. After a human being's soul leaves the body and enters heaven, it lives on; only death dies.

The second poem is written by Emily Dickinson who pays much attention to life and death, time, and eternity. For Dickinson, death is "a dialogue between the spirit and the dust" as in the poem, the spirit and the dust argue over what should happen to a person. To Death's mind, after death men are buried and exist no more, but the spirit argues that human spirit leaves the body and rises to heaven. They do not see eye to eye with each other and begin to debate. Then the spirit proves itself by showing that despite the corpse is buried under ground, the spirit is at full liberty to rise to heaven and finds peace there.

These two poems compare different attitudes toward death. In Donne's poem, human spirit will leave the body and enter eternity while Dickinson thinks that the spirit will go to heaven. They two both believe in a free soul after death. The difference lies in their treatment of the dead body: the former believes in a free body while the latter argues that the body will be buried in the ground with no freedom as that of the spirit.

(本题要求总结和对比两首诗中关于死亡的观点。第一首是约翰·邓恩的《死亡，你莫骄傲》，第二首是艾米莉·狄金森的《死亡是一场对话》。

译文：

1. 死神，你莫骄傲

死神，你莫骄傲，尽管有人说你/如何强大，如何可怕，你并不是这样；/你以为你把谁谁谁打倒了，其实，/可怜的死神，他们没死；你现在也还杀不死我。/休息、睡眠，这些不过是你的写照，/既能给人享受，那你本人提供的一定更多；/我们最美好的人随你去得越早，/越能早日获得身体的休息，灵魂的解脱。/你是命运、机会、君主、亡命徒的奴隶，/你和毒药、战争、疾病同住在一起，/ 罂粟和咒符和你的打击相比，同样，/甚至更能催我入睡；那你何必趾高气扬呢？/睡了一小觉之后，我们便永远觉醒了，/再也不会有死亡，你死

神也将死去。(杨周翰 译)

2. 死亡是一场对话

死亡是一场对话/在灵魂和尘土之间。/"分解吧。"死亡说。灵魂回答，"先生，/我有另外的信念。"/死亡对此怀疑，争辩从头开始。/灵魂转身离开，/为了证明，只留下一件/黏土的外衣。)

V. Essay questions

1. ①Emily Dickinson is the best known American female poet. She penetrates the psychological of the individual mind. A life of seclusion has shaped her poems with intense individuality and a quality of meditativeness. Personifications are often used to illustrate rather abstract concepts. Her poetry embraces a wide range of important issues such as religion, death, immortality, love, and nature.

   ②Her poems have no titles and are always quoted by their first lines. Stylistically, dashes are used to create cadence and capital letters as a means of emphasis. Most of her poems feature heavy uses of repeated four-line, rhymed stanzas of traditional Christian hymns with two lines of four-beat meter alternating with two lines of three-beat meter.

   ③Dickinson is a master who makes spirituality work in surprising ways, managing multiple changes in her simple form: imperfect rhythms, subtle rhythmic breaks, and unique grammar and punctuation are used to create fascinating world puzzles, producing very different interpretations over the years.

   ④Dickinson's poetry, though simple in its form, is remarkably diverse, subtle and rich. Her limited private world never limits the infinite power of her creativity and imagination.

2. "Because I Could Not Stop for Death" portrays Death as the central image and a gentleman. The metaphorical use of an event familiar to people of the nineteenth century constitutes the background of the plot. A gentleman, Death himself, drives a carriage to pick up his lady, an imagined persona of the poet. The whole poem is constructed on this imagination, a dramatic representation of the passage from this world of the secular to the afterlife.

   In the first stanza the gentleman has catered to his intended lady with the prospect of eternity. The second stanza indicates the peacefulness and pleasantness that foreshadows the upcoming journey. By the third stanza, Death and the persona are nearing the edge of town where rich images are presented. The seemingly disparate elements of children, "Gazing Grain", and "Setting Sun", the sensations that dying lady experiences, are transferred to these parts of the world. She is gazing, and the notion is transferred to the grain; she is "setting", and this notion is transferred to the sun. The mention of children "striving" at recess is a subtle preparation for the stasis, or lack of motion, described in the succeeding images. In addition, the three elements are the condensation of the progress and passage of a lifetime, embracing the three states of youth, maturity, and old age, the cycle of day from morning to evening, and even a suggestion of seasonal progression from spring through ripening to decline.

   In the fourth stanza, as "Dews" now grow "quivering and chill" upon her skin, which are traditional associations of the coldness of death, we sense that the lady is getting closer to death. Her tippet made of lace is often perceived as should be placed around the shoulders of a deceased woman lying in repose.

In the fifth stanza, they have arrived at a country cemetery. The House is a fresh grave, the roof a small tombstone, the cornice the molding around a coffin's lid. All have already been placed "in the Ground". The lady is alone now; her gentleman friend has vanished unexplained.

In the sixth stanza it is not until after the school children, the "Gazing Grain", the "Setting Sun", and the "Swelling of the Ground" that the lady begins to realize where she is heading. She has, therefore, apparently been tricked, seduced, and then abandoned.

第20章 哈丽雅特·比彻·斯托

20.1 复习笔记

Harriet Beecher Stowe(1811—1896)	哈丽雅特·比彻·斯托(1811—1896)
1. Life	**1. 生平**
Harriet Beecher Stowe was born into a respectable and famous family. In 1816, she began studying in Litchfield, Connecticut. When Catherine founded Hartford Girls' College in 1824, she transferred to it. In 1836, she married Calvin Ellis Stowe. In 1850, when her husband was hired as a professor at Bowden College, she returned to her native New England. Her previous 18 years of observing Ohio River slaves led her to conceive the popular anti-slavery novel.	斯托夫人出生于名门望族。1816年，她开始在康涅狄格州的利奇菲尔德上学，当凯瑟琳于1824年成立哈特福德女子学院时，她又转入该校。1836年，她嫁给了卡尔文·埃利斯·斯托。1850年，由于丈夫被聘请成为鲍登学院的教授，她又回到家乡新英格兰。她之前18年观察俄亥俄河奴隶的经验让她开始构思这部大受欢迎的反奴小说。
2. Major Works	**2. 主要作品**
Uncle Tom's Cabin(1851) *Dred: A Tale of the Great Dismal Swamp*(1856)	《汤姆叔叔的小屋》(1851) 《德雷德：阴暗大沼地的故事》(1856)
3. Selected Work	**3. 选读作品**
◆*Uncle Tom's Cabin*	**◆《汤姆叔叔的小屋》**
Uncle Tom's Cabin was the best-selling novel of the 19th century and was grounded in a single theme: the evil and immorality of slavery. The novel fueled the abolitionist cause in the 1850s.	《汤姆叔叔的小屋》是19世纪最畅销的小说，它最重要的主题是：奴隶制的罪恶和不道德。这部小说有力地推动了19世纪50年代的废奴主义事业。
The sentimental style and plot characteristics of this novel are very similar to 19th-century sentimental and domestic novels. The novel's success stems from the author's deep feelings about the pain and oppression afflicted on the two heroes, Tom and his friend Eliza.	这部小说的感伤风格和情节特点与19世纪的感伤小说和家庭小说很相似。小说的成功源于该作品倾注了作者对两位主人公汤姆和他的朋友依莱扎所受痛苦和压迫的深刻感受。
Uncle Tom's Cabin outraged people in the American South. The novel was also roundly criticized by slavery supporters.	《汤姆叔叔的小屋》激怒了美国的南方人，也遭到了奴隶制支持者的严厉批判。

20.2 考研真题与典型题详解

Ⅰ. Fill in the blanks.

1. Harriet Beecher Stowe's masterpiece is ________.

2. There was only one female prose writer in the nineteenth century. That was ________.

Ⅱ. Explain the following term.

Uncle Tom(北航2009研)

Ⅲ. Essay question

Analyze *Uncle Tom's Cabin* by Mrs. Stowe.

参考答案及解析

Ⅰ. Fill in the blanks.

1. *Uncle Tom's Cabin*

(哈丽雅特・比彻・斯托(Harriet Beecher Stowe 1811—1896)的名作长篇小说《汤姆叔叔的小屋》(*Uncle Tom's Cabin*)是19世纪最畅销的小说。)

2. Harriet Beecher Stowe

(哈丽雅特・比彻・斯托(Harriet Beecher Stowe 1811—1896)是19世纪美国唯一的女散文作家。她写的长篇小说《汤姆叔叔的小屋》(*Uncle Tom's Cabin*)发表后在国内外引起强烈反响，有力地推动了美国反奴隶制的斗争。)

Ⅱ. Explain the following term.

Uncle Tom: Uncle Tom is used to describe a black man who is seen as subservient to white authority, or who unnecessarily outreaches himself to please the white. The word comes from the title of American writer Harriet Beecher Stowe's 1852 novel *Uncle Tom's Cabin* in which Uncle Tom is a Christian martyr morally superior to his white master. Many adaptations have dramatically changed this description, often making such a figure weak, enslaved, or a racial traitor.

Ⅲ. Essay question

①*Uncle Tom's Cabin* is an antislavery novel that had an impact on national political dissatisfaction with slavery and human rights conditions in the United States. Black slaves are depicted as sympathetic, miserable beings not equally treated as qualified citizens by the white in the novel. By contrast, slave-owners are depicted as extremely cruel without the slightest empathy. This sharp contract exposes the harsh reality of inequality, hierarchy, and racial discrimination entrenched in American society. Largely due to the popularity of the novel, slavery was passionately debated across the country with obvious effect as it has stirred a great nation to reflect on its deep-seated problems and set off a nationwide war.

②The book relates the trials, suffering, and human dignity of Uncle Tom, an old Negro slave. Cruelly treated by a Yankee overseer, Simon Legree, who dies as the result of a fight. Uncle Tom is devoted to Little Eva, the daughter of his white owner, Augustine St. Clare. The two most famous scenes are the death of Little Eva and the pursuit of Eliza and her baby.

③The novel is sometimes regarded as a piece of artistic literature, but its quality is somewhat undermined by unnecessary sentiments, conventional and forced plotting, which gives readers a sense of careless writing efforts. The accuracy of pictures presented in the novel should be under further reflection as the author herself had never lived in the slave states. Nevertheless, the characterization is more successful and touching, distinguishing itself from thousands of others of its kind by showing to readers more than an antislavery tract. The novel has the merits of dramatic intensity, moral earnestness, intense emotionalism and, above all, human interest.

第21章　马克·吐温

21.1　复习笔记

Mark Twain(1835—1910) **1. Life** Samuel Longhorn Clemens, pseudonym Mark Twain, is an American novelist and humorist.	**马克·吐温(1835—1910)** **1. 生平** 塞缪尔·朗赫恩·克莱门斯，笔名马克·吐温，是美国小说家和幽默作家。
Twain grew up in Missouri, where became the setting for the adventures of Huckleberry Finn and Tom Sawyer. At the age of 12, his father died and he was forced to drop out of school and worked as an apprentice at a printing house, a typesetter, a silver miner, a steersman on the Mississippi River, and a journalist in Nevada and California. Such a rich life experience made him deeply understand human nature. While working for *Territorial Enterprise* in Virginia, he gave himself the penname Mark Twain, which means twelve feet. In 1871, he became famous. He bought a villa in Hartford and lived with his wife. He indulged in financial speculation and finally went bankrupt due to the failure of his investment in typesetting and publishing companies. At the same time, he has been pessimistic and suspicious. Mark Twain's late life was bleak. His family members died one after another. His wife died in 1904 and his daughter in 1909. April 21, 1910, Mark Twain died while reading, Connecticut, at the age of 75.	马克·吐温在密苏里州长大，这里成为《哈克贝利·费恩历险记》和《汤姆·索亚历险记》的故事背景。12岁那年，他的父亲去世，他被迫辍学。他当过印刷所学徒、排字工、银矿矿工，在密西西比河当过舵手，在内华达州和加利福尼亚州当过记者。这样丰富的生活经历让他深刻地了解了人性。在弗吉尼亚《地方企业》工作时，他给自己取了"马克·吐温"这个笔名，意为十二英尺。1871年他已声名鹊起，在哈特福德置办了别墅，和妻子一起生活。他沉溺于金融投机，终于因投资排版和出版公司失败而破产。同时他一直情绪悲观，充满怀疑。马克·吐温晚景凄凉，亲人相继离世，妻子1904年去世，女儿1909年去世。1910年4月21日，马克·吐温在康涅狄格的雷丁去世，享年75岁。
2. Literary Achievements Mark Twain is a giant of American literature. He is a great humorist and is regarded as "the real father of our national literature" by Mencken. Before him, American writers were greatly influenced by European literature, but his way of thinking, values, creative language and even his humor were rooted in America.	**2. 文学成就** 马克·吐温是美国的文学巨匠。他是一位幽默大师，被门肯评价为"我们真正的民族文学之父"。在他以前的美国作家受欧洲文学影响较大，而他的思维方式、价值观、创作语言、甚至他的幽默都根植于美国。
(1) "Local colorism" is the most prominent feature of his novels, which shows the language characteristics, customs and lifestyle of a region.	(1)"乡土特色"是他的小说最突出的特点，表现了一个地区的语言特点、习俗和生活方式。

(2) Anderson, Hemingway, Eliot, Faulkner and Salinger are all influenced by him to some extent. Faulkner honored him as "the father of American Literature".	(2)他的口语体散文形式成为美国口语体文学传统的发端，安德森、海明威、艾略特、福克纳、塞林格等都在不同程度上受到他的影响。福克纳将他称为"美国文学之父"。
3. Major Works *The Celebrated Jumping Frog of Calaveras County* (1865) *Innocents Abroad* (1869) *The Gilded Age* (1873) *The Adventures of Tom Sawyer* (1876) *Life on the Mississippi* (1883) *Adventures of Huckleberry Finn* (1884) *A Connecticut Yankee in King Arthur's Court* (1889) *The Tragedy of Pudd'nhead Wilson* (1894) *The Man That Corrupted Hadleyburg* (1900)	**3. 主要作品** 《加拉维拉县驰名的跳蛙》(1865) 《傻子出国记》(1869) 《镀金时代》(1873) 《汤姆·索亚历险记》(1876) 《密西西比河上的生活》(1883) 《哈克贝利·费恩历险记》(1884) 《亚瑟王朝廷上的康涅狄格州美国佬》(1889) 《傻瓜威尔逊》(1894) 《败坏了哈德莱堡的人》(1900)
4. Selected Work ◆***The Adventures of Tom Sawyer*** *The Adventures of Tom Sawyer* is a great children's literature. The major character is an innocent, lively, imaginative and adventurous little boy. Through the protagonist's adventure, the novel satirizes and criticizes the American hypocritical and vulgar social customs, hypocritical religious rituals and stereotyped school education.	**4. 选读作品** ◆**《汤姆·索亚历险记》** 《汤姆·索亚历险记》是一部伟大的儿童文学作品。故事围绕一个天真活泼、富于幻想和冒险的小男孩展开。小说通过主人公的冒险经历，对美国虚伪庸俗的社会习俗、伪善的宗教仪式和刻板陈腐的学校教育进行了讽刺和批判。

21.2 考研真题与典型题详解

Ⅰ. Fill in the blanks.

1. Ernest Hemingway once noted that "all modern American literature comes from one book by Mark Twain". The book Hemingway gave credit to is __________. (天津外国语 2007 研)
2. Mark Twain, pseudonym of Samuel Langhorne __________, started off as a __________ colorist. His novel __________ is the one book from which, as Hemingway noted, "all __________ American literature comes". (国际关系学院 2010 研)
3. The best work that Mark Twain ever produced is __________, which was a success from its fast publication in 1884, and has always been regarded as one of the great books of western literature and western civilization. (人大 2006 研)
4. One of Samuel Langhorne Clemens' best books __________ is built around his experiences as a steamboat pilot.
5. Mark Twain once described the theme of a book as the struggle between a healthy heart and a de-

formed conscience, and he attributed this description to the character __________ in that book. (首师大 2008 研)

6. The result of Mark Twain's European trip was a series of newspaper articles, later published as a book called __________.
7. Mark Twain's first novel, __________ was an artistic failure, but it gave its name to the America of the post bellum period which it attempts to satirize.
8. The Age of Realism is also what Mark Twain referred to as "__________".
9. At the heart of Mark Twain's achievement is his creation of two characters: __________ and __________.
10. __________, breaking out of the narrow limits of local color fiction, described the breadth of American experience as no one had ever done before, or since.

Ⅱ. Multiple Choices

1. West Humor is best represented in __________'s short story writing. (北二外 2007 研)

   A. O. Henry　　B. Flannery O'Connor
   C. Henry James　　D. Mark Twain
2. __________'s stories still had many unrealistic qualities: "tall tales" and unlikely coincidences. He is never a pure realist.

   A. Henry James　　B. Mark Twain
   C. Nathaniel Hawthorne　　D. Henry David Thoreau
3. Mark Twain wrote most of his literary works with a __________ language.

   A. grand　　B. pompous　　C. simple　　D. vernacular
4. Mark Twain was a great social critic and a friend of the Chinese. His *Disgraceful Persecution of a Boy* is a scathing piece of criticism directed against the persecution of the __________ immigrants in California.

   A. Quakers　　B. Chinese　　C. French　　D. Japanese
5. The representative work of Mark Twain is __________. (首师大 2009 研)

   A. *The Notorious Jumping Frog of Calaveras County*
   B. *Innocents Abroad*
   C. *The Adventures of Tom Sawyer*
   D. *Adventures of Huckleberry Finn*
6. With William Dean Howells, Henry James, and Mark Twain active on the scene, __________ became the major trend in the seventies and eighties of the nineteenth century.

   A. sentimentalism　　B. romanticism　　C. realism　　D. naturalism
7. In his later novels, Mark Twain seems less hopeful about democracy, which is reflected in his work, __________.

   A. *The Man That Corrupted Hadleyburg*
   B. *The Mysterious Stranger*
   C. *The Celebrated Jumping Frog of Calaveras Country*
   D. *A Connecticut Yankee in King Arthur's Court*
8. Mark Twain created, in __________, a masterpiece of American realism that is also one of the

great books of world literature.

A. *Adventures of Huckleberry Finn* B. *The Adventures of Tom Sawyer*

C. *The Man That Corrupted Hadleyburg* D. *The Gilded Age*

Ⅲ. Explain the following terms.

1. Local Colorism（北二外 2008 研；四川大学 2009 研；南京师范大学 2018 研）
2. Mark Twain（北航 2007 研）
3. First-person narrative（上海交大 2003 研）

Ⅳ. Read the following quotations and answer the questions.

Passage 1

I took the sack of corn meal and took it to where the canoe was hid, and shoved the vines and branches apart and put it in; then I done the same with the side of bacon; then the whisky-jug. I took all the coffee and sugar there was, and all the ammunition; I took the wadding; I took the bucket and gourd; I took a dipper and a tin cup, and my old saw and two blankets, and the skillet and the coffee-pot. I took fish-lines and matches and other things—everything that was worth a cent. I cleaned out the place. I wanted an ax, but there wasn't any, only the one out at the woodpile, and I knew why I was going to leave that. I fetched out the gun, and now I was done.

Questions:

1. Which novel is this passage taken from?
2. Analyze the language style of this passage.

Passage 2

Now when I had mastered the language of this water, and had come to know every trifling feature that bordered the great river as familiarly as I know the letters of the alphabet, I had made a valuable acquisition. But I had lost something, too. I had lost something which could never be restored to me while I lived. All the grace, the beauty, the poetry, had gone out the majestic river!

Questions:

1. From which novel is this paragraph taken?
2. Who is the author of this novel?
3. What did the author lose when he got to know the river as an experienced pilot should?

Passage 3

YOU don't know about me without you have read a book by the name of *The Adventures of Tom Sawyer*; but that ain't no matter. That book was made by Mr. Mark Twain, and he told the truth, mainly. There were things which he stretched, but mainly he told the truth. That is nothing. I never seen anybody but lied one time or another, without it was Aunt Polly, or the widow, or maybe Mary. Aunt Polly—Tom's Aunt Polly, she is—and Mary, and the Widow Douglas is all told about in that book, which is mostly a true book, with some stretchers, as I said before.

Questions:

1. From which novel is this paragraph taken from?
2. Who is the author of this novel?

Ⅴ. Short answer questions

1. Why is Mark Twain considered a social critic?（国际关系学院 2007 研）

2. In *Adventures of Huckleberry Finn*, Huck Finn is a thirteen-year-old boy. Why does Mark Twain use a child as the center of consciousness in this book?
3. Who are the three dominant figures of the American Realistic Period and what are their literary differences?（国际关系学院 2007 研）
4. How do you understand Mark Twain's use of Local Color in his writing?

Ⅵ. Essay questions

1. Charles Dickens and Mark Twain are both well-known literary realists. Name one of the masterpieces by each of them and make a brief comparison and/or contrast so as to tell the similarities and/or differences between British and American realism.（武汉大学 2007 研）
2. What's the difference between Henry James's realism and Mark Twain's realism?
3. Discuss the themes explored by Mark Twain in *Adventures of Huckleberry Finn.*（大连外国语 2008 研）
4. *Adventures of Huckleberry Finn* was praised by Hemingway as a book from which all modern American literature comes." How do you interpret Hemingway's comment?（中山大学 2004 研）

参考答案及解析

Ⅰ. Fill in the blanks.

1. *Adventures of Huckleberry Finn*

（海明威曾经说"所有现代美国文学都来自马克·吐温的一本书"。这本书是《哈克贝利·费恩历险记》。）

2. Clemens; local; *Adventures of Huckleberry Finn*; modern

（马克·吐温（Mark Twain），原名塞缪尔·朗赫恩·克莱门斯（Samuel Langhorne Clemens），是美国的作家，19 世纪后期美国现实主义文学的杰出代表。开始时他是个乡土作家，《哈克贝利·费恩历险记》被海明威称为"现代美国文学之源"。）

3. *Adventures of Huckleberry Finn*

（马克·吐温最著名的代表作是《哈克贝利·费恩历险记》。）

4. *Life on the Mississippi*

（马克·吐温凭着年轻时驾驶河船的经验，写成了脍炙人口的自传《密西西比河上的生活》。以密西西比河及沿岸的城镇为背景，生动地写下作者的生活体验、童年岁月以及他所热爱的乡土。）

5. Huckleberry Finn

（马克·吐温曾说《哈克贝利·费恩》这部小说的主题是健康的心灵与扭曲的良心之间的斗争，他这段描述是针对小说主人公哈克贝利·费恩而言的。）

6. *Innocents Abroad*

（马克·吐温游历欧洲时写了一系列文章，讽刺而幽默地记录他的所见所闻，这些文章后来整理出版成书，名为《傻子出国记》。）

7. *The Gilded Age*

（1873 年，马克·吐温出版了小说《镀金时代》。所谓"黄金时代"，只不过是个内里虚空，矛盾重重的"镀金时代"——一个时代的梦破灭了。从此，人们用这个词来形容，从南北战争结束到 20 世纪初的那一段美国历史。）

8. The Gilded Age

(现实主义时期被马克·吐温看作“镀金时代”。)

9. Tom Sawyer, Huckleberry Finn

(马克·吐温最著名的作品《汤姆·索亚历险记》和《哈克贝利·费恩历险记》的主角分别是 Tom Sawyer 和 Huckleberry Finn。)

10. Mark Twain

(马克·吐温(Mark Twain, 1835—1910),原名塞缪尔·朗赫恩·克莱门斯(Samuel Langhorne Clemens)是美国的幽默大师、小说家、作家,也是著名演说家,19 世纪后期美国现实主义文学的杰出代表。他的作品突破了地方色彩小说(local color fiction)的限制,描写整个美国社会的经历。)

Ⅱ. Multiple Choices

1. D 美国西部幽默的代表人物是马克·吐温。
2. B 马克·吐温的小说中有很多不现实的特质,荒诞不经的故事和不大可能发生的巧合。
3. D 马克·吐温大多数的作品都是用地方性、口语化的语言写的。
4. B 美国作家马克·吐温是伟大的社会批评家、中国人民的朋友。对于迫害加利福尼亚州华人的行为,马克·吐温在 *Disgraceful Persecution of a Boy* 中给予了辛辣的抨击。
5. D 马克·吐温的代表作是《哈克贝利·费恩历险记》。
6. C 十九世纪七、八十年代现实主义成为美国文学的主流。威廉·豪威尔斯、亨利·詹姆斯和马克·吐温是这一时期的代表作家,他们在理论和实践上都对美国现实主义文学的发展做出了重大贡献。
7. D 《亚瑟王朝廷上的康涅狄格州美国佬》反映出马克·吐温对民主信心渐失。
8. A 马克·吐温的小说《哈克贝利·费恩历险记》展现了美国当时的现实生活,充分体现了马克·吐温的艺术风格,被视为西方文学史上现实主义的杰作。

Ⅲ. Explain the following terms.

1. Local Colorism or Regionalism as a trend first came to prominence in the late 19th century in America. The local colorists were devoted to capturing the unique customs, manners, speech, folklore, and other qualities of a particular regional community, usually in humorous short stories. The most famous of the local colorists was Mark Twain, with his masterpiece *Adventures of Huckleberry Finn*; others, works belonging to Local Colorism included Bret Harte's *The Luck of Roaring Camp*, George Washington Cable's *Kincaid's battery*, Joel Chandler Harris's *Uncle Remus*, Kate Chopin's *The Awakening* and Sarah Orne Jewett's *Country of the Pointed Firs*.

2. Samuel Langhorne Clemens (1835-1910), better known by the pen name Mark Twain, was an American author and humorist. Twain is most noted for his novels *Adventures of Huckleberry Finn* and *The Adventures of Tom Sawyer*. During his lifetime, Twain became a friend to presidents, artists, industrialists, and European royalty. Twain enjoyed immense public popularity. His keen wit and incisive satire earned him praise from both critics and peers. William Faulkner called Twain "the father of American literature."

3. First-person narrative is also called first person point of view, which is used in the analysis and criticism of fiction to describe the way in which the writer presents the reader with the materials of the story. The first person point of view relates events as they are perceived by a single character,

"I". The narrator "I" may be part of the action or an observer, a major or minor participant in the action. As readers, we cannot know or witness anything the narrator does not tell us. We therefore share all the limitations of the narrator. This technique has the advantage of a sharp and precise focus. Moreover, you feel part of the story because the narrator's "I" echoes the "I" already in your own mind. Mark Twain's novel Adventures of Huckleberry Finn is presented from the first person viewpoint.

Ⅳ. Read the following quotations and answer the questions.

Passage 1

1. *Adventures of Huckleberry Finn*
2. In addition to "ammunition", (the etymology of this name is French), most words are Anglo Saxon—short, specific and direct. Most sentences have simple structure. The repetition of the word "took" and the coherence of things gives the impression that Mark Twain's prose is completely dependent on the action and movement of the specific object and body. More importantly, there is also an element of ingratitude, which is the final end of its style. It's available. The whole book corresponds to the actual speaking habits of an uneducated boy from the southern United States in the mid-19th century.

Passage 2

1. *Life on the Mississippi*
2. Mark Twain
3. When he understood the water's language, he began to see it in a scientific way. Knowledge, not its senses, plays a key role in its interpretation, so in his eyes, the river is no longer beautiful, mysterious and charming.

Passage 3

1. *Adventures of Huckleberry Finn*
2. Mark Twain

Ⅴ. Short answer questions

1. As a satirist, Mark Twain criticized many aspects of American society. He mainly focuses on the bottom of society and likes to depict social life through local portraits, which he liked best. Mark Twain strongly opposed to imperialism, abolition, racism and supported feminist movements.
2. When using children's actors, Twain may imply a comparison: before the American Civil War, children and blacks felt powerless and vulnerable.

   Huck and Jim are often in the same situation: both are abused, in danger of losing freedom, and everyone is constantly manipulated by adult white people. How can we see the moral dilemma in Huck, but Jim is also vulnerable to Huck's harm. Although he is the bottom white social leader, he is also white.

   Twain also used his children's actors to bring about a conflict between socialized or recognized morality and another morality based on intuition and experience. Dramatic, such as young Huck is a moral person, his thought is still open and educated, he does not take his principles and values for granted.

   By tracking a boy's education and experience, Twain shows the conclusions about right and wrong based on logic and experience are often contradictory to social rules and moral concepts, which are often hypocritical rather than logical.

3. The three leading writers were William Howells, Mark Twain and Henry James. The three outstanding writers all work for realism. Howell focused on the emerging middle class and its way of life, while Twain put his region and the lower-class people at the top of his story. James mainly wrote about the higher class and rich in American society.
4. Mark Twain's story is to use the local color. It's great. This can be defined as a careful attention to the details of the phycology, as well as the way of speaking, dressing or behaving that is specific to geographical location. Twain insisted that the task of the writer of the local novel is not to generalize the nation, but to put the region and nation of the country in the region and nation. Only in this way can Americans experience the unique diversity of their people and country across a vast continent.

   After the end of the civil war, many American writers used the local color of different parts of the United States.

Ⅵ. Essay questions

1. In the 19th century, many progressive writers wrote to enliven the dark society. Charles Dickens and Mark Twain. *Oliver Twist* is Charles Dickens' masterpiece, and Mark Twain's masterpiece is *The Adventures of Huckleberry Finn*. Both of these books focus on the theme of corrupt society, and the satire tends to focus on racism and religion. Both novels are about children's adventures.

   Oliver Twist is based on real life, including the *New Poor act*. Based on the experience of Oliver, a poor orphan, the author vividly depicts an underworld of thieves and robbers, as well as the terrible cruelty of the Workhouse. Oliver is the first of such characters. They are the image of innocence, love and honesty. The novel has a happy ending. Dickens was in the Victorian era, when British society began to feel change, but still managed to keep the old values. Industrialization began to bring misery, but life was not entirely impossible. Therefore, English realistic writers like Dickens are optimistic. They knew the disadvantages of modern society, and they took the opportunity to denounce them.

   The Adventures of Huckleberry Finn tells a story about the pre-war America, full of huge national defects, violence and even cruelty, but still retains the virtues of "some simplicity, some innocence, some peace". Here is a "hymn" dedicated to this nation before the war, whose moral value disappeared. Machines and money worship are on their way, but the river god, with its "sunshine, space, uncrowded time, tranquility and danger", has not been forgotten. Like British realistic writers, American realistic novelists are helpless or oppressed, fighting against corruption, privilege and social abuse, but civil war and American dream play an important role in their works.
2. Although both Henry James and Mark Twain work for realism, there are obvious differences between them. In terms of theme, James mainly wrote about the wealth of the upper class in American society, while Mark Twain mainly wrote about the wealth of the lower class. Technically speaking, James pursues psychological realism, but Mark Twain's contribution to the development of realism and the whole American literature is partly through his local color theory in American

novels and partly through his oral style.

Henry James thought the only reason novels exist is that they really try to express life. Therefore, this kind of realism is only the obligation of the artist, that is, to express life in the way he sees, and this kind of life may not be the same as "real" life. James transferred the foundation of realistic art from the outside world to the inner world.

Mark Twain preferred to show his social life through the portraits of the places he was most familiar with. He made great use of his rich knowledge of people and places. He confined himself to his familiar life. By quoting his own experience, Mark Twain successfully transformed art into freedom and humor. In short, it is the best element in western culture.

3. There are several themes in the book. The central theme, of course, is the constant struggle between freedom and slavery. This kind of struggle exists for both Jim and Huck. Jim was afraid of the material slavery of the south in the 1840s, while Huck was afraid of the bondage of thought and behavior. He despised Miss Watson and Widow Douglas so much. Obviously, he also wanted to get rid of his father's tyranny. Both Jim and Huck turned to nature to get rid of the shackles of civilization. The raft enabled them to escape the barbarism of society.

   The Adventures of Huckleberry Finn is a novel about growing up. Huck and his friend Jim rafted along the Mississippi River, forcing Huck into the adult world because he had to decide for himself. In the whole story, Huck has moral conflicts with the values accepted by the society he lives in. Although he can't even refute these values consciously, he makes a moral choice based on his own evaluation of Jim's friendship and human values, which is directly opposite to what he has learned. It is also a fable about good and evil. Huck and Jim represent the power of kindness. They fight against those evil people and win the game, which shows that good conquers evil.

4. The book marked the climax of Twain's literary creation. It is important in many ways. First, the novel is written in a rhetorical language quite different from that of Emerson, Poe, and Melville. It is not grand or grandiose, but simple, direct, clear and faithful to colloquial language. This unpretentious spoken style is known as "vernacular". The great thing about the book also comes from the raft's journey down the Mississippi River, where Huck and Jim are searching for their freedom. Twain, who knew the river inside out, used it here in both realistic and symbolic way. The profound description of the book is another great contribution of the book to the American literary heritage. Huck's good nature and humor run through the book. Huck's born goodness has been contrasted with the influence of a corrupt society.

第22章　欧·亨利

22.1　复习笔记

O. Henry (1862—1910)	欧·亨利(1862—1910)
1. Life	**1. 生平**
William Sidney Porter, also known as O. Henry, born in North Carolina in 1862. He had no education, but his aunt read him a lot of stories.	威廉·西德尼·波特，笔名欧·亨利，于1862年出生在北卡罗莱纳州。欧·亨利接受的教育很少，但他姑姑给他读了很多故事。
When he was 20 years old, he went to Texas. He was a good singer and belonged to a quartet. He often took part in church singing in Austin and worked in a drugstore for a while, then in a bank. Eager for independence, he began his literary career, because he and his friends bought a newspaper, in which they humorously published weekly news, as well as short sketches, pictures. He worked hard to write stories for magazines and became rich and famous.	二十岁时，欧·亨利来到德克萨斯州，有着一副好嗓子的他一度在德克萨斯州奥斯汀市的教堂参加定期的四重唱表演。他曾在药店和银行工作。出于对充分独立的渴望，欧·亨利和一位朋友买下一份报纸以幽默的风格出版每周新闻、小品文、绘画和诗歌等，从此他开始了职业作家生涯。之后他又为许多杂志社苦心孤诣地创作小说，收入颇丰，声名鹊起。
2. Characteristics of His Works	**2. 作品特点**
(1) Many of his stories are about New York where poor people live. He sympathized with their fate and hated the rich who exploited and despised them.	(1)他的很多故事讲述的是纽约及其他一些地方穷人的生活。他同情他们的悲惨命运，痛恨那些剥削和轻视他们的人。
(2) His works have unique style and keen observation of details.	(2)他的作品风格明晰，充满对细节的敏锐观察。
(3) His stories are usually short and humorous. All of a sudden, they are very smart and funny, and the ending is always surprising.	(3)他的故事通常短小精悍，透着一种善良的幽默。故事情节十分有趣，引人入胜，结尾总是令人出乎意料。
(4) Many of his stories contain a lot of slang and oral expression, which makes it difficult for people outside the United States to understand. For example, the form of language is based on the characters and scenes described, giving the so-called local color to adapt to the story.	(4)他的很多故事使用大量俚语和口语，给美国之外的读者带来一定的理解难度。这种表达方式有一种本地特色，能更好地将故事中的人物和场景结合起来。
3. Major Works	**3. 主要作品**
The Four Million "The Gift of the Magi"	《四百万》 《麦琪的礼物》

"The Cop and the Anthem" "The Furnished Room" "The Last Leaf"	《警察与赞美诗》 《带家具出租的房间》 《最后一片常春藤叶》
4. Selected Work **◆"The Cop and the Anthem"** This is an interesting short story. It has four obvious characteristics: satirical coincidence, black humor, language, contrast and surprising ending. It reflects the general theme of the story and its fatal satire on the capitalist society: the capitalist class mercilessly exploits and oppresses the common people, and the good and evil are confused in the capitalist society.	**4. 选读作品** **◆《警察与赞美诗》** 这是一个非常有趣的故事，主要有四个特点：讽刺性的巧合、黑色幽默色彩的语言、对比以及出人意料的结局。 故事反映出欧·亨利写作的一般主题和对资本主义社会无情的讽刺：资产阶级残酷地剥削、压迫劳苦大众；资本主义社会是非混淆。

22.2 考研真题与典型题详解

Ⅰ. Fill in the blanks.

1. William Sidney Porter, whose pen name was __________, was the author of "The Cop and the Anthem".
2. Many of O. Henry's stories tell about the life of poor people in __________.
3. O. Henry's __________ is a very moving story of a young couple who sell their best possessions in order to get money for a Christmas present for each other.
4. It is said that O. Henry imitated a French author named __________ as a model, and there is indeed much in common between these two writers.
5. The title of one of O. Henry's books __________ indicates that he considered all the people of New York City worth writing about, instead of only the upper class.

Ⅱ. Short answer questions

1. Discuss the altruistic spirit reflected in O. Henry's short story "Two Thanksgiving Day Gentlemen."（武汉大学 2012 研）
2. What are the characteristics of O. Henry's writing?

参考答案及解析

Ⅰ. Fill in the blanks.

1. O. Henry

（欧·亨利(O. Henry)，原名为威廉·西德尼·波特(William Sydney Porter)，他是美国著名批判现实主义作家，世界三大短篇小说大师之一。《警察与赞美诗》是其著名的短篇小说。）

2. New York

（欧·亨利(O. Henry)善于描写美国社会尤其是纽约(New York)百姓的生活。他的作品构思新颖，语言诙谐，结局总使人“感到在情理之中，又在意料之外”；又因描写了众多的人物，富于生活情趣，被誉为“美国生活的幽默百科全书”。）

3. “The Gift of the Magi”

（《麦琪的礼物》是美国著名文学家欧·亨利的一篇短篇小说，它描写了一个感人的故事：在圣诞节前一天，一对小夫妻互赠礼物，结果阴差阳错，两人珍贵的礼物都变成了无用的东西，而他们却得到了比任何实物都宝贵的东西——爱。）

4. Guy de Maupassant

（欧·亨利(O. Henry)曾被评论界誉为曼哈顿桂冠散文作家和美国现代短篇小说之父，他的文学创作深受法国短篇小说家居伊·德·莫泊桑的影响。）

5. *The Four Million*

（《四百万》是欧·亨利最著名也是最出色的一个集子。取名为“四百万”，其用意在这部集子的前言里有所阐释：“不久前，有人声称纽约只有‘四百人’值得我们关注，但是一个更为聪明的人——一个人口统计者——认为值得我们关注的人的数目要大得多。”由此可见，欧·亨利具有民主主义思想，他要描写的是小人物的喜怒哀乐、悲欢离合。）

Ⅱ. Short answer questions

1. Pete and the old gentleman are characters in the short story, both having a spirit of Altruism. Although the depressed Pete had a big meal before meeting the old man, he tried his best to eat the food that the old man gave him to make the his wish true, Pete wanted to tell that he was full, but he decided to make his deal to comply. Although the old man had some money then, he still invited Peter to dinner. He values honesty very much and would rather starve than break his promise.
2. His stories are ordinary in short, with clever, funny, humorous language, and the ending is always unexpected. It usually has two ends, the first is an unexpected one, and then another, which is completely different, a surprise. Many his stories contain a lot of slang and colloquial expressions that are difficult for people outside the United States to understand. This Language form is used to give the so-called local color, so that the story matches the described characters and scenes. Henry's speech, whether oral or written, is pure and clear.

第 23 章　亨利·詹姆斯

23.1　复习笔记

Henry James(1843—1916)	**亨利·詹姆斯(1843—1916)**
1. Life	**1. 生平**
Henry James was born in a rich family in New York. He had education at home, and traveled with family in Europe, which was another source of education.	亨利·詹姆斯出生在纽约一个富裕、颇有贵族气派的家庭。他主要在家里接受教育，和家人到欧洲旅行也成为其学习的主要途径。
In Boston, he made friends with Howells, and attended Harvard to study law. He lived in Paris and then settled in London for the rest of his life. In 1915, he gave support to England in the First World War and became a British citizen.	他在波士顿与威廉·迪恩·豪威尔斯成为好友，并在哈佛法学院学习。他在巴黎住了一年，之后又搬到伦敦，在英国郊区度过了余生。1915 年，即他去世的前一年，亨利·詹姆斯因在一战中支持英国而成为一名正式的英国公民。
2. Literary Achievements	**2. 文学成就**
(1) Enormously prolific, James authored 22 novels, hundreds of short stories, and many volumes of biographies, travel journals, art and literary criticism, and memoirs.	(1)詹姆斯是一个多产的作家，共创作了 22 部小说，上百篇短篇小说，几十部非小说文学作品，包括传记、游记、文艺批评和回忆录。
(2) James was a pioneer to utilize modernist, stream of consciousness, and he improved a method with a traditional storytelling narrative voice, arguing that writers need "showing" rather than "telling."	(2)詹姆斯是最早运用现代主义和意识流的主要作家之一。他完善了一种审美方式，即避免传统的全知视角叙述，主张作家应采取具有揭示性的"展示"而不是说教性的"讲述"。
(3) James helped to turn novel from journalism and romantic narration into analysis of individuals in the face of society. He defined psychological perceptions as the highest form of experience.	(3)原来小说主要是新闻形式，讲述浪漫的故事，詹姆斯把小说转变成了个人在社会环境中面对种种冲突，进行深刻转变的文学形式，反映人们的心理感受。他认为这就是感受的最高形式。
3. Style and Theme	**3. 风格和主题**
(1) His continuous development of literary style and artistic intention reflects the transition of British and American literature from Victorian to modern times. His early novels	(1)他不断发展的文学风格和艺术意图反映了英美文学从维多利亚时期到现代时期的过渡。他的早

followed the French and Russian realistic writers he admired, while his later works became metaphorical and symbolic due to the in-depth exploration of the characters.

期小说追随了他仰慕的法俄现实主义作家，而他后期的作品则由于深入挖掘人物性格，变得异常具有隐喻性和象征性。

(2) James' reputation is mainly based on the fundamental theme of his works: the collision between the naive vitality of the new world and the degeneration and wisdom of the old world, as well as the moral and psychological complexity. For Americans, it's a process from raw to sophisticated, from naive to mature.

(2)詹姆斯的名声主要是建立在他作品的根本性主题上："新世界"的天真活力与"旧世界"堕落和智慧的碰撞，以及其中道德和心理上的复杂性。对美国人而言，这是一个从生涩走向世故、从天真走向成熟的过程。

(3) James' works are not easy to understand. He has beautiful language, unique vision, rich vocabulary, accurate choice of words, and strives to find the best way to express what he wants.

(3)詹姆斯的作品不易理解。他语言优美，眼光独到，词汇量丰富，选词准确，力求寻找能够表达他所想的最佳表达方式。

4. Major Works

A Passionate Pilgrim (1875)
Roderick Hudson (1875)
The Novels and Tales of Henry James
The American (1877)
Daisy Miller (1878)
The Portrait of a Lady (1881)
The Bostonians (1886)
The Princess Casamassima (1886)
The Spoils of Poynton (1897)
The Turn of the Screw (1898)
The Awkward Age (1899)
The Wings of the Dove (1902)
The Ambassadors (1903)
The Golden Bowl (1904)

4. 主要作品

《热衷游历的人》(1875)
《罗德里克·赫德森》(1875)
《亨利·詹姆斯小说、故事集》
《美国人》(1877)
《黛西·米勒》(1878)
《一个贵妇人的画像》(1881)
《波士顿人》(1886)
《卡萨玛西玛公主》(1886)
《波音顿的珍藏品》(1897)
《螺丝在拧紧》(1898)
《未成熟的少年时代》(1899)
《鸽翼》(1902)
《大使》(1903)
《金碗》(1904)

5. Selected work

◆ ***The Portrait of a Lady***

The novel tells the story of Isabel Archer, a typical American girl, who first came to Europe and lived a free and noble life full of hope, but unfortunately fell into the vicious trap of Mrs. Moore and Gilbert Osmond, who are rude and unscrupulous. Isabel's dreams and expectations are broken: she is unaware that the covetous eyes around her and her wealth lead to her destruction.

5. 选读作品

◆**《一个贵妇人的画像》**

小说讲述了典型的詹姆斯式的美国姑娘伊莎贝尔·阿切尔，初到欧洲，满怀希望过一种自由和高贵的生活，却不幸落入粗野且不择手段的默尔太太和吉尔伯特·奥斯蒙德的歹毒圈套里。伊莎贝尔的美梦和期望破碎了：她毫无察觉周围人对她及她财富的虎视眈眈，最终导致了她的毁灭。

23.2 考研真题与典型题详解

Ⅰ. Fill in the blanks.

1. *Daisy Miller* was written by ________ (大连外国语学院 2007 研)
2. The American novelist ________ probed deeply at the individual psychology of his characters, writing in a rich and intricate style that supported his intense scrutiny of complex human experience. (人大 2006 研)
3. The novel which was described by an American critic as "an outrage to American girlhood" is Henry James' ________.
4. The name of the heroine in *The Portrait of a Lady* is ________. (人大 2006 研)
5. ________ is considered the founder of Psychological realism. He believed that reality lies in the impressions made by life on the spectator.
6. Isabel Archer, who comes to Europe with a will to live a free life only to become the victim of two American expatriates' scheming, is the protagonist of ________ by ________. (天津外国语 2012 研)
7. Henry James's fame rests largely upon his handling of his major fictional theme, ________: the meeting of America and Europe, American innocence in contact and contrast with European decadence, and its moral and psychological complications. (天津外国语 2014 研)
8. Identify the author of the following work. (北师大 2008 研)
   The Turn of the Screw
9. In 1881, Henry James published his novel ________, which is generally considered as his masterpiece.

Ⅱ. Multiple Choices

1. Henry James was fascinated with the "international theme", according to which American innocence is conflicting with European sophistication. In the following novels, ________ does not belong to the type. (首师大 2008 研)
   A. *The Wings of the Dove*　　B. *The Turn of the Screw*
   C. *The Golden Bowl*　　D. *The Portrait of a Lady*
2. Which of the following novels is not written by Henry James? (天津外国语学院 2007 研)
   A. *Daisy Miller*　　B. *The Golden Bowl*
   C. *What Maisie Knew*　　D. *The Rise of Silas Lapham*
3. We usually divide Henry James' career as a writer into three stages: early, middle and mature. Which of the following work belongs to James' early stage?
   A. *The Portrait of a Lady*　　B. *The American*
   C. *The Tragic Muse*　　D. *The Golden Bawl*
4. Which of the following works by Henry James does not deal with "the international theme"? ________ (天津外国语学院 2009 研)
   A. *Daisy Miller*　　B. *The Turn of the Screw*
   C. *The Portrait of a Lady*　　D. *The Ambassadors*
5. Among the three prominent realistic writers, while Mark Twain and Howells seemed to have paid

more attention to the "life" of the Americans, __________ had apparently laid a greater emphasis on the "inner world" of man. (北二外 2013 研)

A. Theodore Dreiser　　B. Frank Norris

C. Henry James　　D. Emily Dickinson

6. Direct psychoanalysis could not possibly be found in the works of __________. (天津外国语 2013 研)

A. Edgar Allan Poe　　B. Washington Irving

C. Henry James　　D. Ernest Hemingway

7. Compared with the writings of Mark Twain's, Henry James's fiction is noted for their __________. (天津外国语 2013 研)

A. frontier vernacular　　B. rich colloquialism

C. refined elegant language　　D. vulgarly descriptive words

8. Choose the novel which is not written by Henry James.

A. *The Ambassadors*　　B. *The Wings of the Dove*

C. *The Bostonians*　　D. *The Mysterious Stranger*

9. The main theme of __________ *The Art of Fiction* reveals his literary credo that representation of life should be the main object of the novel.

A. Henry James'　　B. William Dean Howells'

C. Mark Twain's　　D. O. Henry's

10. With William Dean Howells, James, and Mark Twain active on the scene, __________ became the major trend in the seventies and eighties of the nineteenth century.

A. sentimentalism　B. romanticism　C. realism　D. naturalism

Ⅲ. Explain the following terms.

1. Psychological realism (人大 2007 研)
2. *The Ambassadors* (四川大学 2007 研)
3. Henry James (四川大学 2009 研)

Ⅳ. Read the following quotations and answer the questions.

Passage 1 (人大 2006 研)

Isabel always felt an impulse to pull out the pins; not that she imagined they inflicted any damage on the tough old parchment, but because it seemed to her aunt might make better use of her sharpness. She was very critical herself—it was incidental to her sex, and her nationality; but she was very sentimental as well, and there was something in Mrs. Touchett's dryness that set her own moral fountains flowing.

"Now what's your point of view?" she asked of her aunt. "When you criticize everything here you should have a point of view. Yours doesn't seem to be American you thought everything over there so disagreeable. When I have mine; it's thoroughly American!"

"My dear young lady", said Mrs. Touchett, "there are as many points of view in the world as there are people of sense to take them. You may say that doesn't make them very numerous. American? Never in the world; that's shockingly narrow. My point of view, thank God, is personal!"

Isabel thought this a better answer than she admitted; it was a tolerable description of her own manner of judging, but it would not have sounded well for her to say so.

Questions:

1. Give the title of the work and the full name of the author.
2. Explain the implications of the underlined parts of the passage.
3. Make a brief comment on the heroine Isabel Archer.
4. What is Jamesian theme?

Passage 2

The only obligation to which in advance we may hold a novel, without incurring the accusation of being arbitrary, is that it be interesting. That general responsibility rests upon it, but it is the only one I can think of. The ways in which it is at liberty to accomplish this result (of interesting us) strike me as innumerable, and such as can only suffer from being marked out or fenced in by prescription. They are as various as the temperament of man, and they are successful in proportion as they reveal a particular mind, different from others. A novel is in its broadest definition a personal, a direct impression of life: that, to begin with, constitutes its value, which is greater or less according to the intensity of the impressions. But there will be no intensity at all and therefore no value, unless there is freedom to feel and say. The tracing of a line to be followed, of a tone to be taken, of a form to be filled out, is a limitation of that freedom and a suppression of the very thing that we are most curious about.

Questions:

1. Where is this paragraph from?
2. Who is the author of this article?
3. What is your opinion about the definition of a novel given by the author?

Passage 3

Under certain circumstances there are few hours in life more agreeable than the hour dedicated to the ceremony known as afternoon tea. There are circumstances in which, whether you partake of the tea or not—some people of course never do—the situation is in itself delightful. Those that I have in mind in beginning to unfold this simple history offered an admirable setting to an innocent pastime. The implements of the little feast had been disposed upon the lawn of an old English country-house, in what I should call the perfect middle of a splendid summer afternoon. Part of the afternoon had waned, but much of it was left, and what was left was of the finest and rarest quality. Real dusk would not arrive for many hours; but the flood of summer light had begun to ebb, the air had grown mellow, the shadows were long upon the smooth, dense turf. They lengthened slowly, however, and the scene expressed that sense of leisure still to come which is perhaps the chief source of one's enjoyment of such a scene at such an hour. From five o'clock to eight is on certain occasions a little eternity; but on such an occasion as this the interval could be only an eternity of pleasure.

Questions:

1. From which novel is this paragraph taken from?
2. Who is the author of this novel?
3. What is conveyed in this opening paragraph about English convention?

V. Essay questions

1. According to Henry James's viewpoint, what is the conflict between the American personalities and European personalities?
2. What is the most famous theme in Henry James' fiction? What is his favorite approach in characterization, which makes him different from Mark Twain and W. D. Howells as realists? Please take *The Portrait of a Lady* as an example to give sound ground for your points.

参考答案及解析

I. Fill in the blanks.

1. Henry James
   (《黛西·米勒》是美国作家 Henry James 的国际主题小说。)
2. Henry James
   (美国小说家亨利·詹姆斯的作品善于挖掘人物心理。)
3. *Daisy Miller*
   (《黛西·米勒》是亨利·詹姆斯早期创作的一部优秀中篇小说，该小说一经问世就引起了强烈的社会反响，一位评论家曾评论这本书是“对美国女孩的冒犯(an outrage to American girlhood)”。)
4. Isabel Archer
   (《一个贵妇人的画像》是亨利·詹姆斯的早期代表作，也是他的杰作之一。该小说的女主人公是伊莎贝尔·阿切尔。)
5. Henry James
   (亨利·詹姆斯开创了心理现实主义(Psychological realism)的先河。在小说创作中，将对现实生活的如实描写、心理探测、性格刻画、环境写实与某些象征、怪诞手法融为一体，被称为“心理现实主义”。)
6. *The Portrait of a Lady*, Henry James
   (伊莎贝尔·阿切尔是亨利·詹姆斯名作《一个贵妇人的画像》中的女主人公。)
7. international theme
   (亨利·詹姆斯因其作品中的“国际性主题”而闻名，他关注美国与欧洲文化的碰撞，关注美国的纯洁与欧洲的堕落之间的联系和对照，关注它们的道德和心理并发症。)
8. Henry James
   (《螺丝在拧紧》是美国十九世纪小说家亨利·詹姆斯一部描写心理的恐怖小说。)
9. *The Portrait of a Lady*
   (《一个贵妇人的画像》(1881)是亨利·詹姆斯的早期代表作，也是他的杰作之一。这部作品内涵丰富，结构严谨，对青年女性的心理刻画细致而且精彩，被西方批评家看成是美国现代小说的一个发端。)

II. Multiple Choices

1. B　亨利·詹姆斯喜欢写国际题材的小说，描写美国的天真对抗欧洲的复杂。只有选项 B《螺丝在拧紧》不是国际题材，而是一部描写心理的恐怖小说。
2. D　*The Rise of Silas Lapham*(《塞拉斯·拉帕姆的发迹》是 William Dean Howells(威廉·迪安·豪威尔斯)的作品，其余都是亨利·詹姆斯的作品。

3. B 《美国人》属于亨利·詹姆斯的早期作品。

4. B *The Turn of the Screw*(《螺丝在拧紧》)是亨利·詹姆斯的一部哥特式心理小说，描写的是一位年轻女教师应聘到乡下一家富户照看两个失去双亲的孩子，在其家中见到死去的前任女教师及这家男仆的幽影，气氛越来越紧张，最后，一个孩子死去，另一个精神错乱。其余三个选项都是詹姆斯关于"国际题材"的作品。

5. C 美国现实主义文学时期的三个代表作家是豪威尔斯(William Dean Howells)，亨利·詹姆斯(Henry James)和马克·吐温(Mark Twain)。虽然这三位杰出的作家基本上是同一时期写作的，但他们对"真实"的理解不尽相同。马克·吐温和豪威尔斯似乎注重生活描写，而亨利·詹姆斯则明显强调人类的"内心世界"。

6. C 亨利·詹姆斯是意识流的代表人物。意识流文学泛指注重描绘人物意识流动状态的文学作品，既包括清醒的意识，更包括无意识、梦幻意识和语言前意识。所以他的作品中不会出现直接的心理分析。

7. C 马克·吐温开创了口语化的先河，用词简单、易懂。亨利·詹姆斯出身于纽约的上层知识分子家庭，父兄都是美国颇具声望的哲学家。由于家境富裕，亨利·詹姆斯从小受到良好的教育，掌握多种语言。詹姆斯本人长期旅居欧洲，对19世纪末美国和欧洲的上层生活有细致入微的观察。所以亨利·詹姆斯的用词是精致、高雅的。

8. D 《神秘的陌生人》(*The Mysterious Stranger*)是马克·吐温的作品，其余三项《大使》(*The Ambassadors*)，《鸽翼》(*The Wings of the Dove*)，《波士顿人》(*The Bostonians*)都是亨利·詹姆斯的作品。

9. A 除小说以外，亨利·詹姆斯(Henry James)对文学贡献的另一部分是他的文学批评。在《小说的艺术》(*The Art of Fiction*)中詹姆斯明确指出，小说的目的是反映现实生活。

10. C 十九世纪七、八十年代现实主义成为美国文学的主流。威廉·豪威尔斯、亨利·詹姆斯和马克·吐温是这一时期的代表作家，他们在理论和实践上都对美国现实主义文学的发展做出了重大贡献。

Ⅲ. Explain the following terms.

1. It is the writing of realism that looks deeply into the complexity of psychology. *The Ambassadors* by Henry James is considered to be a masterpiece.
2. *The Ambassadors* is a novel by James, published as a serial. This is one of the masterpieces of James's late period, following the trip of Lewis Lambert Strether in Europe to pursue Chad, his widowed fiancée's son, bringing him to the family business, but he meets unexpected complications.
3. Henry James is an American leading writer in realism of 19th century. He usually describes the upper class of the American society. He is also known for psychological realism. His major works include: *The Portrait of a Lady*, *The Ambassadors*, *Daisy Miller* etc.

Ⅳ. Read the following quotations and answer the questions.

Passage 1

1. *The Portrait of a Lady*, Henry James
2. "parchment": aged culture in Europe having long history.
   "incidental to her sex, and her nationally": it's the nature of her aunt to be sharp as sharpness is the nature of a woman and person from England.

3. She is one of the outstanding Jamesian American girls. She arrives in Europe for the first time with hope, and wanted to live a free life, but eventually becomes the victim of Madam Merle and Gilbert Osmond.
4. Jamesian theme refers to Henry James's major fictional theme, which is "the international theme": the contact of America and Europe, American innocence in contrast to European decay and moral and Psychological complex.

Passage 2

1. *The American Fiction*
2. Henry James
3. In the author's opinion, the novel should reflect life as life really is. It should give a writer freedom to feel and say. This is the essence of realism.

Passage 3

1. *The Portrait of a Lady*
2. Henry James
3. In English world, everything goes in accordance to tradition. Afternoon tea is a routine and English men's seriousness about it reflected their conservative character.

V. Essay questions

1. To a great extent, Henry James' success depends on his handling of the major international themes in American novels and European novels, as well as on the decadence in the European novel the world Almost always made up of American heroes facing the complexity of Europe.

   He believes that Americans often think that Europeans are more elegant, decadent and pretentious, which leads to conflicts and racial differences, and provides an opportunity to compare the typical characters in James' novels. Americans are fresh and perhaps less-educated, but they are eager to learn, which is basically good, even though they ignore the old habits of Europe. On the other hand, Europeans are well-educated and urbanized, Americans are sometimes bored, but they are always tired of their rights. Sometimes they don't have James's principles. Americans are often very moral, while Europeans are very polite.
2. His theme is that the patents of the new world contradict the corruption and wisdom of the old world. Unlike Howell and other realists, he belongs to psychological realism.

   A young American woman, Isabel Archer, has to choose the conflict between independent spirit and social customs She longed to be an independent, independent and responsible woman, fell in love with the evil Gilbert Osmond, married a man who was just for money, and regarded her as a part of his art group closest to Isabel. To decide whether she should fulfill her marriage promise and safeguard social morality, or to let her miserable marriage escape a happier and more independent life, perhaps with the United States.

   The most important part of the book is that she realizes that she is sitting at home alone at midnight, and James shows his thoughts in this quiet moment, with a sense of drama The drama she committed was not to create her work, but through the ideas in her heart.

   James is one of the great American Psychological realists. He uses all creative power to ensure that Isabel's conflict is a natural product.

第 24 章　杰克·伦敦

24.1　复习笔记

Jack London(1876—1916)	杰克·伦敦(1876—1916)
1. Life	**1. 生平**
Jack London (original name John Griffith London) was born on January 12, 1876. He grew up in extreme poverty and from earliest youth supported himself with menial and dangerous jobs, experiencing profoundly the struggle for survival. Once, he was jailed for thirty days for vagrancy, and at this point he determined to educate himself in order to improve his own condition and that of others.	杰克·伦敦(原名约翰·格里菲斯·伦敦)出生于1876年1月12日。他在极度贫困中长大，很小的时候就开始做各种低下危险的工作养活自己，尝尽生存的艰辛。他曾经因流浪罪而被拘捕30天，自此他下定决心通过自学改善自己和他人的境况。
London, with its intelligence and strong body, quickly completed the high school curriculum, and studied in the University of California as a special student for a semester, and gained a lot. At the same time, he believed in the individualism of Nietzsche and Darwin, and the survival of the fittest. He started his literary career after a failed gold rush, and the call of the wild made brought him fame. He continued to write until 1916, when he died.	伦敦凭借着自己的智力和健壮的身体很快完成了高中课程，并以特别生的身份在加利福尼亚大学学习了一个学期，收获颇多。他接受了马克思充满希望的社会主义，同时也相信尼采和达尔文的个人主义观点，相信优胜劣汰适者生存。他在一次失败的淘金后开始了文学创作，《野性的呼唤》使其变得富有。他一直从事写作直至1916年去世。
2. Literary Style and Theme	**2. 文学风格和主题**
(1) Because he wrote fast, Jack London didn't pay much attention to style, form and the characterization that valued by critics.	(1)因为写得太快太多，所以杰克·伦敦不太注重风格、形式以及评论家所看重的人物形象刻画等。
(2) He believes in the fundamental reality of the survival law and the will, and the struggle between them is very dramatic in his most famous novels.	(2)他相信生存法则和权力意志的根本现实，两者的斗争在他最著名的小说中十分具有戏剧性。
(3) There are many themes in his novels, among which the most popular one is the description of primitive and soul stirring contests between the strong and the weak. He always describes these contests in some irresistible scenes, such as the vast sea or the Arctic. He was fascinated by the way violence tests and determines human character.	(3)他的小说主题繁多，其中最受人们欢迎的是关于强者和弱者之间原始又动人心魄的较量的描写，他总是把这些较量放在一些不可抗的场景中来描写，如苍茫的大海或北极的荒野。他着迷于暴力检验并决定人类性格的方式。

3. Major Works *The Son of the Wolf* (1900) *The Call of the Wild* (1903) *The Sea Wolf* (1904) *The White Fang* (1906) *Martin Eden* (1909)	**3. 主要作品** 《狼之子》(1900) 《野性的呼唤》(1903) 《海狼》(1904) 《白牙》(1906) 《马丁·伊登》(1909)
4. Selected Works **◆*The Sea Wolf*** It is a very powerful and exciting novel by Jack London. The hero Humphrey is caught by a whaling ship and forced to become a sailor under the terrible captain wolf Larson. With Larson sailing are some sinister and cunning tramps, but Larson himself is the legendary sea wolf—a violent and cruel man.	**4. 选读作品** **◆《海狼》** 《海狼》是杰克·伦敦非常有力、扣人心弦的小说，主人公汉弗莱被一艘捕鲸船抓住，被迫成为可怕的船长沃尔夫·拉森手下的一名水手。和拉森一块儿航行的都是一些阴险狡诈的流浪汉，但是，拉森自己就是传说中的海狼——一个狂暴残忍的人。
◆*Martin Eden* Martin Eden is an ordinary, rough sailor. He saved a young man once and the young man took him home. His family seemed noble, but in fact it was vulgar. Eden fell in love with the young man's sister at first sight, and in order to be worthy of her, he decided to be outstanding. He read a lot of books and eventually became a famous writer. He is so famous that people even fight with each other to be recommended. However, his indifferent attitude towards life was not changed by fame and fortune. Finally, desperate for everything in his life, he was eager to escape the world and went to the South Pacific. Unable to endure this aimless and painful life any longer, he chose to end his life.	**◆《马丁·伊登》** 主人公马丁·伊登是一位普通、粗野的水手。一次，他救了一个年轻人，年轻人将他带到家里。他的家庭看似尊贵，而实际上庸俗不堪。伊登对年轻人的妹妹一见钟情，为了能配得上她，他决定要出人头地。他阅读大量书籍，最终成为一位著名的作家。他名声大噪，人们甚至为了被推荐和他认识而相互争斗。但是，名声和财富都没能改变他对生活的冷淡态度。最终，他对生活中的一切感到绝望，急切地想要逃离这个世界，于是前往南太平洋。由于再也无法忍受这种无目的、痛苦的生活，他自杀了。

24.2 考研真题与典型题详解

Ⅰ. Fill in the blanks.

1. In the novel entitled __________ written by __________, Thornton saves Buck, and later Buck saves Thornton from drowning in a river.（大连外国语 2008 研）
2. Jack London's masterwork __________ is somewhat autobiographical.
3. __________ is the novel into which Jack London put most of himself.（人大 2006 研）

Ⅱ. Multiple Choices

1. Jack London was at his height of his powers when he wrote __________, which is deeply influ-

enced by Darwinism.

A. *The Sea Wolf* B. *To Build a Fire*

C. *The Call of the Wild* D. *Martin Eden*

2. Jack London: the author of ________, is a naturalist writer.（四川大学2009研）

A. *The Red Badge of Courage* B. *The Octopus*

C. *The Gilded Age* D. *Martin Eden*

3. Which ONE of the following is the author of *The Law of Life*?（四川大学2010研）

A. Mark Twain. B. Frank Norris. C. Edgar Allan Poe. D. Jack London.

4. In 1900, London published his first collection of short stories, named ________.

A. *The Son of the Wolf* B. *The Sea Wolf*

C. *The Law of Life* D. *White Fang*

Ⅲ. Explain the following term.

American Naturalism（北二外2007研；南开大学2008研）

Ⅳ. Read the following quotation and answer the questions.

Buck's first day on the Dyea beach was like a nightmare. Every hour was filled with shock and surprise. He had been suddenly jerked from the heart of civilization and flung into the heart of things primordial. No lazy, sun-kissed life was this, with nothing to do but loaf and be bored. Here was neither peace, nor rest, nor a moment's safety. All was confusion and action, and every moment life and limb were in peril. There was imperative-need to be constantly alert; for these dogs and men were not town dogs and men. They were savages, all of them, who knew no law but the law of club and fang.

He had never seen dogs fight as these wolfish creatures fought, and his first experience taught him an unforgettable lesson. It is true, it was a vicarious experience, else he would not have lived to profit by it. Curly was the victim. They were camped near the log store, where she, in her friendly way, made advances to a husky dog the size of a full-grown wolf, though not half so large as she. There was no warning, only a leap in like a flash, a metallic clip of teeth, a leap out equally swift, and Curly's face was ripped open from eye to jaw.

Questions:

1. From which novel is this paragraph taken?
2. Who is the author of this novel?
3. What lesson did Buck learn?

Ⅴ. Short answer question

Discuss Jack London's writing style and theme.

参考答案及解析

Ⅰ. Fill in the blanks.

1. *The Call of the Wild*; Jack London

（《野性的呼唤》是杰克·伦敦的著名小说，描写了一只狗回归狼群的故事。）

2. *Martin Eden*

（杰克·伦敦名作《马丁·伊登》(*Martin Eden*)是一部带有自传色彩的长篇小说，在该书中杰克·伦敦倾注了他的全部心血，写下了自己如何在平庸的资产阶级的鄙夷下含辛茹苦地读书和写作的经历。)

3. *Martin Eden*

(杰克·伦敦于1909年发表长篇小说《马丁·伊登》(*Martin Eden*)。在这部带有自传色彩小说中，杰克·伦敦倾注了他的全部心血，写下了自己如何在平庸的资产阶级的鄙夷下含辛茹苦地读书和写作的经历，也尽情阐释了他个人的混杂着马克思主义的阶级观、斯宾塞的社会达尔文主义和尼采的“超人”说的社会见解。)

Ⅱ. Multiple Choices

1. C 《野性的呼唤》是杰克·伦敦在其鼎盛时期写的一部深受达尔文主义影响的小说。
2. D 《马丁·伊登》是杰克·伦敦非常著名的一部小说。选项A《红色英勇勋章》是Stephen Crane(斯蒂芬·克莱恩)的作品；选项B《章鱼》是Frank Norris(弗兰克·诺里斯)的代表作；选项C《镀金时代》是Mark Twain (马克·吐温)的第一部长篇小说。
3. D *The Law of Life*(《生命的法则》)是美国作家Jack London(杰克·伦敦)的著名短篇小说。
4. A 杰克·伦敦是美国著名的自然主义作家。1900年他的第一部短篇小说集《狼之子》(*The Son of the Wolf*)的出版使他一举成名。

Ⅲ. Explain the following term.

American Naturalism: The American naturalists accepted the more negative interpretation of Darwin's evolutionary theory and used it to account for the behavior of those characters in literary works who were regarded as more or less complex combinations of inherited attributes, their habits conditioned by social and economic forces. Naturalism is evolved from realism when the author's tone in writing becomes less serious and less sympathetic but more ironic and more pessimistic. It is no more than a gloomy philosophical approach to reality, or to human existence. Dreiser is a leading figure of his school.

Ⅳ. Read the following quotation and answer the questions.

1. *The Call of the Wild*
2. Jack London
3. The core of animal life is harsh competition and survival of the strongest.

Ⅴ. Short answer question

Jack London was a popular writer in the early 20th century. His writing is full of strength and color. He narrated from action, instead of words, and he had little lessons to offer to the reader. Working for a magazine in his early years, he found the author's subjectivity, passion and faithfulness to the works have great attraction. Although his image is often difficult to express, his dialogue is also old-fashioned.

London's themes focus on primitive violence, evolution in biology, wars between classes and mechanical determinism. He believes that man is the victim of forces beyond his control, that to survive is a lasting conflict, and that human beings are the victims of the conflict Animal instinct has been reduced to the lowest level. Strong and weak fight in a cruel way.

第25章 西奥多·德莱塞

25.1 复习笔记

Theodore Dreiser (1871—1945)	西奥多·德莱塞(1871—1945)
1. Life	**1. 生平**
Theodore dresser was born in 1871, ranking 12th among the 13 children at home. Dreiser's early years were doomed to be unhappy. The family moved in Indiana and was plagued by poverty, sense of insecurity and domestic division.	1871年8月27日，西奥多·德莱塞出生在印第安纳州泰瑞豪特，在家中十三个孩子中排行第十二。德莱赛的童年注定是不快乐的。这个大家庭在印第安纳州不断搬家，并被贫困、不安全感和家庭内部分裂等因素困扰着。
Since 15, Dreiser has been independent and has earned a meager salary by doing all kinds of low-cost jobs. In 1889, a high school teacher helped him to read at Indiana University for a year, but Dreiser's knowledge was mainly from his own experience and self-study. After that, he became a journalist, and constantly explored his literary path, and tested his own experience and gained his own knowledge from the view that there was no sacred sanction from nature and society.	从15岁起，德莱赛就独立了，通过干各种低贱的工作挣取微薄的工资。1889年，一位高中老师资助他在印第安纳大学读了一年书，但是，德莱赛的知识主要来源于自己的经历和自学。之后他成了一个记者，并不断摸索自己的文学道路，在自然和社会没有神圣制裁的观点下，检验自己亲身经历获得的见识。
In the last two decades, Dreiser did not write novels, but instead turned to political activity and argumentative writing. In 1927, Dreiser was attracted by communism during his visit to Soviet Union. In 1945, he officially joined the Communist Party of the United States shortly before his death.	最后二十年中，德莱塞不再写小说，而是转向了政治活动和议论文写作。1927年，德莱塞访问苏联，被共产主义所吸引。1945年，他于去世前不久正式加入了美国共产党。
2. Literary Status	**2. 文学地位**
In his life, Dreiser was controversial both as a common man and as a writer. According to the traditional standards, he was accused of being immoral and ideological, and was a dangerous political radical; his works were criticized for its dull style and the narrative of the story was weak. His works describe the real life of immoral characters on a large scale, especially improper sexual behavior, which makes him suffer severe examination.	终其一生，德莱赛不论是作为一个普通人还是作为作家都备受争议。根据传统标准，他被指控为个人行为不道德，缺乏思想，是危险的政治激进派；他的作品被批评风格沉闷，故事的叙事性弱。他的作品中大规模描写不道德人物的真实生活，尤其是不当性行为，使他遭受严厉的审查。

However, over time, Dreiser has been recognized as a well-known critic of American values and a great novelist.	然而，随着时间的流逝，德莱塞已被公认为一位对美国价值观做出深刻批判的有先见之明的批评家，也是一位了不起的小说家。
3. Major Works	**3. 主要作品**
Sister Carrie (1900)	《嘉莉妹妹》(1900)
Jennie Gerhardt (1911)	《珍妮姑娘》(1911)
The Financier (1912)	《金融家》(1912)
The Titan (1914)	《巨人》(1914)
The "Genius" (1915)	《"天才"》(1915)
An American Tragedy (1925)	《美国悲剧》(1925)
Dreiser Looks at Russia (1928)	《德莱塞访苏印象记》(1928)
Tragic America (1931)	《悲剧的美国》(1931)
The Bulwark (1946)	《堡垒》(1946)
The Stoic (1947)	《斯多葛》(1947)
4. Selected Work	**4. 选读作品**
◆***Sister Carrie***	◆**《嘉莉妹妹》**
(1) It is a story of a country girl. She came to Chicago to seek a better life and to realize the American dream.	(1)《嘉莉妹妹》讲述的是一个乡村女孩到芝加哥寻求更好生活，追求"美国梦"的故事。
(2) It presents the author's idea that men are controlled and restricted by genes, instinct and opportunity.	(2)《嘉莉妹妹》体现了德莱塞的自然主义观点，即人总是被遗传、本能和机缘巧合操控及限制。
(3) The world was cold and heartless. Carrie is lonely and lack of help. People are driven by their desire, like a mechanical device, aimlessly seizing any better survival opportunity. She was controlled forces she can't understand.	(3)对嘉莉妹妹来说，世界是残酷冷漠的。孤独无助的她机械地被欲望驱使，盲目地抓取机会以能更好地生存，任她自己被不能理解和控制的力量摆布。
(4) The famous symbol is the rocking chair, which represents life, which is full of uncertain things.	(4)小说中最明显的象征是那把摇椅，它代表了人生的不确定性。

25.2 考研真题与典型题详解

Ⅰ. Fill in the blanks.

1. The identification of potency with money is at the heart of Theodore Dreiser's masterpiece __________.
2. The protagonist of Theodore Dreiser's *Trilogy of Desire* is __________.
3. Dreiser's novel __________, a commercial and critical failure when first published in 1900, was reissued in 1907 and won high praise for its grim, naturalistic portrayal of American society. (人大2006研)

4. The first novel of Theodore Dreiser was ___.
5. Theodore Dreiser visited the Soviet Union in 1927 and published ___ the following year.
6. The impact of Darwin's evolutionary theory on the American thought and the influence of 19th century French literature on the American men of letters gave rise to another school of realism: ___. One of the most familiar themes in this period is the theme of human "bestiality", which is described in *Sister Carrie* by ___.（北师大 2005 研）

Ⅱ. Multiple Choices

1. In the light of American ___, man is living in a cold, indifferent, and essentially Godless world, and is no longer free in any sense of the word.（武汉大学 2010 研）
A. Puritanism　B. Romanticism　C. Realism　D. Naturalism
2. ___ does not belong to Theodore Dreiser's *Trilogy of Desire*.（首师大 2009 研）
A. *The Financier*　B. *The Titan*　C. *The Stoic*　D. *An American Tragedy*
3. The following passage is taken from the novel entitled ___.（大连外国语 2008 研）
A. *Main Street*　B. *An American Tragedy*
C. *Sister Carrie*　D. *Daisy Miller*

To the child, the genius with imagination, or the wholly untraveled, the approach to a great city for the first time is a wonderful thing. Particularly if it be evening—that mystic period between the glare and gloom of the world when life is changing from one sphere or condition to another. Ah, the promise of the night. What does it not hold for the weary! What old illusion of hope is not here forever repeated! Says the soul of the toiler to itself, "I shall soon be free. I shall be in the ways and the hosts of the merry. The streets, the lamps, the lighted chamber set for dining, are for me. The theatre, the halls, the parties, the ways of rest and the paths of song—these are mine in the night."

4. Which of the following figures does not belong to "The Lost Generation"?
A. Ezra Pound.　B. William Carlos Williams.
C. Robert Frost.　D. Theodore Dreiser.
5. With the publication of ___ in 1900, Theodore Dreiser committed his literary force to opening the new ground of American naturalism.
A. *An American Tragedy*　B. *Sister Carrie*
C. *The Bulwark*　D. *The Stoic*
6. In his works, Theodore Dreiser's tone is always ___.
A. sad　B. satirical　C. comic　D. serious

Ⅲ. Explain the following terms.

"*Trilogy of Desire*"（中国人民大学 2006 研）

Ⅳ. Read the following quotation and answer the questions.

When Caroline Meeber boarded the afternoon train for Chicago, her total outfit consisted of a small truck, a cheap imitation alligator-skin satchel, a small lunch in a paper box, and a yellow leather snap purse, containing her ticket, a scrap of paper with her sister's address in Van Buren Street, and four dollars in money. It was in August, 1889. She was eighteen years of age, bright, timid, and full of the illusions of ignorance and youth...When a girl leaves her home at eighteen, she does one of two things. Either she falls into saving hands and becomes better, or she rapidly assumes the cosmopolitan standard of virtue and becomes worse. Of an intermediate balance, under the circumstances, there is no possibility. The city has its cunning wiles, no less than the infinitely smaller and more human tempter. There are large forces which allure with all the soulfulness of expression possible in the most cultured human. The gleam of a thousand lights is often as effective as the persuasive light in a wooing and fascinating eye. Half the undoing of the unsophisticated and natural mind is accomplished by forces wholly superhuman. A blare of sound, a roar of life, a vast array of human hives appeal to the astonished senses in equivocal terms. Without a counselor at hand to whisper cautious interpretations, what falsehoods may not these things breathe into the unguarded ear! Unrecognized for what they are, their beauty, like music, too often relaxes, then weakens, then perverts the simpler human perceptions. (西安交大 2008 研)

Questions:

1. What novel is the above passage taken from? Who is the author?
2. How many types of tempters exist? What are they?
3. Please identify all the instances of "large forces". What can these large forces do?
4. What is suggested as a solution to an eighteen-year-old girl's falling into folly?
5. What realistic features are revealed in the passage? Please expound your argument in detail.
6. What naturalistic ideas are revealed in the passage? Please explain your argument in detail.

V. Short answer question

Make Comments on the following passage. (浙江大学 2007 研)

Oh, Carrie, Carrie! Oh, blind strivings of the human heart! Onward, onward, it saith, and where beauty leads, there it follows. Whether it be the tinkle of a lone sheep bell o'er some quiet landscape, or the glimmer of beauty in sylvan places, or the show of soul in some passing eye, the heart knows and makes answer, following. It is when the feet weary and hope seems vain that the heartaches and the longings arise. Know, then, that for you is neither surfeit nor content. In your rocking-chair, by your window dreaming, shall you long, alone, your rocking-chair, by your window, shall you dream such happiness as you may never feel.

VI. Essay questions

1. In what ways does *Sister Carrie* or some other major works by Theodore Dreiser reveal his perception of the "American Dream"? What do you know and think of the controversy about Dreiser as a man and as a writer? (人大 2007 研)
2. Please briefly comment on Theodore Dreiser's novel *Sister Carrie*. (四川大学 2007 研)

参考答案及解析

I. Fill in the blanks.

1. *An American Tragedy*

   (德莱塞代表作长篇小说《美国悲剧》(1925)通过一个穷教士儿子克莱特·格里菲斯为追逐金钱财势堕落为蓄意杀人犯的故事，揭示了利己主义恶性膨胀的严重后果，同时更揭露了金钱至上的美国生活方式对人的普遍的罪恶性腐蚀毒害。)
2. Frank Cowperwood

（西奥多·德莱塞的《欲望三部曲》（*Trilogy of Desire*）包括《金融家》（*The Financier*），《巨人》（*The Titan*），《斯多葛》（*The Stoic*）。《欲望三部曲》的主人公是法兰克·柯帕乌（Frank Cowperwood）。）

3. *Sister Carrie*

（德莱塞的《嘉莉妹妹》在1900年首次出版时在商业上和文学批评界是失败的，在1907年重新被发现，因其对美国社会的自然描写赢得了很高的评价。）

4. *Sister Carrie*

（西奥多·德莱塞（Theodore Dreiser，1871—1945），美国小说家。其第一部小说《嘉莉妹妹》（1900），通过农村姑娘嘉莉到芝加哥谋生而成为名演员的故事，揭露了资本主义社会繁荣外衣掩盖下的生存斗争，对美国贫富对立的社会作了深刻的描写。）

5. *Dreiser Looks at Russia*

（1927年访苏后，德莱塞发表了一些作品，其中重要的有1928年发表的《德莱塞访苏印象记》。）

6. Naturalism, Theodore Dreiser

（达尔文的进化论对19世纪美国思想影响深远。法国文学对美国作家的影响催生了现实主义的另一流派：自然主义。"人类兽行"成为这一时期的流行主题，西奥多·德莱塞的作品《嘉莉妹妹》很好地反映了这一主题。）

Ⅱ. Multiple Choices

1. D　自然主义作品揭示了一个悲惨的世界，在这样的世界里人类在冷酷、恶劣的环境下与压倒一切的力量做着无望的斗争。
2. D　德莱塞的《欲望三部曲》包括《金融家》《巨人》和《斯多葛》。
3. C　题目中的段落节选自Theodore Dreiser（西奥多·德莱塞）的《嘉莉妹妹》，描写的是嘉莉离开家乡，当火车即将到达芝加哥时候的所见所想。
4. D　西奥多·德莱塞是自然主义作家，他不属于"迷惘的一代"。
5. B　《嘉莉妹妹》的出版让西奥多打开了美国自然主义文学的大门。
6. D　西奥多的作品风格沉闷，故事的叙事性较弱。

Ⅲ. Explain the following terms.

"*Trilogy of Desire*": Theodore Dreiser's serial novels: *The Financier*, *The Titan and The Stoic*. The stories are on the basis of Charles T. Yerkes. a tycoon of transportation in the United State. Dreiser's focus shifted. Firstly, it was about tragedies of people at the lowest level of society. Then it was about the power of titans in the United States in 19th century.

Ⅳ. Read the following quotation and answer the questions.

1. The above passage is taken from Theodore Dreiser's *Sister Carrie*.
2. There are two types of tempters. One is the luxury life in the city; another is the tempter from human.
3. "Large forces" include the gleam of a thousand lights, the persuasive light in a wooing and fascinating eye, a blare of sound, a roar of life and a vast array of human hives. The forces will relax, then waken, then pervert the simpler human perceptions.
4. A counselor who can recognize the tempters tells her all the time and teaches her to recognize the tempters.

5. Realism, stresses that, in the normal form there is a true life. In Sister Carrie, a rural girl came to Chicago to pursue the America dream. What she brings is carefully listed. Secondly, Realism is more objective, instead of idealized. In the description of Carrie, the author is not to judge her morality, but says her position objectively. Thirdly, realism is linked to social problems, revealing the depravity of character disappointment in the environment. In the second part of the paragraph, the author uses several sentences to illustrate the city's temptations and depravity.
6. American naturalists exposed gentility to pieces and wrote the helpless people, and their insignificance in the world, and their lost dignity when facing the crushing forces of environment. In their novels, human beings fight aimlessly against overwhelmingly harsh world, driven by "a wisp of wind," with their lives very much determined by forces they cannot manipulate. In this paragraph, there are two choices for a girl under such condition-she will be better with others' help; she will fall if she assumes the social standard. She can't make a change with her fight alone for there are so many strong forces. Man is reductive to take actions. Furthermore, the cruelty of capitalism, as one part of naturalism, is revealed.

V. Short answer question

This is the last part of *Sister Carrie*. The novel tells the story of a country girl named Carrie who comes to Chicago to make a living in order to pursue her happiness. Through her marriages and extramarital affairs with some wealthy people and her struggles, she became a famous actress in New York. She got what she wanted, but she eventually found that she didn't know what she wanted. This novel concept is a disillusion with the concept of the so-called "American Dream". In this passage, Carrie, sitting in her rocking chair, realizes that it is the blind effort that drives people on, dreaming of happiness that will never come to pass. This is Carrie's dream dashed. "Clink," "shimmer of beauty," and "the apparition of the soul" are all metaphors for the struggle of the blind. In such an American setting, the characters are unable to control their desire for happiness and rocking-chair notions of their own destinies.

VI. Essay questions

1. Every character in *Sister Carrie* is looking for "American Dream" of one's own, which is provided by the expanding democracy. Carrie, a country girl, came to Chicago full of dreams about the good things. She fancies the nice clothes she will be wearing, the exciting places she's going to visit, and the fashionistas she's going to talk with, and thinks that everyone who lives outside the Midwest are in a higher status. Drouet wants a version of his American dream. He has reached some position, which is proved by his clothes. He frequents important institutions in town and makes friends with many people. However, he pursues other dates that represent his dreams, such as a beautiful woman to decorate his arms and his home. Hurstwood has a career, a wife and a family. But he wants more. He knows that his employer keeps him away from making crucial decisions, and he knows that his friends are around him for his status. He wants love and higher prestige. However, in the end, none of them succeeded.

   In his life, Dreiser was controversial both as a common man and as a writer. According to the traditional standards, he was accused of being immoral and ideological, and was a dangerous political radical; his works were criticized for its dull style and the narrative of the story was weak. His works describe the real life of immoral characters on a large scale, especially improper sexual behavior, which makes him suffer severe examination. However, over time, Dreiser has been recognized as a well-known critic of American values and a great novelist.

2. *Sister Carrie* by Theodore Dreiser is a story about a young country girl who came to Chicago to realize her American Dream. She by first became a mistress and later as a popular actress.

With a documentary-like detailed description, Dreiser provides three worlds in Carrie's point of view. They provide a full view of the cruel and passive aspects of society in early 20th century. The first world is life with her working-class sister; then is her life as a mistress of Druet and Hurstwood in Chicago and New York. Every detail is written in amazingly and passively accuracy, thus assuming a sense of being important. Carrie moves forward, like a machine that under the force of lust. She tries to catch any opportunity for a better life blindly. However, like a feather floating in the wind, she is totally pushed by the society that she cannot understand, let alone controlling.

第五部分　20 世纪美国文学

第 26 章　埃兹拉·庞德

26.1　复习笔记

Ⅰ. Historical Introduction	Ⅰ. 历史背景
(1) America's wealth and technological accomplishments had astounded the world.	(1)美国的财富及科技成就让世界瞩目。
(2) The American arts in 1900 were on the threshold of a turbulent modernity which led to the rise of completely new terms, including expressionism, imagism postimpressionism, futurism, dadaism, cubism and surrealism.	(2)1900 年，美国艺术将要迈进动荡的现代性，催生出众多全新的术语：表现主义、意象派、后印象主义、未来主义、达达主义、立体主义和超现实主义。
(3) Before WWI, nineteenth-century realism and naturalism were the major forces in American literature. The nation's literary tastes were still dominated by the genteel tradition and popular romanticism.	(3)第一次世界大战以前，19 世纪的现实主义和自然主义仍是美国文学的主流。美国民众的文学品味仍然由高雅传统和流行的浪漫主义主导。
(4) The mass market of literature expanded with the increasing population, wealth and education, as well as technological developments in printing and publishing.	(4)随着人口增加、财富积累、教育水平提高、印刷业和出版业的科技进步，大众文学市场欣欣向荣。
(5) At the beginning of the new century more and more "little magazines" brought many avant-garde authors to the attention of limited but sophisticated readers who were equipped with modernist sympathies and depper intellectual comprehension.	(5)20 世纪初，越来越多的"小杂志"使众多先锋作家受到一小部分见多识广的读者的关注。这些读者有现代主义者的情怀和更高的理解力。
(6) Writers in the first postwar era self-consciously claimed themselves as a "Lost Generation", who lacked faith and were alienated from civilization.	(6)一战后的作家自觉地将自己称为"迷惘的一代"，他们缺乏信仰，远离人类文明。
(7) American literature during the 1920s presented a new variety and reached its highest peak. Masterpieces of various poem, fiction and drama came out. The "Harlem Renaissance" indicated the rise of black writers.	(7)20 世纪 20 年代，美国文学展现其独特性，并达到顶峰。各种诗歌、小说、戏剧杰作出版。"哈莱姆文艺复兴"预示着黑人作家的崛起。
(8) The 1929 stock market crash and the Great Depression in the 1930s smashed public complacency and induced	(8)1929 年的股市崩盘和 30 年代的"大萧条"粉碎了公众的自

artists to create works about political and social criticism. The literary concerns of the Great Depression and the social turbulence ended by the WWII. A new generation of American writers appeared after the war, called the "Beat Generation", who complied with the skeptical and ironic tradition applied by the earlier realists and naturalists.

满情绪，致使艺术家们创作出政治和社会批判的作品。社会的动荡不安和对"大萧条"时期的文学关注在二战带来的繁荣和骚动中结束了。二战后，出现了新一代美国作家，被称为"垮掉的一代"，继承了早期现实主义作家和自然主义作家怀疑讽刺的写作风格。

Ⅱ. Ezra Pound (1885—1972)

Ⅱ. 埃兹拉·庞德(1885—1972)

1. Life

1. 生平

Born in Hailey, Idaho in 1885, Pound grew up in Pennsylvania. At Hamilton College and the University of Pennsylvania, he majored in Roman language. Pound travelled to Europe in 1908 and published in Venice his first collection of poetry, *A Lume Spento*. When he arrived in London, Pound met T. E. Hulme and joined his Poets' Club, and later he launched Imagism with Richard Aldington and Hilda Doolittle. Pound broke with Amy Lowell in 1914 and then left Imagism for Vorticism: the aesthetics of the two movements permanently influenced his works.

庞德1885年出生于美国爱达荷州的海利镇，在宾夕法尼亚长大。他在汉密尔顿大学和宾夕法尼亚大学学习，主修罗马语。1908年庞德到达欧洲并在威尼斯出版了他的第一部诗集《灯光熄灭之时》。到达伦敦后他结识了休姆并参加了"诗人俱乐部"，后来与希尔达·杜利特尔和理查德·奥尔丁顿发起意象新诗运动。1914年他与艾米·洛厄尔分道扬镳，转向"漩涡主义"，这两个运动的美学思想永久地影响了他的作品。

Pound is also one of the most controversial writers in American literature. He had broadcast pro-Fascist propaganda to Britain and America after the breakout of WWII. After the War Pound was arrested and charged with treason. He was later declared insane and was detained at St. Elizabeths Hospital. Pound was released in 1958 due to the effort of eminent writers such as T. S. Eliot, Robert Frost, and Hemingway. Pound came back to Italy and worked there until his death in 1972.

庞德也是美国文学史上一位饱受争议的作家。二战爆发后，他发表了一些亲法西斯反对英美的演说。战后，他以叛国罪被捕。后来他被宣布精神失常，被拘禁在圣伊丽莎白医院。经过T. S. 艾略特、弗罗斯特和海明威等名人的努力，1958年庞德获释回到意大利，在那里工作直到1972年去世。

2. Poetic Style

2. 作品风格

(1) Pound's poems are derived large from recondite culture, including classics, the works during the Italian and English Renaissance and the works of specific areas of Continental literature such as French symbolists.

(1)庞德的作品大多汲取了深奥的文化，如古典作品，意大利和英国文艺复兴时期的作品，欧洲大陆地区文学，包括法国象征主义。

(2) Most of his works feature "reconstructions" in modern English, and they are developed from earlier literatures in primarily Greek, Latin, Italian, Provencal and Chinese.

(2)他大部分作品都是现代英语的"重建"，主要来源于早期的希腊、拉丁、意大利、普罗旺斯和中国文学。

3. Literary Status and Influence

(1) As the leader of imagist movement, Pound is a giant in English and American Modernist poetry. The Imagist poetry is a type of free verse without the conventional metres and it focuses on the employment of ordinary speech, new rhythms and clear images. Imagism can be seen as an analogy for sculpture, which emphasizes a hard and dry clarity and precision when representing natural items and ideas.

(2) In Pound's view, the West in the beginning of the twentieth century was a world filled with chaos, fragments and barbarism. With saving a tottering civilization as his mission, Pound endeavored to draw standards from past cultures and restore lost order.

(3) He greatly influenced the modernist writers after WW Ⅱ in Britain and America.

4. Major Works

Exultations (1909)

Personae (1909)

Des Imagistes (1914)

Cathay (1915)

The Cantos

"In a Station of the Metro"

5. Selected Works

◆"A Virginal"

The general concept of love is central in this poem. It seems as if this is the narrator's first sexual encounter with a woman, and cannot help but be ecstatic and spellbound about it. The poem is laced with all kinds of vehicles and metaphors.

◆"Salutation the Second"

Time changes, so is the opinions of readers. The poem imagines himself being criticized by people in twenty years because of the lack of imagination and emotion.

◆"A Pact"

Pound makes "a pact" with Whitman here because he was old enough to realize that Whitman was worthy of approving and praising.

3. 文学地位及影响

(1)庞德是英美现代派诗歌的一位巨匠。他是意象派诗歌运动的领袖。意象主义诗歌是一种自由体诗歌，摆脱了传统的音步，强调应用日常语言、新韵律和清晰的意象。意象主义可以与雕塑类比，其目的在于展示自然物体和观念的未加修饰的清晰与准确。

(2)庞德看到20世纪初的西方是一个混乱、破碎、野蛮的世界。他认为有义务保护摇摇欲坠的文明，他试着发掘过去文化的标准、复活失去的秩序。

(3)庞德对二战后英美的现代作家产生深远影响。

4. 主要作品

《狂喜》(1909)

《人物》(1909)

《意象派诗选》(1914)

《中国》(1915)

《诗章》

《在地铁车站》

5. 选读作品

◆《处女琴》

爱是这首诗的主题。这似乎是叙述者第一次和女人发生性行为，禁不住为之欣喜着迷。诗中充满各种修辞和隐喻。

◆《再次致意》

时代不同，读者的观点也不相同，诗人想象自己在二十年后受到世人指责，说自己失去了想象力，作品中没有情感。

◆《盟约》

庞德欲与惠特曼建立"一个盟约"，因为现在他已认识到惠特曼是值得肯定和赞扬的。

◆"In a Station of the Metro" "In a Station of the Metro" is a classic example of the Imagist poetry. Pound was once in a Paris subway station and was struck by the faces of a few pretty women and children hurrying out of the dim, damp, and somber station. So impressed was he by the spectacle that he resolved to bring it out in poetic language. The result was, of course, the poem. "The object" to be treated is the faces in that dim and damp context. The impression is brought out most vividly by the simple, dominant image of flower petals on a wet, black bough, which serves as the most concise, direct, and definite metaphor for the "faces in the crowd."	**◆《在地铁车站》** 《在地铁车站》是印象派诗歌的一首经典佳作。 庞德有次在巴黎地铁站被眼前的景象所打动。在人群中，他看到几个漂亮的女人和孩子的面孔。他们正匆匆忙忙地走出潮湿幽暗的地铁站。这场景给他留下了极其深刻的印象，于是他决定以诗歌的语言来展现这幅画面。最后写成了这首诗。诗中描写的对象是潮湿幽暗环境中的面孔。诗人用一枝湿漉漉的黑色粗枝上的花瓣形象地表达了出这种印象。花瓣简洁、直接、确切地代表了"人群中的面孔"。
◆"The River-Merchant's Wife: A Letter" This is a verse "letter" in which the speaker communicates indirectly, by means of vivid images and shifting tones, the history of her feelings for her absent husband to whom she writes.	**◆《河商之妻》** 这是一首书信体诗歌，说话者通过生动的意象和变化的语气间接地叙述了她对远行的丈夫的感情发展史。

26.2 考研真题与典型题详解

Ⅰ. Fill in the blanks.

1. In his __________, Ezra Pound expresses his fascination with Chinese history and the doctrine of Confucius. (天津外国语大学 2011 研)
2. __________ stands as a great dividing line between the nineteenth century and the contemporary American literature.
3. Author __________ Title __________ (南京大学 2007 研)
   The apparition of these faces in the crowd;
   Petals on a wet, black bough.
4. Ezra Pound's lifelong endeavor had been devoted to the writing of __________, which contains __________ poems. (国际关系学院 2007 研)
5. Pound was the leader of a new movement in poetry which he called the "__________" movement.
6. "In a Station of the Metro" by Ezra Pound goes like this: The apparition of these faces in the crowd; __________. (首师大 2008 研)
7. __________, by Ezra Pound, employs the complex association of scholarly lore, anthropology, modern history and personages, private history and Witticism, and obscure literary interpolations in various languages. (人大 2006 研)
8. According to historians of English literature, the First World War saw the start of a poetic revolu-

tion which was initiated by the imagist movement and the symbolist movement. The imagist movement was led by __________. （天津外国语 2010 研）

9. As Thomas Steams Eliot declared, he followed strictly the advice of his close friend __________ in cutting and concentrating *The Waste Land*.

Ⅱ. Multiple Choices

1. Many people associate __________ with the first half of the 1950s with crime, delinquency, immorality, and amorality, although it has actually made great contributions to American literature. （武汉大学 2011 研）

   A. The Beat Generation B. The Lost Generation

   C. The Sad Young Men D. The Angry Young Men

2. __________ showed great interest in Chinese literature and translated the poetry of Li Po (Li Bai) into English, and was influenced by Confucian ideas.

   A. Ezra Pound B. Robert Frost C. T. S. Eliot D. E. E. Cummings

3. *Exultations* and *Personae* are poetic collections of __________. His last and greatest works is __________.

   A. T. S. Eliot, *The Waste Land* B. Robert Frost, *The Road Not Taken*

   C. Ezra Pound, *The Cantos* D. Wallace Stevens, *Anecdote of the Jar*

4. A(n) __________ usually urges poets to express their momentary impressions through the use of one dominant image. （武汉大学 2011 研）

   A. romanticist B. modernist C. imagist D. transcendentalist

5. Early in the 20th century, __________ published works that would change the nature of American poetry.

   A. Ezra Pound B. T. S. Eliot C. Robert Frost D. Both A and B

6. Ezra Pound's long poem __________ contained more than one hundred poems loosely connected.

   A. *The Waste Land* B. *The Cantos* C. *Don Juan* D. *Queen Mab*

7. __________'s role as a leading spokesman of the famous Imagist Movement in the history of American literature can never be ignored and his one-image poem best demonstrates his principles of what a new poetry should be. （北二外 2013 研）

   A. William Carlos Williams B. Robert Frost

   C. F. Scott Fitzgerald D. Ezra Pound

Ⅲ. Explain the following terms.

1. collage（上海交大 2006 研）
2. Ezra Pound and *The Cantos*（南开大学 2009 研）
3. Imagism（南开大学 2007 研；首师大 2008 研；北外 2009 研；北邮 2010 研；厦门大学 2010 研）
4. Avant-Garde(上海交大 2007 研)
5. Modernism
6. Harlem Renaissance(山东大学 2018 研)

Ⅳ. Read the following quotation and answer the questions.

The apparition of these faces in the crowd;

Petals on a wet, black bough.（北航 2009 研）

Questions:

1. What is the title of this short poem?
2. Who is the author?
3. What two images are juxtaposed or placed next to each other in this poem?

V. Essay questions

1. Choose one of the following authors and make a comment on any one of his/her literary works.（浙江大学 2007 研）

   George Bernard Shaw　　Ralph Waldo Emerson

   Ezra Pound　　Doris Lessing

2. Comment on the artistic features of the poem "In a Station of the Metro" by Ezra Pound.（南京大学 2008 研）

参考答案及解析

I. Fill in the blanks.

1. *The Cantos*

   （Ezra Pound 在长诗《诗章》中阐述孔子学说，他的另一诗集 *Cathay*《华夏》收集并翻译了十几首中国古诗。）

2. The First World War

   （第一次世界大战是 19 世纪美国文学与当代美国文学的重要分界线。）

3. Author: Ezra Pound　　Title: "In a Station of the Metro"

   （题目节选自庞德的《在地铁车站》，该诗是以一个意象作为叙述语言的典型范例。）

4. *The Cantos*; 117

   （庞德把毕生精力都投入到写作《诗章》当中，《诗章》共包括 117 首诗。）

5. imagism

   （庞德是意象主义运动的领军人物。）

6. Petals on a wet, black bough

   （这是意象派诗人庞德的名作，意为：人群中这些面孔幽灵一般显现，湿漉漉的黑色枝条上许多花瓣。）

7. *The Cantos*

   （庞德的《诗章》包罗万象，是庞德的代表作。）

8. Ezra Pound

   （庞德是 20 世纪初"意象派"诗歌的领军人物，其著名的意象派诗歌是《在地铁车站》。）

9. Ezra Pound

   （埃兹拉·庞德(Ezra Pound)，帮助 T. S. 艾略特整理删节《荒原》的初稿，并向出版社推荐出版。）

II. Multiple Choices

1. A　垮掉的一代(Beat Generation)是第二次世界大战之后出现于美国的一群松散结合在一起的年轻诗人和作家的集合体，该流派的作家永远寻求新的刺激，寻求绝对自由，纵欲、吸毒、沉沦，以此向体面的传统价值标准进行挑战，因此被称作垮掉的一代，迷惘的一代(The Lost Generation)指第一次世界大战后美国的一个文学流派。

2. A　庞德对中国文学很感兴趣，他将李白的诗歌翻译成英文，并且深受儒家思想的影响。

3. C　《狂喜》(*Exultations*)和《人物》(*Personae*)是埃兹拉·庞德的诗集，他最后一部也是他最伟大的一部作品是《诗章》(*The Cantos*)。

4. C　意象派是1909年至1917年间一些英美诗人发起并付诸实践的文学运动，其宗旨要求诗人以鲜明、准确、含蓄和高度凝练的意象生动及形象地展现事物，并将诗人瞬息间的思想感情溶化在诗行中。代表人物是Ezra Pound。

5. D　20世纪初，庞德和艾略特发表的诗歌改变美国诗歌的特性，他们是20世纪美国诗坛的开拓者。

6. B　《诗章》(*The Cantos*)是庞德的代表作，其中连同未完成的草稿共有117首。

7. D　埃兹拉·庞德是美国意象派诗歌的代表人物。

Ⅲ. Explain the following terms.

1. collage: Collage refers to a work assembled wholly or partly from fragments of other writings, incorporating allusions, quotations, and foreign phrases. Originally applied to paintings with pasted-on elements, the term has been extended to an important kind of modernist poetry, of which the most significant examples are *The Cantos* of Ezra Pound and T. S. Eliot's *The Waste Land*. The collage technique can also be found sometimes in prose works.

2. Ezra Pound and *The Cantos*: Ezra Weston Loomis Pound (1885—1972) was an American expatriate poet, critic and intellectual who was a major figure of the Modernist movement in the first half of the 20th century. His significant contributions to poetry begin with his promotion of Imagism.

   The Cantos by Ezra Pound is a long, incomplete poem in 120 sections, each of which is a canto. Most of it was written between 1915 and 1962, although much of the early work was abandoned and the early cantos, as finally published, date from 1922 onwards. Strong claims have been made for it as the most significant work of modernist poetry of the twentieth century. The most striking feature of the text, to a casual browser, is the inclusion of Chinese characters as well as quotations in European languages other than English.

3. Imagism: Imagism is a literary movement which came into being in Britain and U. S. around 1910 as a reaction to the traditional English poetry to express the sense of fragmentation and dislocation. The imagists, with Ezra Pound leading the way, hold that the most effective means to express these momentary impressions is through the use of one dominant image. Imagism is characterized by the following three poetic principles: i) direct treatment of subject matter; ii) economy of expression; iii) as regards rhythm, to compose in the sequence of the musical phrase, not in the sequence of metronome. Ezra Pound's "In a Station of the Metro" is a well-known imagist poem.

4. Avant-Garde: Avant-Garde, the French military and political term for the vanguard of an army or political movement, extended since the late 19th century and refers to that body of artists and writers who are dedicated to the idea of art as experiment and revolt against tradition. Ezra Pound's view that "Artists are the antennae of the race", is a distinctly modern one, implying a duty to stay ahead of one's time through constant innovation in forms and subjects.

5. Modernism: It's a general term applied to the wide range of experimental and avant-garde trends in literature of the early 20th century, including Symbolism, Futurism, Expressionism, Imagism, Vorticism, Dada, and Surrealism. Modernist literature is characterized chiefly by a rejection of 19th century traditions: the conventions of realism, for instance, were abandoned by Franz Kafka and other novelists, and by expressionist drama, while several poets rejected traditional meters in favor of free verse. Modernist writers tended to see themselves as an avant-garde disengaged from bourgeois values, and disturbed their readers by adopting complex and difficult new forms and styles. In fiction, the accepted continuity of chronological development was upset by Joseph Conrad, and William Faulkner, while James Joyce and Virginia Woolf attempted new ways of tracing the flow of characters' thoughts in their stream-of-consciousness styles. In poetry, Ezra Pound and T. S. Eliot replaced the logical exposition of thoughts with collages of fragmentary images and complex allusions. Modernist writing is predominantly cosmopolitan, and often expresses a sense of urban cultural dislocation, along with an awareness of new anthropological and psychological theories. Its favored techniques of juxtaposition and multiple points of view challenge the reader to reestablish a coherence of meaning from fragmentary forms.
6. Shortly after WWI, a new black intelligentsia appeared on the scene. They rebelled against the values of their fathers and their way of life. They took an enormous interest in their own lives and values. They tried to solicit the attention of their African American people as well as the whites. And they began a search for a distinct tradition of their own. All these characterized a great movement in the cultural and intellectual history of the African Americans. This new upsurge of African American literature in the 1920s has become to be known as the Harlem Renaissance.

Ⅳ. Read the following quotations and answer the questions.

Passage 1

1. "In a Station of the Metro"
2. Ezra Pound
3. The writer uses the image of "petals" on another image, that is, "wet, black bough". The plosive word "Petals" conjures ideas of delicate, feminine beauty which contrasts with the bleakness of the "wet, black bough".

Ⅴ. Essay questions

1.

In a Station of the Metro

The apparition of these faces in the crowd;
Petals on a wet, black bough.

The poem is considered one of the leading poems of the Imagist tradition. Written in a Japanese haiku style, Pound's process of deletion from thirty lines to only fourteen words typifies Imagism's focus on economy of language, precision of imagery and experimenting with non-traditional verse forms. The poem is Pound's written equivalent for the moment of revelation and intense emotion he felt at the Metro at La Concorde, Paris. Because of the treatment of the subject's appearance by way of the poem's own visuality, it is considered a quintessential Imagist text.

The poem is essentially a set of images that have unexpected likeness and convey the rare emotion that Pound was experiencing at that time. Arguably the heart of the poem is not the first line, nor the second, but the mental process that links the two together. "In a poem of this sort," as Pound explained, "one is trying to record the precise instant when a thing outward and objective transforms itself, or darts into a thing inward and subjective." This darting takes place between the first and second lines. The pivotal semi-colon has stirred debate as to whether the first line is in fact subordinate to the second or both lines are of equal, independent importance.

Pound contrasts the factual, mundane image that he actually witnessed with a metaphor from nature and thus infuses this "apparition" with visual beauty. There is a quick transition from the statement of the first line to the second line's vivid metaphor; this "super-pository" technique exemplifies the Japanese haiku style. The word "apparition" is considered crucial as it evokes a mystical and supernatural sense of imprecision which is then reinforced by the metaphor of the second line. The plosive word "Petals" conjures ideas of delicate, feminine beauty which contrasts with the bleakness of the "wet, black bough". What the poem signifies is questionable; many critics argue that it deliberately transcends traditional form and therefore its meaning is solely found in its technique as opposed to in its content. However when Pound had the inspiration to write this poem few of these considerations came into view. He simply wished to translate his perception of beauty in the midst of ugliness into a single, perfect image in written form.

It is also worth noting that the number of words in the poem (fourteen) is the same as the number of lines in a sonnet. The words are distributed with eight in the first line and six in the second, mirroring the octet-sestet form of the Italian (or Petrarchan) sonnet.

2. ①It is considered as one of the leading poems of the Imagist tradition. Its containing only fourteen words typifies Imagism's focus on economy of language, precision of imagery and experimenting with non-traditional verse forms. ②It is written in a Japanese haiku style. ③It is an early work of Modernist poetry as it attempts to "break from the pentameter", incorporates the use of visual spacing as a poetic device, and contains not a single verb. ④The words in this poem are distributed with eight in the first line and six in the second, mirroring the octet-sestet form of the Italian sonnet.

第27章　埃德温·阿林顿·罗宾逊

27.1　复习笔记

Edwin Arlington Robinson (1869—1935)	埃德温·阿林顿·罗宾逊(1869—1935)
1. Life In 1869, Edwin Arlington Robinson was born in the village of Head Tide, Maine. Robinson is one of the most prolific new poets in the nineteenth century. After his graduation from high school, he entered Harvard, and two years later he left Harvard to devote himself to poetry. Robinson was very poor at the beginning of his career as a poet. In 1905, Robinson was offered a clerk's job in the Customs House in New York by President Theodore Roosevelt who had learned of his difficulties. By 1910 Robinson was able to fully dedicate himself to writing. Robinson won Pulitzer Prize in 1922, 1925, and 1928. Robinson's consistent poetry creation won for him fortune and fame, he became the first important poet in America in the 20th century.	**1. 生平** 1869年，罗宾逊出生在缅因州的海德提德村。他是二十世纪最多产的美国新一代诗人之一。他从加德纳的高中毕业后，进入哈佛学习，两年后离校，随后开始诗歌创作。在他开始诗人职业生涯时，穷困潦倒。罗斯福总统得知他有困难后，于1905年在纽约给他找了一份在海关当职员的工作。直到1910年，他才全身心投入到写作中来。他曾于1922年，1925年和1928年获得普利策奖。罗宾逊持之以恒的诗歌创作使他名利双收，也使他在文学史上占有一席之地，成为二十世纪美国第一位重要诗人。
2. Poetic Style (1) While British poets focused primarily on the grandeur and romance of King Arthur's court, Robinson underlined the dark, latent side in human nature that led to the failure of the Round Table. (2) Robinson's poems sometimes seem simple, yet under the surface simplicity there are intricate and subtle thoughts. (3) Like Robert Frost, Robinson was skilled at the use of New England humor that is dry and sometimes biting.	**2. 诗歌风格** (1)当英国诗人主要侧重于亚瑟王宫廷的壮丽和浪漫时，罗宾逊则主要探究导致“圆桌”败落的人物内心的黑暗以及潜在的缺点。 (2)罗宾逊的诗有时似乎很简单，但是简单的表面下却隐藏着复杂和微妙的思想。 (3)像罗伯特·弗罗斯特一样，罗宾逊也善于运用一种时而干瘪时而辛辣的新英格兰式幽默。
3. Major Works "Man Against the Sky" "Richard Cory" "Miniver Cheevy" "Flammonde"	**3. 主要作品** 《天边人影》 《理查德·科里》 《米尼弗·契维》 《弗拉蒙德》

4. Selected Works	**4. 选读作品**
◆"The House on the Hill" This poem mainly describes the deserted state of the house on the hill, giving readers a sense of desolation and bleakness. It seems to be very simple, but it has many symbolic meanings. It may symbolize the degradation of people, the paralyzed state of human minds, or the declination of a family.	**◆《山上的房子》** 这首诗主要描写了山上房子的衰败景象，给人一种荒凉和萧瑟的感觉。诗歌看起来简单易懂，但却包含着许多象征意义。它可能象征着人的堕落，人的思想的瘫痪，或是一个家族的衰落等。
◆"Richard Cory" It tells that a very decent and rich man in people's eyes finally commits suicide. It shows that we can only know about people in a superficial way, and their inner world is very difficult to reach.	**◆《理查德·科里》** 诗歌讲述的是一个人们眼中十分体面、富有的人却最终自杀了。这表明我们只能从表面上理解一个人，很难真正触及其内心世界。
◆"Miniver Cheevy" The poem, written in iambic tetrameter quatrains, relates the story of a hopeless romantic who spends his days thinking about what might have been if only he had been born earlier in time.	**◆《米尼弗·契维》** 诗歌是以抑扬格四音步的四行诗形式写成的。讲述的是一个无望的浪漫主义者终日在幻想如果自己早出生会是什么样子的故事。

27.2 考研真题与典型题详解

Ⅰ. Fill in the blanks.

1. Edwin Arlington Robinson produced a large body of works and was honored with the ________ Prize in 1922, 1925 and 1928.
2. "The House on the Hill" mainly describes the deserted state of the house on the hill, giving readers a sense of ________.

Ⅱ. Multiple Choices

1. Like Robert Frost, ________ was also noted for his use of a dry, sometimes biting, New England humor.
   A. Carl Sandburg　　B. Wallace Stevens
   C. E. A. Robinson　　D. E. E. Cummings
2. Which is not E. A. Robinson's work?
   A. "Man Against the Sky".　　B. "Richard Cory".
   C. "Miniver Cheevy".　　D. "I'm Nobody".

Ⅲ. Read the following quotation and answer the questions.

And he was rich—yes, richer than a king—
And admirably schooled in every grace:
In fine, we thought that he was everything
To make us wish that we were in his place.
So on we worked, and waited for the light,

And went without the meat, and cursed the bread;
And Richard Cory, one calm summer night,
Went home and put a bullet through his head.

Questions:

1. What is the title of the poem?
2. Who wrote this poem?
3. How are the "we" of the poem different from Richard Cory?
4. Do you think the use of the adjective "calm" in the next-to-last line is an example of verbal irony? What is verbal irony?
5. There is an element of dark humor in the mistaken ideas that the townspeople have of Richard Cory, do you think so?

Ⅳ. Short answer question

Analyze Edwin Arlington Robinson's "Richard Cory".

参考答案及解析

Ⅰ. Fill in the blanks.

1. Pulitzer

(美国诗人埃德温·阿林顿·罗宾逊(Edwin Arlington Robinson)一生创作了很多作品，他于1922年、1925年和1928年三次获得普利策奖。)

2. desolation and bleakness

(《山上的房子》主要描写了山上房子的衰败景象，给人一种荒凉和萧瑟的感觉。它可能象征着人的堕落，人的思想的瘫痪，或是一个家族的衰落等。)

Ⅱ. Multiple Choices

1. C 像罗伯特·弗罗斯特一样，罗宾逊也善于运用一种时而干瘪时而辛辣的新英格兰式幽默。

2. D "I'm Nobody"是 Emily Dickinson 的诗。

Ⅲ. Read the following quotation and answer the questions.

1. "Richard Cory"
2. Edwin Arlington Robinson
3. The "we" in the poem refers to the poor townspeople who live a hard life and admire the rich. But Richard Cory is the rich person who is admired by the poor, and appears to be calm and smart, but with a heart of suicidal despair.
4. Yes, it is an example of verbal irony. Verbal irony occurs when words that appear to be saying one thing are really saying something quite different.
5. Yes. The townspeople think that Richard Cory is rich, educated, elegant and even perfect. But in fact, Richard Cory may have psychological problems and some other miseries which fail to see.

Ⅳ. Short answer question

Robinson's world is naturalistic in nature. Here God is no longer caring, men suffer from frustrations and want of mutual understanding, and life is in general futile and meaningless. These reveal Robinson as a modern poet, capable of a tragic vision in step with the modern spirit, trying to suggest a courage out of despair to seek out the meaning of life.

Take "Richard Cory" for example. Richard Cory is a gentleman, rich and humane and clean and graceful, the way he is dressed, walks downtown, speaks to people, "In fine, we thought that he was everything / To make us wish that we were in his place." But, all of a sudden, we hear of his suicide: "And Richard Cory, one calm summer night, / Went home and put a bullet through his head." The poem does not tell the reader why Richard Cory dies the way he does: it is anybody's guess. The poem is thus also an illustration of Robinson's fascination with "psychological enigmas", enigmas that were the product of modern life.

第 28 章　罗伯特·弗罗斯特

28.1　复习笔记

I. Robert Frost (1874—1963)	罗伯特·弗罗斯特(1874—1963)
1. Life	**1. 生平**
Born in San Francisco, Robert Frost spent his childhood in the Far West. He entered Dartmouth College in 1892, but soon left to write poetry while working at odd jobs. In 1897 he tried academy again, he went to Harvard but left two years later, and acquired a constant distaste for academic convention.	罗伯特·弗罗斯特出生于旧金山，在西部度过了童年。1892 年，他进入达特茅斯学院，但很快就退学做零工并写诗。1897 年，他又尝试上学，并在哈佛大学读书，但是两年后再次退学，从此对学业产生持续的厌恶感。
Frost managed to make a living for the next twelve years by teaching and farming while writing poems. In 1912, Frost determined to risk everything and started a literary career in Britain, where his first published book attracted attention of significant critics. A year later, he went back to America and decided to win recognition there.	此后的 12 年里，弗罗斯通过教书和管理农场勉强维生，并坚持诗歌创作。1912 年，他决定赌上所有，去英国投身文学创作，出版的第一本书便赢得有影响力的评论家的关注。一年后他决定回美国以赢得认可。
After publishing a series of books, Frost gradually became famous. He won the Pulitzer Prize for four times and attained honorary degrees from 44 colleges. In 1961, he was invited to read his own poem at President Kennedy's inauguration.	出版一系列书后，他渐渐声名鹊起。他曾四次获得普利策诗歌奖，并获得了来自 44 所大学的荣誉学位。1961 年他应邀在约翰·肯尼迪总统的就职典礼上朗诵了自己的诗。
2. Poetic Features	**2. 诗歌特点**
(1) Frost's poems are full of wisdom, harmony and delight, which form "a momentary stay against confusion."	(1) 他的诗歌充满机敏与智慧，平静与和谐，祥和与愉悦，使人暂时远离困惑。
(2) Frost viewed nature as a source of analogy and symbol. His focus on nature also indicates his deep moral uncertainties. Frost's poems often explore mysteries of darkness and peculiarity in the desolate and chaotic landscapes of a callous universe where men is alone, helpless and confused.	(2) 弗罗斯特认为自然充满类比和象征。他关注自然也体现了深深的道德模糊。他的诗常常探寻黑暗的神秘，这个冷漠世界上，荒凉混沌景象的不合理，而人类在此孤立无援、迷茫失措。
(3) Most of his poems were set at New England and the subjects center around ordinary people's daily life.	(3) 他的很多诗歌以新英格兰为背景，取材于普通人的日常生活。
(4) Frost had declined the revolutionary principles applied	(4)弗罗斯特反对同时期作家

by his contemporary writers; he was instead in favor of "the old-fashioned way to be new".

(5) Frost's poetry can be appalling and horrifying. He is acutely aware of the fragmentation of modern life. His poems are full of abnormal people.

(6) He uses rural New Englanders' plain speech and prefers the short, conventional styles of lyric and narrative.

3. Major Works

A Boy's Will (1913)
North of Boston (1914)
New Hampshire (1923)
A Witness Tree (1942)
In the Clearing (1962)
"The Road Not Taken"
"Mending Wall"
"After Apple-Picking"
"Birches"
"Stopping by Woods on a Snowy Evening"
"Fire and Ice"

4. Selected Works

◆"After Apple-Picking"

It seems to be a simple poem that talks about the conditions and moods of people after apple-picking, but it is not like this way. In fact, it has much profound symbolic meanings. It symbolizes that an old man is thinking about his life, achievements, and regrets as well.

◆"The Road Not Taken"

The lines present an archetypal human situation where man is faced with the difficulty of making choices. What the speaker is saying is probably that ultimately life would come full circle and the roads make no difference after all. And if we read further, we may find embedded in the texture of the poem a kind of complaint that life is too confining to offer us much leeway for options.

◆"Stopping by Woods on a Snowy Evening"

It is a deceptively simple poem in which the speaker literally stops his horse in the winter twilight to observe the beauty

革新的诗歌原则，选择给传统方式赋予新意。

(5)弗罗斯特的诗歌也描绘了一些黑暗、恐怖的事实或者畸形人。他深切地意识到现代生活的支离破碎。

(6)他采用新英格兰乡村的朴实用语，偏好传统的抒情诗和叙事诗，还喜欢短小精悍的格式。

3. 主要作品

《少年的意志》(1913)
《波士顿以北》(1914)
《新罕布什尔》(1923)
《一棵作证的树》(1942)
《林间空地》(1962)
《未选择的路》
《修墙》
《摘苹果之后》
《白桦树》
《雪夜林边小驻》
《火与冰》

4. 选读作品

◆《摘苹果之后》

《摘苹果之后》看似是一首描述人们摘苹果后的状况和心情的简单诗歌，但事实上，该诗有着深刻的象征意义，象征着暮年之人对人生、取得的成就以及遗憾的思考和反思。

◆《未选择的路》

该诗呈现了一个典型的人生境遇，即面临抉择。诗人似乎在说人生在世诸事皆归于循环，任何选择的结果大概都相去不远。此外，诗中也暗含对人生限制太多、供人选择的余地太少的感叹与抱怨。

◆《雪夜林边小驻》

本诗看似简单，描写了主人公在冬夜来临之时将马停在树林边欣赏雪景，最后又继续赶路的情景。

of the frost scene, and then moves to continue his journey. The poem represents a moment of relaxation from the burdensome journey of life.	诗歌展现的是在繁重的人生旅途中放松的一刻。
Frost frequently uses the techniques of symbolism in this poem: "village" stands for the human world; "woods" for nature; "horse" for the animal world and "promise" for duty and obligation of a person.	弗罗斯特在这首诗中使用了大量的象征手法:"村庄"象征人类社会;"树林"象征自然界;"马"象征动物世界;"承诺"象征一个人的责任和义务。
◆"Department"	**◆《部门》**
The poem is about the life of ants. Ants only do what they regard important but show no interest in the affairs that have nothing to do with them. They had a busy life. However, nobody cares when they passed away, because other ants are also indifferent about the things that are unrelated to them. The poem reflects the indifference of people in reality through describing the life of ants.	本诗描写了蚂蚁的生活,蚂蚁对与自己无关的事情毫无兴趣,只做自己认为重要的事情。蚂蚁一生忙碌,死亡之后却无人在意,因为其它蚂蚁也对和自己无关的事情不感兴趣。整首诗通过描写蚂蚁来影射现实社会中的人们太过冷漠,对别人毫不关心。
◆"Design"	**◆《设计》**
The poem ingeniously implies the possibility of the existence of God. The poet uses "white spider", "moth", "white heal-all" to reveal the opposition between good and evil; light and darkness. The poem expresses that everything includes human self could not dominate their fates. Everything is the design of God. The poem seems short but was designed elaborately.	本诗巧妙构思暗示了上帝存在的可能性。诗人利用"白蜘蛛""蛾子""白花"三个意象揭示了善与恶、光明与黑暗之间的对立,表达了世间万物包括人类自身实际上是不可能主宰自己的命运的,一切都是上天的精心设计。本诗看似简单实则设计精心。
◆"The Most of It"	**◆《它的极限》**
The poem writes about the extremely deep loneliness that makes a person visited by the illusion. All the natural objects are the witness of failed communication that reflects a unique lonely environment.	整首诗写的是异常深刻的孤独。写出了一个人在极度孤独中出现了幻象。诗中所有的自然物都是一种未能达成交流的见证,体现了一种独特的空寂意境。

28.2 考研真题与典型题详解

Ⅰ. Fill in the blanks.

1. "After Apple-Picking" is a well-known poem written by ________.
2. Author ________ Title ________ (南京大学2008研)

   Some say the world will end in fire,

   Some say in ice.
3. Author ________ Title ________ (南京大学2009研)

   I shall be telling this with a sigh

Somewhere ages and ages hence:
Tow roads diverged in a wood, and I—
I took the one less traveled by,
And that has made all the difference.

4. ___________ combined traditional verse forms with a clear American local speech rhythm, forming his own characteristic.
5. In 1993, ___________ became President Clinton's inaugural poet (the second person ever to do so for a president in history, the other being ___________.
6. Robert Frost's first book ___________ brought him to the attention of influential critics, such as Ezra Pound, who praised him as an authentic poet.
7. Robert Frost's second volume of poems was ___________.

Ⅱ. Multiple Choices

1. Which of the following was not written by Robert Frost?
   A. *Tilbury Town.* B. *A Witness Tree.*
   C. *Steeple Bush.* D. *In the Clearing.*
2. The first writer who took the vernacular as a serious way of presenting reality after Mark Twain is ___________. (天津外 2008 研)
   A. Robert Frost B. Ernest Hemingway
   C. William Carlos Williams D. Sherwood Anderson
3. ___________ was regarded as America's poet laureate and invited to read his poem at the inauguration of President Kennedy. (首师大 2009 研)
   A. T. S. Eliot B. E. E. Cummings C. Robert Frost D. Ezra Pound
4. "Two roads diverged in a yellow wood and sorry I could not travel both..." In the above two lines of Robert Frost's "The Road Not Taken", the poet, by implication, was referring to ___________.
   A. a travel experience B. a marriage decision
   C. a middle-age crisis D. one's course of life
5. Robert Frost is famous for his lyric poems. Which of the following lyric poems was not written by Robert Frost?
   A. "Richard Cory". B. "Stopping by Woods on a Snowy Evening".
   C. "After Apple-Picking". D. "The Road Not Taken".

Ⅲ. Read the following quotations and answer the questions.

Passage 1 (首师大 2008 研)

Stopping by Woods on a Snowy Evening

Whose woods these are I think I know.
His house is in the village though;
He will not see me stopping here
To watch his woods fill up with snow.

My little horse must think it queer
To stop without a farmhouse near

Between the woods and frozen lake
The darkest evening of the year.

He gives his harness bells a shake
To ask if there's some mistake.
The only other sound's the sweep
Of easy wind and downy flake.

The woods are lovely, dark and deep,
But I have promises to keep,
And miles to go before I sleep,
And miles to go before I sleep.

1. The author of this poem is __________.
2. "Downy flake" in the third stanza means __________.
3. In this poem, __________ meter is most frequently used.
4. Interpret the main idea of this poem.

Passage 2（上海交大 2007 研）

Stopping by Woods on a Snowy Evening

Whose woods these are I think I know.
His house is in the village though;
He will not see me stopping here
To watch his woods fill up with snow.

My little horse must think it queer
To stop without a farmhouse near
Between the woods and frozen lake
The darkest evening of the year.

He gives his harness bells a shake
To ask if there is some mistake.
The only other sound's the sweep
Of easy wind and downy flake.

The woods are lovely, dark and deep,
But I have promises to keep,
And miles to go before I sleep,
And miles to go before I sleep.
Robert Frost

Questions:

1. What is the theme of the poem? What images does the poet use to express this theme?

2. What are the rhythm and rhyme scheme? In what way do the rhythm and rhyme scheme contribute to the expression of the theme?
3. What is the tone of the poem and how is it established?
4. What is the function of the repetition in the last two lines? What poetic effect does the repetition have?

(Warning: All your answers should be organized into a coherent essay, or marks will be deducted.)

Ⅳ. Short answers questions

1. Analyze Robert Frost's *The Road Not Taken*.
2. Discuss Robert Frost's poetic style.

Ⅴ. Essay question

Robert Frost is said to have "rejected the revolutionary poetic principles of his contemporaries." Prove the validity of the statement with reference to Frost's works.（大连外国语 2007 研）

参考答案及解析

Ⅰ. Fill in the blanks.

1. Robert Frost

（《摘苹果之后》是罗伯特·弗罗斯特(Robert Frost)的名诗。）

2. Author: Robert Frost　　Title: "Fire and Ice"

（题目节选自罗伯特·弗罗斯特的《火与冰》。）

3. Author: Robert Frost　　Title: "The Road Not Taken"

（题目节选自罗伯特·弗罗斯特的《未选择的路》中的最后一节。《未选择的路》是美国著名诗人罗伯特·弗罗斯特的著名诗篇。罗伯特·弗罗斯特堪称美国 20 世纪最受欢迎的诗人之一，是美国非官方的桂冠诗人。）

4. Robert Frost

（弗罗斯特将传统诗歌形式与美国本土话语节奏结合起来，形成了独特的诗歌特点。）

5. Maya Angelou; Robert Frost

（1993 年，黑人女作家玛娅·安杰洛(Maya Angelou)应总统比尔·克林顿的邀请，在其就职仪式上朗诵献诗《清晨的脉搏》("On the Pulse of the Morning")，成为美国历史上继罗伯特·弗罗斯特之后的官方诗人。）

6. *A Boy's Will*

（罗伯特·弗罗斯特(Robert Frost)是 20 世纪最受欢迎的美国诗人。他曾赢得 4 次普利策奖和许多其他的奖励及荣誉，被称之为美国文学中的桂冠诗人。1913 年他在英国出版了他的第一本书《少年的心愿》(*A Boy's Will*)得到了评论界的普遍关注。）

7. *North of Boston*

（罗伯特·弗罗斯特(Robert Frost)是 20 世纪最受欢迎的美国诗人，1914 年他出版了他个人的第二部诗集《波士顿以北》(*North of Boston*)，并获得很高的评价。）

Ⅱ. Multiple Choices

1. A　选项 A *Tilbury Town* 是埃德温·阿林顿·罗宾逊的诗。其余三个选项 *A Witness Tree*,

Steeple Bush, *In the Clearing* 都是罗伯特·弗罗斯特的作品。

2. A 美国诗人 Robert Frost 坚持用美国本土语言写作，把朴素随和、鲜活自然又具有地域特色的新英格兰口语融入了传统的抑扬格律之中，流露出浓重的乡土气息。弗罗斯特被誉为“新英格兰诗人”及“美国民族诗人”。

3. C 罗伯特·弗罗斯特是美国的桂冠诗人，多次获普利策奖，1961 年 87 岁高龄的弗罗斯特应邀在约翰·肯尼迪总统(John. F. Kennedy)的就职典礼上朗诵自己的诗作。

4. D 在《未选择的路》一诗中，作者想要表达的实际是人生的境遇。

5. A 罗伯特·弗罗斯特以抒情诗著称，《雪夜林边小驻》(“Stopping by Woods on a Snowy Evening”)，《摘苹果之后》(“After Apple-Picking”)，和《未选择的路》(“The Road Not Taken”)都是弗罗斯特著名的抒情诗。而选项 A “Richard Cory”的作者是埃德温·阿林顿·罗宾逊。

Ⅲ. Read the following quotations and answer the questions.

Passage 1

1. Robert Frost
2. falling snow
3. iambic tetrameter
4. This poem presents the charm of the nature and the responsibility of the people. The speaker is stopping by woods on a snowy evening. The scene is so lovely that the speaker wants to stay longer, but finally he remembers that he still has a long way to go before he can rest for the night. It also means the speaker has to fulfill his responsibilities before his death.

Passage 2

With very few words, Frost here creates a sense of brooding mystery as the speaker stops his horse in a desolate landscape between woods and frozen lake. The attraction of the woods is their darkness, the intimation they offer of losing oneself in them. The speaker gazes into them with a kind of hopefulness, while his horse shakes his bells, reminding him of getting on with the business of living. The repetition in the last two lines denotes a literal recognition that the speaker must move on and connotes that there is much to be done before life ends. His experience of gazing into the woods is just “a momentary stay against confusion” (Frost's words) that sends the speaker back to life with a sense of renewal. The rhythm of the poem is rigidly regular (iambic tetrameter), and its rhyme scheme is a complex pattern of interlocking stanzas (aaba/bbcb/ccdc/dddd). Each stanza is a complete sentence, and each sentence follows the structure of colloquial English (with the possible exception of the inversion of subject and object in the first line). Such interlocking enclosed rhyme links one stanza with the next one, netting the whole poem together, which indicates that the speaker is murmuring to himself since he is attracted by the scenery. The winter bleakness of the setting (the “Frozen lake”, the “downy flake”, the “lovely, dark and deep” woods) establishes a lonely tone and the symbolic weight of this brief moment when the speaker is drawn to what the woods represent—death, perhaps, or at least a temporary release from life's wearying round of duties and obligations. The speaker's weariness is wonderfully underscored by “downy flake”, a phrase that sets vividly before us the image of snowflake wafting downward.

（译文：

雪夜林畔小驻

想来我认识这座森林，
林主的庄宅就在邻村，
却不会见我在此驻马，
看他林中积雪的美景。

我的小马一定颇惊讶：
四望不见有什么农家，
偏是一年最暗的黄昏，
寒林和冰湖之间停下。

它摇一摇身上的串铃，
问我这地方该不该停。
此外只有轻风拂雪片，
再也听不见其他声音。

森林又暗又深真可羡，
但我还要守一些诺言，
还要赶多少路才安眠，
还要赶多少路才安眠。
余光中译）

Ⅳ. Short answers questions

1. This poem is written in classic five-line stanzas, with the rhyme scheme a-b-a-a-b and conversational rhythm. The poem seems to be about the poet, walking in the woods in autumn, choosing which road he should follow on his walk. In reality, it concerns the important decisions which one must make in life, when one must give up one desirable thing in order to possess another. Then, whatever the outcome, one must accept the consequences of one's choice for it is not possible to go back and have another chance to choose differently.

   In the poem, the poet hesitates for a long time, wondering which road to take, because they are both pretty. In the end, he follows the one which seems to have fewer travelers on it. Symbolically, he chose to follow an unusual, solitary life; perhaps he was speaking of his choice to become a poet rather than some commoner profession. But he always remembers the road which he might have taken, and which would have given him a different kind of life.

2. Frost used simple language, a graceful style and traditional forms of poetry. He achieved an internal dynamics in his poetry by playing the rhythms of ordinary speech against the formal pattern of line and stanza. He often used regular iambic meter. Sometimes he used blank verse. His poem was often deceptively simple, exploring complexity through triviality. He used symbols from everyday life to express profound ideas. He made his poems seem effortless by using colloquial

and direct expressions and conversational rhythms. His success mainly lies in two aspects: he combined traditional poetic forms with American vocabulary and speech rhythms; he worked individual poems into a larger unity by presenting in them a recurrent "persona" in the image of a wise country folk.

V. Essay question

Frost took no part in the literary movement in the 20th century. He did not experiment with form, as many poets did in the 1920s.

Whereas the question for William Carlos Williams and Ezra Pound was how to get out of the "trap" of the traditional rhythm and the iambic pattern which they regarded as not true to contemporary experience, Frost treats form as important as sense. He used familiar, conventional forms, plain language and a graceful style. For example, his poem "The Road Not Taken" is written in classic five-line stanzas, with the rhyme scheme a-b-a-a-b and conversational rhythm and takes road, a very plain image to symbolizing the decision-making in everyday life.

His poems were very carefully constructed yet he made them seem effortless by using colloquial language and American vocabulary. In his poem "Stopping by Woods on Snowy Evening", the rhythm is rigidly regular (iambic tetrameter), and its rhyme scheme is a complex pattern of interlocking stanzas. Each stanza is a complete sentence, and each sentence follows the structure of colloquial English. This renders readers feeling of talking with the poet.

Images and metaphors in his poems are drawn from the simple country life and the pastoral landscape that can be easily understood—mowing, scything, wind's rustling in the grass, bird's singing, as well as ponds, roads, the cycle of the seasons, and the alteration of night and day. In his poem "Mending Wall", he takes the metaphor of mending wall to discuss the relationship between humans. However, profound ideas are delivered under the disguise of the plain language and the simple form.

(本题考查弗罗斯特与同时代诗歌创作的不同之处，可就诗人的诗歌形式、语言特点以及意象三个方面进行分析。)

第29章　卡尔·桑德堡

29.1　复习笔记

Carl Sandburg (1878—1967)	**卡尔·桑德堡（1878—1967）**
1. Life	**1. 生平**
Sandburg was a descendant of Swedish immigrants living in Galesburg, Illinois. His father was a mechanic blacksmith. Sandberg only received intermittent education. He worked as an itinerant laborer in the Midwest and was an "all-rounder". After that, he participated in the Spanish-American War as a reporter for the *Galesburg Evening Mail*. After the war, he entered the University of Lombardy and worked in the fire department to make a living, but he dropped out in 1902 without a degree certificate. He moved to Chicago in 1913 and later became a columnist, editor, and feature writer for the *Chicago Daily News*. Sandburg won the Pulitzer Prize in 1940.	桑德堡是居住在伊利诺斯州盖尔斯堡的瑞典移民的后代，他的父亲是一个机械师铁匠。桑德堡只接受了断断续续的教育，在中西部做过流动工人，是个“多面手”，之后他作为《盖尔斯堡晚邮报》的记者参加了美西战争。战后，他进入伦巴第大学，并在消防部门工作以谋生，但他于1902年退学了，没有拿到学位证书。1913年移居芝加哥，之后成为《芝加哥每日新闻》的专栏作家，编辑和社论作家。1940年，桑德堡获得普利策奖。
2. Poetic Features	**2. 诗歌特点**
(1) Sandburg's most cherished ideal in life was to be "the word of the people." Among his contemporaries, he knew the importance of the people best. His poems expressed the thoughts, emotions and ideals of ordinary people.	(1)桑德堡的理想是成为“人民之声”，在同代人中，他最了解人民大众的重要性。他的诗歌表现了普通人的思想、情感和理想抱负。
(2) Sandburg avoided regular stanza patterns and traditional blank verse, and wrote utterly free verse. He carried forward Whitman's long sentences, but weakened the rhetoric effect and intensity with the style of prose.	(2)桑德堡避免了规律的诗节模式和传统的无韵诗，写的完全是自由体诗。他发扬了惠特曼的长句，但弱化了修辞效果和强度，写出了散文的效果。
(3) He used rich vocabulary of immigrants and the dialects of local residents in his works, and made outstanding contributions to the development of oral style in American literature. However, in his poems, straightforward narratives are more important than subtle images or rhythms.	(3)他作品的语言运用了移民们丰富的词汇和当地居民的方言，对美国文学中的口语体的发展做出了卓越的贡献。但是，在他的诗中，直白的叙述要比微妙的意象或韵律更重要。
(4) The work of Sandburg depicts all aspects of American people's lives, the vast grasslands, the beauty of the east and the west, and the episodes of modern cities.	(4)桑德堡的作品描绘了美国人民生活的方方面面、苍茫的草原、东部和西部的美景以及现代城市的插曲。

3. Major Works

Chicago Poems (1914)
Cornhuskers (1918)
Smoke and Steel (1920)
Slabs of the Sunburnt West (1922)
The People, Yes (1936)
The War Years (1939)
"Fog"
"Lost—"
"The Harbor"
"Cool Tombs"
"I am the People, the Mob"

4. Selected Works

◆"Chicago"

This poem does not follow the conventional writing pattern and rhythm, and depicts the spectacular scene of Chicago. The poet uses the writing technique of personification, taking Chicago as a man who is strong and at the same time has some weakness. The poet, however, thinks that Chicago is glorious, vigorous, hopeful and passionate.

◆"The Harbor"

In this poem, the city and nature are in sharp contrast. The first part of the poem shows us a gloomy picture of city life, the language is depressing and dull. In the second part, the poet uses some images such as "lake", "lake waves", "sun", "shore", "gulls" to describe the beauty of nature, and the tone is light and cheerful. It reveals the poet's dislike to the city and love, longing for nature.

◆"Fog"

The poet describes the static and dynamic of the morning mist by comparing it to a cat.

◆"Cool Tombs"

Death will end everything, both good and bad, and common people of present have their own meanings and values.

◆"Flash Crimson"

No matter how hard life is, as long as you work hard, you will see the dawn of hope.

3. 主要作品

《芝加哥诗集》(1914)
《剥玉米的人》(1918)
《烟与钢》(1920)
《夕阳剪影》(1922)
《人民，是的》(1936)
《战争年代》(1939)
《雾》
《失落——》
《海港》
《清冷的墓》
《我是人民群众》

4. 选读作品

◆《芝加哥》

这首诗没有遵循常规的写作模式和韵律，描绘了芝加哥城的壮观景象。诗人运用拟人手法，把芝加哥城比喻成一个男人，强壮有力而又有着缺点。总之，诗人认为芝加哥光荣辉煌、生机勃勃、充满希望和激情。

◆《海港》

在这首诗中，城市与自然形成鲜明对比。第一部分诗歌向我们展示了一幅阴郁的城市生活画面，语气压抑沉闷。在第二部分中，诗人用了一些意象如"湖""湖面波浪""太阳""湖岸""海鸥"来描绘大自然的美丽，语气轻松愉悦。表达了诗人对城市的厌恶和对大自然的热爱与向往。

◆《雾》

诗人通过将晨雾比作猫来对其静态和动态进行描写。

◆《清冷的墓》

死亡会终结一切，不论好的还是坏的，活着的普通大众有着他们的意义和价值。

◆《闪烁的深红》

再苦难的生活只要努力下去也会看到希望的曙光。

◆*The People, Yes*	◆《人民，是的》
Sandburg had a strong responsibility and sense of justice for the people. He described the life of people and expressed their thoughts, feelings and wish. He praised the people and the spirit of democracy and freedom.	桑德堡对人民怀有强烈的责任心和正义感，他在诗中描写人民的生活，表达人民的思想、感情和愿望，歌颂了人民和民主自由的精神。

29.2 考研真题与典型题详解

Ⅰ. Fill in the blanks.

1. At one time, Sandburg's reputation mainly rested on a multi-volume biography of ________ including *The Prairie Years* and *The War Years*.
2. "After Apple-Picking" is written by ________, who wrote and published in the east, at the same time ________ was making his voice heard in the Mid-west. With the poem "Chicago", he was considered as the only great poet then writing in the Whitmanesque tradition. (北师大 2005 研)

Ⅱ. Multiple Choices

1. To many who read "Fog" (1916), "I Am the People, the Mob" (1916), "Grass" (1918), and the 21 sections of *Good Morning, America*, ________ was successor to 19th-century poet Walt Whitman as the proclaimer of the American spirit.

   A. T. S. Eliot　　B. Ezra Pound　　C. Robert Frost　　D. Carl Sandburg

2. The following lines are taken from ________. (大连外国语 2008 研)

A. "Chicago"　　B. *The People, Yes*

C. "Departmental"　　D. "Salutation the Second"

The people so often sleepy, weary, enigmatic,
is a vast huddle with many units saying:
　"I earn my living.
　I make enough to get by
　and it takes all my time.
　If I had more time
　I could do more for myself
　and maybe for others.
　I could read and study
　and talk things over
　and find out about things.
　It takes time.
　I wish I had the time."

3. Carl Sandburg had also taken interest in folk songs which he tried to collect and sing during his travels. These folk songs appeared eventually in print in his well-known ________.

A. *Good Morning, America*　　B. *The People, Yes*

C. *In Reckless Ecstasy*　　D. *The American Songbag*

4. Which of the following is not Carl Sandburg's work?

A. *Chicago Poems*　　B. *Good Morning, America*

C. *The People, Yes*　　D. *Criterion*

5. __________ are not only poets but also literary critics. (北二外 2007 研)

① Edgar Allan Poe　② Carl Sandburg　③ T. S. Eliot　④ Ezra Pound

A. ①③④　　B. ①②③　　C. ①②④　　D. ①②③④

Ⅲ. Read the following quotation and answer the questions.

Hog Butcher for the World,
Tool Maker, Stacker of Wheat,
Player with Railroads and the Nation's Freight Handler;
Stormy, husky, brawling,
City of the Big Shoulders:

Questions:

1. These lines are talking about a big American city which is also the title of the poem. What is it?
2. Who wrote this poem?
3. What is the city called in the first line?

参考答案及解析

Ⅰ. Fill in the blanks.

1. Abraham Lincoln

(卡尔·桑德堡(Carl Sandburg)美国现代诗人及传记作家。20 世纪 20 和 30 年代，他创作并出版了林肯的传记《草原年代》(*The Prairie Years*)和《战争年代》(*The War Years*)。)

2. Robert Frost; Carl Sandburg

(罗伯特·弗罗斯特的《摘苹果之后》是在美国东部创作并发表的，同时，卡尔·桑德堡在中西部声名鹊起。《芝加哥》发表之后，他被认为是当时沿袭惠特曼风格的最佳诗人。)

Ⅱ. Multiple Choices

1. D　桑德堡的理想是成为"人民之声"，在同代人中，他最了解人民大众的重要性。他的诗歌表现了普通人的思想、情感和理想抱负。

2. B　题目中的诗歌节选自美国诗人 Carl Sandburg (卡尔·桑德堡)的作品"The People, Yes"(《人民，是的》)。该段译文：人看上去老是疲倦，不够睡，像个谜，/ 是很多单位组成的一大堆，都在说：/ 我赚钱过日子。/ 我赚的刚可以过活，/ 却占尽我的时间。/ 要是我有更多的时间/ 我可以为自己多做些事，/ 或者替别人多做些事，/ 我可以读书写字，/可以谈谈天，/ 找出事情的道理来。/ 这需要时间，/ 但愿我有时间。

3. D　美国诗人及传记作家卡尔·桑德堡对民歌很感兴趣，他在旅途中收集和吟唱民歌。这些民歌后来出版名为《美国歌谣集》(*The American Songbag*)。

4. D　*Chicago Poems*(《芝加哥诗集》)，*Good Morning, America*(《早安，美国》)和 *The People, Yes*(《人民，是的》)都是卡尔·桑德堡的作品。

5. A　爱伦·坡、艾略特和庞德都既是诗人，又是文学评论家，只有桑德堡只是诗人。

Ⅲ. Read the following quotation and answer the questions.

1. *Chicago*

2. Carl Sandburg

3. Hog butcher for the world

第 30 章　华莱士·史蒂文斯

30.1　复习笔记

Wallace Stevens (1879—1955)	**华莱士·史蒂文斯（1879—1955）**
1. Life	**1. 生平**
Stevens was born and grew up in Pennsylvania. His father was a prosperous attorney. Stevens's original dream was to become a writer. He studied at Harvard University for three years. During this period, he published poetry works on *Harvard Advocate*. He went to New York in 1900 for a try at journalism. But the following year, on his father's advice, he entered the New York Law School. He was qualified as a lawyer in 1904. After graduation, he worked as a lawyer in several law firms. After marriage, he moved to Connecticut to work for Hartford Insurance Company and finally became the company's vice chairman.	史蒂文斯出生在宾夕法尼亚，并在那里长大。他的父亲是一位成功的律师。史蒂文斯最初的梦想是成为一个作家，他在哈佛大学学习了三年，期间曾在《哈佛呼声》上发表诗歌作品。1900 年他去纽约尝试做新闻工作。但是第二年，他接受父亲的建议，到纽约法律学院学习。1904 年获得律师资格，毕业后在好几家律师事务所当过律师，婚后移居康涅狄格，在哈特福德保险公司任职，最后成了该公司的副董事长。
After the 1930s, Stevens continued to create and publish works. *The Necessary Angel* established him as a major American poet. For his *Collected Poems*, he received the National Book Award and the Pulitzer Price.	20 世纪 30 年代后，史蒂文斯开始持续创作出版。《必要的天使》使他成为美国主要诗人之一。《诗集》则使他收获国家图书奖和普利策奖。
2. Poetic Features	**2. 诗歌的特点**
(1) Stevens pursued the artistic beauty of poetry. He often used music and painting techniques to increase the artistic charm of poetry.	(1)史蒂文斯追求诗歌的艺术美，他经常运用音乐和绘画技术来增加诗歌的艺术魅力。
(2) The motivation of his works originally originated from "ideas of order", which is consistent with the inherent order of nature and the universe. It is the privilege of humans and individuals to find that this consistency.	(2)他的作品的动机最初源于"秩序"的理念，他的"秩序"就是真理，其与自然和宇宙固有的秩序一致，发现这种一致性是人类与个体的特权。
(3) Stevens is a sensory poet like Keats. He delighted in depicting the world as revealed to the sense, hoping to relieve the dullness of daily life by exploring pleasures in the senses.	(3)史蒂文斯如济慈一样是一位感官诗人。他喜欢描绘感官可以感受到的世界，希望通过发掘感官的快乐来缓解每日生活的枯燥沉闷。
(4) He experimented with a series of styles and created elegant French poetry, exotic images, weird sounds, peculiar	(4)他试验了一系列风格，创作出法式优雅的诗意，异域意象，

analogies and incredible topics.

怪异的声音，奇特的类比和不可思议的题目。

(5) In the later stage of his poetry creation, Stevens's poetic style became contemplative, even puzzling, and obscure.

(5)在他的诗歌创作后期，史蒂文斯的诗风变得富于沉思甚至是令人费解、晦涩难懂。

(6) His pursuit of perfection is reflected in his careful thinking, extremely outstanding skills and precise and accurate language.

(6)他追求完美的精神体现在他缜密的思维，极度杰出的技艺和严谨准确的语言。

3. Major Works

"The Snow Man" (1921)
Harmonium (1923)
Ideals of Order (1936)
The Man with the Blue Guitar (1937)
Parts of a World (1942)
Transport to Summer (1947)
The Auroras of Autumn (1950)
The Necessary Angel (1951)
Collected Poems (1954)

3. 主要作品

《雪人》(1921)
《风琴》(1923)
《关于秩序的思想》(1936)
《携蓝色吉他的人》(1937)
《世界的某些部分》(1942)
《转入夏季》(1947)
《秋天的晨曦》(1950)
《必要的天使》(1951)
《诗集》(1954)

4. Selected Works

◆"Peter Quince at the Clavier"

The poem is very sensual—Mark Halliday calls it Stevens' "most convincing expression of sexual desire".

4. 选读作品

◆《彼得·昆斯弹风琴》

这首诗充满欲望——马克·霍立德称该诗是史蒂文斯"表达性欲最有力的证据"。

◆"Anecdote of the Jar"

(1) To some extent, it is a rather strange poem. Wallace Stevens was quite opposed to telling the reader the meaning of the poem. Therefore, we can only understand and interpret in the context of its aesthetic creed and related topics.

◆《坛子的轶事》

(1)在某种程度上，这是一首比较怪异的诗，不容易理解。华莱士·史蒂文斯相当反对向读者直陈诗的含义。因此，我们只能在其美学信条和相关主题的上下文中进行理解和阐释。

(2) The "I" in the poem could be a symbol of the art world and a symbol of imagination. This poem seems to discuss the relationship between art and nature. Art and imagination give form and meaning to nature and the real world. A society without art is a society without order. Man creates order according to his own cognition, and half of the world he lives in is created by himself.

(2)诗中的"我"可能是艺术世界的象征，是想象的象征。这首诗歌似是讨论艺术和自然之间的关系。艺术和想象力赋予自然和现实世界以形式和意义。没有艺术的社会是没有秩序的社会，人按自己的认知创造秩序，人所生活的世界有一半是他自己创造的。

◆"The Emperor of Ice-Cream"

The poem describes two scenes at the funeral of a dead woman: one is that people are busy making ice cream, and the

◆《冰淇淋皇帝》

诗歌描写了一位去世的女人葬礼上的两个情景：一是人们忙着做

other is that people cover her with the sheets she embroidered before.	冰淇淋，二是人们用她之前绣过的床单盖上了她。

30.2 考研真题与典型题详解

Ⅰ. Fill in the blanks.

1. At the age of 44, Wallace Stevens was finally persuaded to publish a book of poems, entitled __________.
2. After his death, Wallace Stevens's previously uncollected works appeared under the title __________.
3. __________ was successful in two different fields which seemed rather incompatible with each other: he was vice-president of an insurance company and a remarkable poet at the same time.
4. Write down the name of the author of the following work.（厦门大学 2010 研）
"Anecdote of the Jar"
5. Wallace Stevens was absolutely committed to the notion that a poet lives in two worlds—the world of reality and the world of __________ and builds bridges between them.（天津外国语 2014 研）
6. For the publication of his *Collected Poems*, __________ received the National Book Award and the Pulitzer Prize.

Ⅱ. Multiple Choices

1. The following selection is from a poem entitled __________.（大连外国语 2008 研）
A. "The Snow Begins" by William C. Williams
B. "The Snow Man" by Wallace Stevens
C. "Mad As the Mist and Snow" by W. B. Yeats
D. "Fire and Ice" by Robert Frost

One must have a mind of winter
To regard the frost and the boughs
Of the pine-trees crusted with snow;

And have been cold a long time
To behold the junipers shagged with ice,
The spruces rough in the distant glitter

Of the January sun; and not to think
Of any misery in the sound of the wind,
In the sound of a few leaves,

Which is the sound of the land
Full of the same wind
That is blowing in the same bare place
For the listener, who listens in the snow,

And, nothing himself, beholds

Nothing that is not there and the nothing that is.

2. Like T. S. Eliot, __________ mainly appealed to the taste of the so-called elites.

A. E. A. Robinson B. Wallace Stevens C. E. E. Cummings D. Carl Sandburg

Ⅲ. Explain the following term.

supreme fiction (人大 2004 研)

Ⅳ. Read the following quotations and answer the questions.

Passage 1 (北航 2007 研)

I placed a jar in Tennessee,
And round it was, upon a hill.
It made the slovenly wilderness
Surrounded that hill.
The wilderness rose up to it,
And sprawled around. no longer wild.
The jar was round upon the ground
And tall and of a port in air.
It took dominion everywhere,
The jar was gray and bare.
It did not give of bird or bush,
Like nothing else in Tennessee.

Questions:

1. This poem's title is "Anecdote of the Jar". Who is the poet?
2. Please analyze the symbols of this poem.
3. What does the "jar" stand for?

Passage 2 (上海交大 2006 研)

The Snow Man

One must have a mind of winter
To regard the frost and the boughs
Of the pine-trees crusted with snow;

And have been cold a long time
To behold the junipers shagged with ice,
The spruces rough in the distant glitter

Of the January sun; and not to think
Of any misery in the sound of the wind,
In the sound of a few leaves,

Which is the sound of the land
Full of the same wind
That is blowing in the same bare place

For the listener, who listens in the snow,
And, nothing himself beholds
Nothing that is not there and the nothing that is.

Wallace Stevens

Questions:

1. How many nouns are there in the poem? How many concrete nouns and abstract nouns are there in the first four stanzas and in the last stanza? What is the significance of the difference in these nouns between the first four stanzas and the last stanza?
2. In the last stanza, the three occurrences of "nothing" suggest that the listener sees everything and yet still sees emptiness. Why does he so?
3. Why does the definite article appear more often than the indefinite article in the poem?
4. What is the theme of the poem?

(Warning: All your answers should be organized into a coherent essay, or marks will be deducted.)

V. Essay question

Analyze Wallace Stevens "Anecdote of the Jar".

参考答案及解析

I. Fill in the blanks.

1. *Harmonium*

(1923年，44岁的华莱士·史蒂文斯出版了他的第一部诗集《风琴》(*Harmonium*)。)

2. *Opus Posthumous*

(华莱士·史蒂文斯死后，其之前未收集的诗作集合成册于1957年发表，名为《遗作》(*Opus Posthumous*)。)

3. Wallace Stevens

(华莱士·史蒂文斯无论是作为一名律师还是作为一名诗人，都成就非凡。)

4. Wallace Stevens

(短诗《坛子的轶事》("Anecdote of the Jar")的作者是华莱士·史蒂文斯(Wallace Stevens)。华莱士既是一位著名的诗人，也是成功的商人。)

5. imagination

(史蒂文斯坚信着这样的准则，诗人来往于两个世界，一个是现实世界，一个是想象的世界，并架起连接他们的桥梁。史蒂文斯的"Anecdote of the Jar"，全篇都贯穿着这样的思想。)

6. Wallace Stevens

(在华莱士的《诗集》出版之后，他荣获了国家图书奖和普利策奖。)

Ⅱ. Multiple Choices

1. B 这是华莱士·斯蒂文斯的名诗《雪人》，译文如下：人必须怀有冬日的心境，/才能去看霜，看那松树上/挂满雪冰的树枝。/人必须长期保持寒冷，/才能欣赏披着冰雪般发丝的杜松，/才能领悟远处粗硬的云杉。/在一月阳光下的闪烁，他才能不去想/那蕴含于风的呼啸声/和树叶飘零中的那份凄凉。/那是大地的声音，/大地刮起同样的风，/在同一个荒野上吹拂。/那风为雪中的聆听者所刮，/他自身虚无，看不见/那些不存在的，却看见存在的虚无。

2. B 和艾略特一样，华莱士·斯蒂文斯主要被所谓的“精英”所欣赏。

Ⅲ. Explain the following term.

supreme fiction: Supreme fiction is the creation, according to Wallace Stevens, upon the belief that poetry or any art creates a meaningful order and pattern in life, an order we accept even while recognizing that it is artificially imposed by humankind. The supreme fiction is a mature reflection on the mind's relation to the world and one way that the imagination can encounter the world.

Ⅳ. Read the following quotations and answer the questions.

Passage 1

1. "Anecdote of the Jar" is written by Wallace Stevens.
2. The wild rural Tennessee, chaotic and formless, is a symbol of the world of nature or the reality. And the jar—a man-made object, is suggestive of the world of art, and by extension, the world of imagination.
3. The "jar" stands for the world of art and imagination. The world of nature, shapeless and slovenly, takes shape and order from the presence of the jar. The world of art and imagination gives form and meaning to that of nature and reality.

(译文：我把一只圆形的坛子/放在田纳西的山顶。/凌乱的荒野/围向山峰。/荒野向坛子涌起，/匍匐在四周，不再荒凉。/圆圆的坛子置在地上，/高高地立于空中。//它君临四界。/这只灰色无釉的坛子。/它不曾产生鸟雀或树丛，/与田纳西的别的事物都不一样。)

Passage 2

The whole poem is a long sentence which describes the scenery in an open wild place in winter. The content is changed as the perspectives change and the focus of the poem changes, which are implied by the differences in the concrete nouns and abstract nouns in the first four stanzas and in the last stanza. In this poem, there are 27 nouns. The corporations between the concrete nouns and abstract nouns in the first four stanzas and in the last stanza are 16:6 and 1:4. The first four stanzas focus on describing the scenery and the last stanza summarizes the previous four stanzas and implies the poet's points. In the last stanza, the three occurrences of "nothing" suggest that the listener sees everything and yet still sees emptiness. For he sees the world as the snow man does, who is free of human biases, he sees everything here. Since this place is a bare natural place with no human biases and the listener's heart is so pure, the listener sees emptiness. Compared with the use of indefinite articles in poems, poets use more definite articles. It shows that perspective is dependent on human prejudice, so everything one sees is specific and certain. To see objective things, one must look at the world like a snowman. The snowman has no prejudices. He knows that the winter days are neither cold nor painful. This poem can be understood as an expression of naturalistic skepticism.

This poem expresses Stevens' perspectives, from relatively objective descriptions of winter scenes to relatively subjective emotional reactions (thinking of the pain in the wind), and finally concludes that the audience and the world itself are "nothing." It also can be said that Stevens' perspectives are construed as commitment to the principle that "instead of facts we have perspectives, none privileged over the others as truer or more nearly in accord with things as they are, although not for that reason all equal."

V. Essay question

To some extent, it is a rather strange poem. Wallace Stevens was quite opposed to telling the reader the meaning of the poem. Therefore, we can only understand and interpret in the context of its aesthetic creed and related topics.

The poem seems to be talking about the relationship between art and nature. The world of nature, shapeless and slovenly, takes shape and order from the presence of the jar. The "I" in the poem could be a symbol of the art world and a symbol of imagination. This poem seems to discuss the relationship between art and nature. Art and imagination give form and meaning to nature and the real world. A society without art is a society without order. Man creates order according to his own cognition, and half of the world he lives in is created by himself. Stevens firmly believes that the poet is the archetype of creative power on which all human understanding depends. His poet is "the necessary angel of the earth", in whose sight man sees the earth again. The poet is, in other words, an instrument by means of which man is made to see life whole again.

第31章 托马斯·斯特恩斯·艾略特

31.1 复习笔记

Thomas Stearns Eliot (1888—1965)	托马斯·斯特恩斯·艾略特(1888—1965)
1. Life	**1. 生平**
Thomas Stearns Eliot, poet, critic and editor, was born in St. Louis, Missouri, on September 26, 1888, of New England stock. He attended a private school and entered Harvard University at the age of 18 to major in language and American literature. He published several poems in *Harvard Advocate* and attained the M. A. degree in 1910. After a year in Paris, he returned to Harvard to pursue a doctorate in philosophy, but settled in England in 1914, where Eliot worked as a teacher, and then for Lloyd's Bank. He befriended Yeats and Pound, and they identified with Eliot's poetic talents. Eliot entered the Anglican Church in 1927 and became a British citizen.	1888年9月26日，诗人、评论家、编辑T. S. 艾略特出生于密苏里州圣路易斯，是新英格兰血统。他就读于私立学校，18岁时进入哈佛大学主修语言和美文学，在《哈佛呼声》上发表了几篇诗作，于1910年获得文学硕士学位。在法国待了一年后，回到哈佛攻读哲学博士学位，于1914年定居英国，当过教师和劳埃德银行职员。同时与叶芝和庞德结交，他们认同艾略特的诗歌才华。艾略特1927年入英国国教，加入英国国籍。
From the mid-1920s, Eliot became famous as a poet and literati. As early as 1926 he delivered the prestigious Clark Lectures at Cambridge University, followed from 1932 to 1933 by the Norton Lectures at Harvard, and just about every other honor the academy or the literary world had to offer. In 1948 Eliot received the Nobel Prize for Literature.	20世纪20年代中期起，艾略特作为诗人和文人名声大振。早在1926年就受邀在剑桥主讲颇具名望的"克拉克讲座"，1932至1933年在哈佛主讲"诺顿讲座"，几乎得遍了所有学术界和文学界的荣誉。1948年艾略特获得诺贝尔文学奖。
2. Literary Achievements	**2. 文学成就**
(1) Eliot transformed his preference for 17th-century English metaphysical poetry (the most famous representative is John Dunn) and 19th-century French symbolist poetry (representatives include Baudelaire and Laforge) into poetry innovation in creative techniques and themes.	(1)艾略特将他对17世纪英国玄学诗派(最著名的是约翰·邓恩)和19世纪法国象征主义诗派(包括波德莱尔和拉佛格)的偏爱转化为诗歌创作技巧和题材的根本革新。
(2) He advocated that poetry should be regarded as an organism, and its specific content is truly related to the author's imagination and experience. He judged the poem by the degree to which fusion and concentration of intellect, feeling, and experience were achieved. These ideas have greatly improved the internal analysis of poetry.	(2)他主张把诗歌视为有机体，其具体内容与作者的想象和经历真正相关。他评价诗歌的标准是智力、感觉、经历相融合集中的程度。这些理念极大地提升了诗歌的内在分析水平。

3. Major Works

Prufrock and Other Observations (1917)

The Waste Land (1922)

Ash-Wednesday (1930)

The Use of Poetry and the Uses of Criticism (1933)

Murder in the Cathedral (1935)

Four Quartets (1943)

The Cocktail Party (1949)

3. 主要作品

《普鲁弗洛克及其它一些观察》(1917)

《荒原》(1922)

《圣灰星期三》(1930)

《诗歌的用法和评论的用法》(1933)

《大教堂里的谋杀案》(1935)

《四个四重奏》(1943)

《鸡尾酒会》(1949)

4. Selected Works

◆"The Love Song of J. Alfred Prufrock"

This poem expresses the fear of facing the true self by describing the inner monologue of Prufrock on the way to the appointment. Through a series of repetitive "how" and "why" self-questions, the protagonist recounts his mediocre life. He wants to sound important, but what will he say if a lady expects him to talk about himself? Any revelation about him could bring indifferent rejection. This is a question that Prufrock has always considered in the poem.

The protagonist Prufrock represents a class of people who lived in modern cities in the 20th century with an empty mind and unable to calm their hearts. Their typical characteristics are world-weariness, depravity, helplessness and incompetence.

The first irony in the poem is the name of the hero. J. Alfred is a noble name while Prufrock, as the author said, is the name of a most common people. The greatest irony of the poem is reflected in the inner monologue of the protagonist. It shows his meaningless life, but he is unable to change the contradiction in this state.

4. 选读作品

◆《J. 阿尔弗雷德·普鲁弗洛克的情歌》

本诗通过描写普鲁弗洛克前去赴约的路上的内心独白，表现了他面对真实自我的恐惧。通过一系列的重复的"怎么样"和"为什么"的自我提问，主人公讲述了他平庸无奇的生活。他想要表现得很重要，但是在面对女士时他应该展现自我，这是普鲁弗洛克在诗中一直考虑的问题。

主人公普鲁弗洛克代表了20世纪生活在现代城市中心灵空虚、无法使自己内心平静的一类人。他们的典型特征是厌世、堕落感、无助感和无能感。

诗中的第一处反讽应该是主人公的名字。J. 阿尔弗雷德(J. Alfred)是一个贵族的名字，而普鲁弗洛克(Prufrock)却是再普通不过的平民的名字，这无疑是主人公矛盾的开始。诗歌最大的反讽应该是主人公内心独白展现出的自己无意义的生活，而自己又无力改变这种状态的矛盾。

◆"Preludes"

"Preludes" is one of the early works of Eliot. This poem is short, which describes the desolate and dilapidated scene in the winter. It shows the contradictory and helpless people in that environment. Eliot intertwined filthy reality and beautiful fantasy in his poems, showing the inevitable connection between beauty and ugliness.

◆《序曲》

《序曲》是艾略特早期的作品。本诗篇幅较短，描述了冬日里荒凉破败的景象以及处于那样环境中矛盾而又无奈的人们。艾略特在诗中将污秽的现实和美好的幻想交织在一起，显示出了美与丑的必然联系。

◆**"Journey of the Magi"** The speaker in this poem is one of the three wise men journeying to Bethlehem, to the birth of Christ. The poem reflects Eliot's consistent theme: feeling powerless against alienation in a changed world.	◆《三贤哲的旅程》 诗歌中的说话者是前往耶稣诞生地——伯利恒的三智者之一。诗歌反映了艾略特一贯的主题：对已经发生变化的世界中的异化感到无能为力。
◆**"The Hollow Men"** The poem is divided into five parts with 98 lines. This poem reflects Europe under the Treaty of Versailles after the First World War, the difficulty of regaining hope and conversion to religion. Some critics pointed out that it also reflects Eliot's own marriage.	◆《空心人》 该诗分五部分，共有 98 行。这首诗反映了一战后《凡尔赛条约》下的欧洲、重拾希望和皈依宗教的困难以及一些批评家所指出的艾略特自己的婚姻。

31.2 考研真题与典型题详解

Ⅰ. Fill in the blanks.

1. Eliot's __________ is a morality play in verse dealing with the assassination of Archbishop Thomas Becket by knights of Henry II.（人大 2006 研）
2. "Impersonal theory" of poetry was developed by __________, a famous poet as well as a distinguished literary critic.（天津外国语学院 2011 研）
3. In 1927, T. S. Eliot announced that he was a royalist in __________, a classicist in __________, and an Anglo-Catholic in __________.（国际关系学院 2007 研；首师大 2008 研）
4. *The Waste Land* was written by __________.（大连外国语学院 2008 研）
5. Taking the form of soliloquy, __________ by T. S. Eliot depicts a timid middle-aged man going (or thinking of going) to propose marriage to a lady but hesitating all the time.（天津外国语学院 2007 研）
6. T. S. Eliot's poem *The Waste Land* is divided into __________ sections. The waste land here stands for __________.（国际关系学院 2009 研）
7. Few men of letters have been more fully honored in their own day than __________, and even those who strongly disagree with him seemed content with his selection for the Nobel Prize in 1948.
8. __________ by T. S. Eliot is regarded as a central text of modernism. It is said to catch precisely the state of culture and society after World War I and graphically illustrate the spiritual poverty of the West of that time.
9. Published in 1917, *Prufrock and Other Observations* immediately established T. S. Eliot as a leading poet of the avant-garde. The most notable poem in this collection is entitled __________.
10. The publication of *The Waste Land*, written by __________, helped to establish a modern tradition of literature rich with learning and allusive thought.

Ⅱ. Multiple Choices

1. The central character J. Alfred Prufrock in T. S. Eliot's famous poem "The Love Song of J. Alfred Prufrock" is __________. (天津外国语学院 2009 研)

   A. an old man　　B. a godlike figure

   C. a restless young man　　D. a muse

2. __________, one of the essays in *The Sacred Wood*, is the earliest statement of Thomas Steams Eliot's aesthetics, which provided a useful instrument for modem criticism.

   A. "Sweeny Agonistes"　　B. "Tradition and the Individual Talent"

   C. "A Primer of Modem Heresy"　　D. "Gerontion"

3. Which of the following poets is a Nobel Prize winner?

   A. Ezra Pound.　　B. Robert Frost.　　C. T. S. Eliot.　　D. Wallace Stevens.

4. T. S. Eliot was a __________.

   A. playwright, critic and poet　　B. critic, poet and novelist

   C. novelist, essayist and poet　　D. poet, novelist and politician

5. Thomas Steams Eliot's second volume of criticism __________ (1914) was much admired for its critical method.

   A. *The Function of Criticism*　　B. *The Metaphysical Poets*

   C. *Homage to John Dryden*　　D. *The Sacred Wood*

Ⅲ. Read the following quotations and answer the questions.

Passage 1

Let us go then, you and I,
When the evening is spread out against the sky
Like a patient etherized upon a table;
Let us go, through certain half-deserted streets,
The muttering retreats
Of restless nights in one-night cheap hotels
And sawdust restaurants with oyster-shells:
Streets that follow like a tedious argument
Of insidious intent
To lead you to an overwhelming question...
Oh, do not ask, "What is it?"
Let us go and make our visit.

In the room the women come and go
Talking of Michelangelo.

Questions:

1. This is the first 14 lines of a famous poem "The Love Song of J. Alfred Prufrock ". What is the name of the poet who wrote it?
2. What image is created in this passage?
3. Do you think Prufrock is a tragic figure? Why?

4. Is this poem a dramatic monologue? Why?

Passage 2

The Burial of the Dead
April is the cruellest month, breeding
Lilacs out of the dead land, mixing
Memory and desire stirring
Duil roots with spring rain.
Winter kept us warm, covering
Earth in forgetful snow, feeding
A little life with dried tubers.

Questions:

1. This is the first seven lines of a masterpiece poem. What is the name of this masterpiece?
2. Who is the author of this masterpiece?
3. What theme can you get from these lines?

Ⅳ. Short answer questions

1. How many parts are there in *The Waste Land*?（国际关系学院 2007 研）
2. Discuss the concept of Wasteland in relation to the works of those writers in the 20th century American literature.

Ⅴ. Essay questions

1. What is the subject of T. S. Eliot's masterpiece *The Waste Land*? What is the significance of the poem? Point out some of the features and innovations that you particularly appreciate in it. Who was T. S. Eliot probably influenced by in creating the poem?（人大 2006 研；南京师范大学 2018 研）
2. Analyze Thomas Steams Eliot's "The Love Song of J. Alfred Prufrock".

参考答案及解析

Ⅰ. Fill in the blanks.

1. *Murder in the Cathedral*
（艾略特的《大教堂里的谋杀案》是一部道德剧，讲述了亨利二世的骑士暗杀托马斯·贝克特大主教的故事。）
2. T. S. Eliot
（"非个性化"理论是艾略特诗歌理论的核心内容，包括艺术情感、传统、客观对应物三个相互影响、相互制约的核心概念，"诗不是表现情感，而是逃避情感；不是表现个性，而是逃避个性。"）
3. politics; literature; religion
（艾略特宣称自己在政治上是个保皇派，文学上是古典主义者，宗教上是英国天主教徒。）
4. T. S. Eliot
（艾略特，英国著名现代派诗人和文艺评论家，《荒原》是其代表作。）
5. "The Love Song of J. Alfred Prufrock"
（艾略特在《J. 阿尔弗雷德·普鲁弗洛克的情歌》中，采用独白的方式，讲述了一个中年男人去(或者想去)向一位女士求婚，但一直犹豫不决的故事。)

6. five; the spiritual ruins in Europe

(艾略特最著名的长诗《荒原》分为五部分：《死者葬礼》《对弈》《火诫》《水里的死亡》和《雷霆的话》，将一战后的欧洲描写为一片人欲横流、精神堕落的荒原，折射出现代西方人的幻灭感和精神危机。)

7. Thomas Stearns Eliot

(T. S. 艾略特(Thomas Stearns Eliot)作为诗人、评论家、剧作家，其作品在二十世纪乃至今日的文学史上影响极为深远。1948 年，60 岁的艾略特迎来了他一生中最大的荣誉——诺贝尔文学奖。)

8. *The Waste Land*

(艾略特的《荒原》是现代主义中最具有代表性的作品，它精确描述了一战之后社会和文化的状态，展示了当时西方社会的精神危机。)

9. "The Love Song of J. Alfred Prufrock"

(《普鲁弗洛克及其它一些观察》的出版奠定了艾略特在先锋派中的领导地位，其中最著名的诗歌是《J. 阿尔弗雷德·普鲁弗洛克的情歌》。)

10. Thomas Stearns Eliot

(托马斯·斯特恩斯·艾略特(T. S. Eliot)的《荒原》(*The Waste Land*)在艺术上的成就超过现代派的其他诗作，是一首具有借鉴价值的杰作。诗中大量的典故、比喻、暗示、联想、对应等象征主义手法及意象叠加，时空交错等现代诗歌表现手段，极大地丰富了诗歌的表现手段，拓展了诗歌的思想内容。)

Ⅱ. Multiple Choices

1. C　艾略特在《J. 阿尔弗雷德·普鲁弗洛克的情歌》中描写了一位焦躁不安的上层社会年轻人求爱的矛盾心理。具有很浓的讽刺意味，刻画了当时社会背景下的人对于爱情对于生活的复杂心理。

2. B　1920 年，T. S. 艾略特的批评文集《圣林》(*The Sacred Wood*)的出版奠定了他在 20 世纪文学理论和批评界的重要地位。其中《传统与个人才能》("Tradition and the Individual Talent")这篇论文最早阐释了他的美学，为现代文学批评提供了有利的工具。

3. C　1948 年，60 岁的艾略特迎来了他一生中最大的荣誉——诺贝尔文学奖。

4. A　艾略特是一位剧作家、评论家和诗人。

5. C　T. S. 艾略特的第二本批评文集《向约翰·德莱顿致敬》(*Homage to John Dryden*)因其批评方法而倍受推崇。

Ⅲ. Read the following quotations and answer the questions.

Passage 1

1. Thomas Stearns Eliot
2. a patient etherized upon a table
3. Yes, Prufrock is the image of an ineffectual, sorrowful, tragic twentieth-century Western man divided between passion and timidity, between desire and impotence. His tragic flaw is timidity; his curse is his idealism. Knowing everything, but able to do nothing. He lives in an area of life and death. He despairs of life. He discovers its emptiness and yet has found nothing to replace it. Thus the poem develops a theme of frustration and emotional conflict.

4. Yes, it is a dramatic monologue. He is a character created by Eliot, and he speaks directly to us. He tells us his thoughts in leaps and bounds, jumping from one image to another, just as a human mind does.

Passage 2

1. *The Waste Land*
2. Thomas Stearns Eliot
3. The theme of the poem is modern spiritual barrenness, the despair and depression that followed the First World War, the sterility and turbulence of the modern world, and the decline and breakdown of Western culture, and the impotence and decadence of modern man.

Ⅳ. Short answer questions

1. *The Waste Land* is a great long poem written by T. S. Eliot. It consists of five parts, which are entitled as "The Burial of the Dead", "A Game of Chess", "The Fire Sermon", "Death by Water" and "What the Thunder Said".
2. *The Waste Land* is a poem written by T. S. Eliot on the theme of the sterility and chaos of the contemporary world. The expression of despair in the postwar era repeatedly appeared in the works of those writers in 20th-century American literature. Faulkner treated modern society as a wasteland in a dramatic way. He condemned the mechanized industrialized society, which dehumanizes mankind by forcing mankind to develop false values and reducing essential values such as courage, tenacity, honesty, and kindness. Fitzgerald tried to portray the spiritual wasteland of the Jazz Age. Under the mask of relaxation and joy, there was only meaninglessness and futile effort. Among the grandeur and luxury, there were only signs of waste and moral decay. Hemingway, the leading spokesman of the Lost Generation, though disillusioned in the post war period, strove to bring about man's "grace under pressure". He tried to bring out the idea that man can be physically destroyed but never defeated spiritually.

Ⅴ. Essay questions

1. (1) The subject: *The Waste Land*, Eliot's most important single poem, has been hailed as a landmark and a model of the 20th-century English poetry, comparable to Wordsworth's *Lyrical Ballads*. With bold technical innovations in versification and style, the poem not only presents a panorama of physical disorder and spiritual desolation in the modern Western world, but also reflects the prevalent mood of disillusionment and despair of a whole post-war generation.

   (2) The poem's significance: *The Waste Land* is a poem concerned with the spiritual breakup of a modern civilization in which human life has lost its meaning, significance and purpose. The poem has developed a whole set of historical, cultural and religious themes; but it is often regarded as being primarily a reflection of the 20th-century people's disillusionment and frustration in a sterile and futile society. The horror and menace, the anguish and dereliction, and the futility and sterility expressed in his poetry had been afflicting all sensitive members of the postwar generation. What's more, the new styles like making use of phrases in foreign languages and rich extensive use of other writers' works, other cultures and classics enlighten the following writers much. This poem is the milestone of modern poetry.

   (3) Feature appreciation: The style of the work in part grows out of Eliot's interest in explo-

ring the possibilities of dramatic monologue. Eliot also enjoyed the music hall, and something of the flavor of this popular form of entertainment gets into the poem. It follows the pattern of the musical fugue, in which many voices enter throughout the piece restating the themes. Above all perhaps it is the disjointed nature of the poem, the way it jumps from one adopted manner to another, the way it moves between different voices and makes use of phrases in foreign languages, that become the most distinctive feature of the poem's style.

(4) Maybe Eliot was influenced by Homer, Sophocles, Petronius, Virgil, Dante Alighieri, William Shakespeare, Edmund Spenser, Geoffrey Chaucer, Thomas Middleton, John Milton, Andrew Marvell, and Walt Whitman for pieces of their works are frequently seen from this poem.

2. This poem expresses the fear of facing the true self by describing the inner monologue of Prufrock on the way to the appointment. Through a series of repetitive "how" and "why" self-questions, the protagonist recounts his mediocre life. He wants to sound important, but what will he say if a lady expects him to talk about himself? Any revelation about him could bring indifferent rejection. This is a question that Prufrock has always considered in the poem. The protagonist Prufrock represents a class of people who lived in modern cities in the 20th century with an empty mind and unable to calm their hearts. Their typical characteristics are world-weariness, depravity, helplessness and incompetence.

The first irony in the poem is the name of the hero. J. Alfred is a noble name while Prufrock, as the author said, is the name of a most common people. The greatest irony of the poem is reflected in the inner monologue of the protagonist. It shows his meaningless life, but he is unable to change the contradiction in this state.

第 32 章　F. 斯科特·菲茨杰拉德

32.1　复习笔记

F. Scott Fitzgerald (1896—1940)	F. 斯科特·菲茨杰拉德（1896—1940）
1. Life	**1. 生平**
F. Scott Fitzgerald was born in St. Paul, Minnesota. His family was considered socially prominent and genteelly poor. He was initially sent to study in a private school and later entered Princeton University. In 1917 he left school to join the army. During military training, he fell in love with the daughter of a judge, Zelda Sale. Zelda told Fitzgerald that he could marry her only after he became prosperous. He worked in an advertising company, writing novels and short stories at night. In 1920 Fitzgerald's *This Side of Paradise* was published and became immensely popular. On the strength of this one successful book, he won the expressive prize of Zelda.	F. 斯科特·菲茨杰拉德出生在明尼苏达州的圣保罗。他的家族有一定的社会声望，但是却很清贫。他最初被送进私立学校学习，后进入普林斯顿大学。1917 年他离校入伍。在军事训练期间，他爱上了一位法官的女儿，泽尔达·赛尔。泽尔达告诉菲茨杰拉德只有他飞黄腾达后才能娶她。他便在广告公司工作，夜间写小说和短篇故事。1920 年菲茨杰拉德的第一部小说《人间天堂》一经出版即大获成功。这部小说的成功使他赢得了泽尔达。
Fitzgerald and his wife lived extravagantly, but they were not happy together. To repay the debt, Fitzgerald went to Hollywood to write scripts in despair to support himself. Zelda later had a mental breakdown and was sent to a mental hospital. Because of loneliness, he often used alcohol to dissipate his sorrows, and he felt that his talent was diminishing. In 1940, he died of a heart attack at the age of 44, while working on *The Last Tycoon*.	菲茨杰拉德夫妇生活奢侈，但在一起并不幸福。为了偿还债务，菲茨杰拉德在绝望中去好莱坞写剧本来养活自己。后来泽尔达精神崩溃，被送进了精神病院。孤独寂寞，常借酒消愁，再加上感到自己才华逐减，最终断送了这位英才。1940 年菲茨杰拉德在写《最后一个大亨》时死于心脏病发，年仅 44 岁。
2. Literary Achievements	**2. 文学成就**
(1) Fitzgerald was one of the great stylists in American literature. His language is fluent, his observations are meticulous, and his words and metaphors are extremely original. Its simplicity and gracefulness, its skill in manipulating the relationship between the general and the specific, its bold impressionistic and colorful quality, in short, its competence to convey the vision of the author all reveal Fitzgerald's consummate artistry.	(1)菲茨杰拉德是美国文学史上一位伟大的文体学家。他的语言通顺流畅，观察细致入微，措辞和比喻极具独创性。他的文章质朴、雅致，较好地把握了整体与细节之间的关系，大胆地运用印象主义手法和绘声绘色的描写，文章充分表现了作者的观点，这些都显示了菲茨杰拉德高超的艺术才能。

(2) Fitzgerald became one of the most important American writers in the 1920s because of his keen social insight and amazing lyricism. He portrayed the emptiness of American money worship and the never-ending American dream of love, glitz, and desire.

(2)菲茨杰拉德因其敏锐的社会洞察力和惊人的抒情，成为20世纪20年代美国最重要的作家之一。他描绘了美国人拜金主义的空虚，以及关于爱、浮华、欲望满足的永不停歇的美国梦。

(3) His *Tales of the Jazz Age* gave its name to this crucial period in the cultural history of America. He was the spokesman of the Jazz Age.

(3)他赋予了其短篇小说集《爵士时代的故事》20年代特有的名字，他本人也成为"爵士乐时代"的代言人。

3. Major Works

This Side of Paradise (1920)
The Beautiful and Damned (1922)
Tales of the Jazz Age (1922)
The Great Gatsby (1925)
Tender is the Night (1934)
The Last Tycoon (*unfinished*)

3. 主要作品

《人间天堂》(1920)
《美丽与毁灭》(1922)
《爵士时代的故事》(1922)
《了不起的盖茨比》(1925)
《夜色温柔》(1934)
《最后一个大亨》(未完成)

4. Selected Work

◆*The Great Gatsby*

(1) Gatsby's personal experience is the same as that of the entire United States in the first few decades of the 20th century. Modern people live in a spiritual wasteland, and life has lost its purpose and meaning. Gatsby's personal life has become a great fable in the cultural history of the entire country. Fitzgerald's greatest cultural achievement lies here.

(2) Fitzgerald was envious of the rich, but more contemptuous. He tried to explain the influence of wealth on the split personality of his characters. In The Great Gatsby we have Tom and Daisy, completely dehumanized and dehumanizing.

(3) Fitzgerald's writing skills are impeccable. He chose Carraway as the dramatic narrator. Through Carraway's consciousness, events are filtered, which ensures a unified and compact structure of the entire story. Carraway's limited right to know about the incidents determined that he seemed to have reservations about the information, which created a sense of mystery and suspense.

4. 选读作品

◆《了不起的盖茨比》

(1)盖茨比的个人经历与20世纪前几十年美国整个国家的经历如出一辙。现代人生活在精神的荒原之上，生活已失去目的和意义。盖茨比的个人生活已成为整个国家文化历史上的伟大寓言。菲茨杰拉德在文化思想领域取得的最大成就正在于此。

(2)菲茨杰拉德对富人和富贵的态度有羡慕，但更多的是鄙夷。他试图解释财富对其笔下人物性格分裂的影响。在《了不起的盖茨比》中，汤姆和黛西这两个人物象征着财富本身，意味着堕落，也诱使他人堕落。

(3)菲茨杰拉德的写作技巧无可挑剔。他选择了卡罗威这一戏剧化的叙述者，通过卡罗威的意识事件得以过滤，这保证了整个故事的结构统一、紧凑。卡罗威有限的知情权决定了他对信息似乎有所保留，这制造了一种神秘及悬念之感。

32.2 考研真题与典型题详解

Ⅰ. Fill in the blanks.

1. Nick Carraway functions as both the narrator and a character in Fitzgerald's best-known work __________. （大连外国语 2008 研：A 卷）
2. F. Scott Fitzgerald's first novel __________, with its portrayal of casual dissipations of "flaming youth", was an immediate commercial success.
3. Author __________ Title __________ （南京大学 2008 研）
   So we beat on, boats against the current, borne back ceaselessly into the past.
4. F. Scott Fitzgerald summarized the experiences and attitudes of the 1920s decade in his masterpiece novel __________.
5. F. Scott Fitzgerald's second novel __________ describes a handsome young man and his beautiful wife, undoubtedly modelled after himself and Zelda.
6. The hero in F. Scott Fitzgerald's novel __________ is a psychiatrist who marries a rich patient. The author condemns the wasted energy of misguided youth.
7. F. Scott Fitzgerald's last novel __________ remained unfinished.
8. In 1925, F. Scott Fitzgerald wrote his best novel __________. It is the story of an idealist who was destroyed by the influence of the wealthy, pleasure-seeking people around him.

Ⅱ. Multiple Choices

1. F. S. Fitzgerald is NOT the writer of __________. （北二外 2010 研）
   A. *The Great Gatsby* B. *The Last Tycoon*
   C. *As I Lay Dying* D. *Tender is the Night*
2. Among the following writers, who is often acclaimed literary spokesman of the Jazz Age?
   A. William Faulkner. B. F. Scott Fitzgerald.
   C. Henry James. D. Eugene O'Neill.
3. "There was music from my neighbor's house through the summer nights. In his blue gardens men and girls came and went like moths among the whisperings and the champagne and the stars..." This quotation is taken from __________.
   A. *Moby Dick* by Herman Melville B. *Daisy Miller* by Henry James
   C. *Sister Carrie* by Theodore Dreiser D. *The Great Gatsby* by F. Scott Fitzgerald
4. Which of the following American writers has NOT been a Nobel Prize winner?
   A. F. Scott Fitzgerald. B. Ernest Hemingway.
   C. William Faulkner. D. John Steinbeck.
5. The Fitzgeralds lived so extravagantly that they frequently spent more money than F. Scot Fitzgerald earned for parties, liquor, entertaining their friends and traveling. It was this living style that nicknamed the decade of the 1920s as __________.
   A. The Roaring Twenties B. The Jazz Age
   C. The Dollar Decade D. all of the above
6. The following selection is taken from __________. （大连外国语 2007 研）
   A. *Sister Carrie* B. *Treasure Island*

C. *The Great Gatsby*　　　　D. *Heart of Darkness*

In my younger and more vulnerable years my father gave me some advice that I've been turning over in my mind ever since. "Whenever you feel like criticizing anyone," he told me, "just remember that all the people in this world haven't had the advantages that you've had."

7. The best dichotomy which can describe about the theme of F. S. Fitzgerald's *The Great Gatsby* is ________. (武汉大学 2011 研)

A. children's innocence VS. adults' decadence

B. spiritual wilderness VS. material civilization

C. the innate evils of man VS. human perfectibility

D. conservatism VS. liberal-mindedness

Ⅲ. Explain the following terms.

1. The Jazz Age(国际关系学院 2007 研；北二外 2009 研；首师大 2009 研)
2. The Lost Generation(北航 2007 研；四川大学 2010 研)

Ⅳ. Read the following quotation and answer the questions. (北航 2007 研)

Most of the big shore places were closed now and there were hardly any lights except the shadowy, moving glow of a ferryboat across the Sound. And as the moon rose higher the inessential houses began to melt away until gradually I became aware of the old island here that flowered once for Dutch sailors' eyes—a fresh, green breast of the new world. Its vanished trees, the trees that had made way for Gatsby's house, had once pandered in whispers to the last and greatest of all human dreams; for a transitory enchanted moment man must have held his breath in the presence of this continent, compelled into all aesthetic contemplation he neither understood nor desired, face to face for the last time in history with something commensurate to his capacity for wonder.

And as I sat there brooding on the old, unknown world, I thought of Gatsby's wonder when he first picked out the green light at the end of Daisy's dock. He had come a long way to this blue lawn, and his dream must have seemed so close that he could hardly fail to grasp it. He did not know that it was already behind him, somewhere back in that vast obscurity beyond the city, where the dark fields of the republic rolled on under the night.

Gatsby believed in the green light, the orgiastic future that year by year recedes before us. It eluded us then, but that's no matter—tomorrow we will run faster, stretch out our arms farther... And one fine morning—

So we beat on, boats against the current, borne back ceaselessly in to the past.

Questions:

1. Which fiction is this excerpt from? Who is the author of the novel?
2. What does "Daisy's dock" stand for?
3. Why are the Dutch sailors mentioned here? In what way does it contribute to the novel?

Ⅴ. Short answer questions

1. Why did F. Scott Fitzgerald use "great" to modify the protagonist's name Gatsby in the title of his novel *The Great Gatsby*? (南京大学 2009 研；南京大学 2007 研；人大 2006 研)
2. Why was Fitzgerald regarded as spokesman of the "Jazz Age"?
3. Comment briefly on the following character. (中山大学 2004 研)

Gatsby

Ⅵ. Essay questions

1. Interpret American Dream by citing several relevant American writers and their works .（武汉大学 2008 研）

2. Irving Howe considers *The Great Gatsby* as a prose version of *The Waste Land*. What do you think of this view?（天津外国语学院 2009 研）

参考答案及解析

Ⅰ. Fill in the blanks.

1. *The Great Gatsby*

（在菲茨杰拉德的名著《了不起的盖茨比》中，Nick Carraway（尼克）既是叙述者，又是小说中的一个角色。）

2. *This Side of Paradise*

（1920 年菲茨杰拉德发表第一部长篇小说《人间天堂》，一举成名。书中描写了一战后年轻一代的精神面貌和生活方式。）

3. Author：F. Scott Fitzgerald　　Title：*The Great Gatsby*

（题目是 F. 斯科特 · 菲茨杰拉德的 *The Great Gatsby*（《了不起的盖茨》）中的最后一句话。）

4. *The Great Gatsby*

（《了不起的盖茨比》是美国作家弗朗西斯 · 斯科特 · 菲茨杰拉德所写的一部以 20 世纪 20 年代的纽约市及长岛为背景的小说，被视为美国文学“爵士时代”的象征。该书敏锐地抓住了当代社会生活的主题，并以象征手法展现了“美国梦”传奇之下的嘲讽及悲怅。）

5. *The Beautiful and Damned*

（1922 年菲茨杰拉德的第二部小说《美丽与毁灭》（*The Beautiful and Damned*）出版。这部小说讲了一个年轻的有钱人，由于婚姻的不幸而导致感情和精神崩溃的故事。书中男女主角无疑是以菲茨杰拉德及其妻子泽尔达为原型而塑造的。）

6. *Tender is the Night*

（菲茨杰拉德的小说《夜色温柔》（*Tender is the Night*）讲述了一个美国精神病医生与一位美丽而又富有的病人结合终遭失败的故事。该小说反映了强烈的怀旧情绪、悔恨心理、失落的希望、破灭的幻想、人格的分裂。）

7. *The Last Tycoon*

（菲茨杰拉德在 44 岁的时候因为心脏病发而去世，留下他最后一本小说《最后一个大亨》（*The Last Tycoon*），这是一本有关好莱坞生活的小说，不过只写了一半。）

8. *The Great Gatsby*

（1925 年出版的《了不起的盖茨比》是菲茨杰拉德写作生涯的顶点。这部小说反映了 20 年代“美国梦”的破灭，深刻地揭示了角色性格的矛盾和内心的冲突。《了不起的盖茨比》被誉为当代最出色的美国小说之一，确立了菲茨杰拉德在文学史上的地位。）

Ⅱ. Multiple Choices

1. C　*As I Lay Dying*（《在我弥留之际》）是 William Faulkner 的作品。

2. B　菲茨杰拉德是爵士时代的发言人。

3. D　这段话选自菲茨杰拉德的《了不起的盖茨比》，描写了盖茨比家举办晚会的情景。

4. A　除菲茨杰拉德外，海明威、福克纳、约翰·斯坦贝克均获过诺贝尔文学奖。

5. D　菲茨杰拉德夫妇生活奢华铺张，沉溺于舞会、酒精、交友及旅行，因而他们常入不敷出。这种生活方式赋予了 20 世纪 20 年代"疯狂的 20 年代"(The Roaring Twenties)，"爵士乐时代"(The Jazz Age)，"美元年代"(The Dollar Decade)等别名。

6. C　题中片段选自美国著名小说家 Francis Scott Key Fitzgerald 的代表作《了不起的盖茨比》，是小说的开头部分，参考译文为：我年纪还轻，阅历不深的时候，我父亲教导过我一句话，我至今还念念不忘。"每逢你想要批评任何人的时候，"他对我说，"你就记住，这个世界上所有的人，并不是个个都有过你拥有的那些优越条件。"

7. A　从盖茨比的成长来看，他年轻时纯洁的美国梦随着他的堕落而消亡。

Ⅲ. Explain the following terms.

1. The Jazz Age: The Jazz Age describes a period in the United States after the end of the First World War, which lasted into the roaring twenties and ended with the outbreak of the Great Depression. It marked a period of constant changes in value, while the stock market soared. From the perspective of historical and cultural studies, it contrasts with the parallel description of the Roaring Twenties, which emphasizes multiple forms of modernism. The name of this era comes from jazz, and the popularity of jazz in many classes of society greatly increased. The public accepted the technological developments include automobiles, air travel and telephones, as well as new trends in modernism in social behavior, art, and culture. One of the most representative literary works of the Jazz age is American writer F. Scott Fitzgerald's *The Great Gatsby* (1925).
2. The Lost Generation: Lost Generation is a literature school that originated in American in the twentieth century. Lost Generation refers to the generation after the World War I. Meanwhile, it also refers to the disillusioned young writers who lived as expatriates in Western Europe for a short time, most notably Paris. Figures identified with the "Lost Generation" included authors and artists such as Ernest Hemingway, F. Scott Fitzgerald, Ezra Pound, Sherwood Anderson, Waldo Peirce, John Dos Passos, John Steinbeck, and Cole Porter.

Ⅳ. Read the following quotation and answer the questions.

1. This excerpt is from *The Great Gatsby* by F. S. Fitzgerald.
2. The green light at the end of Daisy's dock represents Gatsby's hopes and dreams about Daisy. Thus, "Daisy's dock" stands for Daisy and also the American Dream.
3. The Dutch sailors are connected to the early settlement of the New York area. To the Dutch sailors, America is a place full of wonder and promise where they may fulfill their dreams. The same is for Gatsby who newly becomes a millionaire and wants to gain Daisy's love with his wealth. The Dutch sailors can be taken as an allegory in the novel.

Ⅴ. Short answer questions

1. Gatsby is great because he is able to create a new identity for himself when he needs to be someone else. His determination and audacity are amazing since he focuses on a goal of winning Daisy and he does whatever is necessary to attain it. He believes that he needs wealth to keep Daisy in the manner she is accustomed to, and so he attains a "business" that gives him financial wealth. What is more, he studies mannerisms and expressions he thinks is what the social elite says and does.

That Gatsby is great is also because of his unworldly love for Daisy. He takes the blame for Daisy when she commits a crime and that takes a great man.

Gatsby is great because he is a mythical figure whose personal experience approximates a state of mind that embodies America. Gatsby is the last of the romantic hero, whose energy and sense of commitment take him in search of his personal grail.

2. Fitzgerald was a representative figure of the 1920s. He never failed to remain detached and foresee the tragedy of the "Dollar Decade." His works mirror the exciting age in almost every way. Through the glittering world of his fiction run the themes of moral waste, decadence and necessity of personal responsibility. *The Great Gatsby*, a book about the Jazz Age, is a case study in people's pursuit of an elusive American Dream. It is also a powerful criticism of American society. Thus he is often regarded as literary spokesman of the Jazz Age.
3. Gatsby is the protagonist of Fitzgerald's *The Great Gatsby*. He is a mythical figure whose intensity of dream embodies general American's state of mind. Gatsby is the last romantic hero, whose energy and sense of commitment takes him in search of his personal grail. This talent for self-invention is what gives Gatsby his quality of "greatness": Gatsby reveals himself to be an innocent, hopeful young man who stakes everything on his dreams, not realizing that his dreams are unworthy of him.

Ⅵ. Essay questions

1. The American Dream is a national ethos of the United States of America in which democratic ideals are perceived as a promise of prosperity for its people. In the pursuit of American Dream, first expressed by James Truslow Adams in 1931, citizens of every rank feel that they can achieve a "better, richer, and happier life." The idea of the American Dream is rooted in the second sentence of the *Declaration of Independence* which states that "all men are created equal" and that they are "endowed by their Creator with certain inalienable rights" including "Life, Liberty and the pursuit of Happiness." In common parlance, the term American Dream is often used as a synonym for home ownership since homes have historically been seen as status symbols separating the middle classes and the poor. This usage, though, while common, is generally considered a very specific use of a more general term.

   Some authors have written to critique or ridicule the concept, such as John Steinbeck's *Of Mice and Men*. Fitzgerald became one of the most important American writers in the 1920s because of his keen social insight and amazing lyricism. He portrayed the emptiness of American money worship and the never-ending American dream of love, glitz, and desire. F. Scott Fitzgerald wrote *The Great Gatsby* about the extreme selfishness of adultery, bootlegging and social climbing sometimes associated with the American Dream, as did Sinclair Lewis in *Babbitt*, which satirized 20th-century materialism and conformity. Hunter S. Thompson's depicted in *Fear and Loathing in Las Vegas*: *A Savage Journey Into the Heart of the American Dream* a dark view of the search for the American Dream in the early 1970s after the collapse of the counter-culture movement; a vision of the cynical politics of Richard Nixon, violence, avarice, ignorance, vicious patriotism and personal alienation, endemic to American society.
2. Both *The Great Gatsby* and *The Waste Land* are about the loss of an ideal and the disillusionment

that people's incorruptible dream is shattered into pieces by the relentless reality. Both of them reflect a world filled with desire, spirits fall down, moral is lost and life is corrupt. Through the two works, the general disappointment toward reality, world and human civilization are shown. So *The Great Gatsby* interprets *The Wasteland's* theme by the story of Gatsby.

But in another respect, the artistic feature of *The Great Gatsby* is that the language manifests the poetic quality. The style of F. Scott Fitzgerald, closely related to his themes, is explicit and chilly. His accurate dialogues and his sensitive styles provide the reader with a vivid sense of reality. He uses the scenic method in his chapters, each one of which consists of one or more dramatic scenes. Sometimes he inserts passages of narration, leaving the tedious process of transition to the readers' imagination. Fitzgerald's writing skills are impeccable. He chose Carraway as the dramatic narrator. Through Carraway's consciousness, events are filtered, which ensures a unified and compact structure of the entire story. Carraway's limited right to know about the incidents determined that he seemed to have reservations about the information, which created a sense of mystery and suspense. The accurate details, the completely original diction and metaphors, the bold impressionistic and colorful quality have all revealed his consummate artistry. His words are like pieces of poems, provoking reader's imagination and placing them in the beauty of poetry. In this sense, *The Great Gatsby* is a prose version of *The Waste Land*.

第 33 章　欧内斯特·海明威

33.1　复习笔记

Ernest Hemingway (1899—1961)	欧内斯特·海明威（1899—1961）
1. Life	**1. 生平**
Ernest Hemingway was born in Oak Park, near Chicago, on July 21, 1899. In 1917, after graduation from high school, Ernest Hemingway went to work as a reporter for *The Kansas City Star*. Due to poor eyesight, he was refused entry into the army in World War I, and then worked as a volunteer in the American ambulance unit in France as a driver. He was later transferred to Italy, where he was seriously injured. After demobilization, he returned to the United States. The war experience has long affected Hemingway's life and writing like a nightmare.	1899 年 7 月 21 日，海明威出生在芝加哥附近的奥克帕克。1917 年，他高中毕业就去《堪萨斯城星报》当记者了。由于视力差，他在一战中参军遭拒，而后作为志愿者在驻法国的美国救护单位当司机。他后来被调到意大利，在那里受了重伤。复员后，他回到了美国。战争经历如噩梦般长期影响了海明威的生活和写作。
Hemingway was a myth in his own time and a myth in American literature. He was a shining public hero, and his writing style and lifestyle have been imitated by many people. Hemingway is the spokesman for "a lost generation". He won the Nobel Prize for Literature in 1954. In his later years, Hemingway behaved strangely. Possibly because he could not write any more, or possibly because he could not act out his code, or because of both and his ill health, he shot himself on July 2, 1961. The world was shocked into the disconcerting awareness that Hemingway's death marked the end of an era in the history of American literature.	海明威是他所在那个年代的神话，同时也是美国文学的神话。他是星光闪耀的公众英雄，他的写作风格和生活方式受到很多人的模仿。海明威是"迷惘的一代"的发言人。1954 年海明威获得了诺贝尔文学奖。晚年海明威行为古怪。或许因为文思枯竭，或许因为他不能实践自己的行为准则，又或许二者兼有，再加上他疾病缠身，1961 年 7 月 2 日海明威开枪自杀，举世为之震惊，海明威的逝世标志着美国文学史上一个时代的结束。
2. The Hemingway Code Hero	**2. 海明威式英雄**
Hemingway writes all his life about one theme, "grace under pressure". Under this theme, he has created many typical Hemingway heroes. The world described by Hemingway is essentially chaotic and meaningless. In the world he describes, one alone resists forces that he can't understand. He will be extremely disappointed to realize that no matter how hard he tried, he would eventually end in failure. But Hemingway heroes possess a kind of courage. It is this kind of courage that makes him show his manhood and maintain his	海明威的一生都在描写一个主题，即"重压下的优雅"。在这个主题下他塑造了众多典型的海明威式英雄。海明威笔下的世界在本质上混乱不堪，毫无意义可言。在他笔下的世界里，人单枪匹马去抵抗他自己都无法理解的力量。他极其失望地意识到无论自己多么努力，最终还是会以失败告终。但是海明威式英雄具备一种勇气。正是这种

dignity in the face of adversity. This is the essence of a code of honor in which all of Hemingway's heroes believed. Hemingway's characters, Nick Adams, Jake Barnes, Frederic Henry, and Santiago are all typical Hemingway heroes.

勇气使他表现出大丈夫气概，在逆境中保持尊严。这是所有海明威式英雄都相信的荣誉准则的核心。海明威小说中的人物尼克·亚当斯、杰克·巴恩斯、弗瑞德里克·亨利、圣地亚哥等都是典型的海明威式英雄。

3. Writing Style

(1) He promoted the development of reportage. He believed that the sentences of reportage should be simple in structure, limited in words with concise imagination, and adopt a dramatic tone which is not affected by emotions.

(2) In the later part of his life, Hemingway came to be known as "Papa Hemingway". This compliment refers mainly to his contribution to the development of the colloquial style of writing in America. Hemingway's articles are simple, natural, straightforward, clear and easy to understand, novel and lively, and rich in meaning.

3. 写作风格

（1）他推动了报告文学的发展，他认为报告文学的句子应该结构简单，用词有限制，想象要精练，要采用不受感情影响的、戏剧化的语调。

（2）海明威晚年被称作"爸爸海明威"，这一赞誉主要指他为美国文学史上"口语体"这一新的写作风格做出了突出的贡献。海明威的文章简朴、自然，直截了当，清晰易懂，新颖活泼，而且意蕴丰富。

4. Major Works

In Our Time (1925)
The Sun Also Rises (1926)
A Farewell to Arms (1929)
Death in the Afternoon (1932)
The Green Hills of Africa (1935)
For Whom the Bell Tolls (1940)
The Old Man and the Sea (1952)

4. 主要作品

《在我们的时代里》(1925)
《太阳照常升起》(1926)
《永别了，武器》(1929)
《死在午后》(1932)
《非洲的青山》(1935)
《丧钟为谁而鸣》(1940)
《老人与海》(1952)

5. Selected Work

◆*A Farewell to Arms*

A Farewell to Arms can be read as a footnote to *The Sun Also Rises*. Frederic Henry experienced the war firsthand. He found that the war had no sacred glory at all. It was just a living slaughterhouse. Henry fought alone as a typical Hemingway hero. He speaks less and acts decisively. Even with others, he usually acts like an outsider and is good at controlling his feelings. *A Farewell to Arms* caught the mood of the postwar generation and brought international fame to Hemingway.

5. 选读作品

◆《永别了，武器》

《永别了，武器》在某种意义上是《太阳照常升起》的注脚。弗瑞德里克·亨利亲历战争，却发现战争毫无神圣光荣可言，而是活生生的屠宰场。亨利孤军奋战，他是典型的海明威式英雄——少言寡语，行动果断。即使与他人在一起，他也通常表现得像个局外人，善于控制自己的感情。《永别了，武器》反映了战后一代的失望情绪，并令海明威享誉国际。

33.2 考研真题与典型题详解

Ⅰ. Fill in the blanks.

1. American writers of the first postwar era self-consciously acknowledged that they were a "__________", devoid of faith and alienated from a civilization.
2. Author __________ Title __________ （南京大学 2009 研）
   The two waiters inside the café knew that the old man was a little drunk, and while he was a good client they knew that if he became too drunk he would leave without paying, so they kept watch on him.
3. Set in Spain during the Civil War, the novel __________ stated again Hemingway's view of love found and lost, and described the indomitable spirit of the common people. （人大 2006 研）
4. In 1954, Ernest Hemingway was awarded a __________ for his "mastery of the art of modern narration".
5. In the same way that F. Scott Fitzgerald's *Tales of the Jazz Age* became the symbol for an age, Ernest Hemingway's novel __________ painted the image of a whole generation, the Lost Generation.
6. Ernest Hemingway's stature as a writer was confirmed with the publication of his novel __________ in 1929. The novel portrayed a farewell both to war and to love.
7. In the story *The Old Man and the Sea*, Ernest Hemingway portrayed an old fisherman named __________, who is triumphant even in defeat.
8. In 1952, Ernest Hemingway published a successful novel entitled __________, which won the Pulitzer Prize in 1953 and occasioned the award of the Nobel Prize in 1954.
9. Author __________ Title __________（南京大学 2007 研）
   He disliked bars and bodegas. A clean, well-lighted café was a very different thing. Now, without thinking further, he would go home to his room. He would lie in the bed and finally, with daylight, he would go to sleep. After all, he said to himself, it is probably only insomnia. Many must have it.
10. With the publication of *The Sun Also Rises*, __________ became the spokesman for what Gertrude Stein had called "a Lost Generation".
11. Writers like Ernest Hemingway and William Faulkner tried to represent the absurdity theme in __________ novelistic devices, while the writers in the 1960s regard the conventional novel as __________.

Ⅱ. Multiple Choices

1. Ernest Hemingway is noted for the following EXCEPT __________. （首师大 2008 研）
   A. Lost Generation　　B. iceberg theory
   C. American Dream　　D. "grace under pressure"
2. In one sense __________ wrote all his life about one theme, which is neatly summed up in the famous phrase "grace under pressure," and created one hero who acts that theme out. （武汉大学 2010 研）
   A. F. S. Fitzgerald　　B. Ernest Hemingway

C. William Faulkner D. Sinclair Lewis

3. Ernest Hemingway was badly wounded in Italy and sent to a hospital where he fell in love with a nurse. These two persons later became the characters of his novel ________.

A. *The old Man and the Sea* B. *For Whom the Bell Tolls*

C. *The Sun Also Rises* D. *A Farewell to Arms*

4. Who has made the statement that all modern American literature comes from a single book called *Adventure of Huckleberry Finn*?

A. Ernest Hemingway. B. William Faulkner.

C. F. Scott Fitzgerald. D. T. S. Eliot.

5. ________ addressed Ernest Hemingway and his peers as "the lost generation" which entitled a generation in the 1930s. (北二外 2009 研)

A. Gertrude Stein B. William Dean Howells

C. Sherwood Anderson D. Henry James

6. "Nick Adams" is a character who frequently appears in ________'s stories.

A. William Faulkner B. Theodore Dreiser

C. Mark Twain D. Ernest Hemingway

7. In 1954, ________ was awarded the Nobel Prize for Literature for his "mastery of the art of modern narration".

A. Thomas Stearns Eliot B. Ernest Hemingway

C. John Steinbeck D. William Faulkner

Ⅲ. Explain the following terms.

1. "Hemingway Heroes"(武汉大学 2008 年)

2. Ernest Hemingway(四川大学 2010 研)

3. Santiago(北航 2009 研)

Ⅳ. Read the following quotations and answer the questions.

Passage 1(北航 2008 研)

In the later summer of that year we lived in a house in a village that looked across the river and the plain to the mountains. In the bed of the river there were pebbles and boulders, dry and white in the sun, and the water was clear and swiftly moving and blue in the channels. Troops went by the house and down the road and the dust they raised powdered the leaves of the trees. The trunks of the trees too were dusty and the leaves fell early that year and we saw the troops marching along the road and the dust rising and leaves, stirred by the breeze, falling and the soldiers marching and afterward the road bare and white except for the leaves.

…

Poor, poor dear Cat. And this was the price you paid for sleeping together. This was the end of the trap. This was what people got for loving each other. Thank God for gas, anyway. What must it have been like before there were anesthetics? Once it started, they were in the mill-race. Catherine had a good time in the time of pregnancy. It wasn't bad. She was hardly ever sick. She was not awfully uncomfortable until toward the last. So now they got her in the end. You never got away with anything. Get away hell! It would have been the same if we had been married fifty times. And what if she should die? She won't die. People don't die in childbirth nowadays. That was what all husbands thought. Yes, but what if she should die? She won't die. She's just having a bad time. Afterward we'd say what a bad time and Catherine would say it wasn't really so bad. But what if she should die?

Questions:

1. Identify the author and the work from which the passage is selected.
2. What is the symbolic meaning of the title?
3. How do you understand the features of heroes in the author's works?
4. Comment on author's writing style and philosophy underlying all his works?

Passage 2

This passage is an excerpt from Ernest Hemingway's short story "The Killer". Read it and answer the following questions. (北二外 2008 研)

"Talk to me, bright boy," Max said. "What do you think's going to happen?"

George did not say anything.

"I'll tell you," Max said, "We're going to kill a Swede. Do you know a big Swede named Ole Andreson?"

"Yes."

"He comes here to eat every night, doesn't he?"

"Sometimes he comes here."

"He comes here at six o'clock, doesn't he?"

"If he comes."

"We know all that bright boy," Max said. "Talk about something else. Ever go to the movies?"

"Once in a while."

"You ought to go to the movies more. The movies are fine for a bright boy like you."

"What are you going to kill Ole Andreson for? What did he ever do to you?"

"He never had a chance to do anything to us. He never even seen us."

"And he's only going to see us once," Al said from the kitchen.

"What are you going to kill him for, then?" George asked.

"We're killing him for a friend. Just to oblige a friend, bright boy."

"Shut up," said Al from the kitchen. "You talk too goddamn much."

1. Could you summarize the plot in this section?
2. What is the writing style shown in this section?
3. Comment on the construction of the killers' image.

V. Short answer question

Please explain Ernest Hemingway's "iceberg theory" of writing. How does Hemingway's own writing illustrate this theory? Please illustrate your points with examples from one of his novels or short stories. (厦门大学 2010 研)

VI. Essay questions

Hemingway's war novel ends with a scene in a maternity hospital. How does this final topic, the death of a woman and a child in childbirth, force us to enlarge or reconsider what we took to be the central subject of the novel? In what sense is the novel a war novel? What is its subject if it is not war, battle, engagement with the enemy, strategy, etc.? Sufficient textual information is required to illustrate your viewpoints.（南京大学 2007 研）

参考答案及解析

Ⅰ. Fill in the blanks.

1. Lost Generation

（第一次世界大战后以海明威为代表的一些美国作家自称是“迷惘的一代”。所谓“迷惘”，是指他们共有的彷徨和失望情绪。这些作家中，大多数人亲身经历过第一次世界大战。在战场上，他们目睹了战争给人类带来的巨大灾难，经历了战争的折磨。）

2. Author: Ernest Hemingway　　Title: “A Clean, Well-lighted Place”

（题目节选自海明威的“A Clean, Well-lighted Place”（《一个干净明亮的地方》）。这是海明威的一个短篇小说。）

3. *For Whom the Bell Tolls*

（海明威的小说《丧钟为谁而鸣》(*For Whom the Bell Tolls*)以西班牙内战为背景，该小说陈述了海明威对爱与失去的观点，描写了普通人不屈不挠的精神。）

4. Nobel Prize

（1954 年海明威获诺贝尔文学奖。获奖理由：“因为他精通于叙事艺术，突出地表现在其近著《老人与海》之中；同时也因为他对当代文体风格之影响”。）

5. *The Sun Also Rises*

（菲茨杰拉德的短篇小说集《爵士时代的故事》(*Tales of the Jazz Age*)是爵士时代的标志，而海明威的小说《太阳照样升起》(*The Sun Also Rises*)则刻画了整个“迷惘的一代”的形象。）

6. *A Farewell to Arms*

（海明威的第二部力作是 1929 年出版的《永别了，武器》(*A Farewell to Arms*)。此书以爱情与战争两条主线，阐述了作者对战争及人生的看法和态度。）

7. Santiago

（《老人与海》(*The Old Man and the Sea*)是海明威最著名的作品之一，小说讲述了一位老年古巴渔夫圣地亚哥(Santiago)，与一条巨大的马林鱼在离岸很远的湾流中搏斗的故事，表明了人可以被毁灭，但不能被打败的人生态度。）

8. *The Old Man and the Sea*

（1952 年海明威发表了小说《老人与海》，书中竭力表现一种人类战胜和支配自然的强大力量以及一种必胜的信念。这本书是海明威创作的高峰，海明威因此获得 1953 年的普利策奖和 1954 年的诺贝尔文学奖。）

9. Author: Ernest Hemingway　　Title: “A Clean, Well-lighted Place”

（题目节选自海明威的《一个干净明亮的地方》。）

10. Ernest Hemingway

（1926 年欧内斯特·海明威(Ernest Hemingway)的第一部成熟力作《太阳照常升起》(*The Sun Also Rises*)发表。这部小说确立了海明威作为“迷惘的一代”代言人的地位。）

11. traditional, "literature of exhaustion"

(海明威和福克纳等作家用传统小说的手法反映荒诞的主题。而20世纪60年代的作家诸如巴思于1967年在《大西洋》月刊(*The Atlantic*)上发表了堪称后现代主义宣言的文章《枯竭的文学》("The Literature of Exhaustion"),宣告传统小说已经用尽或者某些可能已经枯竭。)

Ⅱ. Multiple Choices

1. C 海明威既是"迷惘的一代"的代表,也是"冰山理论"的提出者,其作品主题不少是关于"压力之下的优雅",但他并非"美国梦"的代表作家。
2. B 海明威的一生都在描写一个主题,即"重压下的优雅"。他同时塑造了典型的海明威式英雄来实践这一主题。
3. D 一战期间,海明威在意大利身受重伤,被送进医院。在那里他爱上了一个护士。海明威本人和这个护士日后成为小说《永别了,武器》(*A Farewell to Arms*)主人公人物的原型。
4. A 海明威曾说,所有的美国现代文学作品都源自马克·吐温的《哈克贝利·费恩历险记》。
5. A 美国作家斯泰因对海明威说:"你们都是迷惘的一代",后来海明威以此作为他的小说《太阳照常升起》的题词。
6. D 尼克·亚当斯是海明威短篇小说集《在我们的时代里》的主人公,通过尼克的成长经历,阐释在尼克身上硬汉精神和硬汉品质特征已具雏形,从而说明尼克是海明威系列硬汉形象第一人。
7. B 1954年海明威获诺贝尔文学奖 。获奖理由:"因为他精通于叙事艺术,突出地表现在其近著《老人与海》之中;同时也因为他对当代文体风格之影响"。

Ⅲ. Explain the following terms.

1. "Hemingway Heroes": The works of Ernest Hemingway generally center on the concept of heroism. Each of his novels contains a "Hemingway hero"—a man of honor and integrity who expresses himself not with words, but with actions. The Hemingway hero is a noble but tragic hero fighting with the overwhelming force; though he knows that he will be defeated at last, he decides to act like a hero.

    He is not a Godlike figure, but an ordinary, often flawed mortal who must look to himself for strength. The Hemingway hero is actually a mirror image of the author himself. Santiago in *The Old Man and the Sea* is a typical Hemingway hero.

2. Ernest Hemingway: Hemingway was a myth in his own time and a myth in American literature. He was a shining public hero, and his writing style and lifestyle was imitated by many people as the spokesman for "a lost generation". He was famous for his novels and short stories written in his spare, laconic, terse, clear, telegraph-like, yet intense prose with short sentences and very specific details. This style is his famous "Iceberg Principle" that emphasizes simplicity and economy of expression. Almost all his stories deal with the theme of courage in the face of tragedy. They reveal man's impotence and courage out of despair to assert himself against overwhelming odds. These heroes are called "The Hemingway Code Heroes".
3. Santiago: Santiago is the protagonist of *The Old Man and the Sea*, written by American novelist

Ernest Hemingway. He is an old man who hasn't caught any fishes for eighty-four days. On the final journey he has a fight with sharks. This character depicted by Hemingway is a typical "tough guy". Santiago embodies Hemingway's definition of courage as "grace under pressure". He never loses dignity in the face of death. The glory and honor Santiago comes not from the battle itself but from his pride and determination to fight. His famous words are "A man is not made for defeat...a man can be destroyed but not defeated."

Ⅳ. Read the following quotations and answer the questions.

Passage 1

1. The passage is selected from *A Farewell to Arms* by Ernest Hemingway.
2. The title has two symbolic meanings: First, it means Henry say goodbye to the war, for the word "arms" has the meaning of "weapon". The second meaning is that Henry say goodbye to his dear wife Catherine Berkley who dies in the hospital. The "arms" also symbolizes Catherine's arms.
3. Hemingway writes all his life about one theme, "grace under pressure". Under this theme, he has created many typical Hemingway heroes. The world described by Hemingway is essentially chaotic and meaningless. In the world he describes, one alone resists forces that he can't understand. He will be extremely disappointed to realize that no matter how hard he tried, he would eventually end in failure. But Hemingway heroes possess a kind of courage. It is this kind of courage that makes him show his manhood and maintain his dignity in the face of adversity. This is the essence of a code of honor in which all of Hemingway's heroes believed. Hemingway's characters, Nick Adams, Jake Barnes, Frederic Henry, and Santiago are all typical Hemingway heroes. A Hemingway code hero can be destroyed but not defeated.
4. He promoted the development of reportage. He believed that the sentences of reportage should be simple in structure, limited in words with concise imagination, and adopt a dramatic tone which is not affected by emotions. In the later part of his life, Hemingway came to be known as "Papa Hemingway". This compliment refers mainly to his contribution to the development of the colloquial style of writing in America. Hemingway's articles are simple, natural, straightforward, clear and easy to understand, novel and lively, and rich in meaning. The philosophy underlying his works is Iceberg Principle. Hemingway said: "If a writer of prose knows enough about what he is writing about he may omit things that will have a feeling of those things as strongly as though the writer had stated them. The dignity of movement of an iceberg is due to only one-eighth of it being above water. A good writer does not need to reveal every detail of a character or action."

Passage 2

1. The story is a conversation between George and two killers in a restaurant. The killers plan to kill one of George's regular customers named Ole Andreson. George wants to know the reason, but he only finds that the killing is to oblige a friend of the killers.
2. Hemingway's words are very simple and plain; his sentences are short and direct. He is skilled at creating the scenes by using dialogues and conversations.
3. The killers' image is constructed through dialogues. There are many wisecracks and slangs in their speech, such as "bright boy" and "You talk too goddamn much". Max seems to be silly, for he talks too much to George. He even tells George their plan to kill Ole Andreson. Al is the

dominating and rude one of the two because he tells Max to shut his mouth. The two killers are all a little bit sentimental, for their killing is only to oblige a friend.

Ⅴ. Short answer question

The Iceberg Theory (also known as the "theory of omission") is a term used to describe the writing style of Ernest Hemingway. Hemingway said: "If a writer of prose knows enough about what he is writing about he may omit things that will have a feeling of those things as strongly as though the writer had stated them. The dignity of movement of an iceberg is due to only one-eighth of it being above water. A good writer does not need to reveal every detail of a character or action." As a journalist he learned to focus only on events being reported, and to omit superfluous and extraneous matter. By "iceberg theory" Hemingway means that writers should get the most from the least, prune language to multiply intensities, and tell nothing but the truth in a way that allowed for telling more than the truth. In his writing the facts float above water; the supporting structure and symbolism operate out-of-sight. Hemingway describes an action such as Nick Adams fishing in "Big Two-Hearted River" while conveying a different message about the action itself—Nick Adams concentrating on fishing to the extent that he does not to think about the unpleasantness of his war experience.

Ⅵ. Essay question

A Farewell to Arms can be read as a footnote to The Sun Also Rises. Frederic Henry experienced the war firsthand. He found that the war had no sacred glory at all. It was just a living slaughterhouse. Henry fought alone as a typical Hemingway hero. He speaks less and acts decisively. Even with others, he usually acts like an outsider and is good at controlling his feelings. *A Farewell to Arms* caught the mood of the post-war generation and brought international fame to Hemingway.

As a nurse, Catherine is able to transfer herself to the hospital where Frederic is recovering. Then, she flees with him to Switzerland where she dies from internal bleeding resulting from a difficult childbirth. In her death she is the picture of heroism and her statements are full of dark humor. "I am not afraid. I just hate it." Concerning this, we can conclude that this novel is also a tragic love story, in which man is doomed to be trapped in difficult situations and in misery.

Besides the subject of war, the novel also explores the searching of identity. Frederick Henry represents the experience of a whole nation, who is wounded in war and disillusioned with the insanity and futility of the universe. This subject is important to the story because it expresses the general question of the individual in the postwar world. Frederic represents this questioning of what is the force that can cause such awful destruction and human suffering. Frederic's identity is displaced by the late introduction of his name to the reader, the fact of his being an American in an Italian army, and his constant play with words. He speaks Italian, but not well enough. All these examples try to show that Frederic does not know who he is.

第 34 章　约翰·斯坦贝克

34.1　复习笔记

John Steinbeck (1902—1968)	约翰·斯坦贝克（1902—1968）
1. Life	**1. 生平**
John Steinbeck was born in Salinas, California, the locale of much of his finest fiction. He was self-reliant in his childhood and worked as a laborer, crew member, newspaper reporter, bricklayer, assistant chemist, surveyor and apple picker.	约翰·斯坦贝克出生在加利福尼亚的萨利纳斯，他的许多最优秀的小说就是以此为故事背景的。他从童年时代起就自力更生，做过劳工、船员、报社记者、砖瓦工、化学家助理、测量员和苹果采摘工人。
He read various British and French classics since he was a child. He later studied at Stanford University, but did not graduate. Later, with the support of his father, he decided to specialize in literary creation. He wrote some romantic works, but none of these works produced any response in the literary world. His works explored the social problems of that era, especially the suffering of poor farmers, which earned him the Pulitzer Prize in 1940 and the Nobel Prize for Literature in 1962.	他从小阅读各种英国和法国的经典文学作品。后来他就读于斯坦福大学，但未毕业。后来在父亲的资助下，他决定专门从事文学创作。他写过一些浪漫主义作品，但这些作品在文坛上都未产生任何反响。他的作品探讨那个年代的社会问题，尤其是一贫如洗的农民遭受的苦难，使他在 1940 年获得了普利策奖，1962 年获得了诺贝尔文学奖。
2. Literary Style	**2. 文学风格**
(1) Steinbeck sympathized with the immigrant workers and the people of the lower class because he had personally experienced the suffering. His work reflected his concerns about the customs of laborers.	(1)斯坦贝克同情那些移民工人和下层社会人民，因为他亲身经历过苦难。他的作品反映了他对劳工们的习俗的担忧。
(2) Steinbeck's lyrical prose vividly captured the unique language, characters, legends and humor of his hometown. He was a superb storyteller whose reforming vision led him to contrast the conflicting moral codes of people in search of permanent ideals.	(2)斯坦贝克的抒情散文生动地捕捉到了他家乡独特的语言、人物、传奇和幽默。他是个优秀的小说家，他革新的洞察力，使其对比了人们在寻求永恒理想中，互相冲突的道德准则。
3. Major Works	**3. 主要作品**
Cup of Gold (1929) *The Pastures of Heaven* (1932) *To a God Unknown* (1933) *Tortilla Flat* (1935) *In Dubious Battle* (1936)	《金杯》(1929) 《天堂牧场》(1932) 《大地的象征》(1933) 《薄饼坪》(1935) 《胜负未决的战斗》(1936)

Of Mice and Men (1937) *The Grapes of Wrath* (1939) *The Moon is Down* (1942) *East of Eden* (1952) *The Winter of Our Discontent* (1961)	《人鼠之间》(1937) 《愤怒的葡萄》(1939) 《月亮下去了》(1942) 《伊甸园以东》(1952) 《烦恼的冬天》(1961)
4. Selected Work	**4. 选读作品**
◆The Grapes of Wrath	**◆《愤怒的葡萄》**
(1) *The Grapes of Wrath* is one of the major American novels. The title of the book comes from "The Battle Hymn of the Republic," a war song of the Civil War, in which there are the lines, "Mine eyes have seen the glory of the coming of the Lord, / He is tramping out the vintage where the grapes of wrath are stored."	(1)《愤怒的葡萄》是美国文学史上一部重要的小说。它的题目取自美国内战时期的《共和国战歌》中的几句"我的眼睛已看到了上帝到来的光环，/他在走遍储存愤怒葡萄的葡萄园。"
(2) This novel portrays the westward journey of the families like the Joads. What Steinbeck wants to express is that when most people are hungry and cold, they will resort to violence to get what they need. The days of anger are coming. The grapes of anger in people's souls are growing more and more heavily. If no measures are taken to prevent them, some kind of social revolution will happen.	(2)这部小说描绘了乔德等家庭西迁的过程。斯坦贝克想要表达的是，当大多数的人们处于饥寒交迫的情况时，他们就会付诸暴力，取其所需。愤怒的日子正在到来，在人们的灵魂中愤怒的葡萄正在成长得越来越沉甸甸，倘不采取措施阻止，某种社会革命将会发生。
(3) In terms of structure, this novel consists of two parts, the process of the Joad family and the Oklahoman's collective westward migration, and the general picture of the Great Depression. The inserting chapters' function as the social and historical background against which the characters move. Many plots in the novel are obviously influenced by the Bible.	(3)在结构上，这部小说由两部分材料组成，乔德一家人和被迫迁移的俄克拉荷马人集体西迁的过程，以及大萧条的概貌。插入章节为人物活动提供了社会和历史背景。另外，小说的结构借鉴了圣经故事的构思轮廓。小说中有很多地方明显受到圣经的影响。
(4) The novel reflects the difference between Steinbeck and other writers who reflected the economic crisis in the 1930s. The works of that era were permeated with depression and defeatism. In such an atmosphere, Steinbeck still believed in human nature. He believed that in the future people could overcome difficulties and the situation would get better.	(4)该小说反映出了斯坦贝克与其他 20 世纪 30 年代反映经济危机的作家有不同之处。那个年代的作品中弥漫着沮丧与失败主义，但在这样的氛围之中，斯坦贝克仍然相信人性，相信未来人们能克服困难，情况会有所好转。

34.2 考研真题与典型题详解

I. Fill in the blanks.

1. The novel set in the American Dust Bowl region, which shows the social significance of the migrant labor problem was written by __________ and the title is __________. (大连外国语学院

2007 研）

2. In the short novel ________, John Steinbeck portrayed the tragic friendship between two migrant workers.

3. In 1935, John Steinbeck published ________, a collection of short stories which vividly described the life of poor Mexican-Americans with affection and humor.

4. John Steinbeck's post-war novel ________ reflected his bitter feelings against those greedy, rapacious elements of society which made the war possible.

5. ________ was the foremost novelist of the American Depression of the 1930s.

Ⅱ. Multiple Choices

1. ________ tells the Joad family's life from the time they were evicted from their farm in Oklahoma until their first winter in California.

   A. *Of Mice and Men* B. *The Grapes of Wrath*
   C. *The Great Gatsby* D. *For Whom the Bell Tolls*

2. His treatment of the social problems of his time, particularly the plight of the dispossessed farmer, earned ________ the Pulitzer Prize in 1940 and the Nobel Prize for Literature in 1962.

   A. William Faulkner B. John Steinbeck
   C. Ernest Hemingway D. F. Scott Fitzgerald

Ⅲ. Read the following quotation and answer the questions.

The migrant people, scuttling for work, scrabbling to live, looked always for pleasure, dug for pleasure, manufactured pleasure, and they were hungry for amusement. Sometimes amusement lay in speech, and they climbed up their lives with jokes. And it came about in the camps along the road, on the ditch banks beside the streams, under the sycamores, that the story-teller grew into being, so that the people gathered in the low firelight to hear the gifted ones.

Questions:

1. Which novel is this passage taken from?
2. Who is the writer of this novel?

Ⅳ. Essay questions

1. What are the major artistic features of John Steinbeck?（北航 2007 研）
2. Anzlyze John Steinbeck's *The Grapes of Wrath*.
3. Respond to the following question in an essay of about 300 words. Please relate your discussion to the textual detail of the works.（武汉大学 2014 研）

   In what ways do you think the story of migrants and working people in John Steinbeck's *The Grapes of Wrath* represent the stereotypical "American" experience? Is it similar to and different from the stories of earlier settlers of the United States, such as the Puritans or those who settled at Jamestown?

参考答案及解析

Ⅰ. Fill in the blanks.

1. John Steinbeck, *The Grapes of Wrath*

（20 世纪 30 年代中期，由于受到沙尘暴的侵袭，美国中部大平原地区变成“尘谷”（Dust

Bowl)，受此影响，大批居民迁徙到加利福尼亚州，被称为“沙尘暴移民”，美国小说家 John Steinbeck 的小说《愤怒的葡萄》正是以此为背景。)

2. *Of Mice and Men*

(约翰·斯坦贝克在 1937 年发表小说《人鼠之间》(*Of Mice and Men*)，描写了两个无家可归、无地可耕、相依为命的流动农业工人的悲惨遭遇。)

3. *Tortilla Flat*

(1935 年约翰·斯坦贝克发表了小说《煎饼坪》(*Tortilla Flat*)。在这部小说里斯坦贝克用幽默的语言善意地描写了居住在蒙特雷城郊煎饼坪的一群贫穷墨西哥裔美国人的生活。)

4. *The Pearl*

(1947 年约翰·斯坦贝克的著名中篇小说《珍珠》出版。这部小说文字洗练，寓意深刻，无情地鞭挞了人世间有钱人的贪婪和凶恶。)

5. John Steinbeck

(约翰·斯坦贝克是 20 世纪 30 年代美国文坛上最活跃、最引人瞩目的作家之一，也是经济大萧条期间最重要的小说家。他的小说《愤怒的葡萄》(*The Grapes of Wrath*)以大萧条为背景，具有史诗般的规模和气魄。)

Ⅱ. Multiple Choices

1. B 《愤怒的葡萄》(*The Grapes of Wrath*)通过乔德一家从俄克拉荷马州向西迁至佛罗里达州的过程，描绘了在 30 年代经济危机和特大旱灾影响下大批农民破产的真实面貌，揭示了人们在苦难历程中精神上的变化。
2. B 约翰·斯坦贝克的作品探讨那个年代的社会问题，尤其是一贫如洗的农民遭受的苦难，使他在 1940 年获得了普利策奖，1962 年获得了诺贝尔文学奖。

Ⅲ. Read the following quotation and answer the questions.

1. *The Grapes of Wrath*
2. John Steinbeck

Ⅳ. Essay questions

1. John Steinbeck was a significant Depression writer. He did all kinds of jobs when he was young, which brought rich materials to his novels. He gives a vivid picture of his time. His works examined the lives of the working class and migrant workers during the Dust Bowl and the Great Depression.

Steinbeck sympathized with the immigrant workers and the people of the lower class because he had personally experienced the suffering. His work reflected his concerns about the customs of laborers.

Steinbeck's lyrical prose vividly captured the unique language, characters, legends and humor of his hometown. He was a superb storyteller whose reforming vision led him to contrast the conflicting moral codes of people in search of permanent ideals.

2. (1) *The Grapes of Wrath* is an important novel in the history of American literature. Its title is taken from a few lines in "The Battle Hymn of the Republic," a war song of the Civil War, "Mine eyes have seen the glory of the coming of the Lord, / He is tramping out the vintage where the grapes of wrath are stored."

(2) This novel depicts the process of Joads and other families moving westward. What

Steinbeck wants to say is that when most people are hungry and cold, they will resort to violence to get what they need. The days of anger are coming. The anger in people's souls is growing heavier and heavier. If no measures are taken to prevent them, the social revolution will occur.

(3) In terms of structure, this novel consists of two parts, the westward trek of the Joads and the dispossessed Oklahomans, and the general picture of the Great Depression. The inserted chapter provides the social and historical background for the character's activities. In addition, the structure of the novel draws on the outlines of the biblical story. There are many places in the novel that are obviously influenced by the Bible.

(4) This novel shows the difference between Steinbeck and other writers who reflected on the economic crisis in the 1930s. Depression and defeatism permeated the works of that era. But in such an atmosphere, Steinbeck believed in human nature and thought that people would overcome difficulties in the future and the situation could get better.

3. In *The Grapes of Wrath*, The Great Depression throws the country into abject chaos and makes life intolerable for the luckless millions. One of the worst stricken areas is the central prairie lands. There the farmers become bankrupt and begin to move in a body toward California, where they hope to have a better life. The westward moving is a most tragic and brutalizing human experience for families like the Joads. There is unspeakable pain and suffering on the road, and death occurs frequently. Everywhere they travel, they see a universal landscape of decay and desolation. When they reach California and try to settle down, they meet with bitter resistance from the local landowners. Iniquity is widespread and wrath is about to overwhelm patience.

This experience is just like the experience of the early Americans, those Puritans who settled at Jamestown. They felt disappointed about the United Kingdom. So they left there and settled at the new land. They hoped they will have a new life. Everyone can get success by his own efforts. This idea is represented by Benjamin Franklin. American Dream appeared. The wilderness filled the Puritans with the hope of restoring the Garden of Eden, and looked like the "Promised land" with which God rewarded His chosen people. Thus for a long time the hope kept floating before the people, keeping them happy and optimistic about the future. The note of pessimism may have made itself first heard and heeded in Mark Twain's *The Gilded Age*. Later, they felt more and more disappointed because of the decadence and corruption. Finally, this American Dream shattered.

So in this way, two experiences have the similar points. However, in *The Grapes of Wrath*, in their westward moving, it was a procession full of pains and sufferings. They were unhappy all the way. But, to the early Americans settlers, there was a period of happiness. The failure of the American Dream is a slow procession. So, in this way, two experiences have the different points.

第 35 章　威廉·福克纳

35.1　复习笔记

William Faulkner (1897—1962)	**威廉·福克纳 (1897—1962)**
1. Life	**1. 生平**
Faulkner was born in New Albany, Mississippi. When he was four or five years old, the family moved to Oxford, Mississippi, where he resided for the rest of his life. Faulkner fictionalized the town of Oxford to become Jefferson Town, located in the mysterious Yoknapatawpha County, which is the background for most of his later works. Although he did not graduate from university, he read a lot and travelled extensively. Faulkner was a poet when he first started his literary creation, but he was unsuccessful. In 1925, he turned to novel creation. After winning the Nobel Prize in Literature in 1949, Faulkner gradually became famous.	福克纳出生在密西西比的新奥尔巴尼，四五岁的时候举家搬到密西西比的牛津镇，之后一直定居于此。福克纳把牛津镇稍作虚构，就成了杰佛逊镇，位于神秘的约克纳帕塔法县，是他之后大部分作品的背景。虽然他没有从大学毕业，但他博览群书且游历甚广。福克纳刚开始从事文学创作时是诗人，但并不成功，1925 年便转向小说创作。1949 年获得诺贝尔文学奖后，福克纳渐渐声名远播。
2. Literary Features	**2. 文学特点**
(1) Faulkner boldly carried out innovative experiments in form, and constantly developed artistic expression techniques to better express his views.	(1)福克纳在形式上大胆地进行创新实验，不断发展艺术表现手法以更好地表达他的观点。
(2) Faulkner attached great importance to the creation of characters, which was the key to his expression of the versatility of characters. He allowed the characters to enjoy a maximum degree of autonomy and independence. There are quite a few devices by means of which the autonomy of the characters is ensured. One of the most important is authorial transcendence by employing a fallible narrator or multiple narrators.	(2)福克纳极重视人物的塑造，这是他表现人物多面性的关键所在。他给予角色最大程度的自主和独立，运用各种写作手法以保证人物的独立性。其中最重要的是，通过不可靠叙事者和多位叙事者的手法来实现“作者的超脱”。
(3) Faulkner's works are somewhat difficult to understand. There are a lot of inner monologues in his works, and he used a lot of modern stream of consciousness techniques. Words are often spelled together without capitalization and punctuation. The meaning of the sentence is unknown, and the long sentences pile up strangely. The use of pronouns also increases the complexity of his article.	(3)福克纳的作品有些不易理解。他的作品里有很多的内心独白，并且运用了大量的现代意识流技巧。单词常拼写到一块，没有大写和标点符号。句子意义指代不明，长句奇怪地堆积到一起。代词的使用也增加了其文章的复杂性。
(4) His works include daily spoken language, local dialects, and standardized literary language, covering multiple “registers” of the English language.	(4)他的作品里包含日常口语，地方方言，又有规范的文学语言，涵盖了英语语言的多种“语域”。

(5) Faulkner's imagination was extremely rich. He created a series of characters set against the background of historical development and the decline of the American South with the family story. His novels gradually developed to the realm of mythology, elevating the simple and true stories in life to the height of mythology.	(5)福克纳的想象力异常丰富。他创造了以历史发展和美国南方衰落为背景的一系列人物，打造了一部家族故事。他的小说逐步向神话的境界发展，把人生中简单而真实的故事提升到神话的高度。
3. Major Works *The Marble Faun* (1924) *The Sound and the Fury* (1929) *As I Lay Dying* (1930) *Sanctuary* (1931) *Light in August* (1932) *Absalom, Absalom!* (1936) *The Hamlet* (1940) *Go Down, Moses* (1942) "A Rose for Emily" (1930)	**3. 主要作品** 《大理石牧神》(1924) 《喧嚣与骚动》(1929) 《在我弥留之际》(1930) 《圣殿》(1931) 《八月之光》(1932) 《押沙龙，押沙龙!》(1936) 《村子》(1940) 《去吧，摩西》(1942) 《献给艾米丽的玫瑰》(1930)
4. Selected Work **◆"A Rose for Emily"** "*A Rose for Emily*" is a very famous gothic short story of Faulkner. The story happens after the American Civil War, in Jefferson Town. It is about the weird and stubborn Miss Emily, who was controlled by her father and was unable to establish a normal relationship with a man. She finally killed the man she loved but could not marry. This story reflects the decline of the South after the Civil War and the conflicts between the past and present values of Southern people. Emily is a representative of southerners and a symbol of old traditions. She refuses to recognize the alternation of the old and the new era. She strives to maintain her status. Emily's death reflects the irresistible historical trend of the collapse of the plantation economy and slavery.	**4. 选读作品** **◆《献给艾米丽的玫瑰》** 《献给艾米丽的玫瑰》是福克纳的一篇经典的哥特式短篇小说。故事发生在美国内战后的杰弗逊镇，讲述的是古怪、固执的艾米丽小姐由于备受父亲掌控而无法与男性建立正常的恋爱关系，最后将自己深爱的却无法与之结婚的男人杀害的故事。 故事反映了内战后美国南方的衰落和南方人过去与现在价值观的冲突。艾米丽是南方人的代表，是旧传统的象征，她拒绝承认新旧时代的交替，力求保持自己的地位。艾米丽的死反映了种植园经济、奴隶制的瓦解是不可抗拒的历史潮流。

35.2 考研真题与典型题详解

I. Fill in the blanks.

1. The works written by ________ may be viewed as a culmination of the development of twentieth-century southern fiction.
2. Author ________ Title ________ (南京大学2008研)
   His mother's hand touched his shoulder.

"Does hit hurt?" she said.

"Naw," he said. "Hit don't hurt. Lemme be."

3. In his novel, William Faulkner has invented a county named ________ and the seat of the county ________. (国际关系学院 2009 研)
4. Quentin is a character in William Faulkner's novel ________.
5. Joe Christmas is a character in William Faulkner's novel ________.
6. Two writers played important roles in making Faulkner what he later became. ________ helped him to write and publish his first novel *Soldier's Pay* and ________ was his idol and inspired him to write creatively.
7. ________ wrote about the disintegration of the old social system in the American Southern States, and its effect on the lives of modern people, both black and white.
8. In ________'s ________, the protagonist begins as a man of integrity and a pillar of his country, but ends with a tragic vision of human existence, voicing that "Life is a tale told by an idiot, full of sound and fury, signifying nothing." (天津外国语 2012 研)
9. The Compsons, the Sartorises, and the Sutpens are representative southern aristocratic families in ________'s novels, and they are all portrayed as prisoners of the past, who cannot reconcile with the fall of the south after ________. (天津外国语 2013 研)
10. Writers like Ernest Hemingway and William Faulkner tried to represent the absurdity theme in ________ novelistic devices, while the writers in the 1960s regard the conventional novel as ________.
11. Write down the names of the authors of the following works (厦门大学 2007 研):

    A. *Go Down, Moses*

    B. *Light in August*
12. William Faulkner was awarded ________ for literature in 1950 because he created a symbolic picture of the remote past "to retell the recurrent story of human dreams, bravery and defeat, to make a statement about the past and use that statement to talk about man's lot in his world."
13. ________ wrote about the society in the South by inventing families which represented different social forces: the old decaying upper class; the rising, ambitious unscrupulous class of the "Poor Whites"; and the Negroes who labored for both of them.

Ⅱ. Multiple Choices

1. Which ONE of the following is the author of *Light in August*? (四川大学 2011 研)

   A. Willia Cather. B. Richard Wright.

   C. Ernest Hemingway. D. William Faulkner.
2. Which writer does the following selection discuss? (大连外国语 2007 研)

   A. William Faulkner. B. Arthur Miller.

   C. Eugene O'Neill. D. Mark Twain.

He was born in New Albany, Mississippi. When he was four or five years old, the family moved to Oxford, Mississippi, where he resided for the rest of his life. Oxford was with some fictional modifications, a prototype of Jefferson, in the mythical country of Yoknapatawpha, the setting of *Sartoris* and most of his subsequent works. His central themes, however, was not Oxford, or Mississippi, or even America. It was, as he put it, the universal theme of "the problems of the human heart in conflict with itself."

3. Among the many novels written by William Faulkner, the title of ________ is associated with the Bible.（首师大 2008 研）

   A. *The Sound and the Fury*　　B. *Absalom, Absalom!*

   C. *As I Lay Dying*　　D. *Light in August*

4. Which of the following is not a theme of *The Sound and the Fury*?

   A. The decline of a family.　　B. The South vs. the North.

   C. The past vs. the present.　　D. Racial problems.

5. Thomas Sutpen is a character in William Faulkner's novel ________.

   A. *Absalom, Absalom!*　　B. *Light in August*

   C. *Go Down, Moses*　　D. *The Sound and the Fury*

6. In William Faulkner's *The Sound and the Fury*, he used a technique called ________, in which the whole story was told through the thoughts of one character.

   A. stream of consciousness　　B. imagism

   C. symbolism　　D. naturalism

7. William Faulkner's novel ________ is about a poor white family's journey through fire and flood to bury the mother in her hometown, Yoknapatawpha.

   A. *Intruder in the Dust*　　B. *As I Lay Dying*

   C. *Absalom, Absalom!*　　D. *Light in August*

8. Which ONE of the following writers is the author of the novel *The Sound and the Fury*?（四川大学 2010 研）

   A. Harriet Beecher Stowe.　　B. Stephen Crane.

   C. William Faulkner.　　D. Henry James.

Ⅲ. Explain the following terms.

1. Yoknapatawpha（北航 2007 研）
2. The Southern Renaissance in American Literature（四川大学 2011 研；北航 2008 研）
3. Multiple point of view

Ⅳ. Read the following quotations and answer the questions.

Passage 1（大连外国语 2007 研）

It tells the remarkable story of an aging spinster in Jefferson whose death and funeral drew the attention of the entire town, "the men through a sort of respectful affection for a fallen monument, the women mostly out of curiosity to see the inside of her house, which no one save an old manservant—a Combined gardener and cook—had seen in at least ten years." The unnamed narrator, which some critics have identified as "the town" or at least a representative voice from it, in a seemingly haphazard manner relates key moments in the heroin's life, including the death of her father and a brief fling with a Yankee road paver, Homer Barron.

1. The title of the story is ________.

   A. "Evelyn"

   B. "Why I Live at the P. O."

C. "A Rose for Emily"

D. "The Story of an Hour"

2. Beyond the literal level of the narrative, the story is sometimes regarded as symbolic of ________.

A. the changing of values and attitudes in American South

B. the disillusion of the American Dream

C. the materialistic pursuit of the Americans

D. alienation of human relationship in a commercialized society

Passage 2

The following is an excerpt from William Faulkner's short story "A Rose for Emily". Please answer the following questions according to the excerpt. (北二外 2010 研)

When Miss Emily Grierson died, our whole town went to her funeral: the men through a sort of respectful affection for a fallen monument, the women mostly out of curiosity to see the inside of her house, which no one save an old manservant—a combined gardener and cook—had seen in at least ten years.

It was a big, squarish frame house and spires and scrolled balconies in the heavily lightsome style of the seventies, set on what had once been our most select street. But garages and cotton gins had encroached and obliterated even the august names of that neighborhood; only Miss Emily's house was left, lifting its stubborn and coquettish decay above the cotton wagons and the gasoline pumps—an eyesore among eyesores. And now Miss Emily had gone to join the representatives of those august names where they lay in the cedar-bemused cemetery among the ranked and anonymous graves of Union and confederate soldiers who fell at the battle of Jefferson (the Town of Jefferson).

Alive, Miss Emily had been a tradition, a duty, and a care; a sort of heredity obligation upon the town, dating from that day in 1894 when Colonel Sartoris invented an involved tale to the effect that Miss Emily's father had loaned money to the town, which the town, as a matter of business, preferred this way of repaying. Only a man of Colonel Sartoris' generation and thought could have invented it, and only a woman could have believed it.

Questions:

1. What is the town people's response toward Emily's death and what's the reason for that? Use your own words to give an illustration.
2. These paragraphs typically show Faulkner's major concern in literary writing. Please explain Faulkner's literary concern in general with one representative work except this short story.
3. In the 3rd paragraph, Miss Emily is referred to as "a tradition". What does this tradition mean? When the paragraph ends with the sentence "Only a man of Colonel Sartoris' generation and thought could have invented it, and only a woman could have believed it", what information does the writer want to give to his readers?

V. Short answer questions

1. In what way is William Faulkner called a Southern writer?
2. Discuss William Faulkner's style.
3. Why is William Faulkner considered by critics a great avant-garde experimenter?

Ⅵ. Essay questions

1. In what way is Emily Grierson a monument of tradition?（天津外国语 2009 研）
2. William Faulkner once said, "She [Caddy Compson] was the beautiful one", "She was my heart's darling. That's what I wrote the book about and I used the tools which seemed to me the proper tools to try to tell, try to draw the picture of Caddy." How do you understand Faulkner's appraisal of Caddy?（天津外国语 2007 研）

参考答案及解析

Ⅰ. Fill in the blanks.

1. William Faulkner

   （威廉·福克纳的作品可以看做是 20 世纪美国南方小说发展的巅峰之作。）
2. Author: William Faulkner　　Title: *Barn Burning*

   （题目节选自福克纳的 *Barn Burning*（《烧牲口棚》）。）
3. Yoknapatawpha; the town of Jefferson

   （福克纳在自己的一系列著作中虚构了位于密西西比州北部的约克纳帕塔法县，这个县的中心是杰弗逊镇。）
4. *The Sound and the Fury*

   （昆丁（Quentin）是威廉·福克纳小说《喧哗与骚动》（*The Sound and the Fury*）中的人物，同时也是该小说第三部分的叙述者。）
5. *Light in August*

   （《八月之光》（*Light in August*）是威廉·福克纳写的一部批判种族主义的小说。乔·克里斯默斯（Joe Christmas）是该小说的主人公。）
6. Sherwood Anderson; James Joyce

   （安德森和乔伊斯对福克纳的文学创作产生了很大影响。前者帮助他出版了第一部小说《士兵的报酬》，后者激发了他进行创造性写作的动力。）
7. William Faulkner

   （美国作家威廉·福克纳（William Faulkner 1897—1962）的作品主要描写美国南方旧社会制度的解体及其对现代人生活的影响。其作品深层次地反映了现代社会中人与人的沟通与疏远，揭示了西方社会中人性受扭曲与异化的问题。）
8. William Faulkner, *The Sound and the Fury*

   （"Life is a tale told by an idiot, full of sound and fury, signifying nothing."是威廉·福克纳著作《喧哗与骚动》中的句子。）
9. William Faulkner; the Civil War

   （这三个家族是福克纳关于南方贵族的三个代表，在这些作品中，主人公们生活在过去的牢笼中，无法接受美国内战后南方的衰落。）
10. traditional, "literature of exhaustion"

    （海明威和福克纳等作家用传统小说的手法反映荒诞的主题。而 20 世纪 60 年代的作家诸如巴思于 1967 年在《大西洋》（*The Atlantic*）月刊上发表了堪称后现代主义宣言的文章《枯竭的文学》（"The Literature of Exhaustion"），宣告传统小说已经用尽或某些可能已经枯竭。）

11. A. William Faulkner

(《去吧，摩西》由7个相互连接的故事构成。作者对黑人和白人两个种族之间充满痛苦和耻辱的关系进行了严肃探讨。)

B. William Faulkner

(福克纳是美国南方文学的代表，《八月之光》是他的一部批判种族主义的小说。)

12. the Nobel Prize

(1949年福克纳获得诺贝尔文学奖，获奖原因为"他对当代美国小说做出了强有力的和艺术上无与伦比的贡献"。)

13. William Faulkner

(福克纳的作品描述了南方社会中代表不同的社会力量的家庭：旧的腐朽的上层阶级；雄心勃勃的"穷白人"和为两者劳动的黑人。)

Ⅱ. Multiple Choices

1. D *Light in August*(《八月之光》)是 William Faulkner(福克纳)的代表作之一。在作家营造的"约克纳帕塔法世系"中占有重要位置。他的另一部出名的作品为 *The Sound and the Fury*(《喧嚣与骚动》)。

2. A 威廉·福克纳(William Faulkner)美国作家，生于美国密西西比州新奥尔巴尼的一个庄园主家庭，南北战争后家道中落。他发现"家乡那块邮票般大小的地方倒也值得一写，只怕一辈子也写不完"。怀着这样的信念，从他的第三部小说《沙多里斯》(*Sartoris*)他把19篇长篇和70多篇短篇小说纺织在"约克纳帕塔法世系"(Yoknapatawpha)里，通过南方贵族世家的兴衰，反映了美国独立战争前夕到第二次世界大战之间的社会现实，创造了20世纪的"人间喜剧"。

3. B 在福克纳的小说中，《押沙龙，押沙龙!》的题目是和圣经有关的，因为押沙龙是旧约里的一个人物，是大卫的儿子。

4. D 《喧嚣与骚动》的主题包括家族的没落、美国南北冲突、内战前后文明的差异，不包括种族问题。

5. A 托马斯·塞德潘(Thomas Sutpen)是威廉·福克纳小说《押沙龙，押沙龙!》中的主人公。

6. A 福克纳在小说《喧嚣与骚动》中运用"意识流"和"多角度"叙述方法产生了强烈的艺术效果，为现代派小说创作做出了卓越贡献。

7. B 福克纳的小说《在我弥留之际》描写了农民安斯按照亡妻的遗愿，经过重重磨难率全家扶送灵柩去杰弗逊镇妻族的墓地安葬。作者通过一些矛盾的、不和谐的和具有反义的事物表明，在现代文明世界里，人的存在没有真正的意义，现代人的命运既是一场悲剧，又是一场滑稽的玩笑。

8. C *The Sound and the Fury*(《喧嚣与骚动》)是 William Faulkner(威廉·福克纳)的代表小说之一。

Ⅲ. Explain the following terms.

1. Yoknapatawpha: Yoknapatawpha is a fictional county created by American author William Faulkner as a setting for many of his novels. It is widely believed by scholars that Lafayette County, Mississippi and its county seat Oxford is the basis for Yoknapatawpha County. Faulkner would often refer to it as "my apocryphal county." Yoknapatawpha is located in northwestern Mississippi and its seat is the town of Jefferson. This fictional county is bounded on the north by the Talla-

hatchie River and on the south by the Yoknapatawpha River.

2. The Southern Renaissance (also known as Southern Renascence) was the reinvigoration of American Southern literature that began in the 1920s and 1930s with the appearance of writers such as William Faulkner, Tennessee Williams, and Robert Penn Warren and so on. Before the Southern Renaissance, the Southern literature was dominated by writers who supported the "Lost Cause"—the heroism of the Confederate army and civilian population during the Civil War and the supposedly "idyllic culture" that existed in the South before the war. The Southern Renaissance changed this by addressing three major themes in their works. they are 1) The burden of history in a place where many people still remembered slavery, Reconstruction, and a devastating military defeat, 2) the South's conservative culture, specifically on how an individual could exist without losing a sense of identity in a region where family, religion, and community were more highly valued than one's personal and social life, 3) the South's troubled history in regards to racial issues. They also brought new modernistic techniques such as stream of consciousness and complex narrative techniques to their works (as Faulkner did in his novel *As I Lay Dying*).
3. Point of view is the vantage point from which a narrative is told. Novels sometimes, but infrequently, mix points of view. The American writer William Faulkner is a master at presenting multiple points of view, showing within the same story how characters react differently to the center and various points of view radiating from it. This technique makes it difficult for the reader to see the truth of the story.

Ⅳ. Read the following quotations and answer the questions.

Passage 1

1. C 这段文字描写了美国作家威廉·福克纳(William Faulkner)的小说《献给艾米丽的玫瑰》中的人物艾米丽的葬礼情景，全镇的人都前往观看。
2. A 这篇小说中艾米丽是旧南方的代表，与来自北方的修路工人荷马以及小镇的变化形成鲜明对比，艾米丽小姐的悲剧说明了旧南方社会制度的腐朽和解体，美国南方价值观和生活态度均已发生变化。

Passage 2

1. The town people's response toward Emily's death is mixed. On one hand, when alive, Emily is an outsider, controlling and limiting the town's access to her true identity by remaining hidden. She is a muted and mysterious figure. Therefore, upon her death, people are curious to see the inside of her house and to know more about her. On the other hand, her death represents the disappearance of a tradition, so it causes the feeling of sympathy and compassion.
2. Faulkner is a major American southern writer. His major concern in writing is about tradition versus change. In this short story, through the mysterious figure of Emily Grierson, Faulkner conveys the struggle that comes from trying to maintain tradition in the face of widespread, radical change. *The Sound and the Fury* is also about this concern. It tells a story of deterioration from the past to the present. The past is idealized to form a striking contrast with the loveless present. There is in the book an acute feeling of nostalgia toward the happy past.
3. This tradition means southern civilization, its morals and ways of behaviors. Although Emily once represented a great southern tradition centering on the landed gentry with their vast holdings and

considerable resources, Emily's legacy has devolved, making her more a duty and an obligation than a romanticized vestige of a dying order. The town leaders conveniently overlook the fact that in her straightened circumstances and solitary life, Emily can no longer meet her tax obligations with the town. Emily emerges as not only a financial burden to the town but a figure of outrage because she unsettles the community's strict social codes.

V. Short answer questions

1. Faulkner is called a Southern writer in that most of Faulkner's works are set in the South. His works have managed successfully to show a panorama of the experience and consciousness of the whole Southern society both before and after the Civil War. Though Faulkner set his works in the South, his concern was always with the general human situation.
2. Faulkner boldly carried out innovative experiments in form, and constantly developed artistic expression techniques to better express his views. He attached great importance to the creation of characters, which was the key to his expression of the versatility of characters. His works are somewhat difficult to understand. There are a lot of inner monologues in his works, and he used a lot of modern stream of consciousness techniques. His works include daily spoken language, local dialects, and standardized literary language, covering multiple "registers" of the English language. Faulkner's imagination was extremely rich. He created a series of characters set against the background of historical development and the decline of the American South with the family story. His novels gradually developed to the realm of mythology, elevating the simple and true stories in life to the height of mythology.
3. Faulkner boldly carried out innovative experiments in form, and constantly developed artistic expression techniques to better express his views.

   ① He used the device of stream of consciousness. Action and plot are less important than the reactions and inner musings of the narrator. Time sequences are often dislocated. In this way, he went deep into the mind and memory of his characters.

   ② He employed multiple points of view and a circular form instead of a linear structure which makes the reader see the difficulty of arriving at a true judgment.

   ③ He stressed authorial transcendence.

   ④ He used an original narrative method which often withholds or gives confusing information. His sentences are not clearly indicated with words running together from time to time without proper punctuation. For him, the long sentence is a technique for compressing the greatest possible amount of time.

   ⑤ The violation of chronology in the narrative structure is matched by a violation of everyday language habits in Faulkner's prose style.

   ⑥ His prose varies from colloquial, regional, to formal diction and cadences of American speech.

VI. Essay questions

1. Emily is a representative of southerners and a symbol of old traditions.

   Firstly, she is the representative of the upper class of southern society which is crumbling. Social class is the typical production of southern tradition and her family is a typical upper-class family. Her father did a special contribution to the town during the war which gained respects from government. Her family members have eccentric temper which is thought understandable for royal family. Standing in the garages and cotton gins, her house is the only building of the old time.

Secondly, she is living in a traditional way which is worshiped by old men in the town. She lived with a black servant, having no tax to the town.

Thirdly, she has the hereditary obligation upon this town which is the core spirit of the southern tradition. According to her obligation, she can't marry the man from north and low class but to bury her love deeply. This is the root of her tragedy.

Fourthly, she rejects advance of society, new life value and locks herself in her big, old house. Though people all begin to live in a new way ignoring the old tradition, they treat Emily as their representative of the vanishing past. Faulkner saw the northern industrialization eroding the southern tradition day after day and set Emily as the monument to fight against it which is in vain finally.

2. According to Faulkner, Caddy Compson is the true hero of *The Sound and the Fury*. She is the second Compson child, a strong-willed yet caring woman. She is Benjy's only real caregiver and Quentin's best friend. Caddy never develops a voice, but rather allows her brothers' emotions towards her to develop her character.

    The first section of the novel is narrated by Benjamin Compson, a source of shame to the family due to his mental retardation; the only characters who evidence a genuine care for him are Caddy, his older sister, and Dilsey, a matriarchal servant. From Benjy's memory we know that Caddy is very kind and caring.

    In the second section, we understand Quentin's feeling about Caddy. He is obsessed with southern ideals of chivalry and is strongly protective of women, especially his sister Caddy. He could protect his sister by joining her in whatever punishment she might have to endure. He is depressed on hearing the sexual affairs of Caddy, and finally kills himself.

    Through the memories of her brothers, the voice of Caddy becomes clear. In fact, the whole story is told by different people, all around Caddy. She is the most active and attractive one of the Compson family, as well as the favorite character of Faulkner in the novel.